LINE
OF
VISION

DAVID
ELLIS

Quercus

First published in Great Britain in 2008 by

Quercus
21 Bloomsbury Square
London
WC1A 2NS

Published by agreement with G. P. Putnam's Sons,
a division of Penguin Putnam Inc.
357 Hudson Street, New York 10014

A CIP catalogue reference for this book is available
from the British Library

ISBN 978 1 84724 570 0

10 9 8 7 6 5 4 3 2 1

Printed and bound in Great Britain by Clays Ltd, St Ives plc.

This book is dedicated to my father, Wayne Ellis.

ACKNOWLEDGMENTS

I owe so much to so many for their support and advice in writing this novel.

To those who read earlier drafts and offered their insight: Missy Thompson, Margi Wilson, Jimmy Timble, Dan and Kristin Collins, and Leslie Breed. The book wouldn't be the same without your help. Special thanks to Krista and Jim Hanson for thoughts that significantly affected the final draft. To Jim Jann, who read several versions from the beginning on, and offered wonderful improvements to each one. To Jim Minton, for all of your encouragement and some exceptional criticism (now it's your turn to write one).

To Anny, for all of your support and ideas all the way through this process, and for everything else you have meant to me.

To Scott Turow, for early advice and encouragement I will never forget.

To my friends at Cahill, Christian & Kunkle, for everything they taught me, and for the warmth they showed me during trying times. To Steve Nieslawski in particular, a great "boss" and an even better friend.

To my agent, Jeff Gerecke, for taking a chance on an unknown writer and showing me the way. To David Highfill, my editor, for endless enthusiasm and outstanding critical analysis.

To my mother, Judy Ellis, the sweetest and most loving person on this planet, for some great feedback in the final stages. (Always listen to your mother.) To my sister, Jennifer, for all the love and support that a brother could ever hope for.

And to Susan, for all your work and insights on the final drafts, and for warming my heart and inspiring me in ways I couldn't translate into words.

FIVE MINUTES TO TEN. I WONDER WHAT SHE'S doing right now. Someday I'll ask her what happens before we start, but in a way it's more fun to imagine. Maybe she's sipping Merlot, closing her eyes as the bitter flavor sinks into her tongue, pondering what's to come. Maybe she already turned on the jazz, the blaring saxophone, the tinny echo of the drummer's high hat. Maybe she's putting on perfume in her cute little way, spraying it in front of her and walking into the mist. That would be interesting, because she will be the only one who smells it.

Does she practice? Maybe she's in the bathroom upstairs, her hands running along the silky outline of her negligee, watching herself in the mirror, moving to the music.

Three minutes to ten. I focus on the silk curtain that covers the glass door. Soon the light will come on in the den. A prelude to our moment.

Maybe she's thinking about me. I admit it, I'd love to think so. I'd love to believe that she doesn't need the wine or the music, that it takes nothing more than the thought of me to unleash her.

The light summer wind glides through my hair, under the short sleeves of my cotton shirt. I cross my arms and lean against the ragged bark of the tree. The darkness is consuming, utter blackness from every side. I can barely make out the back porch, the grand architecture of her house.

Thirty seconds till ten. The light in the den goes on, coloring the silk curtain egg-yellow, one spot of light interrupting the night. Her shapely silhouette appears through the curtain; she reaches for the button by the end table. And now the curtain slides open.

She is the love of my life.

BOOK ONE

1

SOMETHING IS WRONG WITH THIS PICTURE.

The winds on November 18 are unusually strong for this time of year, even by Midwestern standards, carrying mist and some stray leaves in the night air. It doesn't make my journey up the three acres of the Reinardts' backyard any easier. The ground is hard, but still damp from today's rain. My feet keep slipping on the blanket of wet leaves. I silently curse the Midwestern weather, the Indian summer that provides us these leaves that should have disappeared weeks ago, the abrupt plummet of the temperature this week. I feel the near-freezing mist on my cheeks, which are about the only parts of my body exposed to the elements. But even as I trudge up the hill, focused on the ground—both to avoid the wind and to watch my step—I sense that something is out of place. The typical leap of my heart when I make it into the clearing, the dreamy sensation as I approach the house—none of this fills me now. Something is different.

I readjust the wool scarf, wrapped tightly around my face and irritating my skin to no end. Back before I crossed the stream, I was forced to tie it in a knot behind my head, or else it would fly off. Every few steps now, I stop to pull it back over my nose.

I press on, with my head down and eyes open in slants; no angle is safe from the relentless, swirling wind. My hands have curled into fists to keep warm, leaving the finger holes of my gloves empty.

I make it up the hill to within about thirty yards of the old Victorian house. It's been, what, sixteen years since high school, and it feels more like thirty to my legs. I catch my breath next to my favorite oak tree, whose naked branches wave mercilessly from side to side in this wind.

The estate of Dr. Derrick Reinardt and his wife, Rachel, rests triumphantly on top of a small hill in the suburb of Highland Woods. Your basic spread in this north-shore bedroom community: sprawling acreage in the back with no front yard to speak of, a fairly unassuming exterior masking the ornate decor within. This is the upper-class side of the suburb—not mega-rich family money but working-class wealth, CEOs, doctors, personal-injury lawyers, a former governor—and the houses in this neighborhood remind me of tiny fiefdoms, wide plots bordered by trees and shrubbery that serve more to ensure privacy than to impress. This is not a bad thing, mind you; there is no way that a neighbor could see me back here.

The Reinardts have a long, wooden back patio with a surprisingly simple array of wood furniture and a gas barbecue grill that is covered this time of the year with a thick gray tarp. The den is in the back of the house by the patio, separated by a large sliding glass door with a silk curtain that—

The curtain is open.

Wait. Today's Thursday, right? Yeah, of course it is. Am I late? Could she be done already?

I furiously pull back my coat sleeve to look at my watch, which is no small chore wearing these gloves. No. No. I *can't* be late.

No. The fluorescent numbers read 9:34. As usual, I'm way early. Maybe she hasn't set up yet. But—that doesn't make sense, either. She usually has everything ready well before she starts. She knows I get here early, likes the fact that I'm waiting with anticipation. No, the curtain should definitely be *closed*.

I stand around for a couple of minutes, looking over the house, seeing nothing, no sign of Rachel. Tonight the sky offers no light; the warm-weather insects do not provide their creaks and calls. The fury of the wind mutes all sound, leaving me to a silent film with not much for video, either.

Maybe she just got a late start, is all. Maybe she'll come down soon. I yank my scarf down just in time to sneeze into my gloves. Then I sneeze again. I wipe my hands on the tree.

"This is ridiculous," I say to no one, though this is really not the most appropriate word to describe me at this moment, a grown man sneaking around outside a married woman's house. Pathetic. Depraved. Perverted. All of the above?

I consider leaving. It can't be more than twenty degrees out here, well below zero with the windchill. God, the wind is whipping up something awful.

"Story of my life," I mumble, again to an audience of no one. All dressed up and nowhere to go.

My mind drifts from my aborted fantasy show to work tomorrow. I have to get in early anyway, get ready for the presentation. It's probably just as well. Time to turn back, no more jollies, adult responsibility time. But still, my feet remain planted. I think of Rachel's words, almost two weeks ago to the day. I had mentioned her husband in an offhanded way, an innocuous comment, I don't even recall what. Her outburst of tears, the contortion of her face, her eyes squeezed shut.

"Tell me, Rachel," I said.

She shook her head. "No," she whispered.

I sat up on an elbow on the bed, moved the wisps of bangs from her forehead. "Tell me, sweetie. Tell me what's going on."

Her sobbing subsided momentarily. She swallowed hard. "If he ever knew I told someone . . ."

"Oh, honey. He'll never know. You think I'm gonna tell him?" I actually laughed as I said that. Then I took her hand in mine. "Told someone about what?"

The lights are on upstairs. I look up at the windows. No silhouettes. No sign of life.

"Sometimes," she started. "Sometimes he—" Her eyes closed, her mouth turned in a frown.

"Rach, sweetie, it's me. Tell me about it."

She let out a sigh. She had settled on it now. She would tell me. Her eyes opened into mine.

I look back down into the den, the only room I can see into. Nothing. Nada. The staircase that leads to the bottom floor winds around at the last two stairs and ends at the cream tiled hallway, which leads past the living room into the den. From my view, I can see those last two stairs, the hallway, and the den. On the right side of the den is a white, deliciously soft couch. At the back end of the den, opposite the sliding glass door, is the bar, lined with bottles of liquor, oak cabinets underneath.

I do another once-over around the house. Not a creature is stirring.

"It's only sometimes," she said, apologizing for her husband. "Only when he drinks."

"Okay," I said quietly, "it's only sometimes." I brought a hand to her face, then thought the gesture inappropriate. She needed space, time.

She sighed again, her body letting out a tremble.

"He hits me, Marty," she whispered. "My husband beats me."

Still nothing upstairs. It's 9:37. My anxieties getting the better of me, images running wild in my mind, but the truth is, no one's home. She's probably at dinner with him or something. Regardless, the regularly scheduled programming will not be seen tonight, and all I'm gonna have to show for it is hypothermia and a bruised ego. Time to cut my losses. I look back down the hill at the woods that form the name of our town, Highland Woods. The entire suburb has built up around this miniforest, which has made my path to and from the Reinardts' house these many days a conveniently clandestine one. Over the stream and through the woods. To grandmother's house we go. I swear, that stupid song comes into my head every time I make this trip.

I looked over my beautiful Rachel, her neck, her shoulders, her face.

She sensed what I was doing. "No," she said flatly. Her face pale, void of any expression, she lifted herself from the bed and turned, adjusting herself so she sat with her back to me.

Before she had settled I saw them. I brought a trembling hand to her back but didn't make contact. Three, four, five

lacerations, long spindly scars forming a gruesome road map
down the center of her back. I remembered then her wincing
while we had made love earlier, as I sank my fingers into
her back.

Guilt was the first thing that I felt. How had I not noticed
these before? How long had this gone on, and I hadn't no-
ticed?

I brought my arms around her, pulling her backward
against my chest, my face buried in her neck.

"He uses his belt," she said with no inflection. "But never
my face. He's too smart for that. He even keeps it below the
neckline. Scars you can never see."

I look back at the den again. I stuff my hands into my
jacket pockets and stomp my feet in a feeble attempt to keep
warm. I fix on the staircase in the hallway, my eyes tearing
from the wind.

I jump at the sight of her, my one and only, my beautiful
Rachel, the jet-black hair to her shoulders, the shapely outline, even from a distance the shiny amber eyes. My hand
leaves my pocket just in time to grab the tree to keep my
balance. She must have been in the living room, not upstairs.
Or did I miss her coming down the stairs?

I can't make out her features very well; I'm too far away
to see the expression on her face. She's wearing a whitish
blouse and blue slacks, not her ordinary attire for the occasion—she usually opts for a negligee, sometimes surprises
me with an outfit like a schoolgirl skirt and knee-high socks.
But tonight, as she walks along the tiled hallway in a semicrouch, almost tiptoeing yet moving with some urgency, Rachel is anything but provocative, her whole body wearing an
obvious pain, maybe fear.

Scars you can never see.

She reaches the den, still crouching sheepishly, one hand
tucked under her shirt. She walks to the bar. Her back is to
me as she reaches the counter, a deep mahogany brown. She
keeps looking up at the ceiling, probably listening for her
husband upstairs? At the bar, she raises a trembling hand to
the ice bucket. She removes a couple of cubes but knocks

the tumbler sideways, the ice spilling onto the bar and floor.

Her head turns upward again.

It's only when he drinks.

She sets the glass upright, stuffs some more ice into it, and reaches for a bottle of liquor. She fills the glass and tries to gather the spilled ice. But her hand is shaking so hard that she can barely put the cubes back into the container.

The other hand remains tucked under her shirt.

She looks up again, but this time not straight at the ceiling. This time, she looks more toward the staircase in the hallway. Her hands are still now.

A clumsy, uncertain foot stomps onto that last stair, then into the hallway. Dr. Reinardt is wearing an oxford shirt, haphazardly tucked into his pants, with the sleeves rolled up. His movements are slow and awkward. He stops at one point in the hallway and reaches out to the wall to steady himself.

The doctor can't see Rachel yet; she is still by the bar, against the front wall of the den. But now Rachel has placed the drink on the bar; she is reaching behind the bottles of booze that line the back of the countertop. She pulls the bottles back and reaches out with her other hand. I catch a glimpse of shiny steel as she raises the object over and behind the bottles.

I shift and feel the wood from the Reinardts' deck. I'm only about twenty feet from the glass door now. The deck is raised three steps off the grass, leaving me the perfect amount of space to crouch down from their view. I reach up to the deck for balance and realize that my hands, like Rachel's, are trembling.

The outside porch light is off, so they can't see me unless they're looking. And as Dr. Reinardt enters the den, he is not looking out the glass door.

He stops and just stares at Rachel. She reaches for the glass on the bar, but the doctor, without moving, says something to her that makes her put her hands at her side. He says nothing more, just glares at her.

Rachel fidgets. She brushes back a strand of hair from her face, then puts her hands at her side again. She's talking to him, her head moving compliantly, but he doesn't respond. Finally, she picks up the glass and offers it to her husband. When he doesn't take it, she sets it down on the bar near him. The doctor lashes out with his right hand, knocking the glass and its golden contents to the carpet. Rachel instinctively steps back, says something in apology, then crouches down to retrieve the glass and ice. She is facing me now. For the first time, I see her face. I can make out cuts and bruises on her cheeks.

Scars you *can* see.

Rachel stands now, turning away from me and toward her husband. Her hands raise in compromise; she's trying to calm him.

The doctor staggers toward his wife, who holds her ground. They are face-to-face now. As slow as he's moving, his right hand rises in a flash, fist half closed. Rachel's head whips to the right, her hair and arms flying wildly, her knees buckling as she falls backward to the carpet. She lands awkwardly on an elbow, then rolls over so she's facing the carpet. The doctor nods approvingly, that's-what-ya-get, as Rachel brings a hand to the developing bruise below her eye.

Rachel slowly makes it to her feet again, her hand returning to her cheek, her entire body trembling.

"I know how it'll end," she told me only a few days ago. *"He told me how."*

Dr. Reinardt approaches her. He grabs her by both arms, shaking her. Rachel breaks a hand free and swings it lifelessly toward his face.

I am on the deck now, crouched down like a catcher, as I watch this silent horror movie, no sound but the *thump-thump, thump-thump* of my pulse. The only thing separating me from the sliding glass door is the wooden bench and the picnic table.

"Tell me how, Rach."

Dr. Reinardt reasserts his grip on Rachel. He pulls down on her, forcing her to the carpet in a vise grip. Once on the floor, he tears at her blouse.

"He's going to rape me first. He said he'll rape me then kill me."

And then, as I grip the wooden bench and slowly rise, it is suddenly clear to me. And something like calm sweeps over me, a certain focus through the panic. Because now I know how this story will end.

2

THE SHOWER WATER IS MUCH HOTTER THAN I would normally prefer. I stand in the tub for what must be forty-five minutes, obsessively scrubbing my body with soap. The red is now long gone from my skin. Even the bar of soap, reduced to a nub, is restored to its blue-white stripes. My head falls gently against the front wall of the shower and I stare down at the tub, the warm water pulsating on my neck, watching the last of the crimson liquid swirl around the drain and disappear. Finally, I punch off the water, not because I'm clean, or because the water has turned cold, but because I'm simply too tired to stand.

I dry off and make my way through the steamy bathroom. I throw on a pair of sweatpants, and for the first time tonight I let my body collapse, onto the unmade bed.

Think now. Think.

Tomorrow is Friday. Good to be so close to the weekend. Nothing big planned for work. Our meeting with the Texas investors; but I'm ready for that, and it should be over by two.

The next week will be shortened for Thanksgiving. I could make some excuses and skip the holiday dinner.

I force myself to take a deep breath. I can get through this. I close my eyes, which sink into my head as exhaustion sweeps over me. But I can't sleep. Not now. I take inventory of my condition.

My lower back, which has given me fits since high school, is throbbing. My biceps ache. My knuckles are swollen and bruised. My legs, conditioned for jogging only, feel like noodles. My head is congested, and I've been sneezing on and off since I've been home.

And from somewhere deep down, a gathering sense of loss comes over me. I guess I never fully expected that Rachel and I would be a couple. She made a point of promising nothing; I was in no position to push. The truth is, I never really confronted myself on the subject. Caught in the whirlwind, I was living for the moment. But somewhere in the web of elation and ecstasy was some measure of hope. Now I'm left with the irony that, because of what I've done, I may have less of a chance than ever.

Yet in the swirl of emotions surging through me, the prevailing one is not fear, or self-pity, or pain. I am euphoric. I am fulfilled. I have saved Rachel from a horrible man, giving her the chance to be happy. Or at least not miserable.

The repercussions—losing Rachel, not to mention a life spent in a jail cell—form a canopy over me, following me, haunting me, but for the moment I am on a plane that transcends such mortal concerns. I've never been one for religion, but for the first time I can relate to the notion of higher judgment, whether it is that of some god or simply my own.

Or, for the less theological among us, it's like taking a painkiller after breaking an ankle: You're aware of the pain, and you know it's going to hurt like hell in a few hours, but for now it's just a muted throbbing.

Before I start to sound too self-congratulatory, let me add that I have no interest in paying any price for what I have done. I didn't climb the altar until I'd addressed the basics: I've scrubbed all of Dr. Reinardt's blood off my body, stripped off all of my clothes and thrown them into a garbage bag, and now I'm planning the immediate future.

I think of Rachel. When I left her, she was barely conscious. She had taken a brutal beating from her husband, not to mention what happened afterward.

What is she doing right now? Did she call the police? Did someone else? Either way, the police were there; I heard the sirens. What would they make of the scene they found at that house? And then panic. Will they—no—will they suspect *Rachel*?

But it doesn't make sense. They would have no reason to. Nobody knows about us, nor does anyone know about our little secret shows every Thursday night. And the police will find Rachel with bruises on her face, if not her whole body. They will assume that the intruder beat her up. And how will they explain the broken glass door? Rachel is a thin, demure woman. She couldn't break through a thick glass door.

I shake my head forcefully. Jesus, get a grip. They're not going to think she broke into her *own house*!

Concentrate. Think logically, like the police are.

How will Rachel handle the cops? Will she be able to lie to them? The police will want to talk to her right away. Given the scene, with the broken glass door and all, she will certainly have to say that an intruder entered the house. She will probably describe him differently than me. Dark hair, not reddish blond. Dark complexion, not pale Irish. Muscular or fat, not trim. Short, not tall. Or maybe she'll say it was a black guy. That would sell well in an affluent whitebread community like Highland Woods. Tomorrow I might be reading in the *Daily Watch* that a large black man broke into the Reinardt house.

You didn't see his face, I said to Rachel as I left her house.

But I ready myself for the possibility that she might not be able to protect me, especially in an hysterical state only moments after the murder. And I can't *expect* her to lie for me. She didn't ask me to do this. God, she was so scared. Just lying there on the floor by the carpet, watching me, wondering what I was going to do, hoping, I guess, hoping that I would make this all stop for her, make the pain go away—

Stop. Think logically.

Can they trace this to me?

Every criminal makes a mistake. That's what the prosecutor who visited my law school class said. Those words, uttered eight years ago, have stayed with me ever since. Did I know back then that this day would come? Did I know somewhere deep down that I had it in me to—

Stop.

What mistake did I make?

I play this scenario out in my mind, over and over. Standing on the deck. Jumping through the glass. My hands on his chest. The gun in my hand.

Oh, am I a sight, furiously pacing the upstairs, running on empty, powered only by the fumes of fear so deep, so intense, that my body motors forward else it will fall over.

What mistake did I make?

Did my coat catch on a piece of the glass? Did some of my hair fall onto the carpet? Did I leave a boot print on the patio? Did I spill any of my *own* blood?

The patio the wind the glass the gun the blood the body—

But as I run through everything, nothing jumps out at me. I was wearing gloves, and I don't think I touched anything besides the gun and the doctor anyway, so no fingerprints. Most of my hair was covered with the knit cap—I mean, *all* of it was, right? And because I underestimated the cold weather, I wore my leather jacket, not a cloth overcoat, so probably nothing caught on the glass. Right?

I take a deep breath and try to relax a little, my hands gripping the comforter in the spare bedroom. Really, what would the police know? If Rachel played it cool and smart, they would have only a very vague description of the intruder. They would have no prints, no murder weapon.

And if they never find the body, they might not even know that he was murdered at all.

Okay.

I walk to my bedroom closet and run my fingers over the hanging suits. The charcoal suit, that's the one I was wearing today at work. I pull it off the hanger and throw it onto the bed. I wore a cream shirt today, but it's lying in a ball in my laundry, and I don't have any others. Gonna have to go with a white one.

Talk about mistakes. I might be making my biggest one now.

The steam is gone in the bathroom. I knot my tie in the mirror, not caring how bad it looks; anyway, I should pull it down, a hardworking man working late. I look at my sports watch resting on the sink. Shit. I forgot to clean it.

I wet a piece of toilet paper and rub the crusted red off the face and plastic band. I really have to be more careful. Thoughts are swirling in and out of my head now: Rachel, the doctor, the gun. I have to be sure not to miss any detail. The toilet paper gets flushed down the toilet.

I toss the athletic watch in a drawer. I opt for the Gucci timepiece and fasten it around my wrist. The hands on the gold face read just past two-thirty.

I let out a long, nervous sigh, my heartbeat alternating between a flutter and full-throttle pounding. Leave it to me not to leave well enough alone.

_____ 3 _____

THE FIRST THING I TYPICALLY DO WHEN I WALK into the garage is hit the opener, which turns on the overhead light. This time, I go straight to the car in the dark. I open the door and the dome light comes on. I get in and quietly close the door.

I sit inside the car, key in hand, only inches from the ignition.

It's not too late. I don't have to do this.

The inside light stays on a moment, then fades out, leaving me in darkness, consuming blackness, where everything is safe. I could stay safe, safe for tonight, anyway.

Or I could ruin everything.

I grab the lever at my feet and pop the trunk. I reach inside the glove compartment and pull out the flashlight. Then I softly open the door again.

I shine the flashlight over the inside of the trunk, the thin brown carpet. Nothing discernible. Quite well done, I must say. Not a speck of blood, far as I can see. No sign whatsoever that only hours earlier, the dead body of Dr. Derrick Reinardt lay in the fetal position on this carpeted surface. Satisfied, I close the trunk.

All right. Fine. If you're going to do it, *do it*!

And act normal. From this moment on.

I walk over and confidently punch the garage door opener, something a very confident person with nothing to hide would do. The garage is lit now. The grinding sound of the lifting door breaks the quiet of early-morning suburbia, leaving me cringing in a crouch, waiting for the return to silence. I close the car door and start up the car.

The streets are deserted. I keep it under thirty.

I left something at work, I'll say if I'm pulled over. *I've got a big deal going down tomorrow, and I need something from work to finish preparing tonight. Dr. Reinardt, you say? No, sorry, don't know him. Kidnapped, you say? Wouldn't know anything about that. You see, I was going to work because I left something there, you see, and I need it to finish something I was preparing tonight and sure you can look in my trunk but I can tell you this for sure you sure won't find any of his blood in the car because I ALREADY VACUUMED AND WASHED IT OUT!*

The ramp onto the highway is only three blocks away. I let out five minutes' worth of breath as I enter the curve to the right.

I pop on the radio, an all-news station. No. There might be some breaking story I don't really feel like hearing right now. I punch one of my preset buttons to a classical station. Piano music. Fine. Good.

I left something at work. Pause. *I've got a big deal going down tomorrow, and I need something from work to finish preparing tonight.* Shrug. *Big presentation, you see.*

Downtown comes into view, only a handful of lighted squares sprinkled among dozens of buildings. Our offices are at the south end of the commercial district, and I follow the highway to the last exit before it heads out of state.

The Hartz Building is the newest, and among the most modern, of the downtown buildings, said to be the largest all-concrete structure in the state. The atrium houses several little stores and a decent coffee shop. The lobby is an escalator's ride up, where the security guards sit. After seven o'clock, everyone must sign in and out.

It's a big presentation, you understand, and I left something at work.

Seven o'clock is also the time that the building closes, and you need a key card to get in. There's access at the west and south entrances. Once in the building, if you have a card you can walk around the atrium to the back elevators, used for the underground parking garage. You can take that elevator up to the lobby, and if you're really good, you can sneak into the main elevators without being seen by security. Often, when people are leaving work after a long day—after seven, that is—they will get off the main elevators and turn straight to the back elevators to get to the parking garage. This was my shtick, always in a bigger hurry going than coming. You're supposed to sign out, and the guards usually holler after me to come to the desk to sign out and record the time.

I consider parking in the underground lot, but I don't want some attendant remembering me arriving at such a strange hour. I park at a meter on the south side.

I take the stairs up to the building and press the key card against a square sign by the door that reads HARTZ BUILDING. The door pops slightly ajar, and I pull it open.

I left something at work. I've got a big deal going down tomorrow, and I need something from work to finish preparing tonight. I hope I don't have to use this line now; if security sees me walking in, the plan backfires. I'm supposed to be *leaving* work after a long night, not coming *in*.

I walk along the marble floor, each step echoing off the

high ceiling. The atrium is cool and airy, reminding me of other late nights at the office. I look around at the walls and in the store windows, practicing my casual look, waiting at any moment to be accosted by a security guard. I pass the escalator leading up to the lobby. There's a set of stairs there, too, which I usually take up to the lobby, where the main elevators are located. But this time I keep walking and turn down the hall marked PARKING.

I reach the back elevator and press the "up" button. The upper of the two circles next to the elevator flashes red, and the door opens with a chime, a little too loud for my liking, but I'm in my nothing-to-hide mode, so I keep calm. Once in, I hold my key card against an identical HARTZ BUILDING square to send me up to the lobby.

I'll sneak out of the back elevator into the main elevator. This time of night, security won't be paying any attention; they'll never notice me. Then I'll go up to my office, turn on the light and my computer, and come back down after a hard night of work, signing out at around three-thirty. *No, I was nowhere near the Reinardts' house that night. You see, I was at work. I have the sign-out sheet to prove it.*

As the elevator stops, I hear the blaring of a walkie-talkie. A security guard.

A chime, then the door slides open.

I can go back down and out of the building. Abort.

Footsteps on the marble.

Sweat breaking out now, on my forehead, my neck. Panic, all of my deepest fears rising to the base of my throat, loosening my bowels, bringing a quiver to my limbs. What now? If I try to go back downstairs now, the guard will probably find me there, and what kind of song and dance do I do *then*? It's better to stride through the doors with confidence, no, with indifference and maybe a hint of annoyance because I was working at *home,* yeah, and I left something at work and I've had to come all the way back and I'm *so* annoyed but then why am I still wearing my suit—

Act normal.

I step out of the elevator and turn left, toward the main

elevator. A woman in a security uniform is standing by the elevators, her neck craned to look at the intruder, the walkie-talkie dangling from her hand.

"Hello . . . ?" she says uncertainly.

I walk toward her. "Hi." My voice is even. "I—left something upstairs."

"Oh—okay, no problem," she says, and holds her look on me a little longer than normal.

"Did I surprise you?" I ask innocently, as we walk toward the security desk side by side.

"Oh, no." She waves her hand. "I was a little confused, that's all. You came in the south entrance and walked all the way around to the parking elevator."

"Oh, yeah." I laugh. *Fuck.* "My knee's been bothering me. I didn't feel like taking the stairs." *Then why didn't you take the escalator, you dumb-ass?*

But she rescues me. "Yeah. I don't know why they turn off the escalators at night."

My heart is pounding through my chest now. I grab the pen for the sign-out sheet, my hand trembling. "Well, hey, what are you gonna do?" I say calmly, like an innocent person would.

The security lady walks into her little room and watches a tiny TV set that sits next to the black-and-white monitors. It sounds like a comedy she's watching; I can hear a guy's animated voice and a laugh track.

I pull the sign-out sheet along the marble top in front of me. There are three other people's names on this page, none from my office. The last person to sign out left at 12:18. I scribble the name *M. Kalish* on the sheet. I move over to the next line and write *McHS,* for McHenry Stern, the name of my company. The next line is the time of arrival. Anyone arriving after seven P.M. has to fill in this space. Anyone who's been working since that morning, of course, would skip it.

"Three-fourteen," the lady says to me with a sigh; she's probably in midshift. My eyes drift up at her. She is about ten feet away from me.

Here goes nothing.

I skip to the next space on the pad, time of departure. I scribble in *3:20.*

I drop the pen and look up. She's watching her little screen.

"Thanks," she says absently.

I get into the elevator and wipe the sweat off my face. My pulse is thumping through my body.

You came in the south entrance and walked all the way around to the parking elevator. So much for sneaking in. When the key card is activated to get into the building, security sees it. A light probably goes on or something. Of course! A real mastermind, I am. Like I'm gonna sneak into this building in the middle of the night without being seen.

A fleeting thought passes through my mind: *What else have I missed tonight?* But I can't think about that now. No no no. I have to execute this. Just a few more minutes, I can panic all I want.

If she doesn't pay attention to the sign-out sheet, she'll never know that I fudged it. I hope that's one fascinating, hilarious show she's watching.

I look at my watch as the elevator opens into our offices. It is 3:15. I walk through the front doors; my office is close by. I walk into the office, flip on the light, and walk over to my desk. I sit in my chair and turn on the computer. I pull up the contract I've been drafting for tomorrow's meeting. I look over at my phone; the message light is blinking. No time for that. I reach for the coffee cup by the window that holds all my coins.

I leave my office and take the internal stairs two floors up, to sixty-three. I reach the cafeteria and plunk change into the vending machine. I choose a muffin and some potato chips. Then I move to the coffee machine and buy a cappuccino.

It's 3:19 on my watch as I walk back into my office, food in hand. I open the bag of chips and set them on my desk. I take a handful out and stuff them into my mouth. I take the muffin out and toss it into my garbage, leaving the wrapper on the desk. I pour half of my steaming coffee into the sink at the minikitchen on this floor.

I survey my office one last time before leaving. Opened bag of chips, muffin wrapper, half-drunk cup of coffee. The diet of a workaholic, spending half the night on a big project. My computer is on; the screen saver will come on after fifteen minutes. I'll leave the overhead light on, too.

Wait. One last touch.

I walk over to the phone and punch the speed-dial button for my secretary.

"Deb," I say into the phone, "I'm gonna need the revisions on the Madison contract first thing in the morning. I'm done for tonight. I gotta get *some* sleep. Thanks." The message will be recorded as having been made at 3:20 in the morning.

I hustle back to the elevator and make my way down to the lobby. I very casually approach the security desk, careful to walk gingerly. My bad knee and all.

She is still watching her show. She looks up momentarily, to watch me pick up the pen. I hold the pen over the space for time of departure.

"G'night," she says absently, then turns back to the TV.

I make a writing motion with the pen, never touching the paper. Time of departure, 3:20. Time of arrival, blank.

I walk down the dead escalator and out the building.

I start my car, the sound of stringed instruments in short, crisp strokes blaring from the stereo. I lift my arms and conduct the music, my hands moving decisively.

I've been working, I can say now if I'm pulled over. *I've got a big deal going down tomorrow, and I had to finish my proposal. Oh, yes, I've been working all night at my office. Wanna see the sign-out sheet?*

WHAT—WHAT ARE YOU GOING TO DO?

I pop up from my pillow, sucking deep breaths of air. I look at the clock by my nightstand. It's 5:45. I've only been asleep for an hour. It's freezing in here. I pull the blanket from the bed up around my shoulders.

My head feels like it has swelled to balloon size. My nose is congested to the point that I'm breathing through my mouth. My throat is raw. I get out of bed to make some coffee, carrying the blanket over my shoulders. I sneeze, one time after another, and grab a tissue from the bathroom.

The mirror reveals a ghoulish figure. Puffy eyes, pale face, and matted hair with a piece that stands almost straight up in the back. I look at the sports watch, resting on the sink. Last night's events sweep back into my mind like an avalanche.

"What—what are you going to do?" Rachel asked me.

I wonder what she is doing right now. Is she at the police station? Is she scared? Relieved? Does she realize her life will be better now that he's gone?

That almost surreal sense of calm from last night is gone; absolute, pure terror has taken its place. A prominent member of the community is dead, and that community will put intense pressure on the police to find the man. I want to get back into bed. A nightmare would be better than this reality.

I am going to jail.

All the rationalizing and wishful thinking does not change the fact that, at the outset, my fate depends on Rachel. She might crack and identify me. Or she might do a terrible job of lying, which might get her in deep with the police as well. Rachel is an open, honest person who couldn't tell a convincing lie if she planned it out for weeks. With all the stress of last evening, the chances of her credibility are diminished all the more.

At one point last night, I took comfort in the thought that Rachel would be so overcome from the beating, as well as the shock and grief, that the police would not expect her to give any details whatsoever. I envisioned her sitting in a chair covered with a blanket, stunned and disoriented, unable to speak intelligibly. That thought lasted about half an hour. Then I realized that, for all the police knew, Dr. Reinardt was still *alive*. There would be a manhunt for him. They would need to know everything they could immediately.

I shower and dress for work. I'll be there by 6:45, and with such an early start, I can leave early. A lot of people leave early on Friday anyway. That means I will have to spend only about five hours around other people before the weekend.

I step out my door and see the newspaper on the porch in its blue plastic wrapping. My heart skips a beat. The first public description of what I have done is under that blue wrapping. I know that if I read it now, the reality of what happened might unleash some emotions I have bottled up. And I am never one to trust my emotions. It's critical that I act normal today. I'll read it when I get home.

The routine of walking to the train comforts me. I try to think of the things that usually pop into my head during the two-block trek. Deadlines at work. Making partner. The blonde who lives on the corner, who is sometimes stretching for her morning jog as I pass.

But I'm too early for her today. I stand almost alone on the platform, awaiting the train, just me and a guy with a crew cut and a muddy trench coat silently agreeing that it's too cold and too early for conversation. When the train arrives I find a seat. This is the time I typically read the paper, which I have left behind. Other passengers, however, have their papers open. Most have them folded into halves or quarters, but the guy across from me has the front page open fully, so I can see the headlines and the back page. My eyes

catch the large bold print. Something about the economic
summit. For some damn reason, my eyes wander up to the
top column, above that headline. I see the words "Prominent
Surgeon" and look away. My heart starts racing, and I feel
sweat breaking out on my forehead. The train is coming to
a stop. I jump up from my seat and get off. I'll take a cab.
Best thirty dollars I'll ever spend.

McHenry Stern, Ltd., is an established downtown investment banking firm. Michael McHenry founded the firm in
1961, and it has grown to about three hundred people. I'm
in Real Estate. I started with the firm after receiving my
MBA, which I got after I bailed on law school. I'm a year
or two from eligibility for partner, about the most pressurized
time for an investment banker. Doing the legwork to close
deals is no longer the sole criteria. You have to look, think,
and act like a partner. Whatever *that* means.

Frank Tiller and I have been trying to put this deal together
for months with a group of investors from Texas. We're trying to sell them on a piece of suburban real estate that we
proposed would be a nice site for retail outlet stores. Frank
is a partner, but he is also my closest friend at work. He
really wants to make this deal, in part because he knows it
will reflect well on me. This deal alone will get me more
than fifty percent past revenue plan.

I get to work about seven-thirty. I throw my coat on the
back of my office door and survey the scene. Empty wrappers, cold coffee, computer turned on. Yep, a long night indeed at the office. I sit down at my desk. It will be good to
be at work, lose myself in my routine.

The message light on my phone is blinking, as it was last
night, and I activate my voice mail. The first message is from
Penny Quinn in Acquisitions, asking if I know some guy
over at Bennett Stowe, another banking outfit. I don't. The
second message is from Nate Hornsby, a stock analyst in
town who works with me at the Reinardt Family Children's
Foundation.

The foundation is a philanthropic organization that reaches
out to underprivileged and handicapped children in the

county. It consists of businesspeople who like to get together at stuffy cocktail parties to raise money for the kids. Then we give the money to the people who really sacrifice their time and energy by implementing the different programs, spending the time with the kids. The cochairs of the foundation, of course, are Dr. Derrick Reinardt and his wife, Rachel.

". . . tried to reach you at home . . ."

I press 4 on my phone to replay the message from the beginning. The computerized voice tells me that the call was from last night at 9:35. "Marty, it's Nate. Foster bailed on the luncheon next week. You were right. The fucker. I don't know why the hell I thought he'd do it. Anyway, we need another speaker fast. If you have any ideas, let me know. I thought you still might be at work. I just tried to reach you at home, but you weren't around, and you sure as hell don't have a date. I'm still at work, if you wanna give me a call."

Beautiful. He tried to reach me at home last night. *Now that you mention it, Officer, I called Marty at his house Thursday evening, right about the time Dr. Reinardt was abducted. And you know something, he wasn't home. He wasn't at work, either, 'cause I tried him there, too. Nope, I guess Marty wasn't at home or work when the attack occurred. Why, did he tell you he was? Well, then, he's a goddamn liar and a murderer!*

I look out my window to the south. Our building is the farthest south downtown, which leaves me with a view of little more than the expressway that leads out of town and a convention center being built. The cranes are already operating this morning, lifting girders and carrying them off; bulldozers are scooping up earth.

Rachel is the person who makes that foundation run. The doctor is—was, I guess—the figurehead who drew the money. Rachel dutifully appears at the fund-raisers, but her real passion is working with the kids, most of whom come from broken families in the inner city. She's happiest when she plays with the children in the after-school programs designed to keep them focused on something other than smoking dope or gang-banging, or when she visits sick or abused kids in the hospital.

I don't do much hands-on work for the foundation. I'm uncomfortable in those situations. I feel hypocritical, doing this charity work to soothe my conscience. It seems like the kids, much more than adults, can see right through that insincerity.

But the kids really warm up to Rachel. Somehow, this wealthy, educated, beautiful socialite can sit down with a group of disadvantaged children and fit right in. It's because she, unlike me, genuinely enjoys being with them. Maybe it's her way of escaping her personal life. Maybe it gives her a purpose, a center. Whatever the case, I have seen her spend an hour with a child who is struggling to put together the simplest sentence in a picture book, sounding out each syllable and then making the child start again from the beginning, beaming with pride at the slightest hint of progress, cradling the child in praise at a job well done.

A guy on the construction site below is chewing someone out now, pointing angrily as two guys in hard hats get to their feet and start hustling toward a pile of bricks. The sun's peeking out, casting a shadow onto the half-built convention center.

It was about as nice a day as you get in the city, a warm, breezy, sunny Saturday in the park. We had at least fifty kids running around, the girls playing jump rope or hopscotch or some version of tag, the boys either wrestling, throwing around a Nerf football, or just running for the sake of it.

I was in charge of the food, which meant removing the fried chicken from the buckets and placing them into large serving trays lined with aluminum foil. I had even coaxed my friend Jerry Lazarus into helping, and he was dishing potato salad onto plastic trays with little enthusiasm. People were setting up the picnic tables and covering them with red-and-white-checkered tablecloths.

I could see Rachel in my peripheral vision, in a T-shirt and purple shorts, a piece of cloth tied around her neck holding a whistle that dangled at her chest, a clipboard in her hand. She was dictating orders to other volunteers, pointing them in this direction or that and looking around.

"No," she said forcefully to someone, "that's after *lunch. Right before the nature walk. Just let them run around a while."*

I stopped what I was doing and watched her. She was surveying the entire situation with the concentration of a quarterback looking over a defense. She scanned the park, checking each boundary. The kids had specific instructions not to leave the borders, and Rachel the patrol monitor was checking. She turned around, glanced behind her, looked away, then turned back again. I followed her eyes and saw a little boy sitting alone against a tree.

Rachel's posture immediately softened. She slowly walked over to him, me following behind.

The boy didn't even look up at her. She bent down next to him slowly, sitting on both knees. I crept closer.

"Hey, Jacob," she said softly; she knew the name of every child in the foundation. "Don't you want to play? David and Benjamin are playing on the slide. That looks like fun."

The boy couldn't have been more than five or six. He had short, thick curly hair, and he was wearing an orange foundation shirt and stubby little shoes that I knew we had provided him.

"Nope," he said, without taking his eyes off the grass between his spread legs.

"Do you want to help us get the food ready?" Rachel tried. "It's an important job, but I know you can handle it."

"Uh-uh," Jacob mumbled, without moving.

"Okay," Rachel said. "Well, do you mind if I sit here with you?"

Jacob looked up at Rachel. "Where's my mom?" he asked with a trembling voice.

Rachel didn't miss a beat. "She's getting help, Jacob. She loves you a lot, and she doesn't want to hurt you anymore."

Jacob's face wrinkled up. "She didn't mean to," he squealed, before bursting into sobs.

Rachel reached for him. She gently pulled him against her, then she stood up, holding him in her arms, his stubby arms wrapped around her neck, his face snug against her shoulder, his body trembling with each sob. She placed a hand behind his head, cradling him. She turned as she whispered into his ear, and I saw her face next to his. The tears had streaked down her face, fresh ones still coming. Her eyebrows were arched, her eyes dancing, as she spoke quietly to this child, trying to say something that would make him believe that he would have a good life, a future, a mommy who didn't hurt him.

"You there?"

I see Frank Tiller in the reflection off the window. I turn my chair around to face him and note the reaction on his face.

He sizes up my downtrodden appearance, then raises an eyebrow. "I hope you at least had some company."

Frank is a broad-chested man—played ball in college, he'll be the first to remind you, might have gone pro if a torn anterior cruciate ligament hadn't bumped his time in the forty to double digits—whose gut has gained considerable ground in the past few years. He has blond and gray hair, wavy, and way too long, in my opinion. He's a loud, boisterous guy, a back-slapper, with a pretty good business sense, but someone who doesn't sweat the details. Only Frank would imagine that I was up all night screwing my brains out when we have this huge meeting this morning. He would do it, I'm sure, and still give a great presentation the next morning, off the cuff. Me, I don't have the gift.

Today, Frank has a blue striped shirt with white collar and French cuffs, dark blue braces, and a bright red silk tie, an appropriately bold ensemble. He's always in good cheer, and his clothes accentuate the impression. I silently curse him for being in the office so early, but he loves the life.

I shrug at his suggestion that I look tired. I wonder how I appear to him, how I will appear to everyone today. I stare at my half-drunk coffee from last night, the open bag of potato chips, the empty muffin wrapper, hoping that Frank will notice them, too, and ask me about it.

"You're working too damn hard," he tells me. In my tenure with the firm, I have developed a reputation as one of the hardest-working people. A "grinder" is how one of the senior partners described me. The truth of the matter is that I could be a lot more efficient with my time. And unlike many, especially the married ones, I am in no particular hurry to get home at night. A lot of the people around here tell me that I shouldn't let work completely intrude on my personal life, to which I silently reply, *What* personal life?

Tiller has joked that they could board up the window in my office and I wouldn't notice. He says this with an air of sympathy. He knows my parents have passed away, and I have only a sister, whom I see, at most, a couple times a year. So he has taken it upon himself to serve as a surrogate father, a role in which I find him utterly ridiculous.

I shake my head. "I'm not feeling that great. Touch of the flu." The plan had been to act as normally as possible today. Not to say I was tired, or sick, or distracted, or upset. Not to act differently, or draw any attention to myself whatsoever. It took me a grand total of ten minutes to blow that plan. Now I have the flu. And I almost forgot my most important line: "Working late on Madison."

Frank claps his hands with a *whack* and rubs them together, a Boy Scout making fire, his indicator that a hot deal is about to close. "Put on your game face," he says eagerly. Today, he is saying, we may close this deal. I was hoping he'd ask me how late I was working, so I could reluctantly admit that I was here past three. But he's caught up. "Let's do a run-through. Nine-thirty?"

"Great."

He pauses at the door, giving me the once-over. "You hear about that doctor in your town?"

The change of topics throws me, and Jesus, *what* a topic. For some damn reason, it has not occurred to me that everyone will be talking about last night's events. I consider saying

I hadn't heard. "Yeah, I read something briefly." You know, just some light reading I skipped over.

"Briefly? Someone broke into his house and kidnapped him, probably killed him. In *your* quiet little town."

"They don't know where he is?" I ask. Zero for 2 on the intelligent responses. The headline probably said, "Prominent Surgeon Kidnapped."

Frank shakes his head. "Some guy broke in, they think he shot him, and he carried him out of the house."

"Was it for ransom?"

"They don't know. They found his blood all over the carpet."

"Just *his* blood?" I ask. Jesus, what a question.

Frank pauses a moment, not sure what I mean. "Well, I think they've ruled out animal sacrifice." He smiles briefly at his joke. "He beat up the wife, too."

"Who did?"

"What do you mean, *who*?" He measures me. "Are you with us this morning? The bad guys."

I reach for a tissue and blow my nose. "She's alive?" I ask through the Kleenex.

"The wife? Yeah. Although not by much, what I understand."

I just shake my head, hoping the conversation will end. My throat is closing up, my classic reaction to stress. Move on, Frank.

Frank's eyes raise a moment, over my head, then back to me. His expression drops. "Oh, jeez," he says. "You knew them—from that charity, right?"

"Of course I knew them," I say too abruptly. This isn't going well. I throw the tissue into the garbage can behind me. "I mean, not that well. But they seem like nice people." I wave a hand. "No big deal." No big deal that people I know were involved in a brutal break-and-enter.

He appraises me for a moment. "Yeah. Nice fucking world, huh?"

Yeah, Frank. Nice fucking world. Now get out.

"Nine-thirty," he says to me with a pointed finger.

"Nine-thirty." I sneeze into my hands.

Frank cocks his head a little, like he's trying to get a clearer look at me. "You up for it?"

"Sure, sure," I say, my cupped hands full of phlegm. "Nine-thirty."

"You might wanna get a cup a coffee in ya." He taps the door frame and is gone.

Good God, what a lousy performance. *Gee, Officer, now that you mention it, Marty did seem a little distracted that morning. He said he didn't feel good, and he sure didn't look good, like he'd hardly slept. And you know something else? I mentioned the kidnapping to him, you shoulda seen the look on his face. He wanted to know whose blood was on the carpet. He snapped at me when I asked him if he knew the Reinardts.*

I realize that this will be my life post-doctor, at least for the immediate future. Second guessing any conversation I have. Trying to imagine the look on my face. Seeing everything through this prism. The man in the plastic bubble.

Frank is one of my closest friends, probably wouldn't turn me in even if I spilled the whole damn thing to him, and there I was tripping all over myself. I've realized over the years that I have seriously overestimated my poker face and, in fact, that I often give off a misleading expression. Someone takes me seriously when I'm kidding, thinks that I'm mad when I'm not. This is not the most sought-after trait for a person trying to cover up a homicide.

The office starts buzzing a lot earlier than I would have preferred; I guess everyone has the same idea here, cramming in last-minute details to get an early start on the long weekend. I sit in my office, doing next to nothing, until a little before eight. Then my secretary, Debra, pops in. Deb has been my secretary going on four years now. She is a petite woman, five-one at most, with a mass of blond hair covered with hair spray. Deb is a little battleship, a staffer who looks at the white-collars with probably too much distrust, quick to defensiveness except when she's dealing with me. I happen to think she's pretty attractive, but she wears too much makeup and is way too fussy with her appearance.

"Hi" is the extent of her morning greeting, as she fumbles with some papers. She hands me the Madison contract. As she looks up at me, she stops with the papers. "*You* look good. Long night?"

On our office voice mail, you can bypass the computerized message telling you the time of the call by pressing 1. I had hoped that Deb wouldn't do this, that she would hear that I called her past three in the morning.

"Thanks for noticing," I say. Let's see if I can manage not to screw up this conversation. "Tiller's been all over me on this mall deal."

I stare again at my food from last night. *Is someone gonna notice this stuff?*

"You need to exit out of the Madison document," Deb scolds me. On our computer network, only one person can work on a document at a time. So at least I've established something with her: I was working late. Or maybe she'll think I just got into the document this morning. Shit.

"Sorry," I tell her. "At three in the morning I'm not thinking too straight."

She says nothing, much to my chagrin, just reaches around me and taps on the keyboard, exiting the document. I look at the papers she has set in front of me.

"Marty, you really look awful. You should go home."

I grab a tissue in time to catch my sneeze. Then a second one.

"I can't," I say, before blowing my nose. "The Madison meeting is today. That's why I was working so late last night."

She gives me that maternal look she has, arms folded and head cocked. Then she nods at the desk. "Nice breakfast."

So! She noticed. But wait—*breakfast*? "No, no," I correct. "This food is from last night. I was eating this last night."

Deb stares at me, a little curious at my eagerness to explain the prior evening's dinner selection. "Oh-kay," she says cautiously. Sure, Marty, whatever. Weirdo.

Deb reaches down to the contract and flips it open to a

page she has tabbed with a yellow Post-it. "I wasn't sure what you wrote here," she says.

"Where?"

"Here." She runs her long nail under the words. "I thought you wrote 'easements and endorsements.' But that doesn't make sense."

I pick up the paper to read it.

"What happened to your *fingers*?"

I put the contract down and look at my right hand. The index and middle fingers are swollen and have turned a shade of purple.

"Oh, you know," I say casually. But I don't know. "Jammed 'em playing basketball."

She gently puts her hand underneath the fingers. "Did you break them?"

"I don't think so." I pick up the contract with my left hand and read it. "Encroachments. Easements and encroachments." I hand the contract to her.

"Oh. Okay. That makes sense." She snatches the papers from me. "I'll get this right back to you." She starts to walk out and stops. "Sandy has some gauze and tape," she says. "You should get them taped up, at least. I can—"

"Deb, they're fine."

"Are you sure?"

"Just forget it, okay?"

She shrugs and leaves. I sneeze again. Then again. I decide right then that I won't leave my office today unless I have to.

I end up using the crutch of feeling sick to explain my downtrodden appearance today. The meeting with the Texas investors goes fine; in fact, it is about the only time today that the Reinardt incident doesn't come up in conversation.

ABDUCTION OF SURGEON ROCKS QUIET TOWN
Prominent Physician Kidnapped from Home, Believed Dead

Dr. Derrick J. Reinardt, a respected cardiologist and a leading local philanthropist, was abducted from his home in suburban Highland Woods late Thursday night. Police responded to a 911 call from Dr. Reinardt's wife at approximately 10:00 P.M. Investigators believe that the intruder crashed through a glass door dividing the back porch and the den, using a piece of patio furniture to gain entry.

The intruder first attacked Dr. Reinardt's wife, Rachel, in the den. Police suspect that the intruder may have attempted to sexually assault Mrs. Reinardt when he was surprised by Dr. Reinardt. Dr. Reinardt apparently heard a commotion and came to the living room with his handgun.

Police believe that a struggle ensued between the intruder and the victim, in which Dr. Reinardt was thrown to the floor in the den and shot by the perpetrator. The man then carried Dr. Reinardt back out through the same glass door he used to gain entry.

The suspect is described only as a white male, thin build, approximately 6'2". The intruder was wearing a navy-blue ski mask and heavy coat.

Investigators do not believe that this was a kidnapping for ransom, although they concede that they are not ruling out any possibilities at this point. An intensive manhunt is under way for Dr. Reinardt, a cardiovascular surgeon at Mercy Hospital and the founder and cochair of the Reinardt Family Children's Foundation. Mrs. Reinardt was treated at Highland Woods Memorial Hospital for bruises to her face and body.

I set the paper down on the kitchen table and take a long drink of coffee.

I broke in and attacked her. Maybe tried to rape her. Did she give them that idea? They could have come up with that on their own, the way Rachel looked. Then the doctor came down with his gun. I took the gun away, threw him down, and shot him. Rachel called 911 after I left. And I was wearing a ski mask, so she never saw my face.

Not bad. This will throw off suspicion that I broke in with the sole purpose of attacking the doctor. It was just an ordinary rapist who got surprised by the husband. They won't be looking for motive beyond that.

I glance at my watch: 4:25. I wish it were later. In fact, I wish that days and days could go by in seconds. I want to put distance between me and the incident. I'm not sure why; the police could still solve the crime months from now. But the further away I get from this, the better I can handle it.

Almost instinctively, I leave the kitchen table and walk over to the portable phone in the den. I pick it up and punch the numbers I have never dialed but know by heart.

A soft voice answers. "H-Hello?"

"Hello," I say, trying to sound innocent and concerned, but my voice has deepened considerably from my cold, giving off a menacing tone. "This is Marty Kalish. I work with Mrs. Reinardt at the foundation. I was just calling to offer my condolences and to see if there was anything at all I could do."

"Oh, well . . . thank you, Mr. . . . . Kalish? This is Rachel's mother. I'm afraid she isn't up to speaking—" She covers the phone. Voices in the background. "Umm, hold on a minute, please."

My pulse races.

"This is Rachel Reinardt."

"Mrs. Reinardt, this is Marty Kalish. I work at the foundation." I speak with a deliberate formality. Never know who might be listening. "I don't mean to disturb you. I just wanted to tell you that we're all praying for you."

"That's very nice of you, Mr. Kalish. We're all praying, too."

"Do they have any idea who did this?"

"I'm afraid not. All we can do is hope."

I want to say more but don't dare. I cannot, in fact, say another word. An awkward silence hangs over the line. We have so much to say to each other.

"Will you excuse me?" Rachel finally says.

"Of course, of course."

"Thank you for calling." A soft click.

Mr. Kalish. Mrs. Reinardt. This is how it will be from now on.

The cocktail party at the Arnold T. Pierce Museum was one of the most anticipated fund-raisers the foundation has ever put on. It had a national flavor to it, with the invitees including the secretary of education from Washington. It was an election year, and the chance to attend an event filled with wealthy contributors drew most of the public officials from the county.

The theme was casino night, perhaps the most clichéd and least subtle fund-raising theme in history. The museum cleared out the largest exhibit room it had to hold the hundreds of socialites who attended. Dr. Derrick Reinardt was at his best that night, mixing with the politicos and businesspeople from across the nation. The word was that the doctor had a few political aspirations of his own, and it was clear to all that he was in his element that night.

The elegant Mrs. Reinardt wore a long black dress, off the shoulders. Her long black hair was pulled up. She mingled as comfortably as her husband, and probably more effectively as far as fund-raising was concerned. She would move from group to group, always commanding the fixed attention of all. She would playfully hold on to the arms of acquain-

tances, laugh gracefully at the appropriate times.

All of this, of course, I observed from afar, having never met Mrs. Reinardt and seeing her only from across the room. I was not one of the targets tonight. In fact, I was supposed to be doing my share of soliciting.

"It's just not my game," I explained to Jerry Lazarus, who had joined the foundation about the time I did. Jerry went to law school with me, only he graduated and joined a high-powered firm.

Jerry laughed. "You'll never hold public office, Marty," a fate that he and many others had predicted for me in my more vibrant years. "You can't schmooze." Even then, after all the years out of law school, I still had to laugh at these words coming from an ex-hippie like Laz. I always pegged Jerry for public-interest work, legal assistance or NARAL, maybe some tree-hugging group. His long hair from those days was now cropped stylishly, the granola replaced with quiche, the flannel shirts traded in for trendy designer suits and silk ties. He reminded me of so many other students from my law school days, who would moan about civil rights and constitutional protections and join protests about faculty diversity or environmental policy, but when it came time to choose a vocation would become infinitely more fascinated with the finer points of corporate restructuring and vertical monopolies. I never thought I would hear the word "schmooze" from the same guy who almost dropped out of school rather than take a mandatory first-year legislation class, all because the professor had once served in the Nixon administration.

"No, Laz, I'll happily leave the ass-kissing to you," I said to him.

"Unless I'm mistaken"—Jerry smirked—"aren't I talking to a guy who spends his days with one hand jerking off some fat-cat investor, and the other hand reaching for his wallet?"

"That's different. At least it's honest. I'm not pretending to be performing some charitable function."

Jerry's eyes narrowed slightly, the same look he always got when he thought he had me beat in an argument—a not *uncommon situation.* "Yeah, I see that difference," he said. He took a gulp of his scotch. "Don't be so cynical. It's a worthy cause. Who cares how the money gets there?"

"You're falling behind," I said, showing Jerry my empty glass and patting him on the shoulder as I walked to the bar. A typical move for me, retreat before defeat.

I wiggled through some tuxedos to the bar. The bartender was dressed as a Vegas showgirl. I almost couldn't look at her without laughing. I ordered an Absolut with a twist.

I sensed someone behind me but didn't turn around. "I don't believe we've met," said a woman's voice, and I turned to face her. It was her eyes, I think—somewhere between amber and green, almond-shaped, with long eyelashes—that made me step back and utter something guttural. But it was only a split second before I had taken in the whole package. Her thick, even eyebrows arched slightly, the narrow nose, the full lips, the etched cheekbones completed an oval face and strands of black hair fell just past her slender shoulders. She smiled faintly, confidently, without parting her full lips. I realized it right then, without knowing why or how. I realized how desperately I had been waiting for her.

"Marty Kalish, Mrs. Reinardt." I extended a hand. "New guy."

"Rachel." She smiled. Her lips still did not part. "I didn't think I'd seen you here before." She looked me over. I couldn't think of anything clever to say.

"Are you enjoying yourself, Mr. Kalish?" Nice touch. Waiting for permission to address me informally.

"I am, as a matter of fact," I said, and this was more true now than it had been all night. I cast my hand over the room. "Quite a turnout."

"Yes, indeed. You wouldn't think even a room this big could fit all these egos."

I laughed. The bartender handed me my drink. Rachel considered me for a moment. "You have to be the youngest person in this room, Mr. Kalish." Probably not true, but I no doubt looked it, a curse from my father's side.

"Good to learn the game nice and early," I said.

"The game," she repeated.

"The contacts game. Meeting people, getting your name in their heads. Maybe the next time they're looking to put together a deal, they'll remember that eager young gentleman from the foundation."

She sipped her drink, then appraised me again. *"I'm sure they will."* She smiled. *"Will you excuse me, Mr. Kalish?"*

"Of course, Rachel."

The rest of the evening was not nearly as interesting as that brief encounter. I lost some money on blackjack, traded some stories with some bankers about deals that were put together only by the sheer brilliance of whoever was telling the story. But what I did after I met her felt like autopilot— the truth is, her face did not leave my mind for one second.

At around ten o'clock, someone tapped a glass. Dr. Reinardt, microphone in hand in the middle of the room, apologized and said that he had been called away to surgery. He asked us to go on and have a good time. And keep those pledges coming!

The party was set to break up right about that time anyway. I'm sure if it hadn't been, the doctor never would have left. What's one guy with a failing heart, compared to a ballroom full of power brokers?

A good number of the guests began to filter out. The foundation members, at least the junior members like me, were supposed to stick around until the end.

By eleven o'clock, only about twenty of us were left. I was going through some pledge cards that had been dropped into a coffer that looked like a slot machine. I saw Rachel walking toward me. I tried to think of something witty to say.

"Any luck?" she asked.

I waved a pledge card. *"A guy named Samms contributed a thousand dollars."*

"That's not what I meant. Did you make any contacts tonight?"

A good socialite remembers every conversation. I shook my head. *"The bartender seemed pretty impressed with me."*

She laughed. *"That's a start."*

"I'm sorry your husband had to leave."

She looked back absently. "I don't think he's sorry. He likes grand exits. How many other people here were noticed when they left?"

"Are you going to get home all right?" A little forward of me to ask.

This amused her, I think, or maybe she was expecting it. Her eyebrows rose and the faint smile returned. "Why, Mr. Kalish, are you offering me a ride home?"

A little forward of her, but hey, what the hell? I laughed. I felt a stirring in the part of my body that typically got me into trouble. "Call me Marty. And yes."

She accepted with the slightest of blushes, conveying embarrassment, I suppose, but her eyes never left mine, even fixed on me a split second longer than necessary before she walked away.

There was still work left to be done, and I completed it with surprising energy and haste. I saw Rachel talking to some of the other junior members, and I moved into her peripheral vision. I didn't walk all the way up to her; I wasn't sure if she wanted anyone to know I would be driving her home. That gives you an idea of what was going through my mind.

She noticed me and broke away from the others. "All set?" she said to me casually, as she looked into her purse. I was hoping she would have whispered it. Our little secret.

We made small talk on the ride home. We kept it pretty superficial, harmless. But there was something in the way she spoke to me in the car. It wasn't light banter; there was no humor. She spoke slowly, almost seductively (as if I needed to be prodded), using my name in almost every sentence. Innocuous as it was, it was the most titillating fifteen minutes of my life, full of fantasies and expectations and insecurities.

Finally, I pulled into the driveway, hoping that she would speak next.

"Have you ever been to our house, Marty?" The Reinardts often held meetings and little get-togethers at their home. I

*had been there a month earlier, just when I joined the foun-
dation. But Rachel wasn't there that night.*

"No, I haven't."

"Would you like a tour?"

*"Love one." I killed the engine and found myself wonder-
ing how long a doctor takes to perform heart surgery.*

*She took my coat. I followed her past the living room into
the den.*

"Can I fix you a drink?"

*"Please." I sat on the couch. The doorway to the den was
all the tour I needed.*

*She was over at the bar, her back to me. "Absolut with a
twist?" she asked, as she plunked ice cubes into a highball
glass.*

*"I know you probably think those fund-raisers are ridic-
ulous," she said as she poured our drinks. "But they are so
important to the work we do. If I could get that money going
door to door, I would. But this is how it's done. If I have to
snuggle up to some wealthy people to fund these programs
for the kids, it's worth it." She handed me the drink. A good
conversation starter, but I would have preferred something
with explicit sexual overtones.*

*"I understand that. I guess I'm just a little idealistic about
these things."*

*She sat down next to me, folding one leg under herself and
turned toward me. "We could all use a little more idealism."
She clinked her glass to mine. I took a drink, fully aware
that she was watching me as she drank. The vodka eased the
increasing nerves I was feeling.*

*Rachel, on the other hand, was completely calm. She
didn't seem conflicted by what was happening at all. Or
maybe nothing was happening. Maybe, as the adrenaline
rushed to my heart, as my mind danced with images of writhing bodies and soft, luscious moans, Rachel was simply enjoying a peaceful drink to cap off a successful evening.*

*I brought the glass down clumsily. A little vodka spilled
on my tuxedo pants. "Let me get you a napkin," she said,*

and she got up to go to the bar. Once again, her back was to me.

Something made me stand up. To this day, I can't place the moment where the impulses released from my brain to my legs. It just happened. I was trying to interpret signals here, something she was giving off, the extra moment she held the stare, the coy half smiles, like we've-got-a-secret. I'm not sure if I was initiating it, but I had certainly encouraged it. I almost sat right back down, feeling my usual doubts about my ability to read between the lines. I was either right on target or headed for a slap in the face.

Surely this wasn't how these things happened! There was more give-and-take, subtle suggestion topped by a slightly more overt one, slowly closing the gap until the leap was so small that it was practically agreed upon. Surely this was not the way to proceed!

And then I walked to her, suddenly losing any ability or desire to think this through, with an air of detachment, like I was someone else doing this while Marty looked on. "Rachel," I said quietly, hoping to conceal the tremor in my voice, "I have a confession. I didn't come here for a tour." I was delirious, my heart pounding. This would be the defining moment.

Rachel did not share my nervousness. She turned to face me, very slowly, not at all surprised at what I had just told her. Did she know what I was feeling? Did she know the moment she saw me? Was that smile she gave me when she introduced herself more than just social etiquette, more than a flirtation? She couldn't have, of course, but at that moment, as she turned to me, anything was possible.

She raised her hand to my tuxedo button and placed a finger on one of the studs. Then she ran that finger up and down the pleat on my shirt, taking in my reaction.

"You had something else in mind, Mr. Kalish?"

The phone, which rests against my chest now, blares out a dial tone.

Mr. Kalish. Mr. Kalish. She said it then, months ago, with

a sexy formality, the naughty wife who was about to fuck a complete stranger.

But on the phone just now, the formality was real. Mr. Kalish. Mrs. Reinardt. For the rest of our lives?

6

SEVEN O'CLOCK, FRIDAY NIGHT. OUR MONTHLY poker game. I considered bailing but finally decided to go, to do everything I would normally do on a Friday night. Besides, it'll take my mind off things, and I wasn't doing myself any good bouncing off the walls of my house.

So it is that I find myself sitting with Jerry Lazarus, Nate Hornsby, Scott Bryant, and Bill Littman in Scott's musty basement at a ratchety old circular card table, alone with our buckets of coins, six-packs of beer, and cigars that it was Nate's turn to provide.

Littman shuffles the cards while Nate passes out the sto-gies—"Hyde Parks," he informs us. Nate's the self-appointed cigar connoisseur of our tribe. "Not like that candy last time." He means the Avo Uvezians I brought last month. Nate bitched and moaned all night, they were too sweet. *Like chewing on a Tootsie Roll*, he said.

"Five-card draw," Littman announces. "Nothing wild. Nice and simple." Bill went to law school with Jerry and me—unlike me, both of them finished—and did the law-firm life for a couple years before moving in-house to work in risk management. He tells us his stress level dropped several notches with the move, which means he's only a pain in the ass about three quarters of the time now.

I take a swig of the beer and feel that initial little buzz. This is going to be good for me, tonight is.

Scott picks up his cards and groans. He always does that.

"You always do that, Bryant," Nate complains, placing the cigar in his mouth. "You always bitch about your cards and then go home the fucking grand-prize winner." I went to college with Nate. He works for one of the Big Six accounting firms, a senior manager now. His hair has receded painfully, leaving very little on top now, just a few strands of blond, his sides shaved mercilessly. His forehead is prominent and his cheeks are always a shade rosier than normal, so that in his finer moments he could be described as jolly, and at other times a hothead. And he always wears the same brown and yellow flannel to these poker games—his lucky shirt, he tells us.

"You gonna look at your cards, Kalish," Bill Littman says to me, "or you just gonna guess what's under?" You gotta have one Littman at every poker game, the guy who'd play till the sun rises. Hesitate more than five seconds in this game and Littman starts wailing like you stole his firstborn.

"How many cards, Scooter?" Littman barks. He likes calling Scott Bryant "Scooter." It's either that or "pretty boy," because Scott likes to slick his hair back and wear Italian suits. Scott asks for two cards.

I signal for three. I've got a pair of sixes that'll need help. I'm feeling pretty good now. This was a good idea, to come tonight.

"Three." Jerry Lazarus, placing three cards on the table.

"Nice hand." Littman, dishing out the cards with a flick of the wrist.

"Now, *this* is a ci*gar*," Nate Hornsby moans, taking a long draw before removing the stogie to admire it. He holds up two fingers.

This was a good idea to come tonight.

"Who didn't ante?" Littman asks, eyeing only four nickels in the pot. He's got his coins arranged neatly in front of him in little piles.

"Hey." Jerry touches my arm. "What about Dr. *Reinardt*?" Jerry called me today after reading about it in the paper. I didn't return the call. My fingers tighten on the cards. *Yeah,*

I heard something about it. No. *Oh, yeah, can you* believe *it?*

"Unbe-fucking-lievable," Nate answers. Then he points to the cigar lying next to Jerry. "You gonna light that?"

"Who the fuck didn't *ante*?"

"That's the guy in the paper today," Scott Bryant informs us.

Jerry nods. "He was kidnapped."

"He's *lucky* if he was kidnapped," says Nate. "I say he's ten feet under."

More like five or six. I swallow hard, then say, "I don't know who would do something like that." I place the cigar in my mouth, unlit, rotating it. A nice casual thing to do. Something a guy who didn't just commit a crime would do.

"That's a nice town ya got there, Kalish." Nate. "Move outta the big city 'cause ya don't want some lowlife prying open the bars on your window at three A.M., instead ya move into an upper-crust suburb where they just come right through the patio door."

"Was it *you,* Kalish?" asks Littman.

I turn to him, frozen. Was it *me*? Was it—he couldn't possibly couldn't *possibly*—

Littman nods at the center of the table. "The ante, shithead. Someone didn't ante."

"Oh." Relief sweeping over me. I take a deep breath. "No. I anted."

"Was it *you,* Lazarus?"

Scooter tosses in the missing nickel. "You happy now?"

Littman has given me my third six, so I raise Nate to a quarter. Littman takes note of this with a blank expression. His *poker* face. He really takes this so seriously. After a moment's hesitation, he throws in.

"So last week," Scott says. "You gotta hear about this girl."

"Fuckin'-*A*, Scooter." Nate gives us his exasperated tone. "We're trying to have a serious conversation about someone who Laz, Kalish, and I work with"—this really isn't true, of course, we had pretty much moved off the topic; but sometime over the last couple of years Nate has chosen Scooter to be the primary object of his sarcasm/cruelty—"and all *you* can do is think about this junior-high-schooler you corn-holed."

Jerry: "I for one am offended."

I remove the cigar and hold up my hand, happy to keep things moving away from the latest news about the good doctor. "Realizing as I do that a very rare sexual encounter is about the only thing that Scooter has in his life, I suggest we let him tell us about the sixth-grader." A nice little segue into the story Scott is dying to tell, although it isn't really accurate; Scooter's got that teen-idol look, long thick brown hair, chiseled face, and square shoulders that gets him ten times as many women as the rest of us combined.

"Yeah, okay, Don Juan," Hornsby says to me. "You got the next story. Tap that memory bank, kid, 'cause last I looked there weren't any notches on *your* headboard."

"You wound me, Nate." I raise a hand to my heart. This is going well.

"Are we gonna play *cards*?" Littman. With a groan.

"So my boss has a temp fill in for his secretary last week, right?"

"Oh, Christ," says Nate. "Scooter, if you tell me some hot little bombshell led you into the ladies' bathroom and gave you the ride of yer life in a stall, I'm leavin'. I'm gone. That shit happens to me never."

Good, this is good. We've fallen into our familiar give-and-take, four bachelors creeping up on middle age, listening to our gorgeous pal Scooter give us the skinny on sexual encounters that happen to us, like Nate said, never. We'll come through as always, expressing our doubts about the veracity of the story, probing for the sordid details, but in reality not caring about their truth, just happy to be hearing about them, touching them in some way. And *not* talking about my favorite deceased heart surgeon.

"So, I mean, every guy in the firm is inventing excuses to stop by the boss's office and get a look, right?"

"Just tell me ya got video," says Nate. "Give me that much."

I bite off the tip of my cigar and light up. My pulse is under control now. I had to expect that *someone* would bring up Rachel at some point. But we've moved on. This will be good, coming here tonight.

"So, *listen*," Bryant goes on. "So we're talking, right? Small talk. Where do you live, where do you hang out?"

"And there's your story." Littman sighs. "GQ got a hot blonde to talk to him. Can we finish the game now?"

"Brunette. So last Friday I casually mention a bunch of us are going to Flanagan's."

"Call," Littman says.

"I got two pairs." Jerry.

"Three sixes." Me.

Nate throws down his cards in a huff. So does Littman.

Scott looks at his cards. "Three *tens*." He smiles. Then he turns to Littman. "Does that mean I win?" He loves to act stupid about cards, especially when he wins; it really gets a rise out of Littman. We throw the cards to Hornsby, who will shuffle next. Bryant continues as he pulls the coins into his corner.

"So me and my boys are shooting pool, and who shows up but this lady."

"What'd she look like?" Jerry asks.

"Seven-card," says Nate. "Low ace in the hole splits. And she was a toad."

Scooter laughs. "I'm tellin' ya, no way."

"She had an eye patch and a limp." Littman.

"Whatever."

"Just tell me where, Scooter," says Nate. "Give me location and positions. I'll fill in the rest tonight when I'm lying in bed."

Scooter waves his hand casually, but he's beaming.

"Are you gonna smoke that fucking cigar?" Nate says to Laz. "I brought two for each of us. We don't got all night."

Not even two beers in Nate, he's already talking like a southsider with a tenth-grade education. Littman, too, and he grew up in these cozy northern suburbs.

Jerry eyeballs the stogie. He's ready to light up, but he loves getting under Hornsby's skin. "Uhhhhhh, I think I'll hold off for now."

"Don't you want to hear the rest of the story?" Scott has that whiny look now.

"We're giving you time to make the rest of it up," says Littman, touching the first two cards as they are dealt to him. He does that for luck.

Laz turns to me. "You talk to Rachel today?"

"Of *course* he talked to her," Nate says, still dealing. I shoot him a look, but he's not paying attention.

I turn sort of nonchalantly to Jerry. "Um, yeah, I called her."

"How was she?"

"Upset." I shrug. "You know."

"How come you didn't touch the third card?" Scott asks Littman.

Littman gives an exaggerated turn of his head to Scooter. "Because it's *faceup*, dumbshit. What's the point in tapping them when you already know what they *are*?"

Jerry has a pair showing, so he throws in a dime.

"Too rich for *my* blood," Scott says.

Littman turns on him. "You can't fold *now*. There's four more cards comin'." He moves closer to Scott. "You *have* played cards before, haven't ya, Scooter? I swear I seen ya here before."

"Well, I fold."

"Do they have any idea who did it?" Laz asks me.

I shake my head. "No."

Scooter shakes his head, too. "I can't believe you don't wanna hear my story."

"I *know* how it ends, Bryant," Nate says in a tired voice, pitching in his dime. "Yer humpin' and pumpin' in the backseat, top down, she's crying out in pleasure. That's the version we're gonna hear, anyways." He deals the next card, faceup. Littman gets an ace, giving him two showing. He rubs his hands together greedily.

"You might actually win, Litt," Laz says.

Bryant is pouting now, staring down at his coins.

"Oh, *tell* your fucking story," says Nate.

Scooter frowns. "He already guessed it. Location."

Nate turns to him, a hint of admiration crossing his face. "The car, huh?"

Laz gets up with his empty bottle and heads for the fridge. He asks who needs one, and all but Bryant, who's brooding now, give a nod. "None of that micro-yuppie stuff," Nate reminds Jerry. He's a Bud man and goddamn proud of it.

"Can we play cards now?" Littman grunts.

Nate turns on me. "So Rachey didn't say much, huh?"

"Uh, no," I say, a little off guard, my knee suddenly twitching. "Just—you know, she was upset."

"What'd you say to her?"

Jerry returns with fresh beers. I take a drink, too big of one, so that a little spills off my lips. I set down the bottle with a little tremble. I think Nate sees this.

"I—you know—just how ya holding up." Take a deep breath. Take a draw off the cigar and blow smoke rings up at the ceiling. Take another swig of beer. Tell a joke. But what joke? Christ, I got twenty at any given moment, except when I need one. What's the one about the elephant with three balls . . . ?

Nate returns to his cards, rearranging them. "This is your big chance, Kalish."

That one stops me. I try to look confused. Hornsby, thankfully, is not looking for a reply; it was just another off-the-cuff remark he makes all the time. So I just sort of scrunch my face and act like I have no idea what Nate means. Only that won't work with Jerry because he knows or I should say he *suspects* about me and Rachel, so me acting all innocent isn't so believable, but Jerry of all people wouldn't say anything. And Nate is just looking at his cards, so he'll probably let it pass. But I hope it doesn't register with Bryant and Littman, who don't work at the foundation and didn't even know who Rachel *was* until this conversation began. I don't need them remembering this conversation two days or two weeks or two months from now, when the police ask them about me. On the other hand, if things get *that* far I'm probably cooked anyway, but still, if they *do* remember the comment Nate just made—what did he say? Something like, *Now's your big chance,* or something—and they also remember that I didn't *deny* it, they will assume there is some degree of truth to it, but if I *do* deny it, and I go overboard in doing so, I'll seem defensive, and really if it *wasn't* true why would I bother denying it because it would be so obvious that a denial wouldn't be necessary but maybe the best thing to do is to deny it in sort of a flippant casual way, but the other danger there is it might spark *more* conversation about me and Rachel and that's about the *worst* thing that could happen so maybe I'll just blow it off but I think I'm starting to sweat and I don't want to seem nervous but I have this problem that I sweat *so much* that people always notice so maybe I should make some comment about the flu or something to cover it up but my whole plan was to be as normal as possible but I already blew that at work anyway when I told my secretary that I had the flu or was it Frank Tiller I said it to but it doesn't matter because an *innocent* person wouldn't remember that kind of thing anyway because it was such an innocent comment anyway or maybe it was Nate I said it to when I called him back about the foundation speaker who canceled but I don't think so but that still makes Deb and Frank who will be able to tell the police that I was acting strange the day after Dr. Reinardt was murdered and now Scott and Littman will also say whatever *God am* I sweating—

"*What's* his big chance?" Scott Bryant asks Nate.

Nate, still looking at his cards, jabs a thumb in my direction and starts to speak. We're going to talk about this some more now and I have to be ready with an answer a denial is the best thing but a casual denial be very very casual and I wish I could think of a fucking joke because that would be so casual and nonchalant what do you do with an elephant with three balls—

"I almost forgot," Jerry says, snapping his fingers. "I have homecoming tickets next weekend." All eyes, and all attention, turn to Jerry. God, how I love this guy. "Ellen"—his girlfriend—"can't go. I've got three more. Anyone interested?"

"Count me in," Nate says, as the rest of the table joins in as well. Everyone but me, that is. I mumble something about how I can't make it.

"He's got a date with Rachey," Nate says. I turn my attention immediately to my cards, biting my lip in concentration. Shake your head. Laugh. Wave your hand. Tell him to shut his fucking mouth why does he have to keep bringing this back *up*?

Lazarus comes to my rescue. "Hornsby, pick your spots, all right?"

Nate looks up from his cards innocently. "What'd I say?"

"In case you've forgotten," Littman tells Nate, "you're the dealer, pal. Usually that means you deal the cards right about now."

Hornsby throws out card number six. I have nothing showing, and I throw down my cards. I instinctively get up from my chair, my legs a little wobbly.

"Where *you* goin'?" Littman asks.

I point to the fridge.

"You got a fresh one."

I point upstairs.

"Are you telling us you want to take a wee-wee?" Nate asks condescendingly. "It's okay, Kalish. Simon says."

I head up the stairs. I can hear Jerry's voice scolding Hornsby ("You can be such a prick sometimes") and Littman bitching ("Is this a goddamn sewing circle?") as I make it into the bathroom.

I close the door and sit on the toilet, the lid still down. I pull the guest towel off the rack behind me and wipe my face. My hands are trembling, my breathing coming in short gasps, my vision spotty. The floor tile in the bathroom is yellowish circles. Yellowish circles. Count the circles. Focus on the circles. Ten . . . fifteen . . . seventeen circles in a row from the wall to the door. Count the next row. . . .

"What—are you going to do?" Rachel asked me, as I stood over her husband with the gun in my hand.

My heart pounds as the memories flood back; I squeeze my eyes shut to keep them out. God, I was so *calm* last night. Why can't I be now? I look at my watch. I've been in here for five minutes already. I have to go back down. I *have* to.

. . . sixteen seventeen eighteen circles in the next row . . .

They're talking about me downstairs. It was nice of Jerry to come to my rescue but now it looks like I'm upset and I ran off like I have something to hide and maybe Nate is starting to put it together downstairs and Jerry who is smarter than Nate and me *combined* has probably already figured it out but he would never say anything anyway so now I have to go back downstairs and act normal and pray like hell it doesn't come up again maybe I can think of another really good excuse my sister my sister is sick she's very sick and I just found out today and I'm very worried—

A knock on the door. "Hey." Jerry Lazarus. "You okay, man?"

I flush the unused toilet. "Never better." I throw the towel haphazardly on the rack and open the door. The expression on Jerry's face tells me I don't look so hot.

"We don't have to stay," he says. "I'm not feeling so good myself. You want to take off?" This man truly understands me. Probably better than I would prefer.

"Only if *you* want to." Then, to turn the focus to him, "You feel okay?"

"Yeah," he says, "I'm fine."

"You just said you don't feel so good."

"Yeah, well—I'm just saying we don't have to stay."

I flip the back of my hand against his chest. "I'm fine," I say. "I'll see you downstairs."

My sister is very sick. Nod thoughtfully. Sigh. Yeah, just found out today. What's wrong with her? I'd rather not get into it. Is she gonna be all right? We can only hope. Cross your fingers for luck. Anyway, it's got me a little on edge today and that's the reason why I seem so upset it's because of my sister. . . .

7

SATURDAY MORNING TYPICALLY MEANS AN EARLY start for me. Run a few miles before most of the neighborhood is awake. A long breakfast while I read the paper. Then I usually go to work for a few hours. Saturday is the most productive of the workdays. Even when others are in the office, it's only because they have to be. And they want to get out as soon as possible. So socializing is kept to a minimum, and I catch up on the stuff I couldn't get to Monday through Friday.

But no work for this papa-san today. I run my three miles much faster than usual and pick up the Saturday paper on the way back inside. Before I've made it to the kitchen, I've ripped off the blue plastic and started leafing through the front page.

"No Leads in Highland Woods Abduction," the paper announces on the top of section 2. I take a deep breath, adrenaline following a second later. *Abduction,* that's good. They're thinking about a kidnapping. Not a murder by a jealous lover. The article contains nothing new, just a brief overview of the case. So far, so good. I realize that every day will be like this, waiting to see if the cops are getting any warmer.

The doorbell startles me. I open the sports page over the rest of the paper. As I walk to the door I look through the dining room window and find a beige sedan that's seen better days parked in my driveway. I open the door to two men, one squat, one long and lean.

The stockier one flashes a badge, one that resembles the fake tin ones we used as kids, though judging from this guy's sour expression, this isn't playtime. "Mr. Kalish?"

I answer yes as I open the screen door. And I hold my breath. No big deal. Chill.

"Detective Cummings, Highland Woods Police. This is Detective Nicholaos." He nods to his partner. "Could we have a minute of your time?"

Still on pause I am, no good ideas moving about my head yet, just telling him, "Sure," and telling myself, *Calm calm calm.*

I take them into the living room and point to the couch. I sit opposite them in a love seat. I'm very calm. Nicholaos is looking around the room, at the art, the old piano from my parents' house, the framed pictures of my family and my sister's kids.

"I hope we didn't catch you at a bad time," says Cummings, but he knows he did, appraising my outfit and the sweat still clinging to my face. Anyway, it's hard to imagine a good time for meetings like this. Cummings is middle-aged and burly, loose flesh under his chin, bald on top with long hair on the sides that touches his ears, a seen-it-all look shrouded, as far as I can tell, in drowsiness. He reeks of cigar smoke, and it's not ten in the morning. I imagine his days have blended into nights since the good doctor disappeared.

He starts with the obvious, they're investigating the disappearance, just have a few questions. I'm suddenly feeling very fortunate for my recent workout, a convenient excuse for any coloring of my face or, worse, sweat.

I open my hands. "How can I help?"

"How well did you know the Reinardts?"

I tell them what they already know, the reason they're here; I work at the foundation, knew the cochairs in passing.

"What did you do at the foundation?" Cummings will do the talking. I look at the other guy, Nicholaos. He has flipped over a little notepad and started scrawling.

"I was part of the fund-raising committee, mostly. I occasionally work in the programs, too. But basically I work on fund-raising."

Cummings has his hands in his lap, and he's leaned forward on the couch. "Did you have a lot of contact with the Reinardts?"

"Not much. They attended all the functions, of course. But I was just one of about sixty people in fund-raising, which is only a part of the whole foundation. It's a big organization." This is routine Q & A, but I'm still not sure how I'm doing. Should I make eye contact or not? Seem disinterested or concerned? I . . . am . . . calm.

"You didn't know either of them on a personal level?"

You mean besides sleeping with Rachel?

"Not really." I scratch my face. "I'm sure they would recognize me if they saw me, but they probably wouldn't know my name. You know, one of a hundred faces." I wonder if I'm being defensive.

Cummings, looking into my eyes, pauses a split second before continuing. "Well, we're interviewing everyone who worked with the Reinardts. We're tryin' to see if anyone would have any reason to do 'em wrong. Anyone come to mind?"

I crinkle my face and stare at the wall over Cummings's head, at a painting from my house growing up, an abstract piece with violent waves of deep blue and purple. I slowly shake my head. "No. No, I don't think so."

"Anyone at all? Somebody with a grudge? Someone resented them, had an argument with them?" He brings a hand to his face.

"The foundation is not exactly a place that breeds enemies."

"What about *Mrs*. Reinardt?"

"I thought she was included in the last question."

Cummings pauses. He doesn't appreciate the comment, I'm guessing, but he's also wondering if maybe a light has turned on. "Let's just focus on *her,* then."

"I have no idea who would want to hurt her."

"Hmm." Cummings looks like he's feigning disinterest now, a little too casual in his shake of the head. I wonder what his radar's picking up here. Maybe he's just feeling me out. Maybe he really *is* disinterested. "Well, okay," he says. "But maybe someone didn't want to *hurt* her. Maybe someone liked her. Liked her a lot, let's say. Maybe that led to some ill will towards her husband?"

I try to look confused. I just shake my head and open my hands. No verbal answer; I'm afraid the throat might close up if I speak. I'm hunched forward, elbows on my knees, with a suddenly painful knot in the back of my neck and, by my estimate, every ounce of blood in my entire body now gathered in my face.

Cummings leans forward even farther now, his eyes set on mine. "You see what I'm askin', Mr. Kalish. Would you characterize Mrs. Reinardt as flirtatious? Someone who enjoyed the attention of men?"

"No, I wouldn't." My anger strengthens my voice. "I would characterize her as someone who cares deeply about her work. Someone all of us admire and respect. You might show her some respect yourself, Detective."

I see a flash of anger in Cummings's eyes, just a brief clenching of his jaw; cops don't accept disrespect well. He opens his mouth to respond but catches himself. Just like that, the anger is gone, replaced with curiosity. He nods and smiles a little too eagerly at me. "Yeah, you're right," he says amiably. "We've been workin' around the clock, you know how it goes." He keeps his eyes locked on mine, with that fake smile. But he doesn't talk, like if we sit here in silence I'll fill in the space with something helpful.

About sixty seconds pass, me and Cummings playing Mexican, before Detective Nicholaos jumps in. He is still fresh-faced, thick-necked, and athletic in his cheap plaid sport coat and open collar, probably just made detective. "We aren't trying to insult Mrs. Reinardt," he says, "but we need to explore everything. A jealous boyfriend is something we have to look at, or we wouldn't be doing our job."

Jesus. They're talking like it's a given Rachel had a guy

on the side. I swallow hard and try to keep my voice steady. "I highly doubt Rachel is capable of adultery." Rachel, not Mrs. Reinardt. Now I'm calling the person I hardly know by her first name. "Listen, I would love to help you guys. The Reinardts are good people who have done a lot for this city. But I couldn't possibly think of anyone who would want to hurt them." I look at Nicholaos, then Cummings. I pray that we are done. "I mean, we were talking about that. They're such nice people. Who would want to hurt them?"

"Who's *we*?" Cummings asks.

Fuck *me*. "Just some friends."

"Friends with names?"

"Well, I mean, I was talking to Jerry Lazarus"—Nicholaos scribbles the name—"and Nate Hornsby." I watch the detective write these names.

The junior detective looks up. "How do you spell Hornsby?"

"H-O-R—you should already have his name. He's in the foundation."

"H-O-R . . ."

"N-S-B-Y."

"Anyone else? Besides Jerry Lazarus and Nate—Hornsby?"

"Umm. No. That's about it."

Nicholaos nods his head. He claps his hands down on his knees and stands up. "Okay, Mr. Kalish. We appreciate your time."

Cummings is still seated. "You'll let us know if you think of anything." It is not a request.

"Of course," I say as I stand up. "I wish I could've been more help." I wonder just how much help I've been.

8

SATURDAY NIGHT CONSISTS OF MICROWAVE POP-
corn and movies I taped off cable, a typically pathetic weekend night. I start with an old comedy to take my mind off
more sober matters, but I can't shake the overall tension. The
cops shook me up today. I try to put myself in their shoes,
imagine what they thought of me.

I turn off the tape and start watching a late-night police
show. The lead detectives are two handsome guys with expensive haircuts and inane dialogue. They pull up to the
killer's house with a paddy wagon full of cops. The sirens
are blazing all around.

*The first siren had come much earlier than I expected. I was
off the Reinardts' estate and in the woods when I heard it. I
stopped in my tracks and turned, at least as much as I could
turn with Dr. Reinardt's body slumped over my shoulder.*

*I listened for a moment. Just one siren. Just one police
car.*

How had they gotten here so fast?

Run.

*I took off through the woods again, through the branches
that smacked me in the face, over the rough earth littered
with tree roots and rocks, even a stray toy wagon some kid
left here all winter that I kicked about ten feet in the air. The
doctor's arms flopped lifelessly against my back, his chin
bobbing on my shoulder as I ran. I wanted to stop and listen
but didn't dare. My head was bent down; through the wind,
I tried to keep my eyes on the narrow dirt path that spiraled
through the woods. I ran as hard as I could, trying to keep
my balance but too afraid to slow down enough to be careful.*

The wind slammed against my chest, blowing down through my shirt onto my skin. My leather coat was now being worn by the corpse on my shoulder, and all I had on was a thin flannel. The doctor was sliding off my shoulder. I jumped up and lifted him back over my shoulder. He was so heavy.

I've got to find a place to dump him, I thought. Where?

There was a clearing up ahead. It was the one I used to get to my house, a block over. Couldn't leave him there. Keep running. The people who lived by the woods here had a bright light on the back of their house, which shone in my face momentarily.

Keep running.

The woods were thinner here, and I could see all the houses as I ran. My legs were giving out, but I had to keep on. It was too well lit here.

But I couldn't. I stopped and listened. No sirens.

Where was I?

I didn't recognize the house I was behind. But the one next door to it . . .

Yes. Mrs. Krannert's house. A sweet old widow. She wouldn't be awake now.

I carried Dr. Reinardt behind her house. I slipped my way through the trees. She had a brightly lit backyard, but so did everyone else living by these woods, and I was running out of options.

I climbed the hill and dropped the doctor by a row of hedges that separated her yard from the neighbors'. I squatted next to the doctor and listened again for the sirens.

So much for taking my mind off things. I wipe the sweat from my forehead with my shirt. I wander to the kitchen and grab a bottle of Jack and a glass.

I pass the bathroom on the way to the living room and stop at my reflection in the mirror. It's dark enough that the finer features aren't apparent. My face is drawn from lack of sleep; the skin has that almost leathery look that first appeared sometime after my twenty-ninth birthday. The eyes are set back, hollow, my hair falling lifelessly to my eyes.

It's going to be like this from now on, I realize. Everything is going to remind me of that night. Any flashing light, siren, popping sound, scream, bruise, cut, blood. Bottle of scotch, long black hair, belt, flannel, sweatshirt, carpet, window, curtain, wind, cold.

Dirt, shovel, plastic.

The whiskey is warm in my throat. I sit back on my couch and stare at the dark TV set, at my ghoulish reflection.

The doctor looked at me as he lay on the carpet, his eyes wide open, intense, searching my face. I realized after a moment that he didn't see me at all. He was looking through me. His chest, split open and bloody, heaved slowly and deeply. His mouth, which was parted slightly, let out a low sound. A muffled sound. A gurgling sound. A trickle of blood spilled from his lip and down his cheek. His hands gripped the long hairs of the carpet. His right knee raised up; his foot pushed against the carpet. But it didn't catch. It just slipped, and his leg went flat.

I raised the gun up again so he could see it one last time. But his eyes were still.

I bring down the glass with a *clank* on the table and pour a second drink. My throat is raw now, and the whiskey ain't helping.

I've always wondered what it would feel like to have killed someone. Not the feeling of committing the act—that never really interested me—but after. Of carrying that little secret, wondering who knows what, playing the little games with everyone.

I always thought that this would be something I could never live with. That in the end, the better part of myself would force me to come clean. That some inner spirit, some force within that I have never known, would rise up and take hold of me.

Now I know. I *can* live with this. There will be no thumping heart calling to me from the floorboards. No voice tormenting me. No ghosts.

I have crossed over that line, that infinitely thin, often

shifting line that separates the acceptable and the unaccept-
able, the line that so many approach, fantasize about, flirt
with—don't we all flirt with these thoughts?—maybe even
want to cross, but don't. Don't *dare*. That one moment, that
exhilirating, split-second surrender to impulse, and I have
crossed the line, never to look back. I will always be a criminal now. My actions may or may not ever come to light—
I may or may not be judged—but either way, this is who I
am now. And after a day and a half, after getting through
Friday and a visit from Highland Woods's finest, I review
my new position. The first day of the rest of this life.

Everything is different.

My senses are heightened. The air is clearer. The colors
are brighter. The smells are more delicious, or more foul.
There is no such thing as calm now, maybe a dulled awareness at times, but not calm. Because inside me, I have this
knowledge, this little pilot light, that is waiting to be fanned
by any reminder of the doctor, of Rachel, of that night.

I will live with Dr. Reinardt the rest of my life. I will
remember November 18 every day, maybe every hour, that
I live. I will hear the shattering of the glass door as I hurled
the picnic bench against it. I will see the flash from the gun
that first knocked Dr. Reinardt to the carpet. I will feel the
gun itself, heavy in my hand. I will smell the gunpowder,
the putrid odor coming from the doctor's ripped chest. I will
see Rachel, cowering against the oak cabinets, pale, trembling, not knowing what I would do, but not stopping me,
either.

I look back at the blank television. I move the bottle of
Jack so it blocks my reflection.

In the end, my instinct will be the same. Survival. I will
resume my typical mortal concerns. Food, sleep, sex, work.
(Not in that order.) I will make partner at McHenry Stern.
I will continue my modest bachelor ways and save up, so I
can retire at forty-five and move to some island. I will still
send money every month to my sister and tell myself that
I have done my part for her. I will make my goal of running
the marathon. And eventually, someday, I will move on. The

memories will be there, but they will be diluted.

The third drink goes down much smoother. I put the glass down and grab the bottle by the neck, then raise it in a toast to Rachel. This is our bond now. However we may be apart in the end, however many years will separate our lives, we will always have this. We will always share this moment. This is our bond, Rachel. For better or worse.

9

FAR AS I CAN TELL, THE COPS HAVE LITTLE TO show after the first full week following Dr. Reinardt's disappearance. The Sunday paper ran a big article on it. Actually, there were two stories. One was on home security, how the break-in at the Reinardt house was opening some eyes. No neighborhood is safe, if not one in Highland Woods. The other piece was on just the Reinardt case. The police were beginning to rule out kidnapping, the paper said, given the lack of a ransom demand. Interesting.

The Monday *Watch* didn't discuss the case. On Tuesday, there was another good-sized article. The police were shooting blanks, and the reaction from the community was less than tolerant. Dr. Reinardt was one of the most celebrated people in the area. More to the point, this was a respectable doctor who was attacked in a white upper-class suburb. Rich folks don't like the thought of being vulnerable in their own homes. Elected mayors and prosecutors don't like their rich constituents feeling unsafe.

The police chief has been on the news every night, looking grave and increasingly exasperated. At first, the County Attorney, Phillip Everett, played to the cameras as well. Everett is a handsome, fair-haired man in his late thirties who first ran for public office immediately after graduating law school.

After a couple of two-year terms in the state legislature, he ran for County Attorney with the backing of the outgoing guy. He was elected in a surprising landslide, immediately fueling speculation of higher ambitions. He is now serving his second term as the county's top prosecutor and, by all accounts, is ready to go higher. A high-profile murder two years before the next U.S. Senate seat opens up is quite an opportunity. The current senator is widely expected to retire after one question too many about his personal finances, and no successor has jumped out of the pack, just a bunch of formers and saps with family names, circling the ring with hat in hand and one eye on the other guys. Everett will be the hero who makes the rich folks feel safe again.

But as the investigation has worn on with little progress, Everett has played hide-and-seek. He'll be there if a lead breaks, but will lay low until—if—that happens.

The media as a whole is beginning to pay less attention to the investigation. The blood has dried, there are better and more gruesome stories to cover. The less I read in the paper and hear on the tube, the stronger I feel. By today, the Wednesday before Thanksgiving, I have decided that I am up to making my annual trip to my sister's.

I lean back in my recliner and kick my feet up, letting the scotch settle in my gut.

My visit to my sister will be tomorrow. Tonight is for Rachel. Tonight Rachel will be dressed in a long fur coat. She will enter the house without invitation, will find me here in the family room. She will take the remote from my hand and kill the television. Then she will turn on the stereo for soft jazz. She will take the bottle from my hands and bring it to her lips. She will take a sip, close her eyes, and wet her lips, savoring the liquor. She will raise a heel on the recliner, revealing for the first time her long, naked leg through the full-length coat.

Do you want to touch me?

I will start to answer, but she'll bring a finger to her lips.

Where?
Where do you want to touch me?
I will show her. I will show her, over and over again, where I want to touch her.

10

JAMISON KALISH LEYDEN LIVES IN EVEREST PARK, A good ten hours away, with her two children. She and her husband divorced just over a year ago. The kids are four and eight now, real bundles of energy, and the apple of Jamie's eye.

I drove, believing for some reason that it would be therapeutic. And like my father used to, I honk as I pull into the driveway. Jeannette, the little one, is out the door before anyone. A little ball of fire with red pigtails and pink-and-white overalls, she dutifully holds the railing as she comes down the concrete steps to the driveway. I pop out of the car to meet her. She yells, I yell. I gather her in my arms. She squeals and gives me a big kiss, complete with a trace of jelly left over from lunch. I carry her up the steps to the porch and see a boy with a red-and-black basketball T-shirt. Tommy has grown an inch or two since this time last year. At eight, his height has outrun his weight; he is as skinny as I was at that age but with much curlier hair. He throws me a high five, and I pull him against me for a brief hug. He's glad to see me, but by his ripe age is too cool to show much outward affection for an adult. "Mom!" Tommy calls out. "Uncle Marty's here!"

My sister, Jamie, comes out of the kitchen, and despite myself I see my mother. Jamie has inherited her slim build and striking green eyes, Dad's red hair. She smiles sweetly and gives me a big hug. I hold her for a long time. It's always good to see my little sister, but this time seems especially powerful. I stifle the instinct to cry. Times are tough for her, and I haven't exactly enjoyed the past few weeks myself. I am instantly glad I made the trip.

After settling in, I help Jamie in the kitchen. As much as I can, anyway; I slice potatoes. Jeannette, feeling left out, wants to help, too. She's put in charge of folding the napkins.

"So how's the life of a high-powered investment banker?" Jamie asks, as she works on the stuffing. She is petite and athletic, still looking pretty toned after two kids and a nightmare schedule. Her red hair, with new strands of gray, is up in a ponytail.

"Glamorous," I say. "There really is nothing more fulfilling than knowing I helped a millionaire buy a few thousand more acres of land. How 'bout here?"

Jamie smiles. "We're doing okay," says my little sister, as if she's trying to convince herself. "He's doing better." Tommy had a rough go of it when his father left. The school year—first grade—started for him just after his dad moved out, and he would have been better off with a little adjustment before he began.

"I'm in nursery school," Jeannette announces.

I turn to her. "You are? What do you do in class?"

She straightens up. "We paint, and we build, and we draw, and, and we color, and we have story time." I am visibly impressed.

"What does Mrs. Terry say about your drawing, Jeannette?" Mom asks.

"Mrs. Terry says I'm a good artist." She is glowing. Oh, this little kid.

I reach for her nose. "Maybe you could draw something for me." This lights her up. She looks just like her mother, I realize, not just the red hair but her big green eyes. The Kalish women, striking features and luminous hair, all of them. She climbs down from the chair all by herself and runs upstairs to compose her masterpiece.

"Maybe after dinner," Mom says.

Thanksgiving dinner is the first real home-cooked meal I have eaten since—well, since the last time I was here. The menu at chez Marty is, I suppose, your basic bachelor fare. Mac-and-cheese, frozen pizza, pasta with red sauce, Chinese ordered in. Tonight we dine in the small living room next to the kitchen. The table isn't big enough to hold all the food, so Jamie leaves some of it in the kitchen after everyone is served. This house is quite a bit smaller than the one they lived in before Billy left. I am filled with pity and admiration for Jamie, watching her make due with these rather cramped quarters, trying so hard and wanting so much for her children.

Tommy eats sparingly, picking at his plate and humming a song to himself. He participates in the conversation when required, throwing standard one-liners to every query I throw him. What's he been up to? Not much. School? It's fine. His favorite subject? Geography is okay. The only hint of animation he shows is when we talk basketball, so we talk about his team and college ball. Tommy looks like his father, watery blue eyes, sandy, curly hair, and the lean build. He has his dad's sour outlook, too, though I suspect this is less inherited than experiential. He's seen a lot more than many eight-year-olds. He took the brunt of his parents' marital difficulties in a way that Jeannie, then three years old, couldn't. This time last year when I saw him, he was brash and moody, an attention-getter. Now he's reserved, more mature, and maybe more troubled.

Even for kids as well behaved as these, your basic dinner is a chore for Mom. Jamie serves and cuts all of Jeannette's food, which consists of white meat and a roll with brown gravy spilled over it. She wipes Jeannie's mouth, cleans her up when something spills on her lap and she starts crying. I swear, Jamie spends more time watching her children eat than she does eating her own food. No wonder she's so thin.

Tommy and I have dishes detail, while Mommy helps Jeannie with her artwork for my review. I hand Tommy the dishes, he loads.

"Got a girlfriend?" I ask. Now that the girls are away, we can get down to it.

"Gross."

Or maybe not. "Play some one-on-one tomorrow?"

"Okay."

I hand him a dish. "I'll try not to beat you too bad."

No answer. I tell him I'm kidding. He shrugs.

A call from the other room. Jeannette is done with her masterpiece. I sit down on the family room carpet, eager with anticipation, as she triumphantly lays before me her work, composed on a large, thick piece of construction paper, which I haven't seen since grade school. To the right, in brown crayon, is her house. A square with a triangle on top. A red chimney with smoke flowing from it. A rectangular door and three square windows, in black crayon, above it. In the top left corner of the paper is an orange sun with yellow beams. Below the sun, next to the house, is a man with a long stick body, stick arms and legs, dots for eyes and nose, and a smile. Above him, with an arrow pointing down, are the words "Uncle Marty." (Mommy helped with the spelling.)

I am amazed, and I make a point of showing it to Jamie. She is equally impressed. Even Tommy comments on how good it is. Jeannie is positively glowing.

It wasn't my idea to break out the family scrapbook—it was, in fact, over my vigorous protest. Jeannie sits in her mother's lap; Jamie supports one side of the large book, the other ending up on my lap. Tommy sits next to me.

The early photos are black-and-white. They are mostly baby pictures of me, before Jamie was born. One of them is the day I was born.

The next picture, three pages in, is the first one featuring my mother. She is holding me as a newborn: "Marty at 3 days." We are still in the hospital. My mother's dark hair is longer in that picture, I notice in the brief second that I look at the photo before staring at the dark television set.

"That's Gramma," Jeannette announces.

"That's right, honey," says Mom. "And do you know who that little baby is?"

I reach to turn the page. Jamie, somehow ready for it, blocks me.

"That's *you*, Mommy," Jeannie guesses.

"Nooooo."

I reach again, and this time Jamie presses her hand down tightly on the page. "Turn the page," I say.

"Guess again," Mom says.

"It's Uncle Marty," Tommy shouts.

"Right!"

Jeannie squeals with this revelation. Tommy sort of nudges me in the arm.

"Turn it, Jamie."

"He doesn't have any hair!" Jeannie's stubby finger points at me in the photo.

"Jamie—"

She casts me a look.

"She's kissing him!"

"That's right, honey."

"Jamie—"

"You were fat," Tommy observes.

"So were you," I reply with an elbow. "Jamie, turn it."

With a quiet *harrumph* and a sour glance at me, because she never understood, Jamie turns the page. She was always troubled by my lack of a relationship with Adrian—that's our mother, it's the only way I feel comfortable referring to her—but this anxiety grew as Adrian neared death. She was in a nursing home in her last year, and moved to a hospice the last two months as cancer ravaged her body. That whole year, I never visited, talked to her on the phone a handful of times. I made it to her bedside her last day, when she was all but gone. And after she died—this was four years ago—Jamie took a long time before she would talk to me again. My disdain for Adrian, which was once incomprehensible, was now unforgivable to her. I thought she might never speak to me again, but she did, both because she probably wanted to teach me the lesson that blood is thicker than everything else, and because she has an enormous, forgiving heart that I will never have.

I suggest we forget the scrapbook and turn on that animated video Jeannie talked about during dinner. I don't get much of a reception to that, but I keep pressing the idea, as Jamie continues to stroll through the book. Finally, Jeannie decides she's tired of this and warms up to the idea of seeing that video. After even Tommy joins in, Jamie puts away the family album.

So we watch a movie together, some G-rated animation thing featuring a singing mouse. Tommy is restless, but he dutifully watches. Jeannie falls asleep in Jamie's lap and is put to bed. Tommy follows right after, high-fiving me good night.

11

SO I WAIT ALONE IN THE LIVING ROOM AS JAMIE readies the kids for bed, watching the flames of the fireplace dance, eventually allowing my eyes to wander to the mantel above, to the Kalish family pictures. My parents and Jamie and me at some amusement park by a fountain. Jamie and my mother at a ballerina recital, after Jamie had performed. A posed family shot when I was ten, Jamie six. I'm wearing a starched white shirt with black bow tie, Jamie is in a dress that resembles a sailor's outfit. Dad is wearing a sport coat and his typical contented smile. Mother dearest looks as glamorous as ever. The four of us at Jamie's graduation from high school. The four of us at my graduation from college. And finally, side by side, individual black-and-white photos of my parents. My dad's head is turned awkwardly a little too far back at the camera, but he wears that same expression, content, wise, gentle, ignorant. She looks as glamorous as ever.

I look back into my father's eyes in that picture, and for a moment we are looking at each other and having one of our countless conversations in the living room. My dad, in his thoughtful, patient manner, refusing to judge me, laying out the moral map and helping me find my way. I could use his compass right now.

My father was what you would call a sophisticated thinker. Peter Kalish graduated from college with a philosophy degree and headed straight to law school to explore the higher ideals underlying the framework of our society. He was a conservative in an increasingly liberal atmosphere, and my father found this to be the most intellectually stimulating time of his life (as he once told me while explaining the virtues of law school). He was active in several student advocacy organizations in law school, even founded one or two, and dreamed of getting an LLM and returning as a law professor.

That's when he met her.

Peter Kalish met Adrian Vivriano in his third year of law school, and he was immediately taken by her (I supposed if this bio were free from editorialization, I would say he was taken *with* her). She was three years younger, fresh out of college and ready to start her career in social work. Adrian Vivriano was not someone you would expect to find going from one run-down housing project to another checking on the safety and welfare of children in fragmented or abusive homes. She had exotic Italian features, a long but shapely build, and she carried herself with the grace and mannerisms of a woman accustomed to the finer things. It never made sense to me—still doesn't—that she took a job that not only paid so little but that carried with it so little prestige, an absolutely thankless job that must have left her tremendously bruised and sad at the end of each day.

But this was the vocation she chose, and these were the circumstances under which my parents first met: my dad a third-year law student flirting with the idea of sinking into more debt to get another degree, Adrian already a year into her social work.

Funny, I don't know how they met. For some reason, it just never came up. Maybe he stepped into one of those jungle traps where the circular rope suddenly closes around your ankle, and she pounced while he was strung upside down. However it happened, to hear my dad tell it, he flipped over her the moment they met. That was what you did with Adrian, I guess—you flipped over her. There was my love-struck father, already in debt from law school loans and ready to propose after six months. So instead of continuing his schooling, he took a job with one of the big corporate law firms in the city. My dad was a sacrificing sort, someone with incredible inner calm who could be happy in pretty much any situation. He was the peacekeeper in the family, one of the least confrontational people I have ever known when it came to family politics. (This was his failing, I suppose, in her eyes. Or one of them.) So when joining a law firm became the most practical move economically, especially in the opinion of his fiancée, my dad took the path of least resistance. (Dad would always tell me later that this was his choice, that she didn't care what he did or how much money he made. I tend to believe otherwise.)

So my parents got married and lived downtown. She got to continue in the career she wanted, he didn't. To state it mildly, working in a downtown law firm gave my father none of the things that he wanted when he went to law school. It was, as he put it, just another form of business, and he had spent his entire academic career trying to avoid the business sector.

But if my father was not taken with drafting contracts and researching the niceties of antitrust law, he was, as I said, taken with her, and he appreciated the hefty paycheck because *she* did. So along they went for three years, my dad hating his job but loving his wife, his wife loving her job but hating—well, I suppose that's not fair.

Enter yours truly. She quit her job like pregnant women were supposed to do back then. My dad was in his fourth year of toiling in the firm, and he'd pretty much hit his limit when news of my impending arrival hit. Not surprisingly, this is when the problems started. They lost her income at precisely the time when expenses were about to go up, and my dad decided he couldn't take the firm life anymore. He had kept in contact with a conservative advocacy organization that left him an open offer to join, and he told Adrian that he wanted to take it. She was opposed, my dad once admitted to me after one too many scotches, but his thought was that he didn't want his child to grow up thinking that you had to choose a job based on money. What kind of an example would that set for the child? He wanted me to see that what mattered was having a fulfilling career.

Guess who won the argument? So my dad remained miserable for another two years, during which time they saved up all the money they could, and then my dad joined the conservative organization (a couple years later settling in as a law professor at a downtown school). Even then, I think she resented him for it. Maybe that's what did it. Maybe she never forgave him.

That eight-by-ten of my father is so appropriate. The quiet dignity, the scrupulous, good-natured, self-assured man. He only wanted the three of us to be happy. He avoided tension and confrontation like the plague. He approached the typical family squabbles that would arise from time to time with a reasoned, disarming calm. It was only when he talked about the law that a spirit ignited in him, and he spoke with a ferocity and directness that made him virtually unrecognizable from the man who would back down at the slightest hint of tension over the dinner table. Even during those miserable years in the law firm, Peter Kalish continued to be active in legal foundations and published extensively in law reviews, often working well into the early morning on his pieces. If the law is a jealous mistress, she was a mistress who was satiated more often than not. Maybe that's what did it to Adrian. I don't really know what it was, and I've given up trying to guess. And I don't really care. I don't.

I remember touching her hand that last day, four years ago.

Not caressing it, just placing my fingers lightly on top. My mother lay askew on the hospital bed nearly comatose, tubes in her nose, arm, and abdomen, eyes open in immovable slits, her shiny hair spilled over the pillow after a fresh shampooing from Jamie and a nurse.

I'm here, I told her. It's all I said to her, as if by announcing my arrival I was offering some concession. The other words came but never surfaced, as I sat with her. I wonder if she was waiting for them. I wonder if she wanted to say something to me, if she was filled with regret that now, when she wanted to speak, she couldn't.

I hear Jamie in the kitchen now. She walks into the family room with a bottle of wine and two glasses. She notes with approval that I'm looking at the family pictures, but I walk away from them and take the bottle from her hand, lest we start a conversation about our parents.

"The kids are great, Jamie," I say. We sit next to each other on the couch.

She smiles, then sighs. "They really are, aren't they?" She holds out her glass, I pour. "I suppose it could have been a lot worse. When Billy left, Jeannie was barely three. She couldn't understand. She still doesn't, really, but she's accepted it."

"Does Billy see them often?"

"About once every two months." Billy lives out of state now. He didn't contest custody at the divorce. In fact, from what I recall, Jamie was willing to give him more visitation rights than he wanted. "I wish he'd come more often," she says. "He's seeing someone now, it's been about nine months. The more serious it gets, it seems, the less time he has for his children." With the kids in bed and out of earshot, Jamie's words have a decided tension.

So on to something better? "What about you?" I ask. "Anyone in the picture?"

"Oh." She waves a hand dismissively. "Not really. I mean, there's this guy from the office." She is a secretary at a mortgage brokerage firm. "A nice guy. He seems interested. But think about the package he's getting."

"A gorgeous redhead and two dynamite kids. Not a bad package in my book."

She rolls her eyes. "Red-and-*gray*-head," she corrects, holding up a strand of her hair. "And not *his* kids, Marty. Men want their own, not some other guy's."

"Why can't he have both?" It's more of a rhetorical question. I know what she means. Hell, I don't even want kids of my own. The only time I even remotely entertain the notion of children is when I'm with Jeannie and Tommy. Kids are great, after all, when you don't have to do any of the dirty work. That's why grandparents love the role so much.

She sighs again. "Well, I admit, it would be nice. Tommy could use a father right now. And the extra income, for their college."

"I don't hear anything about you in there, little sister." She is just like our dad, subordinating her interests to everyone else's. I certainly did not inherit that trait.

"Sure, it would be nice for me, too." She drifts off for a moment, briefly allowing the thought of another man in her life, a notion that at one time probably would dominate her thoughts, quicken her pulse, but now is nothing more than a piece of a puzzle that must fit perfectly alongside her children. "For the time being, I just want to see how the kids come through this."

"It's been over a year, Jame. The kids are fine. Think about yourself a little."

She considers this momentarily. "By the way, Mr. Single-with-no-kids."

"Oh, yeah, little sister. A real lady-killer, your brother is."

"You're not going to tell me that there are no women interested in a charming, handsome, sensitive man with a six-figure income."

Well, maybe one. But she's married. Or at least she was, until I buried her husband. That thought drifts in and out without much pain; it's probably the change in surroundings that muffles it. Or am I getting over it? Have I put it behind me this quickly? "Tell me about Tommy."

She gets that vacant look again. "Tom is doing much better. He's not fighting anymore. He's in a basketball league, and he's good. He spends hours out on the driveway shooting. It's an escape for him." Her hands cup her glass in her lap, her fingers drumming the sides. "He's doing much better," she repeats.

"He seems al—"

"He needs a father, Marty." Her voice cracks as she says this. She brings her legs up on the couch, so she's sitting Indian style. She brings the glass to her lips but then puts it back down. "I mean, with Jeannette, it's different. She has her mom, and she was so young when he left, she probably won't remember. But Tommy—"

"Has more than most kids could *dream* of, Jame. He has a mother who adores him, and who's always there."

Jamie tightens her shoulders and releases. "I guess. It would be different if he never had a father, but he's out there, you know? And he doesn't care." She pauses. "The truth is, Billy hasn't been here for eight months. Can you imagine what that does to a little boy?"

Now my sister turns to me, and I touch her hair. The same hair that, when Jamie was six, she colored with black magic marker because she wanted to be a brunette. I touch the scar near her ear, where she burned it the first time she used a curling iron, in sixth grade.

Those years are behind Jamie now, and even for someone who has kept her figure, it shows. Lines have formed by her eyes. The gray in her hair, like she said. What really shows through, though, is not something visible. It's the way she carries herself, a complete absence of vanity, her lack of energy for anything unrelated to her kids. It's her spirit, her vibrance, that is gone. She's a divorced secretary trying to hold together a home with two young kids. She no longer dreams of great things for herself. With those bright green eyes, she sees the world only through her children now. I wonder if that's what happens to all women who become mommies. Actually, I can think of one mother who didn't share that trait.

Jamie keeps pace as we down the first bottle. I press her

about this guy she reluctantly told me about. His name is Robert, he's a computer consultant teacher. I ask about the possibilities, but she waves me off.

"I don't know. I have to be careful, Marty, you know? I don't want men coming in and out of their lives. I mean, he seems like a stable guy. He has a good sense of humor. I don't know." She takes another sip. She looks over at me. "Now, don't give me that wrinkled brow," she warns. "I'm *fine*, Marty. Like you said, I have two wonderful kids."

I watch her take another sip, and I reach over and mess her hair. My only sister. My only family. "Did you ever think of moving out by me?" I blurt out unexpectedly, even to myself.

Her response is even more surprising. "You know, I have. I really have. It's not like there's a lot keeping us here. I could find the same job there that I have here. And I'd like Tommy to be closer to you, Marty. Billy is drifting farther and farther away from us. I'd like . . . well, I'd like him to be closer to you." This revelation catches me by complete surprise, and I'm sure my facial expression makes that clear. I've only seen Tommy twice in the past two years, and we really haven't formed much of a bond. But it's obvious that Jamie has been considering this for some time.

I know what the right thing to do is. Encourage her. I could help her with the kids. I could see her more often.

But there will be a responsibility that I'm not ready for. Fuck, that I've *never* been ready for. Doling out some advice over the phone, that's one thing. But being the father figure is another. Setting an example for someone, anyone. I have avoided it, not accidentally, my whole life. It is this fear of responsibility—more of a panic, really—that keeps my mouth shut now. Just a kid myself, frozen, mute, floating in the uncertain world of adulthood, feeling for the landing.

Jamie realizes she has crossed a line, one that I *invited* her to cross. "It's just a thought." She smiles weakly. "Who knows?" She takes another sip of wine so one of us will be doing something besides feeling awkward.

Jesus, I'm still off guard. She's reaching out to me, gauging my reaction, and I sure as hell gave her one. Jamie, bless her heart, manages a little small talk for a few minutes before excusing herself. As she says good night, I pause for a moment, giving her a look that I hope conveys some measure of regret. Regret for being a self-centered asshole. She smiles sweetly at me. Forgiveness. She's seen it before with me. She pats me on the knee and goes to bed.

I sit there on the couch filled with shame. I replay that conversation over and over now; each time, the noble Martin Kiernan Kalish encourages his divorced, single-income sister, Jamie, to move her kids to his hometown. He offers to help her find a job. And he promises to help Tommy and Jeannette grow up. These words will never be spoken.

I think of the bed in the spare bedroom, where I will sleep tonight. Rachel loves strange places. Tonight she will visit me, couldn't stay away for even one night. She will be in workout clothes, loose sweatshirt over an athletic bra, spandex pants. I will give her a look, motioning to the kids' rooms, but she'll give me that smile.

I promise I'll be quiet. I'll be a good girl.

You see, Jamie? Do you see this? Me, a role model?

There isn't much left of the second bottle of wine, but I down what remains. Dirty Uncle Marty. Never married. Never really saw him with a girl, actually. Is he queer? Is *that* his story? No, Tommy, your uncle is not gay. Just a little fucked up, is all. You can shoot the shit, get some advice. But don't get too close to the cage.

I rinse the glasses in the sink and toss the bottle in the garbage. Then I head for the bedroom. To Rachel.

I BEGIN WORK THE NEXT MONDAY REFRESHED AND with new hope. The weekend trip to Jamie's did wonders for my ability to distance myself from what had happened— though I did feel a sinking feeling in my gut as I passed the skyline of downtown.

The office is buzzing as usual, but Christmas is in the air and many partners plan their vacations around the holidays. Very few deals go down this time of year—our fiscal year ends in October, so there's no last-minute rush to make revenue plan—and I can coast through and wait for the new year.

The new year. I think of it longingly. If I can make it until then, it would be a month and a half since the disappearance of Dr. Reinardt. It has to get tougher to solve these things as time wears on, doesn't it? Anyway, judging from the television and newspaper, the police have no idea where to look.

So I throw myself into work this morning, immersing myself in a lease restructuring and trying to believe that I can put this behind me. And there are moments this morning when I *do* believe, where my heart flutters and the words on the contract dance off the page. I just might make it. We just might be together, someday.

My office phone rings around eleven, a double ring that signifies an outside call.

"Marty." Jerry Lazarus.

"What's the word, Laz?"

"Nothing much. Have a nice turkey day?"

"Yeah. Usual family stuff. You?"

"Same. Listen, you going Friday?"

Friday, December 3. The Reinardt Family Children's

Foundation Christmas party. "I guess I thought that would be canceled," I say. The luncheon the Monday before Thanksgiving, for which Nate Hornsby and I were supposed to field a speaker, had been canceled in the wake of Dr. Reinardt's sudden departure. I figured the Christmas party would be, too.

"I did, too," Laz says. "And get this. I heard our chairwoman will be in attendance."

My throat chokes.

"You there?"

"You're kidding."

"No. The show must go on, I guess. So I'm taking Ellen, and she has a friend I've met. We were thinking you might want to double."

Now, that would be something. A woman on my arm with Rachel in the room. Actually, it would be a pretty good cover for me. But I couldn't possibly handle it. Christ, I'm dumbstruck, sweating and mute even now, on the phone with Jerry, while I think about Rachel. Imagine me in a roomful of people, with a blind date, and Rachel.

Jerry describes this woman to me. Fun, I think he said. Great legs. Something about me and a dry spell. I cut him off. Not this time, I say, hanging up the phone to the fading sounds of protest on the other end.

I suppose my first thought should have been how hard it would be for Rachel to attend this party. But the truth is, all I can think about is how excited I am to see her.

The phone rings again. This is the second time Laz has tried to set me up with some woman. He is determined—actually, his girlfriend, Ellen, is determined—to find me someone to settle down with. I haven't had a date, much less a steady girlfriend, for two years. That excludes Rachel, of course, whom no one knows about. Last time, Lazarus had persisted until I agreed to the date, only to have me cancel at the last minute. Laz warned me that my dick was going to fall off.

I let the phone ring three times before lifting the receiver.

Laz isn't going to take no for an answer. I can at least make
him wait before picking up.

"Hel-*lo*," I say in an irritated voice.

"Marty Kalish?" Nothing but air on the other end, just a
faint whisper of a voice.

"Speaking."

"I saw you."

It doesn't register. "You—?"

"I *saw* what you did to him."

The adrenaline outruns the synapses; before I understand
the words, my heart is pounding. My mouth hangs open but
no words come out. Because there *are* no words to answer
this. I spin in my chair so my back is to the door.

The first siren had come earlier than I expected.
How had they gotten here so fast?

"Do the right thing." The line goes dead with a sharp *click*.

I cautiously replace the receiver, like I'm handling a bomb,
and hold my breath. I feel the sweat on my forehead now,
joining the banging pulse. I had covered my tracks that night,
kept a relatively cool head in the panic. No prints. No clues
left behind whatsoever, as far as I could tell. An airtight alibi.
I had controlled the environment. Controlled everything. But
now there is something beyond my control.

Someone saw me.

13

I GO HOME MONDAY AND FIDGET ALL NIGHT. I BOIL
some pasta but can't get it down over the lump in my throat.
I can't read, can't watch TV, can't listen to music. I pace
around the house, going over and over in my mind the path
I traveled after leaving the Reinardts' house. *Where* did he
see me? *When? How?*

I try to make a list of the Reinardts' neighbors, but I know only of a handful. But then, how could *he* recognize *me*? It must be someone I know. Right? Yeah, of course. Dr. Hunt, he's a guy who lives the street over from Rachel. Jason, I think his name is. I found his dog wandering around lost on my street one day, and I checked his tag and returned him to this guy. But would he really remember my name? Susan Rae lives a few houses away from Rachel, we got our masters' together, she works in my building for a development company. But our contact is limited these days to hellos in the building and promises to call each other for lunch. And it was a *man's* voice, for Christ's sake!

Maybe he saw me in the car. But how could he know what I was doing—how could he know there was a dead body in my trunk? Maybe he saw me move Dr. Reinardt. Maybe he saw me in the woods, out his back window, while I carried the doc on my shoulder. Maybe I have no idea how or when or where he saw me, and I need him to *call me back*!

Jesus, only a night earlier, I left Jamie and the kids in Everest Park, actually believing that this thing might be behind me. Less than twenty-four hours later, I feel like someone enjoying his last night of freedom. The fear, the sense of impending doom, is more vibrant now, a more wicked sting, since I've tasted the flavor of survival.

The ring of the phone jolts me. I stare at it in disbelief, as it rings one time and another. Is this him? How do I open him up? What do I say?

A third ring. My answering machine will pick up after the next one.

Pick it up. And keep your head.

"Hello?"

"Uncle Marty?"

"Tommy." I sink into a kitchen chair. "What's going on, little guy?"

"Nothin'. You said I should call anytime."

I mop my face with a dish towel. "Yeah, Tom. Sure. What—what's going on?"

"Nothin'."

I try to slow my breathing. "Okay. Well—how's your basketball team?"

"We won. We're eight and one."

"Cool."

"We're tied with the Barons for first place."

"Good. That's good."

"We play 'em next week."

"Yeah? Good." Bob Fenton. We played on a co-ed softball team two summers ago. I think he still lives a block over from Rachel. But he lives the opposite way from the path I took, right? He couldn't have seen me, could he?

"Mom's sad."

"She—what?"

"Mom's sad."

"No, Tom. She's not sad. Why do you say that?" Sally Martin—but she's another woman! The voice was a *man's*. Jesus, Marty, who else? *Who else?*

"She was crying."

Joey Kellock lives around here somewhere, right? He moved out of the city when his wife got pregnant. He moved to this subdivision—or did he move to Clayton Hills? I think I have his address somewhere—

"I heard her. Last night."

"Yeah?"

But Joey wouldn't pull this shit with me. He'd either keep his mouth shut or just call me up and say, did I see what I thought I saw? Plus I think he lives in Clayton Hills—

"She's sad 'cause of Dad."

"Yeah?"

Call me, goddammit! Call me and tell me what the hell is going on!

"Do you think she's sad?"

I exhale. Concentrate now. For ten seconds, concentrate. "Listen, Tom, I'm sure your mom's not sad. But here's the thing. I really, really can't talk right now. Would it be okay if I called you tomorrow? I really want to talk to you, okay? Tomorrow?"

"Okay."

I hang up and start my pacing again. I go through the night of November 18 step by step, plotting my path, writing down every street I crossed, every name I can think of.

And I stare at the silent phone. The choice is his. He can use it, if he wants, to call me. Or he can use it to call the police.

1 4

 "YOU SEEM TENSE."

"No, not really."

Rachel smiled sweetly, prodding me to fess up. Her hands arched around my left foot, the thumbs pressing into the arch. I laid back against the pillows of my bed, arms propping me up, legs outstretched. The smell of peppermint oil filled the room.

"I just worry," I told her. "About us. I don't think you'll ever leave him."

Rachel frowned. She wore her feelings frequently, not one for airs. Her hair was tied in a ponytail. She wore a powder-blue T-shirt advertising a 5K race the foundation sponsored, blue nylon shorts, and running shoes. I had returned from running as well, thus the foot massage. We had run separately, of course. Couldn't be seen together in public. That was probably the source of my angst.

She continued to work, groping the toes, bending them, running her knuckles along the bottom. "I've never made promises," she said.

"No, I know."

She stopped and looked at me squarely. "I know this isn't fair to you."

"I know, Rach."

"All I can tell you is I love you," she said.

• • •

It is Day Three, postcall. I have jumped out of my seat here at work at least a dozen times at the ring of the phone. I have dreamed of the phone ringing. I have rehearsed my next conversation with him over and over again. Today he will call.

The first three times the phone rings this morning, they are inside calls. The fourth time, I hear the double ring, signifying an outside call. I feel a rush of adrenaline. I take a deep breath, review my lines, and lift the receiver.

"This is Marty Kalish," I say in a grave voice.

"This is Marty Kalish." It's Jerry Lazarus, his voice an authoritative octave lower, mimicking my business voice. "Here now, the news. Our top story . . ."

The tension drains from my body. Lazarus, as usual, is waiting for a reaction from me before he continues.

"Our top story," I play along. "Young lawyer found dead in his office. Phone receiver crammed down his throat."

"Now, now. Is that any way to treat someone who's going to get you laid for the first time in a decade?"

"It hasn't been a decade, it's been twelve years, and it's not gonna happen. No. Are you hearing me? No."

"You haven't even seen her. I'm telling ya, Kalish. Why don't—"

"Jerry. It's not gonna happen."

"I would take this girl out myself."

"Then break up with Ellen and take her out yourself."

"Why can't you give it a *shot*?"

"Think about this, Jerry. My first date with this woman—"

"Joanne."

"My first date with Joanne will be taking her to a party where the head of our group was murdered, and his widow is in attendance. 'Joanne, this is Mrs. Reinardt. Her husband was just killed.' Hey, maybe afterward, we can stop at a morgue."

"Ellen showed her a picture of you. Do you know what she said?"

"I don't care. Don't tell me."

"She said you had intriguing eyes."

"My eyes are not intriguing, Jerry, okay? And anyone who would say that is much too cerebral for me."

"She said she's never dated a man with red hair."

Deb walks into my office with a stack of papers. A contract I've been working on has come back from the lawyers, ravaged in red pen, arrows and circles and deletions. I nod to her, and she sets it down in front of me.

"My hair isn't red," I say to Jerry.

"That's right. It's strawberry blond."

"I'm hanging up."

"Seriously, Marty. You're missing a great opportunity."

"I'm hanging up."

"Your hair *is* red," Deb informs me as she leaves my office.

I move the stack of papers to the bureau behind me. I try to concentrate on the calculations I'm supposed to come up with on a sale-leaseback I'm doing for an oil company. How did I get stuck with this stupid—

The phone double-rings again.

This is him. This is him. Stay focused. Be calm.

"This is Marty Kalish."

"I saw you, Mr. Kalish." The husky, whispering voice.

It's bottom-of-the-ninth time, fastball coming down the pipe, and it's time to take a big swing. "What did you see me do?" I ask. "What are you talking about?" Maybe he isn't sure it was me he saw. A denial might make him reconsider.

"Don't play games." His voice is so quiet I can barely hear him, nothing but air, no hint of the deepness. I have no idea what this guy's real voice sounds like. I guess that's the idea.

"I haven't done anything wrong. What could you have—"

"I saw what you did." His voice is unequivocal.

Get it out before he hangs up. "Do you know Rachel Reinardt?"

No answer.

"Do you? Do you want her to suffer any more than she

already has? Do you want everybody to know what he was doing to her?"

"This isn't about her." The voice is less sure, the first sign of equivocation. I have this guy in a situation he didn't expect to be in: a conversation.

"That's exactly who—"

"I saw what you did. If you don't do the right thing, I'll do it for you."

"Then do it," I say quickly. "Tell the police. Tell them. I won't deny it if you do. But you and I both know what happened in that house before I got there. What happened in that house for a long time before that. You know what the right thing is."

"Your time is running out." A loud *click* on the other end, more violent this time.

I hang up and lean back in my chair. I feel like I just finished a wind sprint, damp and exhausted, jagged nerves burning at my limbs. Truth is, I have no idea whether this guy saw what happened before I broke through the door that night. I have no clue whether he knows that the doctor was beating Rachel. How *could* he know?

But I was trying for something with this guy, a connection, I suppose, a bond, like we're sharing this secret and now we're on the same side. I figured I'd be straightforward, tell him I wasn't ashamed of what I did, sound like I had some principles. Even if he didn't understand what I was talking about, I did whatever I could to plant doubt in his mind about whether to turn me in.

I replay the conversation. I said everything I wanted to say. But something is nagging at me. At the beginning, I played it pretty cool and didn't reveal anything, just like the first conversation. When I started talking about the Reinardts, I kept clear of any admission that I was there or that I did anything at all. But by the end, when he insisted that he would turn me in, I pretty much admitted that I had gone into the house.

I shouldn't have done that. But what's the point of denying it if he knows? That's what I keep telling myself, as the panic rushes to my throat. There's something about releasing a secret, placing information in the hands of another, leaving it to his or her whims. And I have just released it to a complete stranger. The pain in my stomach grows fierce, and I push myself out of the chair to head for the john. Standing in my doorway is the tall, thin frame, the coiffed silver hair, of the senior partner of my firm, with a loose fist poised to tap my door.

"Oh." I stop abruptly, standing uncertainly by my chair. "George."

"Martin. How are you?"

George Renfro walks in and takes a seat as I stand there. I sit back down. When a partner comes into your office, especially the one in charge of compensation, you suddenly have nothing better to do.

I'm working with George on the restructuring of a corporate lease on a downtown building. He is concerned. He speaks gravely about one of the parties getting cold feet, nasty litigation a possibility. I nod importantly and try to keep eye contact, but I'm looking right through him. He might as well be speaking Portuguese. His words just blur into a white noise, providing the background music for my nightmare.

The phone blares out a double ring, and I jump. Is it the caller again? Maybe I'm wrong about him. Maybe he's coming around to my side. Maybe he's someone who's trying to figure out exactly what he saw in the Reinardts' den.

The phone stops in the middle of the fourth ring. George is still talking. I'm still nodding. Then George's voice stops.

I have to talk to the caller again. Maybe I can *meet* with him. Yeah, maybe I can meet with this guy, show him how things are. If he hasn't called the police yet—

The noise is gone. George has stopped talking.

He is staring at me indignantly. I have no idea what to say. Did he ask me a question?

"Martin?"

I shake my head apologetically. "I'm sorry, George. I was just—I understand your concern."

He folds a leg. "Did you hear what I said?"

"I'm sorry, George," I repeat. "This has been a—I've got some—I'm not really here today. I'm really sorry."

He obviously asked me a question, and I obviously have no idea what it was.

He lets up. "Nothing serious, I hope?" His tone is just a slight alteration of his loud, authoritative voice, about as sympathetic as Renfro can be.

"Nothing I can't handle."

I can't bring myself to ask him to repeat the question. We just sit there, staring at each other, the unknown question hanging between us.

"Well, why don't we talk tomorrow?" he says gruffly, as he gets up from the chair.

"Sure, George," I call after him. "I'll stop by first thing."

He gives me the patented Renfro smile, which is not a smile at all, just a brief tightening of the mouth. He is already calling out to someone down the hall before he's left my office.

Deb walks in. "If you're going to ask me who called, I don't know." She normally will give it a good three rings to see if I want to answer it, but she picks up right away if she knows I have someone in my office. She probably didn't see Renfro come in. "I picked up, but whoever it was hung up."

I bury my face in my hands. "Next time get a message."

"He hung *up*. He didn't give—"

"Deb." I stare her down. "Next time, get a message?"

Deb returns the glare, more wounded than mad. "Sure, Marty."

"Thank you."

The outside phone line rings again. I turn to the phone, probably a bit too anxiously, my face hot and moist. Deb takes this in and points to the door. "Should I close this?"

I don't want to confirm my anxiety, but I can't risk someone walking in; as I think about it, I've been lucky enough so far. I tell her to close it. I pick up in the middle of the third ring, as the door closes.

"This is Marty Kalish."

"Talk."

Good. He's rethinking this thing. Control him.

"He beat her," I say quickly. "You hear what I'm saying? He used a leather belt and whipped her on the back." I'm speaking quickly, but trying to keep my voice down. "He'd been doing it for months, maybe years. He was doing it that *night*. Rachel was too scared and humiliated to ever go to the police. She needed someone to help her. Do you think I should spend the rest of my life in jail for saving her life?"

"What was going on in that room?" says the whisper.

"What did I say? He was beating her. Only this time, he was hitting her in the *face*. He was raping her."

No response, but he's listening.

"Don't you see? He was gonna *kill* her."

The line goes dead.

I hang up the phone slowly. I reach for a Kleenex and mop my face. Then I place my hands on my desk to steady myself. *Relax,* Kalish.

I've done everything I can do with the Caller. If he has a conscience—and all indications are that he does—he might let it go. But I have no idea who the Caller is, and he will always be looming over me.

In the two years I spent in law school before getting my master's, I learned about the statute of limitations. The law set an amount of time by which you had to be sued or prosecuted. After that time, you were immune. Among the several purposes for this limitations period was that the law did not want people to live endlessly with the fear of legal action hanging over their heads. In this state, there is no statute of limitations for murder.

I realize that I will always be wondering about the Caller. Even if he decides not to tell the police, I won't know he's made that decision. Maybe that will be punishment enough for me.

I hope he agrees.

THE CHRISTMAS PARTY FOR THE FOUNDATION IS held in the Prentiss Room of the Winston Hotel downtown. I declined an offer from Jerry Lazarus to go with him and Ellen. I want to show up late, not seem too eager.

The outside of the hotel is littered with arrivals and departures, parents yelping at kids, professionals in suits checking their watches. As I push through the crimson doors, it occurs to me that the hotel probably doesn't want us holding our party here, with the taint of scandal. But who wants to be known as the hotel that kicked the charity out?

The Prentiss Room is surprisingly lively. The combination of Christmas music and conversation fills the space. About fifty or so members have shown, a decent turnout. Christmas wreaths hang from the oak wood. A fake tree reaches the twelve-foot ceiling in one corner of the room. I see Laz, who raises a glass to me, and Ellen, who gives me a wink. I grab a hanger for my coat from the coatrack near the entrance.

I give a few hellos, hey-how-ya-doins, as I make my way to Laz. I don't see Rachel, and I don't want to be too eager in my search.

"Nice of you to show," Laz says as I walk up.

I kiss Ellen on the cheek. "Nice threads," she says to me, taking a step back to check me out. I'm wearing a cream shirt and olive tie that she bought me for my birthday.

"You like it?" I ask. "I got it from a girl who has a secret crush on me."

"No doubt." Laz, deadpan. "Must be your winning personality."

"I don't think that's it," I say. "I think it's sexual. She said she wasn't getting any from her boyfriend."

"Are we done yet?" Ellen asks, but I know she enjoys this. She loves sex talk.

"The bar?" I ask, looking around.

Laz points to the back of the room. I make my way through more people I don't feel like talking to. Nate Hornsby is walking around with mistletoe, preying on unsuspecting women. He catches up with me at the bar, a plastic cup of punch in hand.

I look warily at the mistletoe. "Tell me you're not gonna kiss me."

Nate cups his hand around my head and plants one on my cheek. Then he bursts into laughter, unleashing a very, very strong scent of brandy.

"A little overboard on the eggnog, Nater?" I can't help laughing myself, the first time I've laughed since my sister's at Thanksgiving.

He puts his arm around my shoulder and shakes me. Then he puts his head close to mine, his greased hair falling into his face and touching my forehead.

"So, Kalish my boy," he whispers. "Ready to make your move?"

I step back and look at him. *"What?"*

"Now that the hubby's outta the way."

"Scotch on the rocks," I say to the bartender. "Make it two."

"I say seize the day," Nate announces.

I throw back the first drink in one gulp. This pleases Nate.

I turn to him. "I say pick your spots, Nate." Jerry's line from the poker game.

He waves a hand. "Don't get your back up, Kalish. I'd hate to see you miss an opportunity, is all. At least get a good mourning fuck."

I look away. "I think we're done here."

He gets right up next to me again. "The grieving-widow bit suits her."

I follow the direction of Nate's nod across the room. Rachel is talking to a couple of people. Actually, the others are talking, she is listening, smiling politely. I know that face, that forced smile; she's not enjoying herself. I watch her as Nate continues rambling.

Her eyes move across the room. Finally, she sees me. She blinks, then looks away. She takes a deep breath, nods at something the guy next to her is saying. But I can tell she's not hearing him anymore. She steals another look in my direction.

Nate is already gone; I know this because I hear his voice off in the distance, trying to coax someone to kiss him, a woman's giggled protest. I just stand there, watching Rachel. The kick from the first scotch is setting in. It's probably a bad idea to keep drinking, but I gulp the second one and grab a third from the bar. I resume my watch.

Another peek at me. She holds eye contact for a moment. I have to tell her.

She looks back at the people talking to her. She crosses her arms, then puts them down. She runs her hand through her hair. She puts her hands together and fidgets.

"Oh, excuse me," some guy says as he walks past me to the bar.

Rachel looks upset now. She's trying to concentrate on the guy talking to her. Whoever this guy is, he stops talking and puts a hand on her shoulder. She shakes her head and reaches into her purse. She pulls out a tissue and wipes her eyes. She looks over at me quickly, her eyes sullen and brimming.

The wind was whistling inside the den. Rachel was on the hardwood floor in the corner of the den, her mouth wide open, trembling, staring in disbelief at the sight of her dead husband on the carpet.

"An intruder broke in," I said simply as I stood over the doctor. *"You couldn't see who it was."*

Rachel leaves the room. The guys she was talking with watch her walk away, shaking heads and raising eyebrows. Some woman from the foundation walks up to me and asks me how I'm doing. I can hardly speak. I manage to mumble a pleasantry or two and move on.

But I don't know where to go. I walk through the crowd,

like I'm trying to find someone. I keep looking at the door she walked through.

I bump into someone and mumble an apology. Whoever she is knows me and says hi. I keep walking.

I look back at the door. No sign of Rachel.

This is ridiculous. I'm doing laps around the room. I stop and look over heads. Some lady is checking me out, short, middle-aged, gray hair pulled up in a bun. She looks away as we make eye contact. I must look like some crazy man right now.

Rachel is back, holding a cup of purple punch in a clear glass and speaking with a couple of women. One has her hand on Rachel's arm.

I work through the crowd again, keeping Rachel in my sight. She looks up and we make eye contact. I nod to her. She looks away.

Another five minutes, one more conversation I didn't feel like having with someone who works in my building. Rachel's down to one person at her side. Ready for approach.

"Hello, Mrs. Reinardt," I say, extending my hand. "Marty Kalish."

"Sure, Marty," she says, smiling. "Merry Christmas."

The woman next to Rachel, whom I know, also smiles at me, and we shake hands, merry Christmas. She seems relieved that reinforcements have come; her obligatory conversation with the head of the charity—the grieving widow—is over. She excuses herself. It's just Rachel and me now, and I'm unsteady, not sure what to expect. Her look is one for the room, a polite smile, but her eyes are intense, welling with tears.

I wait for the friend to leave earshot. I start quietly, cautiously. "How are things?"

She looks at me with that forced, trembling smile. "Okay, I think."

"Do the police have any idea?"

"Yes, they do," she says, like I've just asked her if she's enjoying her punch.

"Do they know about us?"

She looks down at her drink, pauses, then stirs it with her finger.

"No," she finally mumbles.

"They never will, Rachel. They never will." I want to step closer to her, wrap my arms around her, touch her face, wipe away her tears. But we have an audience. "I'm going to protect you. If I have to come forward, I will."

She looks around the room, blinking at her tears. Anything not to look at me.

I put my hand on her arm. "Listen to me. I'm not sorry I killed him and I'm not afraid of what will happen to me."

She looks back up into my eyes for a long moment. She understands. Her face is fighting contortion; she exhales deeply and swallows hard.

"Do you mean that?" she says quietly.

"I'm not sorry I killed him," I repeat. "And I won't let anything happen to you. Do you hear me?"

She looks back down at her drink. Then, in a whisper, she says, "Are you sure?"

"Of course I am," I answer in a shaky voice. Doesn't she know what she means to me?

Clinks of glass behind us. Laughter. Music. There is nothing left to say, but I just want to look at her. Her chest heaves, her shoulders tremble. She takes a deep breath to hold in her sobbing. And then I walk away from her and out the door, only a few minutes after I arrived at the party.

1 6

THE RIDE HOME FROM THE FOUNDATION PARTY IS A blur. I'm on automatic pilot, making the turns and stopping at the lights, hardly noticing the heavy traffic.

The house is chilly. I feel the heat coming through the

ducts, but it isn't enough. I keep my overcoat on and plop down on the recliner in the family room. I turn on the local all-news cable channel. Nothing on the Reinardt case.

Do the police have any idea?

Yes, they do.

I open the newpaper beside me and reread Friday's article on Dr. Reinardt. No new developments. My throat is painfully dry, but I don't get a drink of water. I can't move from the recliner.

The door opened slowly. She was wearing an oversized sweatshirt, with a stretched-out neck that revealed part of her shoulders. Rachel looked at me with surprise, then a slow smile.

"Mr. Ka-lish." She sang the words.

I stood there, eager as a teenager. "Is your husband home?"

She cocked her head with mock suspicion. "No," she said playfully. "He has late surgery every Thursday night."

"That's too bad," I said. I already knew that he had surgery tonight. I had called the hospital. "Can I come in?"

Her eyes narrowed. "I'm not sure that's a good idea." Still with the half smile.

"Why not?"

"The other night was great—"

"It was more than great—"

"But it was just a night. I am married, after all."

"Just to talk, then," I said.

She considered this, her eyes dancing, flattery and amusement coloring her face.

"I've never really had a full tour of the house."

Her head bowed slightly. "What a tragedy."

"I agree." I smiled. "I walked over, no car. No one knows I'm here."

Her eyebrows arched. "You seem to have certain expectations."

"More like hope." Her expression softened; I was winning her over. "Just to talk, Rachel. Nothing else."

"Just to talk, then," she said, stepping away from the door. Her eyes followed me into the house.

"When is surgery over?" I asked, looking at my watch. It was just past seven-thirty.

"He works past midnight. He performs extra surgeries on Thursday nights so he can work half days on Friday."

"Every Thursday night?"

"Like clockwork."

I'll store that info away, I thought, as I took a seat in the den. Rachel walked over to the coffee table near the sliding glass door. She pushed a button on the table, and the curtains mechanically closed over the glass door with a low hum.

"I'll be back," she told me, dimming the lights on her way out of the room. *"Feel free to fix yourself a drink."*

A minute later, music, jazz, piped into the speakers in each corner of the ceiling. Saxophone, soft bass beat, high hat. I stirred the ice in my scotch with my finger and took a seat on the couch. The room was lit only by the lamp on the coffee table, the outside porch light muted by the closed curtain.

I heard her footsteps on the stairs. Then, as she reached the tiled hallway, the sound of click-click. Dear, sweet, gracious God. High heels. Like she read my mind.

I watched her walk slowly into the den. She wore a purple silk nightie, slightly open to her waist, where it was buttoned once, only lingerie underneath.

I put my glass down awkwardly on the carpet and started to my feet.

"No," she said sternly, wagging a finger at me. *"You sit there."*

She walked over to the bar and poured herself some vodka, her back to me. She took a sip and looked over her shoulder.

"Are you ready, Mr. Kalish?" she said.

I made some kind of sound and nodded.

She walked over to the wall opposite me and stopped, facing me but not looking at me. The music played quietly, the sax blaring over the steady percussion. She closed her eyes *and leaned her head back, running her fingers along the sides of her body. Her hips slowly moving side to side . . .*

The smell of good scotch comes from my mouth, which I realize is wide open. I wipe my forehead with the sleeve of my overcoat. I think of getting a drink, but I still can't move from the chair. I just stare at the walls.

"I love you." That is all I need to say to her tonight, in my semidrunken, wallowing state. I will not tell her that she has made my life real again, passionate, tender, electric. I will not tell her that a world without her is not a world at all. I will not tell her that this is killing me.

17

I GROAN BEFORE I OPEN MY EYES ON SATURDAY morning. I feel the dull pain in my back from spending the night in a recliner. I squint to see the time on the VCR above the TV. It's sometime after eleven. Sunlight has fallen on my patio, the first time it's been out in days. The television is on, a couple of Washington types are debating the pros and cons of affirmative action on a news show.

My shirt is stuck to my chest, my face damp. Sweat, from spending the night in my overcoat. I smack my lips and taste the sour remnants of the scotch.

I finally push myself out of the recliner and head to the front door. But I don't want to open it. I move to the window and look out. Nothing, nobody in my driveway. One car parked up the street, belongs to one of my neighbors.

Nothing better to do, I return to the sweaty recliner, reach for the remote, and surf. Motorbike racing on the sports channel, a little early for the first college hoops of the day. I flip back to the debate on minority set-asides, a topic on which

I typically hold pretty strong views. I want, more than anything, to care about this issue, to care about the same things
everyone else cares about today. Whether my college's football team will win one for the Gipper. Whether I should go
in to work or just enjoy the day outside. Whether I should
clean up the house or wait another week.

But since the evening the esteemed Dr. Reinardt left this
world, I am unable to care about anything but the investigation. I welcome any diversion—work, sports, a conversation with friends—but I can't escape it. With each passing
day, it controls me more. For a moment, here or there, it
leaves my mind, only to return with a jarring force.

I finally get out of my clothes from the night before and
shower. I spend a good half hour in there, scrubbing every
orifice, shampooing my hair over and over. The hot water
finally turns cold, and I punch off the faucet. I step out and
don't even bother with the towel, just stand dripping wet and
naked, staring into the mirror bordered with steam.

*She gently pushed me back a step, her face close to mine.
She looked into my eyes, a calm, steady gaze. I felt her hands
on the buckle of my pants. She pulled the two sides of the
clip apart. Her eyes still on mine, taking in my reaction, her
sweet breath on my face, she reached for my zipper. My
tuxedo pants were a little big for me; I had rented this thing
for the foundation fund-raiser. As she pulled down the zipper,
my pants fell to my ankles. She reached around and un-
hooked the cummerbund, tossing it to the floor. Her hands
ran over my pleated shirt, one hand stopping over my heart,
which pounded through the material. That gave her a little
smile.*

*Her nails wandered down toward my waist. Her fingers
crept inside the elastic of my boxers, pulling them off my skin
and down, over my erection, letting them fall to my ankles.
Her eyes still on me, enjoying my excitement, feeding off it.
Then she took a step back, and her face left mine, down to
my chest, down farther.*

• • •

My eyes return to focus, and I look at the man standing hunched over the bathroom sink, wet hair falling into his face, one hand on the sink, the other out of the mirror's view. Don't adjust your screen; this is your protagonist, in his purest form. Above-average looks, solid job, pretty good intentions all in all, plenty of overtures from the opposite sex over the years, but here I am, standing alone in a bathroom, naked as a jaybird, getting my rocks off while I think of a woman with a future that probably doesn't include me.

I towel off, taking care with my privates, and throw on a flannel shirt and sweats, ritual weekend wear. I look at the overflow of laundry in my closet as I fall onto my bed.

A fear of intimacy, is what one of my old girlfriends in college said about me. It was a pronouncement by Laura Braidwood—the sophomore classics major with a minor in amateur psychology—with a dramatic turn of the head, hands on her hips. A pronouncement to which I laughed out loud, which caused Ms. Braidwood to leave the room in a huff. Why did I laugh? Because it was absurd? Because the truth was worse than her diagnosis? Or was I just laughing at Laura's theatrical, self-important behavior? Probably all of the above.

No, Ms. Braidwood, not a fear of intimacy. Just a lack of desire. I must have been sick the day they passed out the impulses for love and companionship and family, because I have absolutely no desire for any of that. None. Zero. I'm a guy who likes to fly solo, where there's no disappointments, no commitments, no hassles, no expectations, no apologies. The thought of having children, running around after them and watching the clock at work so you can hurry home to wipe their butts or give them the car keys, makes me tired, if not nauseous. I said to Jerry Lazarus once that I refuse to bring a child into this world until I'm prepared to give them the commitment my father gave *me*. But the truth is, I'll never be prepared for that. I just don't want to deal with it. Listen, I'm no rebel. I've done my bit to go along–get along, and then some. College, frat house, master's degree, cushy job in a downtown skyscraper, even joined that charity. I look great on paper. But when the smoke clears, it's just plain old twisted Marty, going about his business and waiting for the day everyone's going to realize the emperor is wearing no clothes.

We're all dying, as they say. I'm just more aware of it than most.

I sit up as the doorbell finally rings. I walk into the bathroom and run my hands through my damp hair, finger-combing it into some semblance of a yuppie hairstyle, off the face with a few bangs falling forward. I find my wallet in the overcoat lying in a ball by my bed. The keys, too. I turn off the bedroom light as the bell rings a second time. The sun probably makes it look warmer than it actually is outside, but I don't bother with a coat. Kind of funny, the sun picks *today* to rear its shiny face.

The bell rings impatiently as I make my way down the stairs. I break from my customary practice of looking through the small rectangular window in the door to see who's calling; even in my distracted state last night, it wasn't hard to notice the car following me. I take one look around; the lights are off, the television silent and looking forward to an extended rest. With a deep breath, I turn the deadbolt and open the door.

I push open the screen door with a smile, more a smile of resignation than one of happiness. Maybe in a sense I am relieved, too.

Detective Cummings grunts a hello. "We'd like to talk some more, Mr. Kalish."

"Fine."

"Down at the station," he says with authority, his chest rising.

"Okay."

"You want a minute to get your stuff together?"

"No," I tell him. I'm ready.

18

HIGHLAND WOODS AND FOUR OTHER UPPER-CRUST suburbs—individually small but collectively populous—have formed a Major Crimes Unit that uses the Highland Woods Police Department when necessary. I say "when necessary" because there aren't a whole lot of major crimes in these here parts. Besides an occasional drug bust, probably little more than disturbing-the-peaces and shoplifting. I've never heard of any murders in any of these towns. This probably accounts for the turned heads as I enter the squad room. The detectives, all three of them, must be green with envy that old Cummings bagged this one.

As I walk through the station, I find myself comparing it to the ones on television. This is cleaner than any of them, nice steel desks each with a computer, large windows that welcome the sun, the scent of flavored coffee in the air.

Alex Nicholaos, the younger detective who showed up with Cummings at my doorstep, offers me a cup of coffee as I sit down in the room. I decline, and Nicholaos leaves me to my worries. I survey my dimly lit quarters. Nothing more than four gray walls, a short table in the middle, and three chairs. Not a bad attempt at intimidation, I suppose, were it not for the lingering scent of Pine-Sol. I wonder which of the walls is the one-way through which other officers can watch and listen.

I wait alone for about twenty minutes. My hands are together, resting calmly on the table. I will not give my secret audience the pleasure of watching me fidget.

The door to the room—an unusually thick wooden door—opens abruptly, and Detective Cummings closes it just as harshly behind him, the sound echoing off the walls. He walks over to the chair across the table from me and plants himself. He sits forward, resting his arms on the table, and looks me in the eyes, measuring me. I return the stare as best I can, which is to say, probably not very convincingly.

"Thanks for coming down, Mr. Kalish," he says to me. "I'm hoping you can help me out. Actually, I'm hoping I can help *you* out."

That's a fresh one. These guys have something more than just a fleeting notion that I'm involved in this. They tailed me last night, I'm not sure how long before that. My guess is they're going to come on strong, maybe bluff a little, and see what I'll give them. I open my hands but say nothing, for no other reason than it seems like the less said, the better. "Call me Marty" is the one thing I do say, which is vintage Kalish, trying to show him from the get-go that I'm not afraid. As if I'm the one who needs to break down the barriers.

"Ted." He points to himself. Now we're Marty and Ted, just two guys looking to help each other out. The detective sighs, running a hand over his mouth as he looks off absently. "This thing," he finally says, waving a hand. "This has been one bitch of a case, Marty. I'll be square with ya on that."

I nod with disinterest, but my heart does a leap with this admission. Even in my state, I realize this could be bullshit, that this is some game he's played a hundred times over. But I hope that it's true nevertheless, that maybe this session won't end with me in handcuffs, that maybe he's just looking to go back over some information and then he'll let me go. Brave, noble, selfless Marty, willing to confess only moments ago when the cops showed up at his doorstep, has now retreated to the familiar form of the man absolutely petrified of going to jail.

Cummings drops his hands flat on the table. "We got a dead doctor. We got a wife who was doin' some side business while the doc was workin' those late hours at Mercy. That's what we got." He sits back in his chair, the hand returning to the mouth. "Now, I've been a cop a pretty long time. I've investigated all sorts a things, right? And if there's one thing I've learned, Marty, it's that things aren't usually all that much of a mystery. Pretty early on, the perp's gonna show himself." He works his mouth. "Or *herself*."

I shift in my seat, the detective's clarification finding its intended mark in the pit of my stomach. As casually as Cummings is taking this, he is no doubt gauging my reaction. The best I can do is look confused, which I am.

"See, when you start lookin' too hard, and you find nothin', sometimes you gotta just step back and look at what's right in front a you."

I nod along with Cummings, the furrowed brow and pursed lips now permanently planted on my face until further notice. "Rachel?" I say, for some reason, like we're just kicking ideas around about how to solve the murder.

He answers with a shrug. "I'm about as bad a gambler as you can find," he says, punctuating it with a grunt-laugh. "I mean, I throw money away on the horses like it's fuckin' toilet paper." He leans forward again and focuses on me. "But I think I'd be ready to bet my mortgage on Rachel goin' down on this."

I swallow hard but remain mum. Cummings has hit me with a roundhouse here—he and I both know it—and the words are rushing up my throat now, along with the bile. *She didn't do it. She couldn't ever do that. It was all me me me.* But as off balance as I am, I will not budge. Not yet. I threw off my fearless mask a moment ago and I'm not all that eager to put it back on.

Cummings runs his tongue over his cheek, like it's just a thought, who knows? For a moment I think that he may actually back off his prediction. "Well, what the hell," he says. "This is against my better judgment, but I'm gonna let you know what we're thinkin' here." His hands are out in front of him, the thick brush of hair on his forearms showing from his shirtsleeves, which are rolled up a painful three tucks. "See, we're makin' Rachel for this thing. I mean, look. We know their marriage was pretty far from a good thing at this point, right?" He makes a face. "And there's this affair. Maybe more than one. For all I know, she's fuckin' four,

five guys on the side." In all his bemusement, his eyes manage to wander over to me with this last comment. "Y'know?"

I let my eyes close for a moment in an effort to contain
myself. I know, fuck, I *know* he's just saying this for my
benefit. But for all his posturing and intermittent cheap shots,
I begin to believe that at the core, Cummings is telling me
what he really thinks here. That Rachel is the killer. I raise
a hand to the table to steady myself.

"What—what are you going to do?" she asked me.

"Don't worry," I said. "It's going to be okay."

Keep steady now, Kalish. Wait him out. Let him show his
hand.

"But here's the thing, Marty. Even if we figure on Rachel,
it's still one down, one to go. She didn't break through that
glass door her pretty little self. Right? So all of the guys
around the station here, they're sayin', look at the guy she
was screwin'."

My eyes rise up abruptly to meet Cummings's.

"So that's what I'm doin'."

Our eyes remain fixed on each other a moment. My move.
I consider a grandiose denial. Indignant protest. But his eyes
are telling me neither is necessary. He already knows it, sure
as he knows that the hair from his eyebrows to the top of
his skull ain't never coming back. He just wants to hear me
say it.

Cummings raises his hands, the white flag. "Like I said,
Marty, I wanna help you. These guys"—he jabs a thumb
toward the door—"these guys already have you sittin' next
to Rachel at the trial."

I clear my throat. "You figure different?"

"Yeah. See, I know somethin' they don't."

"That being?"

"That *being* that you were nowhere near their house that
night."

The adrenaline rush to my heart actually causes a groan
of some kind to leave my mouth, a sound that doesn't escape
my interrogator's attention. I pinch the bridge of my nose.
My alibi seems to have worked. It worked, all right. I do the

math. Kalish is Rachel's boy-toy. Kalish is jealous of hubby, wants Rachel to himself. Kalish did it! Wait. Kalish has alibi. Ergo, Rachel did it! I squeeze my eyes shut. *I'm going to protect you,* I told her that night. Either that, or I'm gonna be responsible for you getting blamed!

"See, here's where we are, Marty. The boyfriend looks guilty. He looks even more guilty if he denies the affair. So I'm sayin', let's get it all aired out. You tell me you were sleepin' with her. And tell me I'm right about you workin' late that night at the office. And then, wa-la." He waves a hand magically.

I study my hands. There is a distinct odor of sweat coming from me now. The smell of fear, I suppose, bitter and scintillating. My insides are cooking, flamed by the truth that has not yet fully reached my brain: I am responsible for Rachel being a suspect.

"Let's start with the affair, Marty. Tell me about it."

Tell him about it and make this go away for Rachel. Tell him more than that. Tell him *you* did it, not her. But still, I can't say it. Maybe it's because I'm not the hero I thought I was, can do the crime but not the time. Maybe that's it, just out-and-out cowardice, that pumps my heart so fiercely that I'm sure Cummings can see it bouncing against my flannel. But there's more to it than that. Something deep within, where my mind is still connecting the dots, tells me to stick to the basic formula: If Cummings wants you to say it, don't.

"What about Rachel?" I ask.

An eyebrow lifts on the detective's considerable forehead. "I think you should be worryin' about *yourself* right now."

I drop my head and close my eyes.

"If you're the boyfriend, which I know you are, and you didn't do it, which I know you didn't—well, hey, maybe this boyfriend-girlfriend theory ain't so grand after all. Maybe Rachel isn't such a good suspect, on second thought."

I can't think straight here, though I'm lucid enough to realize again that this guy might just be playing me—but still, my spirits fly about at the mention of exoneration. For both of us. My face rises to meet Cummings's stare. He can see the hope in my expression. He returns a compromising look. "But none of that can happen 'less you help me. Dig?"

I do a long exhale. "Dig."

"So let's talk about the affair."

Every time we reach this point, the bells and whistles go off. Do-not-tell-him. The control is with me now. As soon as I let go, Cummings is calling the shots. I know it, he knows it. That's what he wants.

"Time's short, kid. These guys are ready to move now. On both of you."

Then let them move! What do they have? Some vague notion that the Reinardts had a bad marriage? Some idea that she was having an affair? That actually provokes a question. "What makes you think I'm the boyfriend?"

Cummings falls back in his chair, like he can't believe we've regressed. He gives me a sour look. "Je-sus Christ, Kalish. If you're not the boyfriend, I'm Peter fuckin' Pan. I'm wearin' fuckin' ballerina slippers." He jerks forward. "Are you shittin' me? You're gonna *deny* this?"

"I just asked a question."

He plants a finger on the table. "Right now, right fuckin' now, I got probable cause on murder one. On you *and* your honey. I'm tryin' to *clear* you, pal. You start denyin' this stuff, it's what I was sayin' before. You're hidin' somethin', you must be dirty."

"I want to know why you think I'm the boyfriend."

"There's no thinkin' about it. I know it."

"Tell me how."

Cummings stares at me a second, then explodes a laugh. "Yeah. Okay. I tell you who helped us out with that, maybe that person has an unfortunate accident the next day or so?"

"The way I see it, Ted, I'm not going anyplace, long as I don't tell you what you wanna hear. So what I can do from this room?" I shrug my shoulders. "You tell me who told you I'm the boyfriend, and maybe I'll tell you something that makes you happy."

Cummings is still now, his bear arms wrapped in front of him, his eyes narrowed with a begrudging smile. "All the same, Marty, I think I'll keep that information to myself."

"Christ." I shake my head and wave him off. "You don't have shit."

The table rocks, and Cummings is out of his seat. I would never have guessed that Cummings could move that frame as quickly as he does now, toward me. He stops in front of me, one hand on the table, one on the back of my chair. He is in my face, all cigar-breath and sweat. "If I give you a list of everyone that's named you, we'll be in here all day." He has my attention, but for good measure he actually moves closer, his nose almost touching my turned cheek. "You didn't notice maybe, along the way while you and Rachey were making goo-goo eyes at your little do-gooder events— you think no one noticed that crap? You don't think your name was the *first* one outta their mouths when we asked 'em?" Even with my face turned away, I feel the eyes boring into me. "I got ten witnesses on a *bad* day." He pushes my chair as he heads for the door.

I holler after him, in a choked voice, I want a lawyer, but he just mumbles under his breath and slams the door behind him.

19

WHEN THE DOOR OPENS AGAIN, A GOOD HALF HOUR later, I smell cologne—Polo, I think—or maybe aftershave. The man who walks in with Cummings is a short, stocky black guy. Unlike Cummings—with the tie pulled down, sleeves bunched up, collar open—this guy is immaculate. He has a short, curly afro and thin, steel-rimmed glasses. He's wearing a charcoal suit and a crisp white shirt with a tab collar that wraps around a sharp purple tie. He carries with him a tape recorder, which he places on the table, taking the cord over to an outlet and plugging it in. Then he sits down at the short side of the table, with the tape recorder right in front of him, and sets down some manila files. Cummings remains standing behind him, arms crossed, eyes never leaving me.

"Mr. Kalish, my name is Walter Denno. I'm a lieutenant here at Area One." He offers a hand, which I accept.

"Very nice," I say.

He cocks his head. "What's that, Mr. Kalish?"

"An equal opportunity interrogation."

I'm out of character here, throwing a racist remark at this cop to get a rise out of him. I want him to get mad. I want him out of control. Because I'm feeling a little that way myself. Thirty minutes alone in a hot, sweaty gray room filled with the ripe odor of adrenaline and fear, sweat dripping from my underarms, my mouth sticky and bitter, my butt raw from this unforgiving wooden chair, and I'm about ready to confess to the Lindbergh kidnapping.

And Cummings shook me up a little, I admit. I've been less than perfectly discreet about my feelings for Rachel, and I've taken enough abuse from my foundation cohorts on this subject to know it's not a quantum leap to put the two of us together. So he's probably got me on that. Fine. Marty and Rachel, sittin'-in-a-tree. But he needs more, I'm figuring.

Denno sighs quietly, like he pities me. "I understand you're denying that you and Mrs. Reinardt were having an affair?"

"I never said that."

"So you admit it."

"No. I didn't answer one way or another."

He waves a hand. "That's the same thing as denying it."

"Really."

Denno moves in a little closer, maintaining his blank expression. He tips the bridge of his glasses with a finger and wets his lips. "Marty. You know, and I know, that you are having an affair with Mrs. Reinardt. This is something that we can prove, right now. Denying this does not help you, or her, one bit." His voice is strong but steady, almost gentle. Professorial.

"It makes me wonder, then," I say. "Why do you need me?"

"We need your help in understanding this."

"You want me to make your job easier."

Denno considers this a moment, then gives a grand nod. "All right. Yes. We're still fuzzy on some details. For instance, where *you* come in." He flips open one of his files, leafs through a few pages, and pulls one to his face. "Looks to me like you have a solid alibi here. You're checking out of work around three-thirty in the morning. You have that big multimillion-dollar deal with your boss—what's his name?" Denno looks over his shoulder at Cummings. "Frank somebody, right?"

"Tiller," Cummings says, never leaving my eyes. I do a slow burn.

"The way I see it," Denno says, "you have no worries, Marty. You tell us the truth, you walk out of here today. We cross you off the list."

"And if I don't talk?"

"Then I wonder why." Denno leans back in his chair, waving a hand. "The first part of that answer's simple enough. You're protecting Rachel. You think, as long as Rachel has no boyfriend, she's clean. No motive, right?"

"And the second part?"

"The second part is *you* have something to hide."

I shrug. "Solid alibi, right?"

"Oh, you weren't *there*," he says. "Doesn't mean you're not an accomplice. Before or after." It's his turn to shrug. "Doesn't matter to me. Either way, it's the same as pulling the trigger. You know how the law on accessory works, right? Didn't they teach you that in law school?" This guy is telling me matter-of-factly that he's been all over my life. "That call you made to Rachel the day after? 'Do they have any leads?' You're asking her, is everything cool, baby?"

I bring a hand to my forehead, the thumping of my pulse vibrating my palm. I need to think. Think think think.

"You talk to us, you straighten things out. Help us understand. Forget about all this accessory stuff. Maybe you *are* clean. Personally, that's what I believe. But we know she would've talked to you about what happened. Am I right?"

I give him a look.

"I wonder what she told you. Maybe she shot him in self-defense."

That one hits me. "What?"

"Self-defense," he says calmly.

"Maybe she didn't shoot him at all."

Denno gives a dismissive shake of the head. "No, she's the shooter. We know that for a fact."

"How could you possibly?"

He stares me down with a warning: Do Not Enter. There will be no answer to that question, nor room for debate. Then the expression softens again. "I think Rachel told you that she killed her husband, Marty. Didn't she?"

"No."

"Then what did she tell you?"

"Nothing."

Denno blows out, his head shaking absently. "We know the Reinardts didn't have a good marriage. Marty"—now it's his earnest look, right at me—"we know he beat her up. We know about that."

My mouth drops. "How could you—what makes you say that?"

"C'mon, Marty." His voice is almost soothing. "Girls talk. Some of her friends at the foundation. She told them. I think she told you, too."

His right hand rose in a flash, fist half closed. Rachel's head whipped to the right, her hair and arms flying wildly, her knees buckling as she fell backward to the carpet.

"Maybe after all that time," Denno says, "Rachel couldn't take it anymore. Maybe she shouldn't *have* to."

"It's getting worse," she told me.

"We have to do something, Rachel. Right now."

If you hadn't broken through the door, this wouldn't be happening. If you hadn't called her the day after, this wouldn't be happening. If you hadn't made up such a good alibi—

"Those bruises on Rachel's face," Denno continues in that voice. "Those were from Dr. Reinardt, weren't they?"

This is happening too fast. I need time to *think*.

"That makes me think, Marty. It makes me think that maybe she was in fear for her life. It makes me think of self-defense."

Dr. Reinardt slapped her again, hard against the cheek, then seized her by the arms. With his grip tight, he forced her down to the carpet, falling on top of her.

"Is that what she told you, Marty? That it was self-defense? That he was going to kill her?"

She didn't have to tell me. I saw it.

I saw you, Mr. Kalish.

"That's what I want to believe, Marty. I really, truly do. Sounds to me like this guy was scum. Beating on a pretty lady like that. Raping her." He closes a fist and leans back a moment. Then he comes forward again, pointing a finger with conviction. "You convince me it was self-defense, I don't charge her. She walks, you walk."

"You're wrong about that. She didn't do it."

My eyes are closed as I say this, but the lack of a response tells me I have commanded the attention of the room. I hear a creak in Denno's chair and open my eyes. He has turned to look back at Cummings.

I bring my hands to my face again and do a long exhale. Am I ready to do this?

"Let's talk about that," Denno says.

I am unsure of the words that will next come from my mouth, as I drop my hands and stare into Denno's eyes. My calculations have taken several forks in the road, the different angles swirling about wildly. The only thing that is clear to me now is that I have no idea what the right thing to do is, and that every decision I have made so far has come back to bite Rachel. I answer him quietly. "I think I should have a lawyer."

Denno deflates, but he hardly misses a beat. "Then you're

both under arrest." He holds out his hands in apology. "You don't give me a choice. We go to our corners and come out swinging. I don't like your chances, Marty. I like hers even less." He sighs and reaches for the tape recorder. "So here's what we do. I'm gonna turn this thing on and ask you if you are, or were, having an affair with Rachel. You can deny it, or refuse to answer, or ask for a lawyer. They're all the same answer to the jury, Marty. You're obstructing this investigation, and you're an accessory to murder. And then I arrest you and Rachel."

"You can't arrest her. She didn't do it."

Denno lowers his eyes a moment, his lips pursed, his body tense. His index finger rises off the table. He speaks slowly. "Tell me *why*."

I pull on my hair and squeeze my eyes shut. There's always more time to do it. I can wait minutes, hours, days to do this, if it's the right thing. Yeah. There you go. I clear my throat. "I have nothing to say. I don't want to talk to you anymore." I open my eyes to a disappointed lieutenant with a clenched jaw and narrow eyes. "I am unequivocally requesting a lawyer." I give him a sour look. "They taught me that in law school."

Denno stares at me, then nods solemnly. He gives a half turn of his head toward Cummings. As if on cue, Cummings uncrosses his big arms and steps away from the wall.

"Will you excuse us, Lieutenant?" Cummings says as he looks right at me.

Denno stands up, watches me for a second, then leaves the room.

"Ted, your turn again," I say, feeling momentarily empowered by Denno's departure. One interrogator down, one to go? "And for the record, that's three times I asked for a lawyer. I think the case was called *Miranda*."

"Yeah, it rings a bell."

Cummings paces around, reasserting himself as the big man in the room. He walks over to one of the walls and picks at some peeling paint. "You know we got a death penalty in this state," he offers. "Juries *love* to give the death penalty on murder one. We haven't done a woman in a long time."

"If you can prove it."

Cummings smiles at the wall. "Can't say I'm too worried about that, Marty."

"Even if you can prove it, she's got self-defense."

Cummings makes a big point of laughing. "Self-defense," he repeats mockingly. "I love it."

"You said yourself. He was beating her. That night, too." I am quick to add, "Probably."

Cummings takes his seat back across the table from me. "Sure, Marty. Sure. Only, help me with this." He runs his finger on the table, like he's trying to figure the equation. "How's the gun get downstairs? Huh? How many people you know keep loaded guns in their *den*?"

Checkmate.

"I mean, people have guns in their houses for home protection. Right? In case someone breaks in while they're asleep or somethin'. Where would you keep that gun, Marty, if it was you?" He holds out a hand. "The bedroom, maybe? Locked in a closet upstairs, maybe? Answer me that one, Marty, 'cause I don't have an MBA like you. What the fuck good is a gun if you have to go downstairs to get it?"

"So they kept it in an odd place. So what?"

"Yeah, okay. Good counterpoint, Marty. Oh"—he snaps his fingers and directs a finger at me—"except the maid tells us the doctor kept it in his nightstand. Right there by his bed. Yeah. The *nightstand*." His eyes bulge. "Go figger. So how's that gun get downstairs, Marty?"

"Maybe the doctor takes it."

"'Cause why? He's gonna shoot Rachel?"

"Yeah, maybe."

"Yeah maybe. Then she disarms him, right? He's got, what, six inches, about a hundred pounds on her? But she disarms him. Okay, sure. Then she shoots him in self-defense. Oh, and *then*, God, I *love* this"—his hands move about expressively, then freeze in midair like he's delivering a punch line—"then a stranger happens by—right?—he's out

for a stroll in her backyard on a freezin', windy night, sure—
and this stranger sees this whole thing, and says, what the
hell, I'm feelin' generous, I'm gonna break in, take the body
and the gun, and skedaddle. And then Rachel, who has acted
in self-defense—right?—she *changes* her story and tells the
coppers that some guy broke in and shot her husband." He
leans back in his chair with a satisfied smirk. "Yeah, that
must be what happened here."

We let a good five minutes pass, Cummings letting this
sink in for me. Jesus, the blind spots I have. Self-defense
doesn't work here, not with a broken door and a missing
body. And the *gun*. If only they knew that she really *did*
bring the gun downstairs to protect herself. But no cop is
ever gonna buy that. And me taking the body away afterward—*this* is how I help Rachel? *This* is how I make everything okay?

Cummings leaves his chair and drops himself on the table
right next to me. His hands rest on his knee, which is eye-
level to me; he lowers his chin and looks at me sympathetically. "You and I both know your alibi is a fix-up," he says
quietly. "You coulda doctored that time sheet six ways to
Sunday."

I start to protest, but he raises a hand slightly off his knee.
"Just listen. Now, you knew the doctor was beatin' her.
Right? You can admit that much. You foundation people
seemed to share your secrets." He pauses until he's sure I
won't answer. "Okay. So you knew. You knew he was takin'
a belt to her. I mean, Christ, you can't hardly do that to *circus*
animals anymore, he's doin' it to her in their bedroom every
night. Night after night, humiliatin' her like that. And all the
sexual stuff, too. *Jesus*. Rape, is what it is.

"And it bothered you, just like it bothered everyone else.
Right? Forget about Rachel bein' your girlfriend. I can prove
that, but forget about it. You're still a friend, and it bothered
you. So maybe you're just tryin' to help her outta this. This
isn't some cold-blooded murder. This is you tryin' to help
someone who needs it. Needs it *bad*. Marty, however this

turns out, with or without Rachel, I got you. The only question is, do I got Rachel, too?"

"I'm not sorry I killed him," I told Rachel last night.

"Are you sure?" she said.

I saw you, Mr. Kalish.

"No," I whisper, my voice a tremble.

"No?" says Cummings. "Then tell me why not. Or get your lawyer, and I'll arrest Rachel and ask her myself. Is that what you want?"

"No."

Cummings adjusts his hands but remains calm. "The gun didn't jump into your hands," he says. "She gave it to you."

"No," I repeat.

"Then tell me how I'm wrong."

Are you sure?

I'm sure. Yes, I'm sure now. I'm not sorry. No, Rachel, I'm not sorry. Everything is quiet now, peaceful at last, dawn breaking over the horizon. I'm not sorry.

20

 "HELLO?"

"Jerry."

"Marty?"

"Yeah."

"Are you watching the game? I'm gonna lose fifty bucks—"

"Jerry."

"—because we have a coach who doesn't understand the forward pass is part—"

"Jerry. Listen to me."

"Yeah, okay. What—what's up? You okay?"

"No, I'm not okay. I need a lawyer, Jerry. A criminal
defense attorney."

"You need a—what're you talking about?"

"You guys do some criminal, right?"

"Jesus, what's happened?"

"Don't you?"

"Yeah, yeah, sure we do. Talk to me, Marty."

"I'm being held."

"Held? Where—where are you?"

"The police station."

"Oh my God. Listen—don't say a word to them."

"Little late for that."

"Jesus—don't—don't say anything else to me. Keep your
mouth shut and just listen to me. I can be down there in ten
minutes. I'm gonna call Paul Riley. He's the guy you want.
Don't say a fucking word until I get there. Do you understand
me, Marty? Do not open your mouth."

---

2 1

"BACK UP AND PUT YOUR HANDS BETWEEN THE
bars."

I obligingly take two steps back. The police officer, my
escort to my new home, grabs the chain between my handcuffs. I hear his keys at work as he slips the cuffs off each
hand.

Highland Woods keeps its prisoners beneath the police station, four identical holding cells of concrete, in each a cement
slab with a thin cushion passing for a mattress, a shiny white
toilet in the corner, a single lightbulb hanging nakedly from
the center of the ceiling. I consider asking this cop, a heavy
guy with a thick mustache and a nasty cough, if he decorated
the place himself, if I can have a room with a view. But I'm

not feeling too flippant at the moment, and these guys have decided that a murder suspect is not to be treated too tenderly. Through the booking, the fingerprinting, and now the escort to the cell, they have been gruff, a little aggressive in their handling of me. I don't know if this is sincere or practiced, something they've heard about in the big city. Above the nasty attitude I've sensed almost a reverence toward me, an eagerness to be a part, any part, of my arrest. I'm the biggest thing these guys have seen here, a murderer in this little upscale town, and all of them want to have some story about me when their friends ask. *Yeah, I printed him. He got a little wise, but I set him straight.*

The cop tells me, the sole occupant down here, to behave myself before he leaves. My cell is spotless and smells of disinfectant. Say this for them, these guys know how to run a sanitary jail. I expected dingy, graffiti-laden walls and the occasional insect. With absolutely nothing else to do, I settle on the flimsy cushion and stare at the walls, bring my feet up on the bed and sit against the wall. I check my watch and the date in the corner. Today's Saturday, right?

And with that, with that one innocuous thought, it staggers me, a chokehold on my throat, the breath whisked from my lungs, the first realization of the irreversible process I have set in motion. Which day of the week it is will no longer hold much meaning to me. There will be no weekdays and weekends. Just days. Just one day after another. Say good-bye to job, friends, life. Say good-bye to choices. Say good-bye to Rachel. Just like that, five minutes in the Reinardts' den, an hour in a room with a couple of cops, and my life has been rewritten.

This much I know about myself: I am a coward. I can put up the brash front, soothe myself with rationalizations, but when the shadows chase the light, when the truth visits me in the still of night, it is this simple fact alone that remains. And it visits me now. Not worrying about my sister, or Tommy, not worrying about Rachel, who is far from in the clear at this point. I am worrying about myself. Me, myself, and I, no room on the boat for anyone else. The question has always been out there: When push comes to shove, can Marty stand down the bad guys? Can Marty do the right thing?

I think the jury's still out. Was I brave on November 18? I've told myself yes, over and over, the dashing prince rescuing the girl. But the truth is, I was reacting, working on impulse, and if I was motivated by anything else, it was selfish. Get rid of the doctor. Have Rachel to myself. Was I brave with the cops just now? Hell no, I just couldn't keep ahead of them, and they had their sights on me anyhow. My confession, as it were, didn't tell them anything they didn't already know. And as far as I can tell, I didn't necessarily help out Rachel, either—for the time being maybe, and hopefully for good, but I'm not exactly in control of what the cops will do.

I just hope she knows I tried. I hope she realizes that I was just trying to help, that I don't want her to get mixed up with this. That I don't want her to try to help me now.

The key jangles in the door by the entrance. Jerry Lazarus steps through cautiously. Christ, he must've broken thirty traffic laws getting up here from the city so fast. He's decked out in weekend wear, a forest-green sweatshirt and baggy gray sweatpants. He has his game face on, calm and reassuring, but the color drains from his already pale mug as our eyes meet. His curly hair is matted and unkempt; he hasn't showered, was spending a lazy afternoon watching college football on the tube.

The same cop follows Jerry in. He steps past him with a beat-up wooden chair, which he places by my cell.

"Can I sit inside with him?" Jerry asks the cop.

"No."

Jerry waits until the officer has left the corridor before he speaks. His facial expression softens. He sits down in the chair and puts his hands together like he's praying. "*Tell me* you didn't confess to killing him."

I say nothing, just watch him. He doesn't look up, just sits frozen with his head falling forward, gently touching the bars. His expression quickly changes to despair, despair for the loss of a good friend. I smile sadly at him. I wouldn't blame him if he wanted nothing to do with me right now. But he is there for me, and not just as my attorney. I appreciate this more than I could possibly express.

"I'm under arrest."

He looks up at me. "Yeah." His eyes run over the little cage I'm in now. He is pale, beads of sweat on his brow. With nothing better to say, he asks, "Are you okay?"

"Better than I've been the last few weeks."

Laz ponders that for a moment; I have already admitted something. "How did—did you turn yourself in?"

I shake my head and give him the *Reader's Digest*. Cops at my door, wanted a little visit downtown, called my bluff.

Laz nods, much longer than necessary. He is visibly shaken, the typically unflappable expression replaced with genuine horror. We sit in silence for several minutes, staring at the floor. I imagine the conflict is raging inside my friend the lawyer right now, wondering whether I'm capable of murder, wondering whether our friendship is thicker than that.

"Thanks for coming, Jerry," I whisper, still with my head down. My voice is hoarse, almost gone. I see Laz lift his head. The tears drop off my cheeks to the floor.

"Did they hurt you? Rough you up or—"

I shake my head no.

"Did they read you your rights?"

It doesn't matter.

"Did you tell them you wanted an attor—"

"Jerry, what's the point? I mean, really."

"We have to consider every angle, Marty. If they coerced a confession—"

"Please, Jerry, okay?" The Constitution seems about as distant as Mars right now. "It doesn't matter. It's over."

How to answer that one, Laz wonders. Finally, he says, "Let's just wait for Paul."

Another long stretch of silence. Jerry is wearing leather moccasins and no socks. He must have jumped right in the car after I called.

"Did you sign anything?"

"No. I didn't put anything in writing."

He nods again. "Anything recorded?"

Cummings slid the tape recorder in front of me. "You and I are going to have a conversation, and you are going to repeat, in a calm voice, what you just told me." Then he turned it on and started talking, reciting the date, time, and parties present.

I stared at the tape recorder. There was something about making a permanent record. Everything was clearer now, after I had finally told Cummings what he wanted to hear. And something told me not to confess on tape.

"No. Nothing tape-recorded."

"Good." He says this without conviction. Then he sighs, gives a curt shake of his head. "Good."

"So you called that attorney?"

"Yeah," Jerry says with the first trace of enthusiasm since he walked in. "You're getting the best, Marty. Paul Riley's the best."

2 2

PAUL RILEY LOOKS LIKE A LAWYER EVEN WITHOUT a suit: tall, lean, and well manicured. He's got about an inch on me—makes him about six-two—with wavy brown hair that hasn't receded yet. He has pronounced cheekbones, and a boyish face that battles the cracks along his eyes. Mid-forties, I'm thinking.

It's just me and Paul Riley. Jerry left when he heard Paul was here, and one of them has decided that it's better just the two of us.

Riley, in his navy turtleneck and khakis, offers his hand through the cell bars. How many times, under more desirable circumstances, have I taken the hand of a colleague, client, friend. This is my first one through bars. Visible ones, at least.

"Jerry has a lot of nice things to say about you," I say.

Riley smiles graciously. "Jerry's well regarded at our firm." The firm is Shaker, Riley and Flemming, a high-powered litigation firm in the city. Most of their work, Jerry has told me, is on the commercial side, representing Fortune 500 companies in employment cases, regulatory fights with Uncle Sam, and insurance disputes. But there are a few ex-prosecutors at the firm who take on criminal work when it comes and when it fits their criteria, namely, clients who can afford their rates.

"Tell me about yourself," I say, like I'm interviewing him for a job.

"May I call you Marty?"

"Everyone else here does."

He smiles. "Okay, Marty, I practiced as a public defender for five years, worked the felony call a good three and a half years, then I was an assistant U.S. attorney for six years. I prosecuted primarily white-collar crime. Tax evasion, insider trading, the like. Then I served as the first Assistant County Attorney for seven years under Edward Mullaney."

"You prosecuted Terry Burgos." I knew I'd seen him before. He was lead prosecutor in the Burgos case. Terry Burgos had killed something like eight students at a private college on the west side of the county over the course of six weeks. The school practically came to a standstill during the murder spree. Burgos was a high school dropout who lived in town, had a dad who didn't treat him so good. It was a sensational case that got big headlines. For Burgos and for Riley, who got convictions on all counts for first-degree murder. That was about nine years ago. The whole thing was rehashed last year, when Burgos died in the electric chair.

"Yes, I prosecuted Terry Burgos."

"Do you believe in the death penalty?"

"Yes, I do," he says without a trace of apology. "Except for my clients."

The joke is not funny, at least not to me, but I find relief in the fact that Paul Riley feels comfortable enough in these intimidating surroundings to say something humorous.

"Are you going to be my lawyer?"

"Is that what you want?"

"Jerry says you're the guy. So that's what I want. Under one condition." Riley sits patiently, ready to hear me, the desperate felon, lay down the law to him. "Rachel Reinardt is off-limits. She had absolutely nothing to do with this, and I won't allow you to conjure up some sexy argument to the jury that she did. I'd rather get the chair." I startle myself with that last comment.

Riley sits stoically, almost amused by this.

"That's the only condition. I'm not interested in being a hero and spending my life in prison, or taking a couple thousand volts like your pal Burgos. If you can get me off, I want off. But not at Rachel's expense."

Paul waits a moment, to be sure I'm finished. He chews on his lower lip and leans forward. "Marty, if I take this case, I will be interested in one thing. That is clearing you of any charges. You are far too intelligent a person to think the criminal justice system is about truth. It is certainly not. It's about what the prosecution can or cannot prove in a court of law."

Paul Riley crosses a leg. He has been here before, giving the lay of the land to the unwashed, the nonlawyers who need his help, and he enjoys the upper hand.

"Now," he says, "I have no interest in getting another person in trouble with the law or exposing her personal life. But I have *every* interest in seeing you acquitted. It is my *duty* to do everything within the law to accomplish that. Everything. I will not start my representation of you by agreeing that I will be deprived of what could be—I have no idea at this point, mind you—a very critical weapon. If suggesting that Mrs. Reinardt was somehow responsible for the death of her husband will win you a 'not guilty,' then that is *precisely* what I intend to do."

I ponder this, actually smile at this guy's conviction. Under no circumstances can I tolerate my lawyer pointing the finger at Rachel. But I like this guy; maybe a little too Ivy-League prissy for my taste, but a guy who doesn't answer to anyone. Here's the chance to get a case that will be all over the papers and a client who can afford to pay, a case most defense attorneys would jump at, and Riley is telling me to stick my "condition" up my ass.

And in the end, Riley will never try to implicate Rachel anyway. The jury will have to look at her sympathetically for my defense to have any chance.

I ask him if he has any conditions of his own. Just that I always tell him the complete truth, he says without hesitation.

2 3

RACHEL WATCHED ME EXPECTANTLY, HER EYE-
brows arched, her eyes dancing.

I took the first bite. Brownies with cherries inside. I didn't think it could be done. I'm not sure it should have been.

"You said you like cherry, right?"

I smiled with the mouthful. "They're delicious," I said, bringing her close to me. They weren't, but the thought was beyond sweet.

"I'm not much of a cook," she apologized.

"I love them," I said. "And I love you."

I shake my head, blink out of the trance. Back to reality. And what a reality. I am famous now, or infamous. I know this, not because the jailhouse sergeant who dropped my breakfast tray on the floor of my cell Sunday morning told me so with a grunt ("Yer a regular celebrity"), but because my face was splashed on the Sunday edition of the *Watch*. Lazarus showed me the paper, at my insistence, when he visited Sun-day. "Confession in Reinardt Murder," the headline announced, right there on page one, bottom fold, beneath which they ran a picture of me taken, of all places, at a downtown hotel at a foundation function. Wearing a tux and a stupid grin.

I saw my celebrity firsthand the following week at my preliminary hearing. The courtroom was full and electric, I could tell even from the waiting room while the court came to order. From there into the standing-room-only courtroom I walked, Martin Kalish, MBA-educated, respectable, philanthropic downtown businessman, hands in shackles with an escort from a county deputy.

As Paul predicted, the judge found probable cause to hold me over for trial on charges of first-degree homicide. I pleaded not guilty at my arraignment two days later. I was lucky to get bail, although it was set at one million dollars. That meant that I had to come up with a hundred thousand dollars. Being a well-paid bachelor with a modest mortgage and a handsome 401(k) had paid off. I liquidated nearly every investment I had and tapped my grandfather's inheritance, which I had planned to use to subsidize the later years of my life lying on a beach in the Caribbean.

Now I'm standing in a conference room at the law offices of Shaker, Riley and Flemming, waiting for my lawyers to join me. From the window I look out east, the remainder of downtown and the lake. It strikes me that the city is gorgeous from this view, grand, dynamic, buzzing, yet something I had never considered as anything more than a nice decoration for my office. Now there is newfound appreciation for the shiny silver and black buildings, the sharp geometry of the newer ones, the fountain in the downtown square.

I get up close to the window and look down forty-two floors at the people walking on the street. A lunch appointment. A business meeting. That was me only weeks ago.

Last week, I put my house on the market. I will need the proceeds to pay off my lawyers. Frank Tiller called me from McHenry Stern to offer his best wishes. And to tell me that I was being suspended with pay from the firm. I already knew that my future at McHenry Stern was over; Frank must have twisted more than a few arms to keep me on paid leave for a while. The presumption of innocence has its financial rewards.

I have moved to a hotel in a suburb a few miles west of the city. The police ransacked my house looking for evidence. Technically, I could stay there, but I have no interest in returning. Paul told me to lay low until he could gain a better understanding of the state's case. So I do just that. I go for walks during the day. I'm catching up on the countless books I've promised myself I would read. I found a decent Mexican restaurant near the hotel and eat almost every meal there, an enchilada special for $3.99.

And I wait. I wait for the paper every day, to see what they'll say about me. I wait for the calls from my attorneys, with news that they've found more evidence against me. I wait for the trial. And now I'm waiting for my lawyers.

The first one to arrive is Mandy Tanner, a junior partner at the firm who's working with Paul on this case. Like Paul, she's a former prosecutor, only she just recently left the office. Mandy's an interesting contrast. On the one hand, she has a very tomboyish quality, one of those women who looks like she could take me in a bar fight, plays shortstop on the softball team. She's slim but hard, on the tall side, more athletic than feminine in her walk. But she's pretty cute, too, in her own way. She has shoulder-length light brown hair, very thick and wavy. Her face is tiny and oval, with prominent brown eyes and a flat nose. She has a healthy laugh, too (I base this on the one time I heard her laugh, while she was talking with the prosecutor, her former coworker; our time together thus far has been anything but a laugh-riot).

I like Mandy, even though I've met her only in my two court appearances. She has a comfortable manner, much like Paul Riley's, but not polished like his. And comfort is one thing that I could use right about now. As we sit here doing small talk, I feel a measure of relief. Maybe this is the same feeling that overcomes any criminal defendant when he is with his lawyer. It's funny, Paul and Mandy, two people whom I had never met two weeks ago, are now my most trusted friends, my saviors, the guides through a process that is fairly unknown to me.

The prosecution has turned over all of its evidence to my lawyers; this is why I'm here. Paul and Mandy have spent the last few days reviewing the material, which is now compiled neatly in two banker's boxes in the corner of this conference room, with colored tabs sticking out everywhere.

"So tell me your life story," I say, once we've thoroughly covered the weather.

She smiles. "Not much of a story. More like a paragraph."

"What kind of work did you do over at the prosecutor's office?"

"All kinds of felonies. Whatever came into my courtroom."

"Murder trials?"

"Sure."

"Win?"

She tilts her head, her thumbs rising from her clasped hands. This is her way of saying yes. She probably figures if she makes a point of saying, *Oh, yeah, the State always wins,* I'll freak out like this thing is a done deal. And if she says, *No, I lost a lot of them,* I'll worry about the competency of my lawyers. More likely, she's just being humble.

"Why'd you leave?"

She shrugs her shoulders. "Change of scenery." It strikes me as a forced answer.

"Pretty nice scenery," I say, waving my hand around the room.

"It's a good place to work." She doesn't seem too interested in elaborating.

"Do you know my prosecutor?"

She smiles. "Roger Ogren? Yeah, I know him. He's an up-and-comer. I worked with him on one case."

"He's good?"

She takes a moment before answering. "He's *thorough.* He's pretty good on his feet, but he's a little tight in front of juries."

"My apologies," Paul Riley says as he enters the room

with a broad grin, probably one better suited for lunch with a CEO than for a guy whose life hangs in the balance. Paul is in full corporate mode, a crisp white shirt with thin burgundy lines, a blue silk tie. His cuff links are gold circles with a small ruby in the center. A little flashier than the plain white shirt and navy tie he wore to my preliminary hearing. We shake hands. With a comforting pat on my shoulder and a ripple in his forehead, he asks me how I'm holding up.

We take our seats, and Paul tells me that they've had a chance to review the evidence. But first, he wants to know what I've been doing. I assure him that, pursuant to his strict orders, I have not discussed this case with anyone, especially with the press. But he goes ahead and gives me the lecture again.

This is the first time I've been with Paul when I wasn't in jail or in court, and I appraise him with a new eye. He really is the classic image of the silk-stocking corporate lawyer, precise in his movements, clear in his enunciation, careful in his choice of words, and meticulous to a fault in his appearance. His hair is the color of sand, with streaks of gray on the sides, parted sharply, not a strand out of place save for one stray bang falling on his forehead to give off the spontaneous, windblown look. Though I suspect that if I touched it, it would be brittle from hair spray. A tornado couldn't blow it awry.

In the handful of days I have spent with Paul, I have learned only a few things about the man I will ask to save my life. First, Paul knows the criminal justice system in this county inside and out. He knows all of the judges on a first-name basis; Christ, he seems to know just about every employee in the criminal courts building. He understands the politics, particularly those of a county prosecutor who is seeking higher office. He tells me that there may be moments in this ordeal where this advantage could be utilized.

Second, he is very, very bright. He is a quick learner on the facts, asks all the right questions. He is patient and intent and discerning.

Third, he is confident to a fault. He is more aware than anyone of point number two above.

And finally, he has a habit that has already found its way under my skin: He likes to ask himself questions and answer them. *Would I prefer that you hadn't spoken to the police?* he asks. *Yes. But do I think it's fatal to our case? No.*

Paul asks Mandy to present a summary of the evidence.

"The state's theory," Mandy begins, "is that you broke into the Reinardts' house with the intent to murder Dr. Derrick Reinardt, that you shot him twice, and that you removed his body from the house." Mandy gets out of her chair and paces behind it.

"The forced entry is easily proven from the state of things at the home, the broken glass door. The state will offer a 911 call from Rachel Reinardt, saying that someone's attacking her husband."

At my preliminary hearing, the prosecutor played Rachel's 911 call. We were given a copy of the transcript from emergency dispatch. I have my own copy, which I've kept with me. I pull it out again as Mandy continues.

OPERATOR: 911.
CALLER: Please . . . please . . . come quick . . . he's going to hurt me.
OPERATOR: Ma'am, where are you?
CALLER: He's going to hurt me.
OPERATOR: Who is going to hurt you? Ma'am, where are you?
CALLER: Please . . . my husband . . . please . . . oh God.

(END OF RECORDING)

God, she tried so hard to cover for me. I imagine her, as I have so many times since that night, lying in that room. Her body trembling, her blouse torn, her face battered, her entire world shaken. No doubt the thought had crossed her mind, during the endless episodes of abuse, while she clutched the pillow or ran from her husband as he wielded the belt. No doubt she had considered the possibility of a life without him; maybe she had even fantasized of his death. But she saw the good in him, the helplessness and desperation and insecurity that drove him to the abuse. And then she did the same for me. She tried to help him, tried to reach him even then. There she lay in that room, as the brutal November wind blew through the shattered glass door, left only with her husband's blood on the carpet, a victim of my choice, not hers. She could have been angry with me, or she could have saved herself from any risk and turned me in. God knows, there was little time for deliberation. But all she did at that point was protect me. She crawled into her living room and made this phony emergency call, like it was some unknown intruder who had attacked her husband. During the swirl that was her life coming undone, she thought of me. She covered for me. She became an unwitting accomplice, endangered herself, for me.

"Intent," says Mandy, "will be proven by the fact that you immediately attacked Dr. Reinardt. You didn't pursue Mrs. Reinardt, at least not in any measurable way. You didn't steal anything. You simply shot him in cold blood and then picked him up and hauled him away." A little blunt for my liking; Mandy is in her prosecutor's role.

"That is what the prosecution has to prove under the law. What they don't technically *have* to prove, but will usually *need* to prove to convince a jury, is motive. Why did you do this? The state will argue that you were having an affair with Rachel Reinardt. You killed Dr. Reinardt so you and Rachel could be together with his money." Mandy's eyes catch mine, then move away. She does not want to confront me on this point, at least not yet.

Mandy looks at Paul, who is seated opposite me on the long marble table. "Now," he says to Mandy, "let's talk about the holes in the state's case." I have the distinct impression at that moment that Mandy has reviewed the evidence much more thoroughly than Paul.

Mandy takes the cue, first tucking a stray hair behind her ear, a rather endearing habit of hers. "The state has not pro-

duced the gun used to kill Dr. Reinardt. They found no fingerprints at the scene. Although they have not taken any
samples of your blood yet, they do not believe that they have
found any blood in his house besides his own." She begins
pacing again. This is her opening statement in my defense.
"Nor did they find any traces of Dr. Reinardt's blood in *your*
house. Nothing in your car. Nothing in the *trunk* of the car,
which is significant because that's where they would expect
you to put the doctor to take him . . . wherever it is they think
you took him. The detectives' report says the trunk and in-
terior were 'impeccably clean.' To them, of course, that
means that you cleaned out the car feverishly after you got
rid of the body. But in the end, all it proves is that there is
absolutely no evidence that Dr. Reinardt was ever in that car.

"Another gaping hole in their case is the body." She
shrugs. "They don't have one. They can't even say for certain
that Dr. Reinardt is dead. The only reason they even think
he was shot is that Rachel said so, and that neighbor heard
gunshots. And Dr. Reinardt's gun is missing.

"Finally, there's the fact that your name is signed out of
your office building that night—actually, the following
morning—as leaving work at three-twenty A.M. Which puts
you at work at the time Dr. Reinardt disappeared."

Yeah, I was feeling pretty good about that myself.

"Unfortunately, the prosecution has gotten hold of the
building security records."

Uh-oh.

"The building security records show that on November
nineteenth, someone using a McHenry Stern building card
entered the building at three-thirteen in the morning. *Which*
McHenry Stern employee, no one knows from the card itself,
because they're not personalized cards."

"It could have been *any* McHenry Stern employee," I say.

"Well"—Mandy starts to make a face, then gives an apologetic tilt of the head—"yes, no one can say for sure who
used the card. But there was only one McHenry Stern employee whose name appeared on the sign-out sheet during
the early morning of November nineteenth. If someone other

than you used the card, they never signed in."

"It would be like they just came in the building and then turned around and left," I groan.

"Exactly."

A dumbshit, that Kalish kid is.

Mandy shrugs. "But still, Marty, all in all, it's a pretty weak case. Besides that little piece of evidence, which is far from direct evidence of guilt, they don't have much at all. In fact, the *only* other thing they have is the alleged confession."

"Yes," Paul agrees, "they do have that." I turn to Paul to hear his input, but he sits silent. Apparently this was the only observation he wanted to make.

"Now," Mandy says, "our theory of the case."

I nod. "You want to hear my story?"

"No," Paul jumps in. "We'll get to that. I want to outline our possible theories."

"Fine."

Paul clears his throat. "The first one is, plain and simple, that you didn't do it. They have the wrong person. With what they have now, it's a strong argument. Now the downside, as we said, is the alleged confession. If they can convince the jury that you said you did it, then we have some explaining to do."

"And the sign-out sheet at the building?" I ask.

Paul shrugs. "Who knows? Maybe it *was* you who came into the building with that card. So what? You came in to get something from work—we've all done that."

"I had a big project going down. A big meeting the next day. I can prove that."

Paul points at me. "There you go. You were working all hours that night, at home. You came back to work to get something you forgot."

"But then I should have signed *in,* too," I say, "when I first entered the building. The fact that I didn't might suggest I was concocting an alibi."

He waves me off. "I hate signing those things. You blew it off."

This guy's all right.

"The other angle they have is the romantic link. They are going to try to put you and Mrs. Reinardt together. If they succeed, they can make a good case based on motive. And that will go a long way, Marty. If a jury thinks you had good reason to want Dr. Reinardt dead, they might overlook some of the other deficiencies in the proof.

"Okay. Now. Rachel has denied that you and she were involved. She has some friends who think she was having an affair with *someone,* they don't know who. The Reinardts' maid said she had seen you at the house before. But that's not saying much. Even Detective Cummings said that all you foundation members were at that house periodically."

Yeah. Right. Good.

"The other potential defense theory," Paul says, "is justification. We concede that you did forcibly enter the house and shoot Dr. Reinardt. But we argue that you are not guilty by reason of defense-of-another. The law in this state recognizes the defense-of-another as a complete justification for killing. We would argue that you reasonably feared for the immediate safety of Rachel."

This defense comes from my comments to Paul when we discussed bail. I told him that if all I was doing was trying to save someone, how could I be a threat to society? Paul didn't want to hear it, in part because, as he said, he didn't want to give the prosecution a preview of our defense, and in part because I don't think he wanted to hear my story until he knew the evidence.

"Now, we haven't talked yet about what happened that night. But there is a good indication that Dr. Reinardt was abusing his wife. She was pretty bruised up. The police were following this lead, they had talked to some people. Maybe you were saving Rachel from the doctor. Maybe you thought he was going to kill her."

Something stirs within me. At this moment I believe that Paul thinks I'm the killer.

"What are the holes in *that* theory?" I ask.

"First," Paul starts, "Rachel Reinardt told the police that a man in a ski mask broke into the house, attacked her, and ultimately killed her husband. She didn't say she was being attacked by her husband when you valiantly came to her rescue. If that's what really happened, we will have to deal with the fact that she lied to the police."

Mandy pipes in. "That could be explained. Many victims of domestic violence deny the abuse. We could argue that she was in denial."

"True," Paul agrees. "On the other hand, there would be the impression that she was covering for you. The state would try to tie in Rachel to some alleged conspiracy with you to kill her husband. Another flaw in this theory: Why were you there? What were you doing so close to the Reinardts' house at ten o'clock? It would be hard to tell a jury that you just happened by their house and saw what was going on. They're going to think you were there for a reason." He pauses on that thought. My heartbeat does a little pause of its own. "*Another* problem. Dr. Reinardt was shot twice. Why shoot him a second time? You probably had removed Mrs. Reinardt from danger with the first shot. Why keep shooting?"

Paul catches the look on my face and holds up his hand. "Marty, I'm just telling you what the prosecution will say. We could argue that firing twice in a row was just a reaction. It could be consistent with defending Mrs. Reinardt."

"And the sign-out sheet . . ."

"Well, that's another problem. It's one thing if you're a perfectly innocent person, running to work to grab something. But if you *did* shoot the doctor, it will look like you went to work to create the alibi. It looks like you had a guilty mind."

This is not going well. I ask if there are any other problems.

Apparently there are. "The fact that you fled. Of course, you would have been scared. Didn't know what to do. Again, we can argue that these actions were consistent with trying to save Mrs. Reinardt's life. But the prosecution will say it was part of your scheme with Mrs. Reinardt.

"And the final, and potentially greatest, flaw is that by admitting you killed Dr. Reinardt, you are admitting you took him from the house and disposed of his body. And no matter how great your motives were in killing him, there is no justification for kidnapping him. He was not a threat to Mrs. Reinardt once he had been shot, and maybe was already dead. And if he *wasn't* already dead, you let him die."

I close my eyes for a moment. Ideas are swirling in and out, as I try to consume everything he's told me. A brief surge of panic comes to my throat, and I fear for a moment that I will lose my lunch on this beautiful marble table. Paul offers to get me a glass of water, but I decline. For several minutes Paul and Mandy sit silently, busying themselves with nothing, waiting for me to gather my thoughts.

"Let's assume," I finally say with a deep exhale, "that Rachel sticks to her story. She didn't see the guy's face. Let's assume that's the truth." I have my attorneys' full attention. "Assuming that, which is the stronger theory? That I didn't do it, or that I did but I was defending Rachel?"

Paul clears his throat. "If I had my choice"—I consider this an appropriate preface—"based on the evidence we have now, I'd say our best bet is arguing that you didn't do it." He looks at Mandy, who nods.

"And if I tell you I didn't do it, how do you defend me?"

"Simple. We go hard on the alibi and point out the lack of physical evidence."

"And that's it."

"More or less."

"Tell me about the 'more.' "

Paul leans back in his chair. "You have something in mind."

"Yes, I do. Does this 'simple' case include pointing the finger at Rachel?"

Paul meets my stare. "It might."

"That's not acceptable."

Paul wets his lips and clasps his hands over his folded leg. "We've had this conversation before, Marty. I will not accept any restrictions on my defense of you. I have no idea at this moment what our investigation will turn up. I will tell you this: As of this moment, having done very little investigation, there is clearly some reason to believe that Mrs. Reinardt is implicated in this. The police were certainly looking at her. If I have to point the finger at her, I will do it in a heartbeat. As long as it doesn't hurt you."

Fair enough. I get up from my chair, my legs wobbly, and wander to the window. It's windy today, the lake is kicking the buoys up and down in the water. I sit on the short bookcase against the window.

"Maybe you should be less worried about Mrs. Reinardt," I hear Paul say, "and more worried about yourself."

A defense attorney's worst enemy is his client. I vividly remember these words from Professor Tice in my criminal procedure course in law school. Most defendants are guilty of the crimes of which they're accused, and many are unwilling to admit as much even to their own lawyer. And at least in theory, defense attorneys aren't supposed to let their clients perjure themselves; if the lawyer knows the client did it, he can't let him take the stand and say he didn't. So lawyers don't want to hear their clients confess, and the clients are even less willing. As a result, defendants will often fail to tell attorneys things they need to know to prepare a proper defense.

"We don't have to decide this right now," says Mandy.

If I lie to Paul now, I might be setting traps for him, and me, at trial. If I am caught lying about anything, anything at all, the jury will probably not believe a word I say.

"I killed him," I announce to the room. The lake, I swear, seems to kick up ever so slightly higher.

I LEAVE MY ATTORNEYS AFTER A GOOD TWO-HOUR meeting that turned decidedly sour once I confessed. Paul looked like he wanted to strangle me, like I had upset his planned defense for me. I told them that—to quote the legal language—I reasonably believed that Rachel was in fear of death or grave bodily harm, and I acted to save her life. At times during the session, I thought Paul was more drilling holes into our defense than building it. What was I doing there in the first place? Why was I wearing a ski mask, as Rachel told the police? Did Rachel know it was me? Why did Rachel call 911 if she wasn't in any danger? Where's the gun?

Paul kept all of these questions in a hypothetical form, like he still wasn't willing to concede that this would be my testimony. *Assuming this is true,* he would say, *how would you have known to go there at nine-thirty? Assuming we go this route, why wouldn't Rachel have recognized you?*

The best question Paul asked was the last one. It was put in the perfect way to avoid confirming my story. He did not ask, *Where did you take Dr. Reinardt's body?* He asked, *Will they ever find his body?*

I sure hope not, I told him.

I'm still reeling a little, not entirely sure that I've made the right decision. I guess maybe I just needed to know that my defense was heading in some direction, if maybe the wrong one.

So I need a little pick-me-up. I dial information on my car phone and try to remember the name of the reporter who has covered my story in the *Watch.* After a long delay from the dispatch, I finally get him.

"This is Andy Karras."

"This is Marty Kalish."

"Oh." Karras has made a couple of attempts to talk to me, but I referred him to Paul. Now that he's got me on the line, he's probably scrambling for his notepad. "I'm glad to hear from you, Mr. Kalish."

"It's Marty. I just wanted to tell you I'm innocent."

"Okay. Well—that's what you pleaded."

"I pleaded not guilty. I'm *innocent.*"

A pause. "Can we meet?"

"No. That's it."

"Listen, Marty, I appreciate your calling. But 'I'm innocent' isn't much to print."

"You'll print it," I say and hang up.

And he does. It appears in the next day's *Watch,* Metro section, as part of a five-paragraph summary of the case.

It prompts a rather heated phone call from my lawyer, Paul Riley. Talking to the press is a big no-no, even if what I had to say was innocuous. The prosecutor won't have much to work with from a declaration of innocence. I think what upset Paul most was that I broke his rules. I consider telling him so but don't.

"I just wanted it on the record," I explain.

"The only record that matters," says Paul, "is the court record. And they've already got you down as not guilty."

Okay. Mea culpa. I'll make a note of it, I promise him.

"Believe it or not, I didn't call you for the sole purpose of scolding you. I wanted to ask you about Rachel." No longer "Mrs. Reinardt." There is no need to ignore our relationship now.

"Shoot."

"I wanted to ask you: Did you know Rachel was seeing a psychiatrist?"

I SPEND THE EVENING IN THE HOTEL ROOM WATCH-ing movies. There's an adult movie on; one of the girls looks kind of like Rachel. I've watched it about five times this month, though I mute the sound because she doesn't sound like Rachel, and that kills the illusion.

So I'm doing the crossword puzzle at about eleven when the phone rings.

Even as a whisper, the voice is unmistakable. "I saw you, Mr. Kalish."

So! My friend the Caller has decided to grace me with another contact. I wasn't sure I'd be hearing from him now that I've been arrested. I've been waiting for the call, *hoping* for it, maybe, but until this moment I don't realize how unlikely I thought it was.

"Are you doing the right thing?"

"You must have read the papers," I say. "I confessed, remember?"

"You pleaded not guilty. You told the paper you're innocent. But I know you're *guilty*." A little bit of voice has crept into the breathy sound. He's mad. I figured seeing the article in the paper might get a rise out of him.

"Says you."

"Don't make me come forward."

"Hey, bud." I am almost playful. "I've already been arrested. Turning me in isn't exactly a *threat*."

"I'll tell them everything. Is that what you want?"

"What did you see?"

"You know what I saw."

"Tell me."

"Quit playing games," he whispers harshly, though I detect a hint of uncertainty.

"*You* quit playing games. How do I know you saw anything at all? How do I know you're not full of shit? How do I—"

"*I saw you kill him.*"

My enemy has blinked. I am frozen for a second, surprised by these words, maybe even more surprised at their effect on me. I figured he would say this to me, but, more than I ever realized, I was hoping he wouldn't. The stirring inside me now is familiar, all *too* familiar. He's got a full house, but at least I've seen his hand.

I hang up the phone and let out an audible sigh. I pinch the bridge of my nose and close my eyes. I can't decide if I'm more disappointed or relieved.

But at least now, finally, I know what I have to do.

2 6

THE OFFICES OF GREGORY D. QUILLAR AND ASSOCI-ates are located in a suburb that I didn't even know existed, twenty-some miles outside the city. The downtown is all of four square blocks of redbrick roads, with mostly clothing stores and banks. I park at a meter right in front of the office.

The reception area is empty, with the exception of a spider climbing the back wall. On the lone desk are a phone and a legal pad, nothing more. People are not breaking down this guy's door. And I don't see any "associates."

There are two offices to the left of the dingy reception. A man steps out of one of them, almost surprised to see someone else in the place. He is black, heavyset, with dark-rimmed glasses and the stub of a cigar protruding from his mouth. I can smell the aftershave before he's within five feet of me. He wears a blue plaid shirt and beige khakis, similar to what I'm wearing. "You the guy who called?" he says, removing the cigar from his mouth.

I introduce myself.

"Greg Quillar," he says, shaking my hand. "Come in, we'll find you a seat." Which won't be easy in this office. The place looks like it barely survived a tornado. Along the back wall is a short bookcase cluttered with loose papers piled high. A round table rests near the shaded window, covered with stacks of manila envelopes, decorated with stripes of light from the midmorning sun coming through the shades. On the floor next to the table is an assortment of camera equipment, sprawled about carelessly. The heater sitting in the corner, with paint peeling all around it, is working overtime, leaving the room oppressively hot.

Quillar removes some files from the one chair he has, exposing dirty red cloth. He wipes at it with his hand, as if this will erase the embedded stain. Then he sits behind his desk and flips open a pad of paper. The combination of cologne and cigar smoke takes little time to reach the back of my throat.

"Your ad said you do surveillance," I say, taking my seat.

"That's right."

"Following around cheating husbands?"

He smiles, flicks his cigar into a tin ashtray filled with other stubs. "Among other things."

"I need you to find out the identity of someone."

He nods importantly, scribbling who knows what on the yellow pad. "Okay," he says patiently, "what can you tell me about this person?"

"Nothing. I don't even know what he looks like."

"You've never seen him?"

"No. But I know how to find him."

"Well, Mr. Kalish—" He catches himself uttering the name. His brow wrinkles and his lips purse as he stares at me a moment. He looks down at his notepad, where my name is probably written. His jaw drops slightly.

"Yes," I say simply, "I'm the one they're accusing of killing that doctor in Highland Woods. Will that be a problem?"

Quillar surveys the room, suddenly aware that he's alone with a killer. He starts shuffling some papers. His eyes drop down below the desk; he's probably got a gun in one of the drawers. Right now he's wondering if he remembered to load the chamber. "That will, uh"—he clears his throat—"that'll depend on what you're asking me to do."

"I told you. I want you to find out who this guy is."

Quillar just sits there, with a troubled look on his face. The pencil falls out of his hand onto the pad of paper.

I lean forward in my chair. "Do you want me to tell you I'm innocent?"

He shakes his head without speaking, still more than a little wary of me.

"Well, I am." I pause, and he nods agreeably. He's going to take this slow with me. "And I think this person has something to do with the crime," I continue. "I'm not asking you to tangle with this guy. I just want to know who he is. If I'm right, and you help me catch this guy, you could be in for a good deal of publicity."

Quillar sighs. Now he is rearranging the pencils on his desk. Finally, he nods. "Well, I suppose if that's all . . ."

"That's all. Tell me who he is. Name and address."

"And what, if you don't mind my asking, do you plan to do with this information?"

"Actually, I *do* mind."

He ponders this.

"I'm not going to *kill* him," I say, not hiding my irritation. It has come to this for me—I have to convince someone that I'm *not* going to commit murder. "I didn't kill the doctor, and I'm certainly not going to kill this guy."

His lips curl into his mouth. "Okay, Mr. Kalish. Okay." My money's as green as anyone else's, and from what I've seen, there hasn't been much pouring in. He picks up his pencil again. "You say you know how to find this guy?"

"I APPRECIATE YOUR SEEING US, DOCTOR," PAUL RI-
ley says to Benjamin Garrett. We sit in Garrett's office, Paul,
Mandy, Garrett, and I.

Dr. Garrett is a lanky man, with only a few strands of
white hair on the top of his head and a long face. Like many
who lose it on top, Garrett compensates by growing it long
and bushy on the sides and back. Pine green and hardwood
are the fashion choices in the office of Rachel's psychiatrist.
I feel like I'm in a cabin in the woods. My lawyers and I sit
on a long, cushy leather couch. I wonder if patients really
lie down on these couches, if Rachel ever lay on this one.

Dr. Garrett sits across from us, his diplomas covering the
wall behind him. The blinds on the large window are pulled
but flipped open, allowing sunlight to filter through and hit
the floor in stripes at my feet.

Paul is the one who will do the talking. He expresses his
gratitude to Garrett for taking time out of his schedule for
us.

Garrett doesn't seem to carry a torch for lawyers. "Obviously, the only reason I've agreed to speak with you is that
Mrs. Reinardt has given me her permission." And she insisted that I be there, along with my lawyers.

Paul promises to be brief. "When did Mrs. Reinardt first
begin seeing you?"

"It would have been May, I think, of last year."

"Can you tell me her reason for seeing you?"

"She said her friends had recommended the idea to her.
She was very slow to open up to me. We would just talk
about her and her husband, her charity work. It took probably
three sessions for her to tell me why she had come to me."

"And that was?"

Garrett sighs. "Her husband had been abusing her. Phys-ically and sexually, for the last several months." These words bring a charge in the air; neither Paul nor Mandy alter their facial expressions, but I know that this was what they wanted to hear. They need this testimony for our defense to have any prayer. Mandy glances over at me, and I make a point of looking unsurprised. Told you so.

"Can you tell us how he abused her?" Paul asks.

"His abuse took two forms: physical abuse by using a leather belt to whip her on the back; or sexual abuse, with no distinguishing characteristics, just classic nonconsensual intercourse." He speaks clinically, no trace of emotion.

My lawyers are far less concerned with this man's sensi-bilities; he is building them a case. "How often did this hap-pen?"

"It happened whenever Dr. Reinardt was intoxicated. Which seemed to be at least one or two evenings a week."

"Was it always associated with alcohol?"

"It's only when he drinks," Rachel told me, apologizing for her husband.

"Apparently," says the psychiatrist.

"No exceptions that you know about?"

"None."

"Doctor," Mandy says, "when you say that there were no distinguishing characteristics associated with the sexual as-saults, what do you mean? Can you describe how they took place?"

"What I mean is that Dr. Reinardt would have sex with her whenever he pleased, without her consent. I wouldn't say there was any pattern to it, although, again, I understand he was intoxicated every time."

"Was there force?" Paul asks.

Garrett flashes him a cold smile. "Force," he says, with a note of disdain. "An interesting word. Do you mean did he strike her before assaulting her sexually? No, he did not. Did he pry her legs open? No, he did not. But he unquestionably took her body for his own pleasure without her consent.

Without *seeking* consent. That, in my mind, constitutes rape."

"And in mine as well, Doctor," Paul says quickly. "I didn't mean to suggest otherwise. I spent many years prosecuting people who did these things." He pauses, and then speaks more quietly. "I'm just trying to understand the context, part of which is whether Dr. Reinardt used physical violence during the sexual abuse. He did not?"

"She didn't mention that."

"Do you know," Paul says a little more cautiously, "whether he took her clothes off, or whether Mrs. Reinardt undressed?"

Garrett puts his hands together, forming a temple. "Sometimes he told her to disrobe, and she complied. Other times he ripped the clothes. Other times, it was merely oral copulation, and I don't suppose her state of dress was of concern."

"I see." Paul shakes his head, pausing to show the proper respect, and then starts a new line of inquiry. "What did Mrs. Reinardt have to say about this?"

Garrett's hands come apart. "It's difficult to know where to begin. She had lost any sense of herself. She considered herself an object of her husband's, nothing more. I asked her whom she blamed for the attacks, and she couldn't answer. She certainly didn't blame him."

Paul nods. "Did she tell anyone else, to your knowledge, about this abuse?"

"To my knowledge, no." I notice Paul cut a glance in my direction.

"Was she afraid of her husband?"

"When the abuse first began, yes. But by the time she began to see me, she appeared to have resigned herself to it. She certainly didn't enjoy it, but she seemed to accept it. However, about two months ago"—about a month before the shooting—"things did change somewhat. She began to fear for her life." Mandy's back straightens a notch or two. "The abuse became more pronounced, and more focused on the physical aspect. In fact, they had not had intercourse for about six weeks. But the beatings became more frequent, more severe. He would strike her with the belt more times, and he was beginning to shout at her as well. He would tell her his problems were her fault, that she didn't understand him and could not help him."

The room is quiet for a few moments. I find myself staring at the window blinds, listening to Garrett's every word, and thinking of Rachel. The abuse she endured, the panic and hopelessness and fear, that no one in this room could ever comprehend.

Paul finally speaks. "Did she actually say she feared for her life?"

"Not in those words, no. She said he was becoming more violent, that he was scaring her. *I* asked *her* if she feared for her life. She said sometimes it seemed like he was enraged enough to kill her, especially the way he yelled at her. But she always came back to the same conclusion: that he would never be able to do it."

"Did you believe that?"

"No. And I told her so. She was in denial."

Paul nods and looks at Mandy briefly. "Did Rachel ever have an affair?" The question brings me back to the reason why we are here, my criminal prosecution. The jury will be quite interested in this answer. My attorneys sure are. So am I, actually—I wonder how far Rachel went with her shrink.

Garrett shakes his head. "She was faithful to her husband. She had absolutely no sense of her sexuality. Sex to her was punishment. In fact, when we would discuss it, she wouldn't even call it sex. To her, it was just 'penetration.' It was nothing more than the physical act of Dr. Reinardt putting himself into her body."

"Did she ever mention Marty Kalish?" Paul asks without looking at me.

I don't know if it's better for our case if he says yes or no. But I know what I want so desperately to hear: *Yes, she talked about him all the time.*

"Not until after Mr. Kalish was arrested," Garrett says to Paul, as if I'm not sitting next to him on the couch. "And only then, just to mention he'd been arrested."

"That was it?"

"That was it."

"Did you get any sense of her feelings about that? Her feelings about Marty?"

"I wasn't looking for that, Mr. Riley. I wasn't investigating a murder. The patient will generally control the topics and pace."

"So you would say you gained no sense of her feelings about Marty."

"Correct."

"Or if she even knew him."

"Correct."

Those exchanges, I imagine, will be repeated almost verbatim at my trial. Paul studies his hands a moment. "Did she ever mention leaving her husband?"

"We certainly discussed it. But it wasn't an option, in her opinion."

"Did you suggest that she leave him?"

"It's not customarily my practice to tell people what to do. I usually hope that they will reach these conclusions on their own, with my guidance."

"Sure."

"But there are exceptions," says Garrett. "This case called for one. Yes, I urged her to leave him for quite some time, and more urgently so near the end." Garrett is emphatic on this last point; whether it's the truth or just convenient for his professional reputation, it's helpful.

"What did she say?"

"She said she couldn't. Her husband needed her. She experienced severe guilt about his problems and her inability to help him."

"Even though she thought he might kill her?"

"She didn't really think he would do it. She wanted to try to help him."

"What exactly were Dr. Reinardt's problems?"

"He was a heart surgeon. He lost a lot of his patients. He was, in a sense, their savior, and when he could not save them, he felt he had failed them." He paused. "That was how Rachel explained it to me."

"Did you ever talk to Dr. Reinardt about this?"

Garrett crosses a leg. "No. I strongly recommended group sessions. But Rachel was adamant. Her husband could never know about our visits."

"When was the last time you spoke with her before Dr. Reinardt's death?"

"It would have been the Tuesday before. We met every Tuesday. That would make it two days before his death, I believe."

"Can you describe that session?"

Garrett stares up at the ceiling. After Dr. Reinardt's disappearance, Garrett had probably thought long and hard about his meeting with Rachel two days before. "It was one of our more troubling sessions, I would say. Mostly she just talked about how much she worried about him. I tried to steer the conversation to her and whether she was afraid. She expressed her fears about the violence, as she had for the prior few weeks. She felt like he was losing control. Apart from the violence, he was communicating with her less and less. She would reach out to him, and he would reject her. She felt he was shutting her out, losing hope. He was losing weight, drinking more, hardly sleeping."

He told me how he's gonna do it.

He's going to rape me first. He said he'll rape me then kill me.

We have to do something, Rachel. Right now.

Paul waits in silence. When he is confident that Garrett is finished, he starts again. "When did you next see her?"

Garrett sighs. "The next Tuesday, as always."

"Can you tell us about that session?"

Garrett is pensive. He wets his lips. "The best word I can use to describe her at that session is 'lost.' She was calm. She wasn't afraid. But she didn't know what to do with herself. A common enough reaction for someone who has lost a—well, a loved one. Her life was defined by his; she felt like she was on this earth for him. Without him, she felt like she had no purpose for living."

"He can't be serious," she said, apologizing again for the

*man responsible for the hideous road map of scars on her
back.*

"He can *be, Rach. You want to wait around to find out?"*

*She pulled away from me. "No," she said. "I have to help
him first. If I leave him now, I don't know what—" Her voice
choked off; she wept softly. "Things will change," she said
finally. "He'll get better."*

"Was she suicidal?"

"Not in my opinion. Confused, and plagued with guilt. But
not suicidal."

"Did she tell you what happened the night of her husband's death?"

"Not really. All she told me was he normally wasn't home
on Thursday nights, that he typically performed surgeries that
night so he could leave earlier on Fridays. But earlier that
week, Dr. Reinardt had lost a patient in surgery. He was
terribly distraught, as he was every time he lost a patient."

Garrett blinks, returning to the topic that brings my attorneys here. "But as for what happened that night, she didn't
want to discuss it. Actually, it was the first session in a long
time in which she talked about herself. I saw it as a positive
development; she was thinking about herself again. Over the
next couple of sessions, we made tremendous progress. Not
in the sense that she was happy; she was not. She missed her
husband. But she was developing a sense of herself. She said
to me at one point something that I thought summed up her
prognosis perfectly: She wasn't happy, but for the first time,
she felt that she had the *possibility* of being happy. She had
hope."

"And during these, say, two or three sessions after her
husband's death," says Paul, "she never mentioned the events
of that night?"

"No. Not until the week the police began to question her
as a suspect."

"The police questioned Rachel." Paul says it like he already knows it, but he wants to know what they said to her.

"They'd been in contact with her off and on," Garrett says.
"But then one day they said they wanted to go over a few

things. One of the things they brought up was the abuse. She didn't know how they even knew about it, but they asked her about it. And she told them."

Paul nods. He's calm, but he wants more. "Rachel was a suspect?"

The doctor shrugs. "I don't know. I asked her that. She said she didn't know. But then she wondered if maybe she *was* to blame. She didn't pull the trigger, of course. But she wondered if maybe there was something she could have done to save him. I considered it a significant setback in her progress."

"What did she tell you about the events that night?"

"She never actually gave me a chronological story. As I said, I'm not a police detective. It wasn't my place to ask. But I can tell you what I gathered from her comments. Her husband was beating her that night. And it was different than ever before. He was striking her in the face. She ran from him, which was also unique. She usually just endured the abuse. He caught her in the den, and he knocked her to the floor. She was hardly conscious at this point. And most significantly, she believes he was about to rape her." The doctor crosses a leg. "I say that this is significant because the rapes and the physical abuse were always kept distinct. The fact that he would combine the beating and the rape suggests to me an obvious escalation in his behavior."

He said he'll rape me then kill me.

We sit on that a moment. Paul urges the doctor to continue.

"She recalls hearing broken glass. Someone struggled with her husband. She crawled into the living room and called the police. Then the police came, too late, it seems."

"What did Mrs. Reinardt think about the fact that her husband was striking her in the face?"

Garrett pauses a moment. "She thought he was going to kill her."

"She told you that?"

"Yes. It was the only time, before or after, that she acknowledged it."

"Do you believe her?"

"Absolutely. The things Dr. Reinardt did to Rachel were private scars. A bruised face was not private. Her husband had given up, for whatever reason."

Paul nods solemnly. "Rachel gave a different story to the police."

"Yes."

"Did she tell you why?"

"No. In her mind, I think, she was protecting her husband. I would imagine she also felt ashamed that she was abused. Most battered women are. It's a sad commentary that women are ashamed of something that isn't their fault, but it is very much a reality."

"And she never mentioned Marty when she described that night?"

Garrett looks at me briefly. "Only when he was arrested. She said she didn't know who broke in to her house. She had no idea."

Paul stiffens slightly. "She said to you that she didn't know who came through the glass door?"

"That's right."

Paul considers this, the wheels turning in his head.

"And Rachel's husband didn't know she was seeing you?" Paul asks.

"She said he didn't know. As I said, she was adamant that he *not* know."

"Did anyone know?"

"I'm not aware of anyone. That's not uncommon," he adds.

"No, I suppose not," Paul agrees. "I wonder, how did Rachel pay you?"

"She paid with cash."

The sober face Paul wore inside Garrett's office, the crumpled brow, the intent eyes, relaxes as soon as the elevator doors close. It's a subtle change; he maintains his formal posture, one hand resting over the other in front of him. But there's a twinkle in his eye now, and the sides of his mouth curl slightly upward. He is looking at Mandy, who is standing next to me.

"This is good," Mandy says quietly.

Paul closes his eyes and nods slowly.

It is not until we are inside Mandy's Jeep that we discuss the meeting. It's Mandy who leads. "These statements," she says, turning to Paul with a glance back at me, "are more powerful than if they came from Rachel's mouth. This is a man she *confided* in, who she bared her soul to. And they support our theory one hundred percent.

"Dr. Reinardt had brutally and systematically abused Rachel; lately, he had been more violent with her. She was *not* having an affair, which undercuts the prosecution's theory. And most important, her story of what happened that night matches our theory perfectly."

The revelations I have just heard in the psychiatrist's office, the story of the suffering Rachel endured, leave me less enthusiastic than my lawyers. But the effect is not lost on me. No matter my feelings for Rachel, my instinct for self-preservation has not been turned off. Dr. Garrett will be a critical witness for me. My defense has been given new life.

"We might have a theory here," Paul says. Now that we have corroboration, he means. Apparently, he wasn't ready to act on my testimony alone, though he never said that.

"So now do we change our plea?" I ask. If we are going to argue that I committed the crime but did it to protect Rachel, we have to formally change our plea.

"Let's give it a while yet," says Paul. "Let's see if we can't get that confession kicked."

28

OUR FOUNDING FATHERS GAVE US CONSTITUTIONAL rights, such as the right against self-incrimination and the right to a lawyer during police questioning. The Supreme Court gave us the concept of a "suppression," where the court would exclude from evidence any confession that was co-erced. To stop there, in my mind, would have been sufficient. But the Court, bless their souls, took it another step. In the landmark decision of *Miranda* v. *Arizona,* the Court laid out a litany of rights that had to be explained to a criminal sus-pect prior to interrogation.

In my law school classes, I had always taken the pro-police view on civil liberties, like my dad. I considered the most important liberty to be the right to be safe from people who break in to your house, or rob you, or kill you. And the Bill of Rights was abridging that liberty. I was willing to accept the remote possibility that the cops might mistakenly break down my door in the middle of the night in order to live in a safe community.

Viewpoints change, of course.

As my lawyers explained it to me, *Miranda* laid out a seemingly simple rule: If a suspect is in "custody"—and law-yers could argue for days about the meaning of that word—then they have to be told about their right to remain silent, and their right to a lawyer, before they are "interrogated." A suspect is "interrogated" if he is asked a question that, if answered, will be likely to incriminate him. As Paul put it, if a cop asks you if it's sunny outside, no interrogation, no *Miranda* warnings necessary. If a cop asks you if you killed the wife's husband, interrogation.

So today, Paul will try to paint me as someone whom Cummings suspected in the murder. He will try to point out all the reasons for suspecting me. Because if I was a legiti-mate suspect, it makes Cummings's questions to me all the more likely "to elicit an incriminating response." In other words, my defense lawyer is going to try with all his might to make me appear guilty in Cummings's eyes that day, and the cop who arrested me is going to make it look like he thought I was a patron saint up until that moment when I stunned him by blurting out a confession. Our system of justice in action.

We have filed this motion—called a motion to suppress—for two reasons. First, if we knock out the confession, the prosecution's case is devastated. Second, even if we lose, Paul gets a preview of how Cummings will testify at trial. We discussed the possibility of my testifying, too, but Paul dismissed it. It's not so much that he's afraid I'll blow the case—they can't ask me if I killed the doctor, their questions have to be limited to the confession. It's more that Paul hasn't decided how I will testify about that confession, and if the judge lets the evidence in—the more likely outcome, Paul told me—we might have a surprise for the prosecution at trial.

The judge presiding over this hearing is not my trial judge. He is Henry R. Schueler, a short man with tired eyes and white hair. He seems to be quite attentive, in part, I assume, because Paul Riley is in the courtroom. Paul is in his element here, a place where he is as big a player as there is, and he seems to live for these moments. Before we started today, he walked over to the prosecution table and shook hands with the opposition. He is their adversary, but he is also their former boss, and a legend at the Prosecutor's Office, from what I gather. If nothing else, he will be forever remembered as the man who sent Terry Burgos, the mass murderer, to the chair.

I get to see Roger Ogren, the prosecutor, for the first time. A pudgy, bespectacled man with watery eyes and greased hair, an unimaginative wardrobe, and a limp in his gait. We skipped formal intros and settled for one very brief moment of eye contact.

Detective Theodore Cummings is decked out in a steel-blue suit and gray tie. His hair, what little remains on top, is well combed. Paul has already covered the preliminaries with him, the initial investigation, his first trip to my house.

Paul is all business once the hearing begins, not playing the glad-hander, not flashy. During the examination of Cummings, he stands at the lectern that divides the prosecution and defense tables. He delivers his questions in crisp bites.

"Detective, you had begun to suspect Mrs. Reinardt in the attack on her husband."

"We were investigating the possibility, yes."

"Based, in part, on the fact that she had been abused by her husband."

"That was part of it, yes."

"And you thought Mrs. Reinardt had a lover," he says.

"We thought it was possible."

"You had heard some talk to that effect from Rachel's friends."

"Yeah."

"And you thought this lover, if he existed, might be involved in the attack on Dr. Reinardt."

Cummings leans forward. "I wouldn't go that far. We thought this person might be able to shed some light on things for us. Maybe she told him somethin', is all."

"But it was also possible this lover was involved in the attack, true?"

"True."

Paul drops both hands on the lectern. "Okay. Now, after your first visit with Mr. Kalish, at his house, you showed a spread of photos to the Reinardts' maid, Agnes Clorissa."

"That's correct."

"These were people who you thought might be the supposed lover?"

"That's right."

"You included Marty's photo in there."

"Yeah."

"There were ten photos?"

"Right."

"How did you show them to her? All spread out on a table?"

"No. One after the other."

"Do you remember the order, Detective? Which photo was first, which was second?"

"No."

"Was Marty's photo first?"

"No."

"Oh. Was it last?"

"No, sir. It was somewhere in the middle."

"Well." Paul holds his hand out. "How can you be so sure?

You just said you don't remember the order."

"I remember *his* photo."

"But not the other nine?"

"Not offhand."

"Not offhand," Paul repeats. "Well, is there *any* way you can remember the order? Did you make a list? Anything?"

Cummings blinks and considers this. "No."

"But Marty's photo stands out in your mind."

"Yeah. I put his photo in the middle of the pack."

"So it wouldn't stand out?"

"Right."

"So I wouldn't accuse you of trying to bias the maid."

"I wanted her identification to be clean. Without any suggestion from me."

A nice answer, Teddy. A nice one for the *trial,* that is, and therefore the answer you have to give. But not so good for this hearing. I look over at the prosecutor, Roger Ogren, who is scribbling busily.

"So you have no memory at all of the other nine photos."

"Like I said."

"But a *specific* memory of Marty's photo."

"Yeah."

"Because of the care you took in not wanting to bias the maid."

"Like I said."

Paul lets that linger a moment, nodding as if he's considering his next question. He will not ask the follow-up to this line of questions—*why was Marty's photo the only one singled out for special treatment?*—but will save it for his closing argument—*because they had set their sights on Marty, and only Marty. He was the prime suspect, and anything they asked him at the police station should have been accompanied by* Miranda *warnings.*

"The maid identified Marty, didn't she?"

"Yes. She said he had been to the house. For the charity stuff. Like dozens of other people."

Paul smiles at Cummings's clarification. "But she seemed disturbed when she saw his photo, right?"

"I would say she got all quiet."

Paul grabs a sheet of paper off the lectern. "That's exactly what you *did* say, Detective. You've just quoted your report verbatim. I congratulate you."

The judge makes a face but decides not to protest. I imagine this is because there is no jury present, and because Paul is the attorney.

Paul sets down the paper. "All right. The day after you talked to the maid was the Christmas party for the Reinardts' charity."

"That's right. At the Winston Hotel."

"You sent someone there. An undercover detective."

"Yes. Detective Brewer was at the party."

"And after the party, Detective Brewer wrote up a report."

"Yeah, she did."

"And in that report"—Paul flips open to his copy—"she stated that Marty came to the party, walked around for about twenty minutes, then talked to Rachel."

"Yes."

"Then he left the party."

"I believe that's right."

"Didn't she also say that Mr. Kalish looked *upset* when he left the party?"

"I believe she mentioned that."

Paul looks down again, reading his copy of the report. "Didn't she also say that, during the first half hour that he was at the party, Mr. Kalish repeatedly glanced over in Mrs. Reinardt's direction?"

What can Cummings do but admit it? "She said that."

"Do you know what Mr. Kalish did after the party?"

Cummings pauses. "I believe he went home."

"You know that for a fact, don't you, Detective?"

"I guess I do."

"Because after the party, you followed Marty."

"Not personally."

The judge, who has been looking indifferently at Paul, makes a quick turn toward Cummings. "You had him followed?"

Cummings turns and looks up at the judge. "Yes, Your Honor."

The judge ponders this for a moment. I feel a surge of adrenaline. We're making our case. They were targeting me, and *only* me.

Paul lets this last revelation sink in a moment. A very long moment. And then Paul moves to the "interview," as Cummings calls it, with me at the police station.

Cummings tells a story that is based in truth, but that omits some of the finer details. Like when I asked for a lawyer. That part, he doesn't seem to recall. His primary focus, he says, was to find out who was sleeping with Rachel. He wasn't sure it was me—he is quick to remind Paul that he had no solid evidence that implicated me.

"In fact," Cummings adds, "like I've been sayin', I didn't even know if she was having an affair with *anyone*."

"But if, in fact, she did have a lover, Marty was your prime suspect, isn't that so?"

"He coulda been her lover, is all I'm sayin'." Cummings fiddles with his tie, knotted so uncharacteristically tight. We've done some research on the detective. He spent three years as a beat officer in the city, the West Side—the toughest part of town you can find. He took a bullet in the shoulder in an exchange with a gangbanger and left the force, moved up to the south side of Highland Woods. I knew this guy was city, from his speech and mannerisms.

"You told Marty you thought he was the lover, didn't you, Detective?" says Paul. "You said you were sure of it."

Cummings pauses. "I don't know if I ever said I was sure. But even if I did, I definitely was *not* sure. That's why I was askin'."

Paul steps back from the lectern. "So you don't deny telling Marty that you were *sure*. Whether you were or not."

"Like I say. I don't recall."

Paul starts to move now, walking behind the prosecutors. "But you *do* recall telling him that Mrs. Reinardt was a suspect, don't you?"

"I said that. That's when he confessed."

Paul stops. "That's when—"

"That's when he said, 'I'm not sorry I killed him.' "

I let out a noise. Cummings has graduated from small fibs to huge lies. It's not unexpected, I guess, and it's a pretty good story. As soon as he mentioned Rachel being involved, Marty, the protective lover, confessed. And jeez, how could Cummings have known that this statement would lead to me confessing? How could the law require Cummings to give *Miranda* warnings when all he was doing was outlining his case?

Paul goes to work on him now, trying to corner his testimony, talking about the fact that Cummings never turned on the tape recorder they had. Talking about how Lieutenant Denno didn't hear all of my confession, even though he was standing just outside the interrogation room. But I can tell now, Paul thinks we've lost. So now he's just working up Cummings's story for our trial, where Cummings will be forced to repeat today's testimony: that I wasn't really a suspect, that they didn't have much on me.

Roger Ogren, the prosecutor, just bolsters this story, probably more than he needs to. *I was as surprised as anyone,* Cummings tells him, *when Mr. Kalish just blurted it out. We were just talking about the case, and boom—he confessed.*

The judge says he'll take it under advisement and issue a written ruling. But I'm not holding my breath. We were swinging for the fences, Paul tells me afterward, acknowledging the obvious, and we've still got a whole game to play. I tell him I want to say I did it—especially now that the confession will probably be admitted to the jury. Paul just sticks to his stupid baseball analogy: Let's see how the game unfolds.

29

PAUL RILEY SHIFTS AT THE LECTERN, THEN PULLS on a cuff link before turning on me.

"Tell us, Mr. Kalish, why did you think that Dr. Reinardt was about to kill his wife?"

"Because I saw it," I tell the empty courtroom, a mock job that's been set up near the lobby in Paul's law firm, sure to impress the corporate types who want to be reminded how sophisticated their attorneys are. "I watched him beat Rachel up that night. And then I saw him rip her clothes. That's when I came through the glass door."

"And Mrs. Reinardt? She didn't see you?"

"I couldn't say. I don't think so. She was lying on the carpet. I wasn't even sure if she was conscious."

"I see."

"Plus, I was wearing a ski mask, like she told the police." Rachel stuck me with that one. I've never owned a ski mask in my life. I hate skiing.

"Fine." Paul considers his next question. "Well, what exactly brought you to the house that night, sir? Why were you there?"

Because Rachel did a striptease for me every Thursday night, ten o'clock? I'll bet Paul would fall over if he heard that one.

"I was worried about Rachel. Her husband had been beating her, pretty badly. It had been getting worse."

"Okay, but why did you go there that particular night?"

"I was worried. See, he had lost a patient that week. He was very upset."

"How did you know that? About the patient?"

"Well—she told me."

"When did she tell you?"

"Oh—that day."

"She call you?"

"Um. Yeah. She called."

"What time?"

"I don't really remember."

"Your best estimate."

"I guess—the afternoon?"

"Uh-huh. What time did you go over there?"

"About nine-thirty."

"Okay. So—" Paul moves toward me, in the witness stand. "So you were worried he might be beating her at nine-thirty, but not at six-thirty? Not at eight o'clock? Something just came over you about nine-thirty, and you went there?"

The man is good. "Well, I just finally got worried enough that I went over there."

"Wow—just in the nick of time, it turns out. Right?"

"Yeah, I guess so."

"When you went there, you planned on stopping him."

"You're not gonna hurt her again," I told the doctor, the gun directed at his face.

"I didn't know what I was gonna do."

"Then why were you wearing a ski mask?"

Because it was a cold night? "Well, I didn't think it was a great idea standing outside someone's house. I didn't want to be seen. So I wore it."

"You didn't want to be seen."

"No."

"And it's your testimony that Rachel never saw that it was you?"

"Move out of the way, Rachel," I said, as she rose to her feet, standing behind her husband.

"Yes. Yes. She had no idea it was me."

"So after shooting the doctor, you didn't go to her. You didn't say, 'It'll be okay, Rachel.' "

"It's over now," I told her.

"No."

"You didn't say, 'Don't worry, Rachel, you're safe.' "

"No."

"How do you explain the 911 call?"

"What about it?"

"Well, you've told us that you were fighting to save Rachel. You said you fought with the doctor to save *her*."

"That's right."

"She called 911 to ask the police to come protect her from someone who was protecting *her*?" Paul picks up an invisible phone. " 'Hello, 911? Please help me. Someone's trying to save my life.' "

"I really can't explain it. You'd have to ask her."

"Wasn't she covering for you, Mr. Kalish? She waited until you left, then she made a fake 911 call to pretend that some unknown assailant had broken into her house?"

"She wasn't covering for me."

"And then you took Dr. Reinardt's body and left."

"Yeah."

"Why didn't you stay?"

"I was scared. I just ran."

"You were afraid of who? The police?"

"Yeah."

"Because you knew you had committed a crime, and you wanted to cover it up."

"I thought it would look bad. I wasn't thinking."

"You were thinking quite *well*, weren't you, Mr. Kalish? Well enough to remove the body, hide the gun, and concoct an alibi at work. You did those things, didn't you?"

"Yes, I did."

"Was Dr. Reinardt alive when you left the house with him?"

"He was . . . I'm not sure."

"So he might have been alive?"

"I don't think so."

"Why? You check his pulse? Feel his heart?"

"No."

"So he might have been alive, right? That's possible?"

"I suppose."

Paul drops his hands and deflates; rehearsal is over. "If he

was alive when you left, then you can forget about any affirmative defense. Because then you deprived him of medical
help that led to his death, at a time when he was absolutely
not a threat to Rachel."

"Okay. Then he was definitely dead when I carried him
out."

"And I haven't even asked you about the body. Or why
you shot him twice instead of once. And they'll pull her
phone records to see if she called you that day." Paul plants
himself in a chair. "We need some work, Marty, before we
assert this affirmative defense. We need a lot of work."

30

"MR. KALISH," GREG QUILLAR SAYS WITH A NOD. HE
walks around to the other side of the booth, throws his briefcase on the seat, and sits across from me. "Sorry I'm late."

It's just past six-thirty. The restaurant in my hotel has
reached its maximum, which is to say it's about half full.
There's a fairly trashy-looking lady sitting at the bar who's
been glancing my way. Forty-something, leathery face, too
much makeup, and decent legs. Could be promising. Who
am I kidding.

"Hope you don't mind," I say, holding up my glass of
scotch. "I started without you."

"Oh, well, I didn't plan on staying long," he says quickly.
He casts a wary eye on my drink, which he can gather from
my speech pattern is not my first.

"Mission accomplished?" I ask.

"Uh, yeah, yeah." He reaches into the side fold of his
briefcase and removes a manila envelope. He places it on the
wood table and slides it across.

"What's in here?"

"Name, address, even got a couple photos."

"Impressive." I stare at the envelope, not sure if I'm happy or depressed.

"Any trouble finding him?"

"No, no. Just like you said."

I reach into the inner pocket of my jacket and pull out a bundle of cash.

"Mr. Kalish," Quillar says, "you paid me in advance."

"I know." I slide the money across to him.

He looks down at the green in front of him. "Then what is this for?"

"That," I say, "is for your next job."

31

THE RED BMW PULLS INTO HIS GARAGE A LITTLE after seven-thirty at night. The bottom floor is already lit. A few minutes later, the lights are on upstairs as well. He walks into the bedroom, yanks off his tie, unbuttons his shirt, changes into a turtleneck and sweatpants. Then he disappears.

He's in the family room now. He's holding a bowl in his hands. He takes a seat on an off-white love seat and reaches for the television remote. The glow from the set flickers repeatedly until he finds the channel he is seeking. He shovels spaghetti into his mouth and watches.

His hair is dark and curly, very short on the sides. The turtleneck doesn't hide his wide neck and thick shoulders. He has a strong-looking face with a five-o'clock shadow. Classic good looks.

The walls are filled with colorful, expensive art. Near the fireplace is an antique grandfather clock that doesn't quite fit the decor. A family relic.

She is in the kitchen, wiping a yellow tile counter. She wears an oversize red flannel with gray sweats. Her dark hair is up in a ponytail. She walks into the family room and says something to him while she wipes her hands on a rag. He looks over at her briefly, says something, and then returns to the television. She watches him for a second longer, then heads back to the kitchen. A moment later, she's upstairs.

The bedroom light goes out at ten. He is still downstairs in the den. The television is still on, but he's reading something now. About midnight, he places the bookmark in the novel and sets it on the table next to him. He lies flat on the couch, turns over away from my view, and is motionless a few minutes later.

32

THE WORDS "PEOPLE V. KALISH," TYPED IN BOLD ON a piece of white cardboard, fit nicely in the slot by the door that's normally reserved for an associate's nameplate. I receive a jolt upon seeing this, my name announced to all the lawyers in this law firm as a criminal. I move into the room to disassociate myself, like it's a sign with an arrow pointing down at me that I have to escape. The room is already filled with boxes, primarily on two sets of cabinets. The left cabinets are apparently the prosecution's case; the defense's are on the right. My trial is still two months away, and the lawyers I am paying have already accumulated cartons full of research and notes. Along with Paul and Mandy, I have two young associates on my case and a private investigator. One of the associates, a stocky, fresh-faced kid named Colgan, shows me to this room while I wait to meet with Mandy. I tabulate that this escort to the file room probably ran me twenty-five bucks.

Each box lined up on the shelves bears that caption: PEO-PLE V. KALISH. This is the same caption, of course, that I see on every legal document in this case, but even now I cringe at the sight. The People. As if the entire state has gathered together, huddled around me, hurling accusations and raising their torches as they march me to the village square and put me in one of those wooden contraptions where my head and hands are locked down, where I will be spat on and ridiculed until the next day, when I am hanged at high noon.

I look through the prosecution's boxes in a casual manner, like I'm just strolling through them randomly. I finally find the file I want, "Neighborhood Canvass." The file is a green pressboard, the pieces of paper bound at the top. I flip through page after page until I find the right one. It's a type-written summary of some cop's notes, fills half a page.

He works in management information systems for an in-surance company downtown, name of Redish Mutual. He didn't hear anything on November 18, because he was out drinking with some friends. He went to bed somewhere be-tween eleven-thirty and twelve. He knows of the Reinardts but has never met them.

She didn't hear anything, either, wasn't even home. She manages an art gallery, has a show every Thursday night that keeps her there until midnight.

I hear Mandy's voice in the hallway, laughing with some-one. I yank at the piece of paper and rip it unevenly off the pressboard. Then I fold it up and shove it in my pocket.

She appears in the doorway. "How are you, Marty?" Her eyes fall to the green pressboard in my hand.

"Better," I say to her, closing up the folder. I am feeling better.

I pour a glass of juice and plant myself in the conference room. A couple of young lawyers wander past the room and glance at me. I can imagine their whispers as they walk on. A murder case is probably far more interesting than a share-holder derivative suit or a products liability action. And here is the murderer himself, in the flesh, in their cushy downtown office. *That's the guy. The guy who offed the doctor.*

I think of Jerry Lazarus. At my insistence, we haven't talked in the law firm since I became a client. Laz is doing well here, a few years from making partner. However he may try to rationalize it, it can't look too good, him being best buddies with a guy on trial for murder. Being the stand-up guy that he is, he will never let that keep him from showing me his undying friendship. So I made a point of telling him that I didn't want to see him at the office.

Mandy takes a seat across from me. She is wearing a blue suit today, with gold buttons that run all the way up and close the suit jacket at the neck. She has pulled her hair back in a clip, temporarily restraining the unmanageable locks.

Mandy holds up a paper with my caption on it. "They want your blood."

"Tell me about it."

"I mean literally. They want samples of hair and blood."

"But if I admit I was there, what's the point?" I watch her eyes fall. She nods without much enthusiasm.

"Unless," I continue, "that's not what I'm going to say."

Mandy plays with a file. "We need to keep our options open, Marty."

"You don't believe me? Even after the shrink?"

She starts, then chews her lip. "It's not that. It's a question of what's the best defense for you. The state doesn't have a strong case against you, Marty. It might be better to just sit back and make them prove it."

I work this over in my mind. "It's because of Rachel and me."

Mandy puts her hands together in front of her, choosing her words carefully. "If we say that you were trying to save Rachel's life, and the state can prove that you two were having an affair, we get hurt. Very bad. Especially if we deny it."

"We *should* deny it," I say. "Because it's not true. How many times am I going to have to say it, Mandy? Rachel and I were not having an affair."

Mandy raises her hands in surrender. "I'm on your side, Marty."

"Why don't you believe me?"

She sighs. "I'm not saying I don't believe you. But it's pretty clear that you have strong feelings for her, Marty. Maybe you think you're protecting her by denying it. You're a nice guy who's trying to do the right thing. But Rachel is not on trial here. You are. And if you two were having an affair, I imagine Roger Ogren will find out. What I'm trying to tell you is you'd only be hurting yourself."

I shrug my shoulders. "Well, this conversation is pointless. Because it's not true."

She appraises me. She has seen more than her share of liars, and she probably fancies herself pretty apt at spotting them. "Let me ask you this, then," she says. "We know they're going to try to prove this relationship, whether it's true or not. Right?"

"Right."

"What will they come up with?"

"You mean, like, credit card receipts from hotels or something?"

Mandy holds her hands out. "Anything."

"Nothing." I shake my head defiantly. "Nothing."

"Roger Ogren will ask around the foundation. What are people going to say?"

"I don't know. No one will say we were sleeping together."

"But he'll ask about little things. How often did you interact? Were you flirtatious? Did you arrive at functions together? Leave together?"

I think of that first night, at the casino fund-raiser. When I drove Rachel home. And the next Monday, when I had lunch with Jerry Lazarus, Nate Hornsby, and another guy from the foundation, Vic Silas, whom Nate had brought along.

The three of them were waiting for me at the table in the tiny Chinese restaurant near my building. We made it through five minutes of small talk, with Laz and Hornsby wearing smug expressions, before they got to the point. Boy, that fund-raiser last weekend was something, wasn't it? Have a good time, did ya? And all that cleaning up to do?

Jerry Lazarus looked over at Nate. *"Now, Nater, Marty left a little before us, didn't he?"*

He had me smiling now; I kind of enjoyed the fact that I had left with Rachel.

"I think he gave someone a ride home," said Nate.

"A woman . . ." Jerry mumbled, turning his hand in little circles. *"A woman . . . on the tall side, real good-looking . . ."*

"All right," I said. *"You had a point to make, Jerry?"*

He waved his hand. *"Not at all."* But I saw the twinkle in his eye. *"I was just wondering how your ride home with Rachel was."*

It was the reason, I realized, that a lunch had been scheduled so soon after we were all together. They were looking for the dope on Rachel and me, like schoolgirls awaiting the latest gossip. Did you just drop her off? Did she invite you in for a nightcap? I knew I had to keep it cool, lest I be accused of protesting too much.

"Hey," Laz said, showing me his palms, *"you don't want to tell us what happened, that's your business."*

I cocked my head at Jerry. *"Enough."*

"No reason to be defensive." Jerry, of course, did his best to egg me on.

"Listen," I said. *"I wish I had a story to tell. But I don't. Okay?"*

All three of them assured me it was okay.

"Like I said," Jerry drew a horizontal line in the air. *"None of my business."*

I admit, I was enjoying this. But I'm not a kiss-and-tell type, especially when I was looking for a lot more than one night with Rachel. Something told me that full disclosure was not advisable here.

"I was worried about you, that's all," Jerry said. *"I mean, when I got home, a good* two and a half hours *after you left, and I called your house"*—he made eye contact with me and

smiled—*"and no one answered, I thought maybe you had car trouble or something."*

I know that at that moment, I turned a bright shade of red. Nate and Vic enjoyed watching me squirm. And Laz smelled blood.

"And I figured Rachel wouldn't know anything about cars. And her husband, of course, had been called away to surgery. Those things can take hours."

I dropped my head but tried to maintain a poker face. Silas was snickering.

"So what was it?" Nate joined in. "What was the delay?"

"Was it car trouble?" Laz asked. "Is that what it was?"

I looked up at them. I scanned the table again to look at my attackers, three guys in suits and ties who were nothing more than little kids playing grown-ups. Three hunters who had just trapped their prey. With all the seriousness I could muster, I said, "Yeah, it was car trouble," before I burst into laughter.

"I fucking knew it," Nate said, pounding the table. Vic Silas smiled broadly. Laz just threw his napkin at me.

"Anything come to mind?" Mandy asks. "Anything anyone could've seen?"

"I think I drove Rachel home once or twice."

"Did anyone see you?"

"Well, sure, Mandy, I'm sure a lot of people saw us. We weren't being secretive or anything. There was no *reason* to be secretive."

"Would it strike anyone as unusual that you were driving her home?"

I shake my head. "I don't know why it would. We live by each other."

"Well, did anyone *else* ever drive her home?"

"Jesus, Mandy, what am I, her social coordinator? I'm sure from time to time, other people drove her home, too. Honestly, I have no idea."

Mandy straightens up in her chair. "I'm not asking you

these questions to annoy you, Marty. I just want to know what Roger Ogren is going to find out."

I rest my hands on the marble table. "Okay. We were friendly, I would say that. I would say I was one of her closer friends. I imagine that Ogren will find people who said we were good friends. Were we flirtatious? I don't know. Rachel, she's one of those people who's very outgoing. You could probably say she flirts with a *lot* of people." I smile at Mandy and rest a hand on my chest. "I, on the other hand, do not flirt."

Mandy's eyes narrow. "Please."

"I'm wounded. Me, flirt?"

She jabs a finger in my direction. She likes to do that. "I've seen your act, Kalish. You're the worst *kind* of flirt. The kind that acts all serious, low-key, the brooding type. The *sincere* type. The most dangerous kind."

It's always interesting, the things people say about you. I don't know if she's right or not. But what I do know is, I'm suddenly enjoying this conversation. It's one of the subtle things I've missed since I was arrested, the give-and-take. Even with the few remaining friends I have, the most I get is sympathy, a caution in their choice of words and topics. Nothing but somber conversations. Mandy treats me like a normal person. She makes fun of me, she argues with me.

"Do I flirt with *you*?" I ask.

"You probably flirt with every woman you meet."

"Including *you*?"

Mandy flashes me a look, blushes a little. "You're doing it right now." She allows a smile to creep in. "Now, back to the subject. What else will Ogren find out?"

"So, I ask you about yourself, get to know you a little. That's flirting?"

"Marty. Change of subject."

"I compliment you on your clothes. *That* makes me a flirt."

"Did you ever see Rachel outside the foundation work?"

"*That's* no fun. Tell me what I do. How I flirt."

Mandy rests her hands on the table and tightens her mouth. "I will not indulge you, Mr. Kaliss. We are here to discuss some things having to do with your case. Not to analyze your social skills."

I give in. "Suit yourself."

"Did you ever see Rachel outside the foundation work?"

I lose my smile. "No."

"Never?"

I pause before repeating it. "No. Really, Mandy. I've told you everything."

Mandy's eyes narrow slightly as she returns to her notes. "Oh. We got our judge. You'll be tried before Judge Mackiewicz."

"Is that good?"

She smiles. "Jake is a pretty good draw, yeah. He used to be sheriff. Pretty hard-nosed guy, but a decent judge. Not a Rhodes scholar. But fair."

"You tried cases in front of him?"

"Yeah. My first felony assignment was in front of him."

"So when do I get the pleasure?"

"In a couple of weeks. Knowing Judge Mack, he'll push for an early trial date."

"Is that what we want?"

"Oh, sure."

"Why?"

Mandy leans back in her chair. "They're still building their case. See, usually they gather the evidence and then arrest the suspect. Here, it didn't really work that way. They had some suspicions about you, sure, but not connected to the murder. They just thought you might be her lover. So they tried to get you to admit that."

"Yeah. They kept coming back to that."

She opens her hands. "Sure. Once you admit to the affair, then the ball starts rolling. If you're the lover, then you're the one who came through the door. Or, you know who did." She leans back in her chair. "My point is, they have almost nothing connecting you to the murder. The quicker we try this case, the better."

I raise a hand. "Wait a minute. If I admit I did it, then we gain nothing by moving fast. Because we've done the work *for* them."

Mandy looks away. A hand comes off the table and hangs precariously before closing to a fist. "That's true. . . ."

"Why is it, Mandy, that you guys are so convinced I'm gonna say I didn't do it when I'm telling you I *did*?"

"You wouldn't take the stand, Marty. Not if we go that way. But if they can't prove a romantic link between you and Rachel, and they don't come up with any other evidence between now and the trial, then their case is weak. Really, it's almost nothing."

I get out of my chair and move to the window. Late morning, and the streets below are littered with hurried bodies. "So the quicker we try this, the less likely they'll find the body. Or the gun."

"Right."

"And you don't have a problem with saying I didn't do it when you know different."

"I don't have a problem with starting with the presumption of innocence and making them prove otherwise," she says. "I have no problem saying to the jury, the state has failed to show beyond a reasonable doubt that Marty is the killer. That's why you hired us, Marty."

I feel the sudden desire to leave. To leave this room, to leave this case. I check my watch. It's not quite eleven in the morning. "Early lunch?" I ask.

33

AFTER A CAB RIDE OVER THE RIVER, MANDY AND I are in a dark restaurant with grungy wooden tables, even dirtier floors, and country rock blaring out of the speakers. We've beaten the lunch rush, leaving Mandy, me, and a waitress in her mid-fifties with way too much bleached-blond hair who smacks her bubble gum.

Mandy has promised me that this place has the best sloppy barbecue pork sandwiches in town. Maybe not my first choice for lunch, but I'm pretty excited about doing anything social with another human being.

"This isn't a place I would expect my lawyer to take me," I say.

"No?" Mandy puts her mouth over the straw. Strictly soft drinks. This is a working lunch.

"You think Paul would come here with us?"

Mandy starts to laugh, pulling her lips away from the straw just in time. "This isn't exactly his kind of place," she agrees. "Actually, it's hard to get anyone from the firm over to this place."

"They prefer white tablecloths and waiters in red jackets."

"Oh, come on, they're not all *that* bad." She rolls her eyes.

I smile at her and sip from my drink. She looks around the restaurant, humming with the music.

"Don't tell me you like this music," I warn her.

"Don't tell me you *don't*!" she says with a laugh. She points over to an open area in the restaurant, separated by railings that form a square. "Every Thursday night, a bunch of the Assistant County Attorneys come here for the two-step."

I put a hand on my face, weary. "I'm gonna try not to picture that in my head."

"Oh, Mr. Kalish. You horribly sheltered man."

I study her a minute, while she takes another sip and continues to hum. I don't know what is most impressive about her. At moments I think it is her animation, how easily she lights up at humor, how willingly she allows in happiness. At other times it's just the fact that she is so comfortable around me, a confessed murderer.

"You don't really strike me as a big-firm lawyer," I observe.

She looks at me suspiciously, eyebrows crooked. "No?"

"No."

She turns her face, so she's staring at me sideways, almost threatening were it not for the wry smile. "Why not?"

"I don't know. You're not—you're so—"

"Plain-Jane?"

"Well, in a good way, yeah. I mean, earthy, you know? You're not stuffy or artificial. Not like some of your co-workers."

She smirks. "*You* said that, not me."

"Why did you join this firm?"

She shrugs her shoulders. "I don't know. Change of scenery."

This time I point the finger. "That's the same thing you said last time I asked you."

She blanches. "Yeah?"

"Yeah. You've got that line down pretty well."

She gives a half smile and tucks her hair behind her ear. "Okay, how's this: It's the best civil litigation shop in town." She uses her straw to chop at the ice in her glass.

Here I go again, pushing. But this is the first normal conversation I've had with someone besides myself in weeks, and I hate to see it end abruptly.

The waitress shows up and drops a tray of food in front of me that could literally make my heart stop. An unbelievably large stack of shredded pork smothered in barbecue sauce, a side of potato slices dripping with cheddar cheese. Mandy already has her napkin stuffed in her blouse, and she dives in.

"Why did you become a lawyer?" I ask with a mouthful of food. I always find it interesting why people choose the jobs they do.

"It's the closest thing in adult life to a contact sport."

I laugh at this. True enough.

"Why *didn't* you want to be a lawyer?" she asks.

"Because it's the closest thing in adult life to a contact sport."

She wipes the red sauce from her mouth. "No, really. You started law school."

"I went to law school because my dad was a lawyer."

"Why'd you leave? After two years? The last year is *cake*."

I take a wipe at my hands. "When I was a second-year, I interviewed with firms for a summer position. One of the lawyers on campus asked me why I wanted to be an attorney. I didn't have an answer."

Mandy nods, chopping at her ice again. "So why did you become an investment banker?"

"Nobody ever asked me why I wanted to be one."

She laughs, one of those little polite noises, but she looks a little concerned. "Fair enough."

I push my food away and throw my napkin on the plate. "My father died during my first year of law school. I kept plugging along, thinking I wanted to do this for him. But then I realized he wouldn't want me to do something that I didn't want to do. So I quit, and joined an MBA program. The truth is, it was the fastest way to make a lot of money." I make an apologetic face. "You know, retire at forty-five and all that."

Mandy gives me a sympathetic smile. "There's nothing wrong with wanting to make money."

"It's no reason to choose a career. If there's one good thing that has come out of all this, it's that I've realized that much."

She smiles at me. "There's hope for you yet."

"It's the only thing keeping me going."

"What about your mom?" Mandy asks. "Is she still alive?"

"No." I wipe my hands once again on the napkin. "No."

Mandy expects more, but when nothing comes, just says, "I'm sorry."

"Yeah, well." I shrug.

"You lost your parents pretty young."

"I lost my dad when I was twenty-three. I guess that's pretty young."

Mandy watches me, the curiosity showing only in a brief twitch of her thick eyebrows.

"She died when I was eight," I say in a flat voice.

"Oh. I—didn't mean to pry."

I wave her off; no problem. "You know. What doesn't kill us . . ."

She starts to nod, then freezes. She looks at me.

"Bad choice of words," I say.

She raises her drink. "To a brighter future, Marty. After you beat this."

I nod without feeling. That hope is out there, I know, just out of my reach, where it belongs. And where it will stay. Reaching for it is like reaching for a hot iron. Instead I will do what I've been doing, holding my breath. Avoiding, not hoping. Pulling the blanket over my eyes. So now I raise my glass with Mandy, on the surface acknowledging the good thought, in my mind willfully blocking it. But in the deep recesses, silently begging Mandy to save me, please save me.

34

DECEMBER 17 IS A LITTLE LATE NOT TO HAVE A Christmas tree up. Then again, maybe they don't observe. He's standing on his deck, lifting firewood off a considerable stack. He lives on a hill, so the deck is about twelve stairs from the ground. Let's see . . . yes, twelve.

He is almost as tall as the door. The light is on, and he is using a flashlight. This time of night, can't be more than twenty degrees outside. I know this better than anyone.

They came home around nine that night, together. A holiday dinner with friends, I imagine, things that the average suburban couple is doing this time of year. I haven't seen her since they came home; she must be somewhere in the front part of the house.

He goes inside with three logs and shuts the door behind him.

The lights go out on the bottom floor. She is in the bedroom, and he is up there a minute later. My heartbeat quickens when I see him through the window. Here we go.

He pulls off his shirt and pants and walks into the bathroom wearing only boxers. She has her head tilted to one side and is running a brush through the long brown hair that falls over her shoulder. He comes out five minutes later with a toothbrush in his mouth, removing it momentarily to speak to her. She pulls back the covers on the bed while she answers him, then moves into the walk-in closet, out of view. He heads back to the bathroom with his toothbrush as she gets into bed, wearing some flannel nightshirt. He comes back out and walks over past the bed, to the doorway. He reaches up to the burglar alarm pad on the wall, that has a green light glowing. I grip the binoculars tighter.

With his index finger, he punches in four numbers to activate the alarm: 3-1-6-1. The light turns from green to red and blinks on and off. Then he hits the light switch and the room is dark. Except for the light, which blinks, by my count, for forty-five seconds before remaining a solid red.

35

THE LAW FIRM OF BRANDON AND SALTERS IS IN THE holiday spirit, as much as a law firm can be, anyway. A Christmas tree adorns the lobby, wreaths and tinsel are scattered around the hallways. The young lawyers mill about in rolled-up shirtsleeves and slacks, one chap with his hair in a ponytail, looking up but hardly noticing me and my lawyers, as the receptionist takes us through their small law library to a conference room.

The office occupies less than one floor of the high-rise, no more than ten lawyers. The secretaries and clerks are dressed just as casually. This is in stark contrast to the buttoned-up look at Shaker, Riley and Flemming. I guess it's the clientele; this is a small criminal defense firm, and even though it has its share of white-collar clients, there is necessarily the typical array of lowlifes who find their way into this office and don't take much to appearances. Lowlifes like me.

A guy like Paul Riley probably isn't accustomed to working so close to Christmas, or to being in an office like this one. But here he is, wearing a brown turtleneck and tweed coat, being led to a conference room for one of the most critical interviews in the case of *People* v. *Kalish.*

Rachel's attorney, Gerald Salters, rises to greet us, shaking hands with Riley like they're old friends. Intros are made for me and Mandy.

Salters turns the program over to Paul. The plan is that we'll tell them what we claim happened, and then Salters will tell Rachel's side. A nice, tidy plan to wrinkle out any inconsistencies, to make sure Rachel's story will jibe with mine. Everyone knows, of course, that we've already met with Rachel's shrink, Dr. Garrett. Shit, Salters is the one who told us about him.

I won't speak in this meeting. If I say anything to anyone besides my attorneys, it is discoverable by the prosecution; no attorney-client privilege. According to Mandy, Paul lobbied hard to get Rachel herself to speak to us. But Salters flatly refused. His client was loath to make any statements to anyone. The police were still on her back, trying to figure if, and where, she fit into all this. What could we do? We took what they gave us.

Paul begins his narrative, explaining that we are still "feeling out" various theories. He speaks "hypothetically" of a man who was concerned about Rachel, who went over to her house out of concern, who broke into the house and wrestled the gun out of the doctor's hands. His story paints me in a far more sympathetic and heroic light than I ever could have. I guess that's what I'm paying him for.

Salters starts slowly. He explains that Mrs. Reinardt regrets that she could not be here herself, but that he is speaking with her full authority. He begins by confirming that Rachel had been abused for just under a year, physically and sexually. He then proceeds to discuss this history almost exactly like Rachel's shrink, Dr. Garrett, had in his office; I'm thinking this is not a coincidence.

"On November eighteenth," says Salters, "Dr. Reinardt flared up again. To be specific, Dr. Reinardt struck Mrs. Reinardt in the face repeatedly. He shouted at her. He told her it was—too late for him, he said. She couldn't help him, he kept saying to her. She had failed him. She was supposed to help him, and she had failed him." Salters waves his hands unenthusiastically.

"Mrs. Reinardt ran from her husband. She ran from the bedroom. He grabbed her from behind and knocked her down, but she broke free from him and ran downstairs. He brought his gun from upstairs and found her in the den. He began to beat her again. Then he began to tear at her clothes, with the gun pointed at her. She feels sure he was about to rape her. At some point shortly thereafter, while she lay on the carpet in the den, she heard someone enter the house through the glass door. There was a struggle between Dr. Reinardt and—and the intruder." He looks apologetically at me. "She crawled into the living room and called 911. She never saw her husband again."

Paul waits to be sure Salters was finished. "Did she know the person who entered the house?"

"No."

Good. Like she told the shrink.

"Let's talk about her relationship with Marty Kalish. It was a platonic one."

I hold my breath on this one. I'm quite sure my attorneys aren't breathing, either.

Salters nods. "Strictly."

Exhale.

"She had confided in him about the abuse?"

"As you said."

"And on November eighteenth," says Paul, "the day of Dr. Reinardt's death, she spoke with Marty about the fact that the abuse had become more severe."

Salters looks at Paul thoughtfully, searching his memory. "I don't believe Mrs. Reinardt mentioned that."

"That's my understanding," Paul says rather forcefully. "And it's an important fact. I wonder if you couldn't verify this with your client."

Of course, Salters says, and he excuses himself. Paul looks at me, as if he is about to speak, and then turns away. Paul, no doubt, is remembering our first conversation on this subject, how I jumped back and forth as to when Rachel last talked to me about the abuse, finally settling on the day of the murder. Paul must have had a strong feeling I was lying, which I was, but I guess he was hoping somehow that Rachel would agree to this now.

Salters returns, stops in the doorway, and clears his throat.

"Mrs. Reinardt has no memory of making a phone call to Mr. Kalish on that day." He looks from Paul to me, and then back at Paul. "She has no memory of speaking with him that day."

36

I TWIST OPEN THE BOTTLE OFFERED TO ME AND drink down half the beer in my first take. I take a look at the label and note the final rite of passage for Jerry Lazarus, from law school rebel to corporate lawyer: The Old Style is replaced with some yuppie microbrew.

I make a point of mentioning this to Laz; he always gets a kick out of jokes about himself. It is, in a sense, like old times for us, back in the first year of law school, fretting over finals and capping off a night of cramming with a cold one. Only this time, it is high-powered lawyer and ex-investment-banker-turned-accused-felon, sitting on a couple of comfortable sofas in Jerry's high-rise condo downtown.

We order in Chinese and try like hell not to talk about my case. We are at the point in our lives where our friends, people who started law school with us, are beginning to make something of themselves. Some have made partner at law firms, not the bigger firms, where you're looking at a minimum of eight years before you touch the purse, but smaller shops. A couple are actually state court judges, guys with ethnic names who were lucky enough to draw first spot on the ballot. We laugh about Gino Cicarelli, your basic slick Italian, grew up out East, played cards every night of the week, and smashed his beer cans with his elbow when he was finished. Guy was lucky if he made three classes a week in school. This guy is wearing a robe now. Looking down earnestly at people caught doing the same things he used to do, and giving them jail time for it.

Jerry has taken the conventional route, up next year for junior partner at his firm. I wonder for the umpteenth time whether I have blown this for him. Guilt by association.

Laz's curly black hair is allowing some gray in on the sides. He's put on about twenty pounds since law school, which moves him from terribly skinny to trim. The crow's feet have deepened; and that little bit of slackness beneath the chin that arrives in the mid-thirties, I don't care how good of shape you're in, has finally begun to take form with Jerry. Tonight, however, he looks more like the guy in law school, when it was all long hair and grunge. He's wearing a T-shirt that says MAKE LOVE, NOT LAW REVIEW, covered with a plaid cotton shirt that he doesn't bother to button.

We make it through about two hours, and five beers each, before my case comes up. We have made the vow not to discuss it, but the alcohol has eroded our restraint. Jerry is looking quite emotional. Never could hold his liquor.

"Sorry about the ruling," he says. Today, Judge Schueler handed down his written opinion: The questions the cops put to me did not rise to the level of an interrogation. No *Miranda* warnings were required. My confession would be admissible at my trial.

I wave a hand.

"But the case is looking good," Laz says.

"I don't want you to get involved, Jerry. We agreed on that."

"What, involved? I hear things." He and Mandy are pretty close, from what I gather. I could see that, too. Laz is all sarcasm, probably has Mandy in stitches when he's on a roll.

"The psychiatrist corroborates everything," he says. "So does Rachel." *Corroborates.* A lawyer word for, they finally believe what I've been telling them.

"We'll see where it gets me," I say.

"It gets you a long way. The jury will be looking at a guy who beat his wife on a daily basis, pulled a gun on her that night. No way they convict. They put you on a fucking altar, is what they do." He accents that last point with a stab of his finger. There's more hope than conviction in his voice, but God bless the man, he's trying. They can put me in the chair and throw the switch, but we won't be denied this night of bravado.

"You're a good man, Laz."

He's got a mouthful of beer; he shakes his head furiously and swallows. "It's what a man *does,*" he says. "And I'll tell you something, Marty, I could never have done what you did. You risk your life to save this woman? You get arrested? Then you get charged with felony counts. And what do you do? You worry about whether *she*'s gonna be okay with it." He thinks about that, then shakes his head. "You're a piece of work, my man."

I nod graciously and fetch some more beers. We down another one in silence. Jerry reaches for another, then, without looking at me, asks, "Was she worth it?"

I take a sip and study that one, wondering if my answer has changed over the last few days. I take another swig and sit back in the chair.

"Forget it," Laz says, waving his hand. "I don't wanna know."

"The answer to your question," I say, "is it doesn't matter. Doesn't matter. It's done, and I have to answer for it. I have to look twelve citizens in the eye and tell them what I did, why I did it, and hope they'll see it my way. We all make choices, I made mine. And now I have to live with it." Amazing what a six-pack can do for your courage.

"It's crazy how fucked-up things can get," Laz offers. "One mistake, Marty." He holds up a finger. "A guy like you, a good guy, minds his own business. One mistake, and they want to take away everything." So much for the pep talks; now he is giving my eulogy. Such is the emotional roller-coaster ride of a drunk person.

"Everything," I repeat sarcastically, jumping on that ride myself. "What did I have, Jerry? Really, when you get down to it. What? A wife? A family? All I had was my job. Chasing around rich guys, trying to get them to give me their money to spend, so the partners at McHenry Stern would like me enough to let me join their club. Seventy hours a week, kissing tail, putting up fronts, when deep down, I'm scared as hell. Lying in my bed at three in the morning, scared they won't accept me. They'll pat you on the back, nice work, Marty my boy, thanks for lining our pockets with another million. Maybe you're lucky, we'll throw an extra ten grand your way in the bonus. Thanks a bunch, but don't fucking *dare* try to join the partnership."

Jerry sets down his beer now, just watching me. "Can't be all that bad," he says.

I make a noise as I take a drink. "Last year, a guy named Sutter, Ray Sutter, a real workhorse, guy makes revenue plan by month eight. He's got a wife and three kids, fourth on the way, it's his turn to await the call from higher up. They turn this guy down, sorry, Ray. You know why, Jerry? Ray lacked vision. That's what they said to this guy. He lacked *vision*. Oh, you're welcome to stick around, make about one percent on the profit you generate. After all, we're a family here, Ray. We take care of our own. Just don't get too close to the purse. And you know where Ray's gonna be come Monday? Bright and early, in the office, making deals for these leeches. I don't need that. At least with Roger Ogren, there's no pretense. He makes no bones about wanting my blood."

Jerry smirks at this. "Well *that's* turning a negative into a positive."

"And even Ray, at least he can look himself in the mirror. He's got a family. He has to play the game, follow the rules, because he's stuck. Me, what's *my* excuse? I have no one to worry about except myself."

Jerry looks at me earnestly, then picks up his beer. I take a deep breath, calming after that outburst that came from somewhere unknown within my conscience. It's funny, the kind of revelations that spew forth when you're in a position like mine.

We sit in silence for a moment. I empty another beer. Jerry is staring at the wall, at what, I have no idea. He clears his throat, like he's going to say something. Then he raises the bottle to his mouth. "They're gonna go hard on motive," he says, the bottle dangling by his lips. He takes a swig.

"So I hear. Marty and Rachel, the happy couple." I look over at Laz, and he's staring back. This isn't idle conversation. He's got a point. The lunch with the two of us, and Nate Hornsby, and Vic Silas. And the various stray comments from each of them, especially Laz and Nate, over the next months. *How's Rachel?* they would say. *Seen Rachel lately? Boy, Rachel sure looks good today, don't ya think, Marty?*

"I never once told you that we were having an affair," I say.

"No, I know," Jerry says forcefully. "You never once did. Far as I'm concerned, I have absolutely no reason to think you were sleeping with her. None whatsoever."

That's what I expected from Jerry. It's pure bullshit, of course. Maybe he doesn't know the sordid details, but that's only because he had too much discretion to ask.

"I wonder how Nate feels about all this," I say.

"The same. He has no reason to think that you two were having an affair."

I narrow my eyes. "And how might you know that, Jerry?"

He shrugs his shoulders. "These things come up in conversation."

Jerry is getting involved in this, something I don't want. There could be trouble for him that even I can't see. He has talked to Nate, gotten him to agree that he had no reason to suspect that Rachel and I were together. I wonder what, exactly, he said to Nate. How he smoothed this over. But I will never ask him. All I can feel for Jerry at this moment is gratitude.

"It's not Nate I'm worried about," he continues.

I feel a knot in my stomach. "Vic."

"Vic." Deep sigh. "*Vic* could be a problem."

I don't know Victor Silas very well; he's really Nate's friend. He's a good enough guy, a little mousy for my taste, not exactly your guy's guy. But a decent enough sort. I've never really gone out of my way to be friends with him. Suddenly, I wish that I had. Even more, I wish that Nate hadn't brought him along to that lunch.

"What does Vic say about all this?"

Laz shakes his head. "He's just a little wigged-out about it. I mean, he doesn't know you like Nate and I do. He doesn't really know what to think. Or what to do." He runs his hand through his hair nervously, then pats it down.

"Has he said anything to the police?"

"No. He doesn't know what to do. I hope I can talk some sense into him."

"Jerry," I say. He looks at me. "You did what you could. But don't push it. If he says something, he says something. You can't get *yourself* in trouble."

"No," Jerry says, shaking his head furiously. "This is my fault. I never should have brought it up at lunch. Why did I have to bring it up? Just couldn't resist a chance to display my wit and sarcasm, could I? I just had to force the issue."

"Jerry. No one could've seen this coming. I would've done the same thing."

"Yeah, well . . ."

"Promise me you won't talk to him about this again."

He runs his finger over the rim of the beer bottle.

"Even if Silas talks, what can he say? I laughed when you suggested I slept with Rachel. I laughed. I didn't admit it."

"True," Jerry says, nodding with me. "You laughed because it was so ridiculous."

"Ridiculous? You saying a guy like me couldn't get a woman like Rachel?"

Jerry gives a weak smile, probably more out of appreciation that I'm trying to lighten the mood. "What are you going to do when this thing's all over?" he asks.

The question comes out of nowhere, but it is a welcome one, a generous one, making the assumption that I will be acquitted. I tell him the truth: I'd be happy if I could be sitting here again next year, same time, same place, same microbrewed beer.

37

THE COURTROOM, AS ALWAYS, IS FULL, EVEN FOR A routine hearing like this one. It's two-thirty in the afternoon. Actually, it's 2:42; the Honorable Jonathan R. Mackiewicz is late. I shift in my seat anxiously, not because there's any suspense, but because I just want to get this over with and get out of here.

I try to take my attention off the reason I am here by studying my surroundings. The courtroom is all dark wood, like the others I've been in since this started. To the left of the judge's raised bench is a woman busy typing on her computer. Stacks of paper are piled up next to her, and she is going through them one by one, completely oblivious to the rest of us. On one side of the courtroom is a long desk with black plastic trays, filled with more stacks of papers and disordered sheets of black carbon paper. A tired-looking black guy in uniform, receding gray hair, and a considerable paunch sits on the other side of the room in a chair, wiping his eyes while he holds his glasses. On his hip is a .38 revolver in his holster, probably hasn't been used in years. Ten bucks says that from my chair I could get to that gun before he could.

The door in the back of the courtroom opens, and another tired-looking person, this time a woman pushing sixty, walks out and holds the door behind her. The cop hurriedly puts on his glasses, stands up, and announces, "All rise."

Behind the woman is the Honorable Judge Mack. He slowly, and I mean slow-ly, steps up to his chair.

The cop continues. "The Circuit Court, Criminal Felony Division, is now in session. The Honorable Jonathan R. Mackiewicz, presiding. All those having business in this court, draw near and you shall be heard."

Judge Mack is about halfway up the steps to his chair when the cop has finished his preamble. We wait for him to take his seat, adjust his glasses, lean over, and peer at the documents in front of him.

Judge Mack is lucky if he has retained ten percent of his hair by now. His face is weathered, his skinny neck rising from narrow, crooked shoulders. His skin hangs from his face like it doesn't fit anymore.

But his voice is surprisingly strong. "Good afternoon, ladies and gentlemen." The lawyers respond in kind.

It is now the lady's turn sitting next to, and below, Judge Mack. She picks up a piece of computer paper and announces, "People versus Martin Kiernan Kalish, Case Number 95 CR 103067."

Judge Mack peers over his glasses at Paul and smiles. "Mr. Riley, nice to see you back in the criminal courts."

Paul stands again and tells the judge it is his pleasure.

His Honor looks down at some document and then at the prosecutor, Roger Ogren. "Before the state proceeds, since this is the first time for all of you before me, let's set a trial date. Does the defense wish to waive the speedy trial?"

"No, Your Honor," Paul says, on his feet once more.

"All right. I'm going to set a trial date of Monday, March fourteenth."

Mandy scribbles this down in her calendar book. Paul thanks the judge.

"Is there anything else," Judge Mack says, "before we proceed with the 311 notice?"

"I don't believe so, Your Honor," Paul says.

"No, Judge," says Ogren, also on his feet. He is holding a piece of paper in his hands. I feel the adrenaline now, the drumming of my heart audible.

"Let's get on with it, then." The judge waves his hand.

Ogren walks over to Paul and hands him the paper, carefully avoiding the stare I have trained on him. "Let the record reflect," Ogren says, now walking toward the judge's bench, "that the People have handed counsel for the defendant its Rule 311 Notice." He hands another copy to the judge.

"The record will so reflect."

A Rule 311 Notice, my lawyers have explained, has to be given to the defense within a reasonable time prior to trial. And it has to be done in open court, on the record.

Ogren is back at his chair now, still on his feet, and he looks down at the document lying on the table. Paul keeps his copy in his hand, away from me.

Ogren clears his throat and begins.

"Pursuant to Section 5, Paragraph 311 of the Code of Criminal Procedure, in the case of the People versus Martin Kiernan Kalish, Case Number CR 00103067, the People hereby give notice to the defendant, Martin Kiernan Kalish, that they will be seeking the sentence of death by electrocution. May the record reflect that the defendant has been fully advised thereof in open court."

The judge looks at Paul, who stands. "The defense is so advised."

38

THE WEEK OF JANUARY 3 BRINGS THE TYPICAL WIN-
ter trade-off in the county: The temperatures rise, the snow
falls. It makes it easier for me to be outside at seven-thirty
in the evening, but harder to sit in my little spot, between
the two shrubs.

Highland Woods is a town of rolling hills, and the yard
where I sit is on one of the tallest. The yard is bordered by
shrubbery, and stacked railroad ties provide the wall between
it and the neighbor's yard five feet below. I've had my escape
planned from the first time I sat here: If the people who live
here see me, I can jump down to the neighbor's yard and
run; their view would be blocked by the shrubs.

Tonight my seat is damp from the snow. I can only imagine how I look, sitting Indian style on this railroad tie, leaves
and sticks poking my face, peering through my binoculars at
his house about a hundred yards away, hoping he'll leave
sooner than later so my butt won't be totally soaked.

He's getting ready for a Friday night out. He walks into
the bedroom in a towel, grabs a sweater from a drawer, and
goes back out of sight, into the bathroom. He comes back
out about twenty minutes later, combed and dressed. He
grabs his wallet from the dresser and stuffs it in his trousers.
He hits the light and it's dark upstairs. Except for the small
green light on the alarm pad.

In another minute, the green light turns red and blinks.
The downstairs goes dark. Good thing, because my legs are
cramping up something awful. Indian style is for kids.

The neighbor's houses are spread pretty far apart, and I
expect I won't be noticed. At any rate, I don't plan to be
here long enough to get caught.

The front door opens with surprising ease. If he had bolted it I never could have gotten in. As I had hoped, he left through the garage door and didn't bother with the deadbolt on the front door. I guess people with alarms don't worry about that stuff.

The shrill sound comes an instant later. I flip on the light, look around in a panic but, as expected, find the alarm pad on the wall, identical to the one upstairs. I quickly punch in the digits 3-1-6-1. The shrill sound switches to three quick beeps, and the red blinking light becomes a steady green.

I am still for a moment, taking in the surroundings of another man's dwelling. My heart leaps, my body filled with a sensation that is part curiosity, part fear, part voyeuristic. I am inside his house.

I walk down the hallway to the den. I reach the glass door that leads to the deck. I unlock the screen door, then open it to reach the thick glass. I flip the latch down to the "unlock" position but do not open the door. I close the screen door again and check it out: When the screen is closed, its frame blocks the view of the lock on the glass door. He won't know the door's unlocked. And this time of year, he shouldn't be using this door much.

I walk back to the front door and lock it back up. Then I go to the telephone in the kitchen. I dial it and wait.

"Hello?"

Hearing the voice brings a rush to my throat, sweat on my forehead. "Yes," I say in a voice much deeper than my real voice, "may I speak to Jane?"

"I think you have the wrong number, sir."

"Huh! Isn't this the home of Jane Paulson?"

"No, it's not. This is the Reinardt residence."

"My mistake, ma'am. So sorry to inconvenience you."

"That's quite all right."

"Bye-bye now."

I hang up the phone and return to the front door. I punch in 3-1-6-1 and watch the green light turn to a blinking red. In much less than forty-five seconds, I return to the den, go through the screen and glass doors, and run down the stairs of the back porch.

I am back at my vantage point less than six minutes after I left it. I jump up on the railroad ties and look through the binoculars. The burglar alarm in his bedroom stares back at me with a solid red light.

39

"HEY, TOM. IT'S YOUR FAVORITE UNCLE."

I'm sitting in my hotel room, as always, staring at the room service that now rests half eaten on top of my television. The screen is showing a college basketball game, the sound muted.

"You didn't call." The voice of a scorned eight-year-old. Scorned first by a father who's moved on to another life, then by the uncle who blew him off on the phone a week or so ago and never called back.

"I know, Tom. I meant to. I just had a lot of things to do. I'm sorry."

Silence at the other end.

"Tommy, I'm really sorry and I want to talk to you. How's your mom doing?"

"She's okay."

"You still think she's sad."

"Yeah."

"Why?"

"I *told* you."

"Because she cries sometimes?"

"Yeah."

"Okay. Well, why do you think she cries?"

"Dad."

"Yeah, huh? Well, you know what I think?"

"What?"

Well, here I go, way out of my league here, trying to counsel a little boy on the difficulties of growing up in a broken family. But I've figured out one thing about Tommy: He will not bring this up with his mother. I have to try.

"I think your mom loves you and Jeannie a lot. But sometimes it gets kind of hard, y'know? So sometimes, maybe, she gets a little sad. But the thing is, most of the time she's really happy, because of you and your sister."

"He's an asshole," he says.

Was I saying that at age eight? Did I have the level of spite, much less the vocabulary? "Well, it was tough when your dad left. But they did what they thought was best for you and Jeannie."

"They always yelled."

"I know. That's why they thought it would be better if they didn't live together anymore. They wanted you guys to be happy. They didn't want you and Jeannie to grow up with them shouting at each other all the time."

I've heard kids blame themselves a lot when parents split. This was Dr. Kalish's shot at erasing this possibility. Any luck?

"He doesn't come around anymore."

"Yeah."

"He's got a new girlfriend."

Okay, Dr. K. How to handle that one. "Your dad is busy, Tom. And he lives out of state now. It's hard for him. I'm sure he visits as often as he can."

"He doesn't give a shit about us," he says. "Mom said so."

I consider my next move. Tommy is sniffling, and his voice has grown harder. I should be an expert on the permanent imprints our early years leave. But not on how to erase them.

"She said it on the phone," he continues. "She was talking to Dad. She said he didn't give a *shit* about us."

"She didn't mean it, Tom. She was probably just mad. She wants him to come visit more, and it's hard for him. But she understands. She'd want you to understand, too."

"He should be nicer to Mom." Christ, can this little guy tug at me. The little man of the house. Protecting Mom.

"You know, Tommy," I say, "your mom really depends on you. She knows you're a strong little man, and she needs you a lot."

It's hard to tell whether I'm reaching him, especially the way he keeps on with his revelations as if I'm not talking. Kids aren't so good with this kind of conversation. And I sure as hell am not. But he seems to be considering what I said. "You think?" he asks.

"Yeah, I think. You're the man of the house now. Jeannie looks up to you. You need to set a good example for her."

"I got a check-plus in math." His grades, along with his attitude, have been bad the last year or so. "But I wasn't so good in science. I hate science."

I laugh. "I did, too." He laughs along; a bond has formed, two men who hate science. This is the first sign from Tommy that I've hit a button.

"But I tried hard anyway, Tommy, because my mom wanted me to. She wanted me to do well so I could get a good education, so I could have a good life when I grew up. And I wanted to make her proud."

"Yeah?"

"Yeah. That's what your mom wants, too, you know. For you and Jeannie to do well. To do your best, whatever that is. Just to try hard." This is going well. I think.

"Mrs. Evans says I'm getting better at spelling."

"Yeah, see, there you go." I think I'm trying harder to convince myself that I'm helping than to actually help. But Tommy seems to be responding. Maybe he just needs a guy to talk to. I can do that, sure.

"Are you gonna come visit?"

Now what, smart guy? Jamie hasn't told the kids about my arrest, and this is the last thing he needs to hear now. I give him something vague, lot of really important stuff going on, I'll try to make it as soon as I can.

I stare into the darkness of my hotel room as we speak, wondering how all of this has come down to making a kid's life a little harder. How I backed off when Jamie talked to me about moving her family to my town, how I've escaped every commitment in my life, as if my only goal was not to have anyone depend on me. Not to be trapped.

I think of Rachel, the only woman I have ever wanted to commit to. But was that just because I knew she could never commit to me? I wonder what it was I felt for her. "Love" is just a word, empty, void of meaning, an overused term. She gave me something, ever since that first night. She energized me, flicked the "on" button. She gave me a center. I've drifted through life, just going along, doing what I'm told, accepting the rules without complaint, like some human automaton. But always thinking, somewhere, somehow, something better would come my way. Waiting for that moment, that glorious moment, when it will all dawn on me, why I'm here and what it is that I want.

I guess that's what Rachel gave me. That glorious moment. I wanted her, I wanted to spend my life with her. If I play things right, maybe I still can.

Tonight Rachel will come to my hotel room. When I open the door I will see a woman, back turned, in the cleaning lady's uniform, a scanty black piece with a white collar, a very seductive pose. Then she will turn around and move the pink duster that obscures her face. And she will smile that smile.

Would you like your bed turned down?

I will say yes.

40

NO SNOW TONIGHT, BUT THE RAILROAD TIES ARE slick and cold, and I fear that with one false move I'll do a freefall onto the frozen yard below. Twenty minutes I spend in this awkward spot, peering through my binoculars at his house, until he leaves.

My walk is a series of shortcuts through common areas and backyards. The homes in the upper-crust section of Highland Woods are peaceful on a below-freezing night, patches of snow resting on the rooftops like half-finished jigsaw puzzles, smoke curling from the chimneys. I move at a normal pace, crunching on the hard inch or two of snow, with the attitude that I'm not doing anything but strolling through the neighborhood if someone inquires. That doesn't stop me from pulling the scarf up over my face, reminiscent of another night not so long ago when I didn't fully appreciate the advantages of anonymity.

There is no secret getaway path here, no woods to shelter me. But I should be okay. My plans do not include carrying a dead body around with me again. Worst-case, I'm a burglar, and I've been accused of worse. Still, there's a caution in my stride, my eyes darting about. I'd rather not be seen.

If a man's true character can be judged by what he does when no one's looking, what does that say about me? I like to watch. I'm a grown-up with an adolescent's thoughts, peeking out from my hiding place, lurking about in shadows, playing let's-pretend with human dolls. I'm this guy, I'm that guy. I'm you.

I take the twelve steps up to the deck as gingerly as possible, slowly putting my weight on each one as I climb. I glance over once or twice at the neighbors behind his house.

The lights are out in their top floor, and with his long back-yard and theirs, they are far away from me, anyway. They'll never see me. This is a much more private entrance than his front door.

I reach the deck and walk over to the glass door. What are the odds that he would have opened this door last night, with near-freezing temperatures? And with the screen closed, he wouldn't notice the lock on the glass door, pushed to the "unlock" position.

Bingo.

The door slides open, and the shrill alarm sounds. I pull open the screen and go to the front door, disarming the alarm with four quick punches of my index finger. I walk past the stairs into the kitchen. They have a walk-in pantry with all sorts of dry food on the shelves. On one shelf is a bunch of phone books, with a little dark brown wicker basket that holds a ring of keys. Spare keys, no doubt. I'll have them copied tonight and returned before they miss them.

The second floor is home to three bedrooms and two baths. One of the rooms is a study, with a black L-shaped desk that hugs the back corners of the room. A computer sits atop the ledge of the desk, next to a series of hardcover books held together by marble bookends. A picture of him and his wife on the wall; he's wearing a cap and gown, she is smiling broadly next to him, her head on his shoulder. His diplomas are on the wall, Yale undergrad and the state university for his MBA, the name MICHAEL RUDOLPH SPROVIERI embla-zoned on each in a thick, fancy font.

The second bedroom must be the guest room, with an iron-ing table set up and a twin bed, which sits under a window with a closed blind. On the bed are five opened boxes with various items, mostly clothes, half covered in the wrapping tissue. Holiday presents destined for a return. In a long thin box is a tie, maybe the ugliest I've ever seen, a solid purple with one very big silver star in the middle. I try to envision the senile aunt who could have thought this was just darling.

The master bedroom has the walk-in closets I saw from my little perch outside. There's the queen-size bed; a water bed, it turns out, as I poke it. The alarm is on the wall by the door, the small light solid green.

His dresser is next to the alarm. Not much inside. Socks . . . underwear . . . sweaters . . . turtlenecks. His summer clothes aren't in this room. Probably in the basement. Good.

I walk over to the window and look out with my binoculars. Highland Woods is really quite scenic this time of year, the snow clinging to the trees, the quiet elegance provided by the winter blanket. But in the dark, there is little to see.

He has quite a view from this window. I move the binoculars around, peering into house after house. I can see people in their kitchens, their playrooms, even one couple fooling around in their bedroom. Amazing what people will do with the curtains wide open. Don't they know there are people like me out there? I keep the binoculars moving until I find what I'm looking for.

I have to stand to the far left side of the window and look almost as far to the right as possible, but I can see it. The oak tree I always stand by, set back about twenty yards off the house, just over the hill that leads down into the woods. The gas grill on the back porch is still there. The little patio table with an umbrella in the middle. Wooden benches around the table, but with one missing on the right side. It's probably locked up in some evidence room.

I saw you, Mr. Kalish.

The sliding glass door has been replaced. From what I heard, the police finished all their investigating of that room about a week ago. Rachel has replaced the door, probably replaced the carpet. I can't tell, because the curtain is pulled closed.

He has a phone by his bed. I dial the number and stretch the cord over to my spot by the window. I lift the binoculars to my eyes with my left hand, taking a moment to find her house again. There she is, upstairs in her bedroom, in a green sweater; her long dark hair hangs lifelessly at her shoulders. I hear a *click* as I watch her pick up the phone.

"Hello?"

"Rachel Reinardt?" This time, a southern drawl. I can't let

my voice shake here, though I'm once again knocked on my heels at the sound of her voice. Even when she answers the phone she is so damn sexy.

"Yes." A very hesitant yes. Her eyes narrow, her brow wrinkles.

"My name is Jeffrey Flowers. I'm a reporter for KTEL-TV in Louisiana."

"I'm referring all calls—"

"To your attorney, ma'am, yes, I know. I'm not asking you to say a word to me. Let me just explain my proposition to you, and then you can hang up on me if you like." I go into some song and dance about a documentary I'm doing that I want to sell to the network, domestic abuse turned bad, and that it will paint her in a most enviable light. I consider reaching for my zipper but decide against it. Can't be caught with your pants down.

She lets me go on for about two minutes before interrupting me, thanks but no thanks, and hanging up. She walks away from the window, out of my view.

41

MANDY'S PLACE IS A LOFT DOWNTOWN, ON THE West Side, where the smokestacks made room about ten years ago for a few buildings full of yuppies who think they aren't yuppies, who wanted to walk to work and steer clear of the trendier neighborhoods. Her loft is a thousand square feet on a good day, but the maple floors, cathedral ceilings, and bay windows give it an airy feel. Dinner was my idea, after a long afternoon of going through prosecution files. Mandy declined at first with a smile. The second time she turned me down, she was a little less glib, telling me in as casual a way as she could that it was probably not a good idea. We both have to eat, I said, so why not just grab something quick? So she finally relented.

Once we agreed, it was only a quick mention of the new Thai restaurant in her neighborhood that turned this quick bite into a long dinner. After a bottle of wine that she ordered, it became an after-dinner drink at her place.

I compliment her on her condo. She says she bought it less than a year ago, just after her salary skyrocketed from the mid-fifties to six figures at the new firm. Mandy can say these things, talk about her salary and things like that, in a way that I never could. I live my life with a constant shield wrapped around me, a Do Not Enter sign permanently etched on my chest. Mandy's says Come On In.

Mandy tells me about her family (two parents, still living, retired in Arizona; two brothers, one playing minor league baseball in Oklahoma, the other teaching high school social studies in Iowa). She tells me about her childhood (tomboy who played baseball and football, moved on to varsity tennis, a scholarship at Iowa State, then law school at Michigan). I find myself fascinated by these things, wanting to know all I can about this woman who is, really, nothing more than my lawyer. I ask questions, make my usual number of wise-cracks. It is a truly enjoyable evening, mostly because we have not said a word about me.

But then there's the inevitable lull in the conversation. We each sip at our wine quietly. I look out the window at a high-rise, filled with people who have less complicated and happier lives. I notice, more than once, Mandy turning to look at me.

"I suppose it's my turn," I say. "My life story."

Mandy smiles. "We don't have to." She has seen a glimpse into my world; I've given her little tidbits about my father and my background. It doesn't take someone of Mandy's intelligence to discern that my least favorite direction is backward.

"Actually," she says, "I just wanted to ask you one thing."

"Go ahead."

"I hope you don't mind."

"Anything."

"This may sound like a silly thing to ask."

"Pop always said, the only dumb questions are the ones you don't ask."

She gives a perfunctory smile, then turns solemn, curious. Her eyes drop from mine; she runs her finger over the rim of her glass. "Are you afraid?" she asks.

"Of course I am."

"Yeah. Of course. You just don't seem like it."

"It's the fatalism in me. Like I saw this coming, in some way, some form."

That's the truth. This is Kalish on Life 101: I do not subscribe to the belief that all humans, at their core, are good. I believe that at my core, in the dark recesses that boil deep within, is a cesspool of all that is—for lack of a better word—bad. A literal pool of insecurity, fear, prejudice, anger, revenge, surrender. And life is nothing more than climbing the very steep hill to the promised land, self-actualization, I suppose, or contentment. The hill is rocky, giving me ample opportunity to find my grip as I lift myself against the very strong gravitational force pulling me back down. And when I do fall back, the landing is soft, the pool refreshing and soothing and nourishing. Sometimes I think I will never actually start the climb back up. Not when the water is so warm.

"I think you're very hard on yourself," Mandy says.

"That's probably true." I turn to her now, lifting a leg onto the couch. The doors this woman opens up. "Truth is, Mandy, there are nights when I stay awake and just cry, and pray, and wonder why this has happened to me. I'm placing my life in the hands of two people who I didn't know from Adam two months ago. This mess, this whole complicated mess that I live with day in and day out, I am now handing over to complete strangers and asking them to clean it up. It's rather unsettling, to say the least."

Mandy, who has never hidden a single emotion or expression, now looks at me with sad eyes, pursed lips. She tells me resolutely, "We'll do everything we can."

"Oh, I know that. I have no complaints about my lawyers, believe me."

"And I'm not a stranger."

"No, you're not." I smile at her, suddenly sorry that I have cast a pall on the evening. She leans back on the couch and crosses a leg. We stare out toward the window, like two teenage kids staring up at the stars, waiting for a surprisingly awkward moment to pass. No, Mandy, you're not a stranger.

"Tell me something you've never told anyone else," I say to her.

She smiles.

"If that's possible," I add.

A wider smile, a turn of the head. "I tend to run on a little, don't I?"

"No, no. I like that."

She sips her wine and mulls this over. This makes a good two and a half bottles we have shared, and any inhibitions Mandy might possibly possess have vanished by now.

She turns to me, leaning on a cushion with her elbow. "You asked me once why I left the County Attorney's Office."

" 'Change of scenery,' " I say, repeating her words.

"Yeah, well." She lifts her glass and takes a sip. Her face grows tense, her eyes glazing over with a haunted stare. Then her stare breaks; she blinks and looks into her drink. "I've tried all these cases, right? And sometimes, I'm not entirely sure the guy's the guy. Don't get me wrong, ninety-five percent of the cases, I have no doubt in my mind. None. But that still leaves five percent, you know? I've got more than probable cause, but I have some doubt. You know, maybe this guy got himself in a pickle, tried to b.s. his way out, one-upped the coppers one time too many and found himself on the wrong side of a charge. What's one street punk from another anyway? Right? They didn't do this one, they probably did a lotta others they walked from. Right? The great equalizer."

Mandy sits on that. She looks like she's got a lot more,

but she's holding back, something I'm not used to seeing in her. I prod her on.

"That's the mind-set," she says. "I mean, these people I work with, they're great, y'know? Great guys, great women. But they're in this fucking *mind-set*." That's the first time I've heard Mandy curse. She raises a finger. "I have never *once* heard someone explain away an acquittal by saying, hey, maybe the guy was innocent. It's always, the jury nullified, the guy lied up and down, judge was an idiot, defense attorney was a crook. No one will admit that maybe they were wrong."

"Maybe they don't *want* to."

"That's right." Her hands wave, her glass spilling some wine onto the floor without Mandy noticing. "They're so scared silly that they're putting someone away for something they didn't do, they convince themselves that their judgment is infallible."

"Mandy—"

"And most of these defendants—including the five percent—well, they don't exactly have *Paul Riley* defending them. These lawyers have a hundred cases a week, they're running from courtroom to courtroom, checking their calendars in the hallways to remind themselves of who their client is this morning. I've had lawyers approach me and say they're here on the Ryan matter, and point to one of the defendants sitting in the holding cell, and I say, no, that guy's Manning, and they say, oh yeah yeah, *Manning*, and they run back to their briefcase and pull a different file. Some of their clients don't have a snowball's chance."

She takes another sip, her hands shaking slightly. She is staring off now, and as she continues, I wonder if she's still talking to me.

"I had a case a few months before I left. Three counts, aggravated sexual abuse. We have testimony from a fourteen-year-old girl that the defendant, her stepfather, had intercourse with the girl. We interview the stepdad. He says she's lying. He says his stepdaughter has a grudge, they don't get along. But he swears they never had sex."

"Was that true?"

"I don't know. He said so. But anyway, we say no, we file on this guy, and we go to trial. We've had the girl examined, and we find evidence of a torn hymenal membrane. In other words, proof that this fourteen-year-old girl did, in fact, have intercourse. So obviously, this corroborates her story, and we turn this evidence over to the defense.

"The stepdad says that the torn hymen proves nothing, because his stepdaughter had had sex many times with her boyfriend. We talk to the boyfriend, who eventually admits to having sex with her. So there is an alternative explanation for the physical evidence. Another reason, besides the stepfather, for the torn hymen. Right?"

"Right."

"Right. Okay, there's a law in this state that says in a rape case, you can't introduce evidence of the victim's past sexual conduct. You know, just because a woman's had sex sometime in the past doesn't make her willing for every guy who comes along. It's a good law, a *great* law, but there's an exception for evidence that is so important that justice requires it be admitted. So I'm thinking, the defense has a dead-bang pretrial motion to admit the evidence of this girl sleeping with her boyfriend. It's not like they're trying to make her out as promiscuous—they just want to be able to explain to the jury that the torn hymenal membrane does not conclusively prove that the stepdad was the one who had intercourse with her. Of *course* this evidence should be admitted."

She pauses a moment, stifling a sob, then waves her hand about.

"But is it my job to say, sure, fine, the evidence comes in? No. My job is to oppose them. For the good of the People, you see. I try to keep out all their stuff, they try to keep out all my stuff, and somewhere in the middle lies the truth. A nice little moral whiteout.

"So it's time for the pretrial motions. First off, the defense attorney is twenty minutes late, and with Judge Donohan, that means you're *already* in a hole. Second, this particular lawyer was once brought up on disciplinary charges, so he's got strike two. And I know for a fact that Judge Donohan had held this guy in contempt before.

"So the lawyer makes his motion to allow in this evidence. He starts arguing about this exception in the rape-shield law. The judge doesn't even let him finish. Dee-nied. Denied! The stepdad has no defense now. He can't even *mention* his step-daughter sleeping with her boyfriend. The jury will hear this physical evidence about the torn hymen, look at this suppos-edly innocent fourteen-year-old, and say, *who else* could have been responsible?"

"Maybe he'll win that argument on appeal," I offer.

Mandy shakes her head slowly and gives a fateful smile. "No appeal." Her voice is flat. "When he lost that motion, he knew he was dead in the water. His client was looking at twenty-five years minimum. We cut a deal for twelve. You know what my supervisor said? He thought twelve was a little soft." She lets out a breath. "A little *soft*. Do you have any idea how child rapists are treated in jail?"

I touch her arm. "You don't blame *yourself*."

She laughs. "Just doing my job, right, right." She empties her glass of wine. "I shouldn't have opposed the motion. I mean, they probably would've thrown me out of the office for letting in prior sex without a fight. But this guy spends at least six years in jail because his lawyer's watch is slow and the judge hates him." She bites her lip. "I had the power to do something there, Marty."

"Did you really believe the stepdad's story?"

"I don't know. I think I didn't *want* to believe him. You get so caught up in the adversarial nature of the thing, you know? I'm the noble prosecutor; anything *I* do is for the good of the People, but anything the defense does is to distort the truth."

"That doesn't sound like you, Mandy."

"It's *not* me. But I let it *become* me."

I reach out to touch her arm and draw closer to her.

"The day I left—we'd convicted on an aggravated battery earlier that month. The defense attorney comes into court to file his posttrial motion for a new trial. This is his written motion." She raises a finger. "Sentence one: The defendant was denied his right to a fair trial. Sentence two: The defendant was denied due process of law. Sentence three: The defendant was not proven guilty beyond a reasonable doubt. The end. No elaboration on the facts of the case. No citation to court decisions. That was the whole motion! *This* is the representation this guy gets." Mandy's shoulders raise. "I— I just couldn't *do* it anymore."

I edge closer. "There's only so much one person can do," I say softly.

"Well, it wasn't going to be me. Not anymore."

I let my hand rest on Mandy's arm a second longer, then remove it, as Mandy weeps quietly. Quite a pair, the two of us, two people with unfulfilling careers, the only difference being Mandy did something about it, if only by escaping. Me, I dragged along with no plans to make the bold move, waiting out my days and letting myself believe the fat salary was worth it. I want, like her, to hit the "rewind" button. Even if I'm convicted—Christ, *especially* if I'm convicted— I want to be able to look back and smile.

42

THE BUILDING AT 211 SOUTH WALTER DRIVE IS ONE of the newest downtown high-rises, just a block off the river that provides the western border to the commercial district. Redish Mutual Life Insurance occupies floors fifty-three through sixty-seven.

The spacious lobby is filled with boutique stores, a couple restaurants, and a decent coffee shop. I walk along the marble floor, past the ATM machines, to the three pay phones. I could walk the path in my sleep by now.

I drop a quarter into one of the phones and dial. Rachel isn't home. Her answering machine picks up. It is Rachel's voice, but she doesn't identify herself by name. She just re-states her phone number but adds that any calls from the media should be directed to Gerald Salters at phone number such and such. It's silly, I know, that I am so desperate to hear her voice that I call her answering machine. But still, I simply cannot control myself, I don't *want* to control myself.

Sometimes when her machine answers, I say nothing, just stand there with heart palpitations, drinking her in, yearning for more but happy for at least this. Sometimes her maid answers, and I don't have to worry about my voice then. The maid is there in the daytime, although I think Rachel has cut her hours. Those are good calls, too, when the maid answers; I can spend several minutes on the phone with her, telling her I'm a repair guy, or I'm taking a survey, or whatever. Her English isn't so good, and most of the time I just end up confusing her. But still. It's almost like I'm in Rachel's house, making conversation with the housekeeper while Rachel is upstairs getting ready for our date. I am touching some part of Rachel's life with these calls.

Other times, when Rachel answers, I use a fake voice, and again ask for Jane Paulson or pretend I'm a reporter. These are difficult calls, because I want so much to use my real voice, talk to her, see how she's doing, tell her what she means to me. But I stifle the urge every time, secure in the knowledge that it would lead to an immediate *click* on the other line and probably to a changing of her home phone number.

This time, I use a recording I have made. I listen to her softly ask that I leave a message before holding my dicta-phone up to the phone and pressing play.

Jane Paulson, this is your chance to win a million dollars! If you return this phone call, you'll be eligible for prizes ranging from a new sport utility vehicle to. . . .

The tape goes on for over thirty seconds. Rachel won't call the number, of course. If she did, she would reach Dewey's Pizzeria. Pizza at your door, thirty minutes or less.

43

TONIGHT'S DINNER IS FILET AND STEAMED VEGE-
tables. I enjoy a couple of bites of the steak until I realize
that this is what my flesh may look like after Roger Ogren
and his cronies are done with me.

The phone rings early in the evening. It's Paul Riley.

"Marty. I have some bad news."

"Yeah?"

A sigh comes through the phone; this is a sound you do not
enjoy hearing from your defense attorney. "Marty. They've
indicted Rachel." I grip the phone tighter. "Murder in the first
degree, conspiracy to commit murder in the first degree."

I close my eyes and take a deep breath. I am numb for a
moment, in disbelief. I feel the constriction in my stomach
before his words even register.

This wasn't supposed to happen.

"Marty? Mar—"

"I'm here."

"I'm going to get in touch with Gerry Salters, her lawyer.
I just wanted to let you know as soon as possible. I wanted
you to hear it from me."

"What do they have on her?"

"I don't know."

"Where is she?"

"She's—well, I—you're not planning on *speaking* with
her—"

"Do you think she's okay?"

"I imagine she's not."

"Is she in jail?"

"No. Gerry's agreed to bring her into custody tomorrow."
Rachel. Oh, Rachel. This is my fault. This wasn't supposed

to happen. No matter how it would turn out, no matter who else got hurt, it was never supposed to be *you*.

"You okay, Marty?"

"This isn't right. She didn't do anything, Paul. She didn't *do* anything!"

"Marty. Listen to me. I want you to calm down. I want you to relax. She has a very good lawyer. She's in good hands."

I can't let this happen to you, Rachel. I will do whatever it takes. Still, after everything. I will keep my promise to you.

"Marty? Are you okay? Marty?"

"What if I just say I did it?"

"Listen to me, okay? You're not thinking clearly here. I—I know this is upsetting to you. But this is not the moment to make any kind of decision. Promise me you won't do anything rash.

"Will you promise me that? Marty? Will you promise me that?

"Marty?"

44

I AM BACK IN MY LAWYERS' OFFICE BY NINE IN THE morning. I look out the window of the lobby, waiting for Mandy Tanner. It's cloudy today, with intermittent rain. The street below is littered with the tops of umbrellas.

I cover a nervous yawn. I slept in fits last night, thoughts of Rachel in a jail cell dominating my mind. I wrestled with the idea of going to the cops last night and writing out a full confession, making it clear that Rachel had nothing to do with this. I made it to the hotel lobby, but I couldn't take the plunge. The only reason I stopped, really, was that every time I've made a rash decision, I've regretted it. There will be time enough to plead guilty if necessary. But the clock is ticking, in big, booming chimes.

Footsteps on the marble behind me. I turn to see Mandy, a gray turtleneck touching her chin. She stops and appraises me a moment. "Hey."

"Have we heard anything?"

"Paul's talking to Rachel's lawyer right now."

We walk to the conference room in silence. And we take our seats in silence. I stare off into space, imagining Rachel walking out of her house through a throng of reporters. The cop taking her fingers and sticking them, one by one, on an ink blotter and then onto a fingerprint pad. The jail cell slamming shut.

"Marty?" Mandy says cautiously. "You hanging in there?"

I run my hand over my unshaven face. "How are they gonna kill me?"

Her lips part, then close. She deflates. "I don't think—"

"Tell me. Please—please tell me."

She puts her hands together on the table and clears her throat. She pauses before starting, quietly, robotic. "The presumptive method is—electrocution. But the inmate may choose lethal gas."

I turn to her. "My choice?"

"We've got a good case, Marty."

I run my fingers through my hair, the bangs falling into my face. "Have you ever sent someone to the chair?"

She stares at me; her eyes glaze over, as if she's looking right through me. She bites her lip and nods. "Yeah," she says evenly.

I whisper back. "How did it make you feel?" I spin my chair around and look out the window. It's dark enough outside that I can see my reflection, barely, a thin face, big mop of hair on top. I hold my breath, trying to imagine what it feels like not to have another one coming. Then I let out a long exhale, and then I smell Mandy's perfume. She sits next to me and takes my hand into hers.

"You want to confess," she says. "You want to make this all go away for Rachel." I look into her eyes. Tears have formed.

"Let them judge you. Let twelve people tell you what you did was right or wrong. Don't make that decision yourself."

I squeeze her hand and look back out the window. "I can't let them hurt her."

"If we plead that you did it, that you were saving her life, you'll tell them. You'll tell them she wasn't involved. You don't have to give up to protect her."

"Then we have to go that way. Or else I plead guilty." Mandy doesn't respond. I turn to her. "Those are the only two choices."

Her eyes run over my face. "Do you trust me?"

"What I trust you with is getting me out of this jam. But I'm not sure I *want* out."

A tear falls onto her cheek now, but she doesn't brush it away. She just looks into my eyes. "I don't want to see—" Her whisper cuts off.

I start to speak but my throat closes up as well. I'm touched by Mandy's compassion, even more so by her ability to care about me at all, her willingness to reach out to someone who is hanging by a string. I realize at that moment that we have made a connection, somewhere along the line. I've felt it for a while now, but only now do I realize that she has, too.

I finish the sentence for her. "You don't want to see me die."

45

Inmates who are put to death in the gas chamber do not become immediately unconscious upon the first breath of lethal gas. An inmate probably remains conscious anywhere from fifteen seconds to one minute, and there is a substantial likelihood that consciousness, or a waxing and waning of consciousness, persists for several additional minutes. During this time, inmates suffer intense, visceral pain, primarily as a result of lack of oxygen to the cells. The experience of "air hunger" is akin to the experience of a major heart attack, or to being held under water. Other possible effects of the cyanide gas include tetany, an exquisitely painful contraction of the muscles, and painful buildup of lactic acid and adrenaline. Cyanide-induced cellular suffocation causes anxiety, panic, terror, and pain.

I close out of the Federal court opinion I pulled up on-line and log off the Internet. I suck in a big breath and hold it. I count backward from one hundred.

I'm not sorry I killed him.
I'm not afraid of what will happen to me.
Are you sure?
Ninety . . .
I saw you, Mr. Kalish.
I'll come forward.
Eighty . . .
Rachel says she didn't see the intruder.
Marty?
What are you doing here?
Are you sure?
Seventy . . .
Are you sure?

46

MY DAILY RUN AT THE HIGH SCHOOL. IT'S OVER forty today, and I run six miles on the quarter-mile cinder track. My headphones are blaring Vivaldi, and I'm lost in my little world of strings and percussion and sweat. I've come to relish my daily jog. I've made a deal with myself that I won't think about the case when I run, and I've kept to it.

The pressure is mounting, though, and manifesting itself physically now. The last few days, my shoulders have tightened up; I wake up every morning with a stiff neck. My appetite is gone, my stomach preferring to twist and turn itself into knots.

The track surrounds the school's football field; as the snow has melted the last few days, the yard lines have begun to appear. Today, a few eager students are out throwing around a baseball, getting loose for the upcoming tryouts, trying not to slip on the field as they hop in place and wing the ball to each other, their breath visible with their effort.

I complete lap twenty-four and break to a walk. I notice by the spectator stands a man in a long olive coat, standing and watching me, smoking a cigarette. As we make eye contact, he nods and walks toward me, dropping his cigarette and crunching it out with his foot, a last stream of smoke curling from his nostrils and mouth. I've had reporters follow me here before, and I've always given the same line: No comment, talk to Paul Riley.

As he approaches, I consider leaving my headphones on and ignoring him completely. But I've been inclined lately to treat these guys more respectfully, hoping they'll return the favor. They rarely do.

"Mr. Kalish?" He extends a hand. He has receding curly hair, a Mediterranean complexion. "Andrew Karras."

"The *Watch*," I say. He's the reporter I called that time, declaring my innocence.

"Yeah. Listen, I was hoping for a comment from you."

I wipe my forehead with my arm. "You know the drill by now. Talk to Riley."

"I'm giving you the chance to hear something in advance, Mr. Kalish."

"Keeping your nose to the ground, huh? Good for you." I pull the hood on my sweatshirt and turn away.

"Okay," he calls out. "You'll find out about Rachel just like everyone else, in a few days."

That one stops me. I turn back to him. "Talk."

"We have a deal? You'll give me a comment?"

"Talk."

Karras blinks and considers his options. He sees he's not gonna get any guarantees. He finally decides he's got nothing to lose. "Rachel's cutting a deal."

I stumble back a step at these words, maybe to make sure the ground is still beneath me, that I am really standing here and I have truly heard what I think I heard. I swallow hard and search the face of my informant for confirmation. His expression tells me he is not kidding, not pulling a fast one. His expression also tells me he is very satisfied with himself, but he manages a solemn face.

"She's pleading guilty?"

Karras shakes his head slowly. He seems surprised that I don't understand. And something more than surprise. Sympathy. Apology. "No, Mr. Kalish, she's not pleading guilty. She's—getting immunity."

I squint my eyes, still not catching the drift.

"They're going to drop the charges in exchange for her testifying against you."

A quick gasp, just a brief intake of air, is the only sound that comes from me. I am frozen, paralyzed, as these words float through my mind. And then, through the echo of the words comes the adrenaline, acid cutting through my veins, a searing rush to my heart, rage and bitterness and shame mixing together in thick black spots before my eyes. And even though this feeling is not foreign, even though I realize I should have seen it coming, even as I chastise myself for having this blind spot, I still can't believe I am uttering the words: "*She*'s going to testify against *me*?"

He says something in reply, but I don't hear it. I throw off my headphones and jump the fence surrounding the track. He is calling to me for a comment, but I just run.

BOOK TWO

THE LAST BOX DROPS WITH A MUTED *THUD* ON THE carpet in my bedroom. Four boxes and this little suitcase, these have been my life for the last two months. I look over at the dresser by the window, the picture of my family on the beach in Florida taken about twenty-five years ago: Jamie waving eagerly at the camera, my father standing behind her in his long plaid shorts and sunglasses perched on top of his head, me scooping up sand to pile on top of the castle. As always, I find relief, a rush of warmth, in this photo, a time when life was simple and ideal and full of hope. It's good to be home.

As I survey the bedroom, I remember the place after the cops were done with it. The bedspread lying in a heap on the floor, the mattress tossed haphazardly back onto the wooden bed frame. The dresser pulled back from the wall, the drawers open, their contents spilled on the floor.

When I came home after my arrest, I stayed a grand total of twenty minutes, just long enough to throw together a suitcase of clothes and a few boxes of toiletries and other items. I left a key with Mandy, who led a photographer around the house taking shots of the place. I paid my maid, Alice, who comes every other week to clean, two hundred dollars to clean up the entire house. And it seems she did a pretty nice job.

Official word of the deal between the prosecution and Rachel Reinardt came down on Saturday. The *Watch* ran the story with very few details. The terms of the plea bargain were not disclosed, only that Rachel was being granted full immunity from prosecution in exchange for testifying against me.

County Attorney Phillip K. Everett's mug was plastered next to Rachel's on the front page. The sober expression he wore, along with the press comments he made, reflected the perfect image: This law-and-order stuff is a tough business, and he's not doing it for his own personal gain, you understand, but for the good people of this fine county who put their trust in him. The new developments have stirred the media awake, so once more I'm fielding a dozen phone calls a day.

Anyway, I'm not going to think about that now. Yesterday, I called my Realtor and told her to take my house off the market. This is my home, and I'm not running anymore.

Tonight I'm going to cook a huge bowl of pasta in *my* house, with *my* pan, on *my* stove.

With a leap, I land on my bed, arms and legs sprawled like I'm making a snow angel. I consider stripping off my clothes and running around the house, because I can. Because I *can*.

I visit every room. I hang my clothes back up in the spare bedroom. I replace my pictures on the dresser. Everything back back back, same as it ever was. No more shitty hotel. No more hiding. No more running.

I go to the basement and do pull-ups on the bar that extends between the beams supporting the staircase. I don't know why. Because I can. I can't do too many, with all the strength I've lost. But I do a few. The sweat feels good. I'm going to throw on a flannel shirt, no shower, and stay up all night watching movies. I'm going to shout at the top of my lungs, and no one from the front desk is going to call with complaints. No one is going to stop me from doing anything I want.

"I'm not gonna let them," I grunt out loud, my arms trembling as my chin reaches out for the bar.

"MR. KALISH," SAYS GREG QUILLAR. "YOU GOT HERE fast."

"Yeah, well." I stand near the door of his office, hands stuffed in my jacket, indicating I'm not interested in pleasantries or small talk. Just give them to me.

Quillar wears a satisfied smirk as he hands me a shoe box. "You don't pay for packaging," he apologizes.

I shake the box, rattling the contents. "Good?"

"Yeah, good. Two's enough, huh?"

I nod. "Two's better than none."

"There's a little surprise in there for you."

"Yeah?"

"Yeah." Quillar smiles. "I got some audio."

"Wonderful." I hand him some extra cash. "A job well done."

He accepts the money with reluctance. "Another job?"

"No. Just to make sure we understand each other. Absolute confidentiality."

"You have my word."

"Then your job is done, sir."

Quillar allows a small grin. An alliance has formed. "I take it your job is *not* done."

I turn as I'm leaving. "I have not yet begun to fight," I say.

PAUL RILEY OFFERS HIS APOLOGIES. HE'S TEN minutes late for our meeting, where Paul will summarize his conversation with Rachel's lawyer about the terms of her deal. Mandy is nowhere in sight. Paul thought it might be better, just the two of us.

As always, Paul cuts to the chase. "Rachel isn't going to testify that you two were having an affair. She still denies this." There hasn't been a day since this thing started that Riley wasn't sure we were sleeping together. "So that's good."

"And?" I run my hands over the marble table. If that's as good as it gets, I don't want to hear what's bad.

Paul's eyebrows raise. "She says you were infatuated with her."

My eyebrows lift as well. *Infatuated*. I never thought of it that way. "Ridiculous," I say with a shake of the head, hoping my facial expression is consistent with my denial.

"She says that you followed her around like a lovesick kid. That you continually asked her out. That you told her to leave her husband." There is a hint of scorn in Paul's voice. Have I been keeping something from him, he wonders, definitely not for the first time. "She also told the C.A. that sometimes you would stand outside her house at night, literally just standing around out there, looking through windows and trying to signal her."

I move my tongue against my cheek. "Is that all?"

"No. She also will testify that on the night of the shooting, her husband wasn't about to kill her. He did beat her up, yes. But in her opinion, he was not going to kill her. He hit her once or twice, but that was all."

I see that the prosecution has anticipated one of our possible defenses, that I was rescuing Rachel from a life-threatening beating. Or maybe this testimony is just to make the doc look like not so bad a guy, after all. Either way, I don't really care. There's only one more thing I want to know. I steady myself. "Did she see who came into her house?"

Paul meets my stare. "No."

"She said no?"

"She said no. She doesn't know who it was."

I take a moment to consider this. Rachel's told them I was a pathetic, lovesick puppy who would die for just a glimpse of her inside her house. That will go to motive, but it's nothing too damaging. She said I mentioned her leaving her husband, which is getting a little more dangerous, but still not too bad. And she said her husband wasn't a threat to her life.

All in all, she could have done a lot worse by me. We weren't having an affair, she said. And she didn't see who came through the door. Truth is, she probably gave them as little as possible to get her deal. It seems she's done her best to straddle the line, saving herself without doing too much damage to me. The fact that Roger Ogren took this deal, with what little Rachel gave him, shows his desperation. Nice work, Rachel.

I bring a hand to my chin. "So there's no evidence that I was at the house that night."

"That's right, Marty. Nothing." Paul, as always, maintains his Solomonic poker face, but I can see he's eager. He has just explained to me that our affirmative defense, that I was saving Rachel's life, has taken a severe blow with Rachel's testimony. Now he's gauging my reaction, wondering if our paths have finally met.

"That's good," I say finally. "Because I didn't do it."

50

THURSDAY NIGHT'S A GOOD TIME TO BE DRIVING out of the city, if you're hoping for traffic. For someone who's lived in and around this area as long as I, I'm surprisingly unfamiliar with the outlying area. I'm not one of these guys who can explain the three fastest routes to the Calder Theater out in Lindenwood or to the stadium downtown, who can make one trip someplace and then recite the directions ten different ways. Mine is not an attentive eye, not as far as streets and towns and directions go. Put me inside a building and I couldn't tell you which way's north any more than I could name you the capital of Togo. Give me directions to someplace, you better give me directions back, too, or I'm lost. One could say—many *have* said—that my head's in the clouds, I have no practical sense. I'd say that's half right. I just don't really care. I don't care if First Avenue intersects the expressway north of Clinton and beats the bottleneck. I don't care if taking the 280 is a faster route as long as you're heading south of Oak Hills.

But this route, this one I remember.

The gas station, Guenther's Body Work, was just a repair shop with a couple of pumps as an afterthought. The lights were off in the store and the main garage; the place looked deserted. I half expected it to be open; a station off the highway could be doing decent business, even past midnight on a Thursday. Off to the side of the garage were several rows of cars, junkers the owner would sell off part by part and a couple of decent foreign ones. I parked my car and killed the lights. Someone driving by, seeing my car, would take it for just another car in for repair.

I found a deep trash can by the gas pumps. With little enthusiasm, I reached in, fished around until I felt some paper. I pulled out a fast-food restaurant bag and a brown paper bag from some drugstore. I looked around, seeing nothing, hearing nothing.

I popped the trunk and reached under the cardboard floor I'd replaced after burying the doc. I lifted the gun with two fingers on the handle. I wiped it best I could with my flannel shirt, then wrapped the gun in one bag, then the other.

Behind the store was a row of trees, bare now for the winter. I stepped into the thicket, careful not to lose an eye on a stray branch, and stomped my foot at the base of one of the trees. The ground was hard, but I could manage. Keeping the shovel with me in the car probably wasn't the smartest idea, if I'd been pulled over, but I was glad to have it now. I found a good spot on the hard ground and started digging.

I'm off the ramp now. The light turns green, and I follow another car in making a right turn. It's just a half block down here. No one behind me.

The sign, GUENTHER'S BODY WORK, is turned off, the letters nothing but sticks of metal. The rest of the station is dark. It's safe to turn in. But I don't. I check the rearview as I drive past the gas station. There's a restaurant down the way, maybe fifty yards. It's still pretty busy, just past ten. I pull in and park my car between two others. Then I kill the engine and wait.

Five minutes pass. No cars have gone by.

Another five minutes. Some people come out of the restaurant, walking to a car on the other side of the lot.

Christ, am I paranoid. I look at my watch: 10:23. It's starting to get cold in here. The sign says, restaurant patrons parking only. Violators will be towed!

Well, I won't be long.

I reach under the front seat for the little garden shovel. Then the adrenaline hits me, like it did on November 18, when I was sitting in my garage, wondering if I should drive to work for an alibi, wondering whether I was about to make one wise move too many. It's not too late to turn back, I told myself then. It's not too late now, either.

I reach for the door handle and pull my hand away, like I just touched a hot stove. The left side of my brain is telling me I'm making a big mistake. The right is telling me how brilliant I'll be. If I don't get caught, the left reminds.

I slowly reach for the handle. My fingers curl around the leather bar. My heart is racing, the sweat forming on my face. If I get caught, it's sayonara. Marty's gonna have a tough time explaining what he's doing with Dr. Reinardt's gun.

But if I don't do it, I'll always wonder if I should have. That sounds familiar.

It's about fifty feet to the station. I walk casually to the rear of the garage, collar turned up, treading carefully to soften the echo of my shoes on the concrete. I inch sideways through the narrow space between the back of the station and the trees, taking a couple of stray branches in the face. It smells like human waste back here, and I don't even want to think about what my feet are stepping in.

Last time I was here, all the trees looked alike. But I have no trouble recognizing the spot. There's not much for lighting, but what the hell, I'm only digging a hole.

I plunge the little shovel into the earth. The tool's not made for ground this hard, I soon realize, as the handle bends backward. Adapt and overcome. I cup my hand around the metal part of the shovel, like it's an extension of my hand. I feel the dirt sink into my fingernails. And I scratch and claw with the little scooper part of the shovel.

Almost ten minutes and one very sore wrist later, the shovel hits metal. I use my hands now, gently sweeping away the dirt. I can feel the trigger. Careful. Last I remember, this thing's still loaded. I lift it out of the ground gingerly by the handle. I put the gun in my right hand, the hand I held it in as I stood over Dr. Reinardt.

I place the gun down gently next to the hole and reach into my jacket pocket. The photo is from the basketball league this past summer. Rachel is holding a little boy's hand, I'm standing next to them with a beaming smile. I'd like to take one last look at the photo before I drop it into the hole, but I can't make it out even as my eyes adjust to the darkness. It's okay, I've got every picture of me and Rachel etched in my mind.

I place the photo carefully into my minitrench, so it's not bent. We are one in the earth now, Rachel. Whatever may happen above ground, we are together here.

51

I SIT ALONE IN MY LAWYERS' CONFERENCE ROOM, tapping my fingers on the marble and humming to myself. It's a bright, sunny day today, the sky glowing with happiness, and they're saying temperatures will hit fifty by week's end.

Mandy hustles into the room and spreads a pile of accordion folders on the table. She mumbles an apology and takes a seat, not even looking at me. She busies herself pulling papers out of the folders and arranging them.

"Top of the morning," I say.

She looks up briefly. "What?"

"Hi."

She looks down at her papers. "Hi." Her voice is flat, dull, not the typically vibrant Mandy Tanner. She mentions the witness list, slides a copy in front of me. We start in on the people on the list.

She's keeping her distance from me a little, listening politely but making things more formal than befits her. Her eyes stay down, at any rate, avoiding contact with mine. Her face is tight, her hands nervous. She's mad.

This, basically, is how Paul Riley has treated me from the

start, someone who's really no better than the scumbags he used to put away, someone who doesn't deserve to be in the same room with the corporate general counsels with whom he typically brushes elbows. Someone, to be sure, who will give him the spotlight again, a high-profile murder case, but who is deserving of nothing more than his tolerance.

But Mandy has always been different. Mandy has always felt a genuine concern for me, she's opened up to me when everybody else's door has closed. It's something to which I've resigned myself with everybody else, old acquaintances who offer little more than a grim handshake, some lame mutterings like "Tough break" or "Hang in there," who are counting the seconds until they can get away from me, the guy who they're *not quite sure* did it. But Mandy has always been different, until today. Now she's tolerating me.

We're talking about Angela Siedlecki, the Reinardts' neighbor who called the police the night of the shooting.

"I think I met her once," I say. "There was a meeting in our subdivision. She was on the board or something. She gave a speech."

"Where was the meeting?"

"At the clubhouse."

She stares at me, then holds out her hands. "Well?"

"Well what?"

"You said you *met* her. Describe that."

"Oh. It was really nothing. There was a buffet. I just talked to her briefly in line."

"And?"

"That was it."

"Well, what did you *say*?"

I hold my stare on her. "Just small talk. We introduced ourselves."

"That's *all* you remember."

"Yes, Mandy, that's all I remember."

"Was Rachel there?"

"I don't know. I didn't even know who Rachel was back then."

"Well, *think*."

"I said I don't remember."

"Well, will Mrs. Siedlecki remember?"

"How should—*Jesus*, Mandy." I open my hands. "What do you want me to say?"

"I just want to be sure she won't remember something significant that you don't seem to recall."

"Oh, you mean, like, Rachel and me holding hands? Snuggling in the corner? I told you, I didn't even know who Rachel was back then. It was before I worked at the foundation. It was years ago. For all I know, Rachel didn't even live there yet."

Mandy turns to her notepad and starts writing. "Fine."

"The truth is, she won't even remember our little conversation at the buffet. The only reason *I* remember it is she was one of the speakers at the meeting."

Mandy nods her head, keeping her eyes on the notepad.

"Have I convinced you?" I ask, exasperated.

"You've convinced me." She stops writing and looks up at me. "I just want to make sure your story's not going to change."

Okay. I'm slow, but okay. I get it. "You're mad about me changing my testimony."

Mandy's expression is tight, her eyes cold. "I guess I don't like to see people playing fast and loose with the system."

"The system."

"Yes, the system."

"You *must* be kidding."

She drops her pen. "What, I guess anything goes? Is that how you figure it? You just tell us anything that's convenient, and we'll buy into it because it's the best story to win? Truth or not, whatever works?"

I sit forward. "You were the one who always told me to go with a straight denial. *You* were the one who didn't like that affirmative defense stuff. So what's the deal?"

"I had no problem with making them prove their case," she says with no small amount of force. "I had no problem with you sitting back in silence, like every defendant should have the right to do, and making them prove their case."

I open my hands. "And this is different how?"

"This is different *how*?" She turns her head a moment, wetting her lips. "This is you taking the witness stand and committing perjury."

"You don't know it's perjury."

"I have a pretty darn good idea."

"Paul believes me."

"Paul—" Mandy pauses a moment, then lowers her voice. "Paul *wants* to believe you. I already told him, I won't be the one putting you on the stand."

I fall back against the chair, suppressing initial anger and speaking in a measured tone. "This isn't gin rummy, Mandy. This is my *life*. Pardon me if I'm more worried about staying alive than fitting into your idealistic concept of the criminal justice system. 'Cause I gotta tell you, it don't look so idealistic from *this* side."

Mandy deflates, not satisfied but quieted. She slowly shakes her head.

"I want to show you something," I tell her. I pull from my pocket a copy of the passage from the court opinion I read about lethal gas and slide it across the table to her. "Please, just take two minutes and read this."

She moves it in front of her. Her head goes down, showing me the uneven part in that mass of thick, coarse, curly red and brown hair. I watch her eyes move from line to line. Her eyebrows move together, then up. She runs her teeth over her bottom lip, swallows hard, curls her hair behind her ear. When she's done, she looks up.

"That's what I'm looking at," I say. "I'm playing fast and loose with a system that wants to do *that* to me."

She looks down at the table, searching for the words. Finally, she straightens in her chair, takes a deep breath. "Okay," she says. "This is my problem, not yours. I guess I thought I'd gotten away from all this when I left the office. But my career anxiety shouldn't be your concern."

"Well." I give her a faint smile. "I'd be lying if I said it was."

Her eyes are apologetic. She smiles weakly. I sense that

there's more here than she's said, that she's not just mad that her client lied, but that *I* lied. The words will never come from her mouth, but I realize that I have betrayed her, not as lawyer to client, but as one friend to another. I have lied to her, made her believe in me as someone who did a heroic thing, only to retreat to a cowardly position the moment the going got tough. I feel a rush to my heart, a tingly, dizzying sensation, emotions suppressed for so long that I've forgotten they exist, that I am a man and that I can care. And more than that, that I can express myself. I want to tell her what she's meant to me, I want to tell her that she is the only one who has treated me like a human being these last months. That she is the only one who's shown an interest. I want to tell her more than that, too, but I know that, like Mandy, I will keep it beneath the surface. She has let the door open too far once, and the brutal slap of wind will prevent her from doing it again. And I will keep my door open just a crack, as always, so I can look through without feeling the breeze.

"So," Mandy says, her tone flat. "You didn't do it."

52

GOOD THING FOR ME, HE'S A SOCIAL GUY, GOES OUT every Friday night. It's tough going into his house during daytime, however easily I manage to slip in with the copy of the key I now have. Nighttime is much better.

I go upstairs to his bedroom window and look over at Rachel's house. Her place is dark. I set the binoculars down on the nightstand and pick up his phone.

I dial the number and get her machine. I leave some message about a charity drive, would she be interested? I talk until the machine cuts me off; ninety seconds. I wait a few minutes and call again. I don't say anything this time; I'm running out of disguised voices. The machine cuts off after ten seconds.

I go back downstairs to the closet by the front door. I leaf through the coats until I find the leather jacket I had noticed before. It's in the back part of the closet, by the lighter-weight coats. It's not a coat he's wearing this time of the year. I grab the zipper of the jacket and hold it up. From the zipper dangles a copper triangle with the name of the man-ufacturer, Drifters, enscribed on it. I've heard the name, seen the commercials: emaciated, brooding models, hair in their faces. *Très* chic, Mr. Sprovieri.

I fish in the outer pockets of the jacket, unable to contain the voyeuristic thrill of going through his things. Stick of gum, a couple of stray mints covered with lint, about thirty-five cents in coins, and a couple pieces of crunched-up paper. I unravel the first piece. It's a receipt from his ATM, showing in faded green print that he withdrew a hundred dollars from his checking account on September 11. I make out part of his account number, too. This is much better.

My next trip is to the basement. I unlock the door and take the stairs, my feet loud on the wood. It looks like the base-ment in the house I grew up in, in a time when most people didn't furnish them with entertainment centers and exercise equipment. Concrete floor, dusty old couches, workbench with a power saw. To the right of the stairs is a weight set, a few barbells and a bench, an old brown couch with some punctures in the fabric, an electronic dartboard with only two darts stuck in it. To the left is a pool table and an old dusty mirror leaning against the wall.

I walk along the concrete floor to the back part of the basement. Near the corner, along the wall, is an oak cabinet. Next to it sits a short, wide wooden chest.

We had an antique chest in the basement of the house I grew up in, kind of like this one. A creaky old thing that my parents filled with childhood souvenirs. I remember when we moved across town when I was in high school, and my mother followed after the movers shouting orders, making sure nothing happened to her precious chest.

I open the chest with a cloud of dust but no creaking sound. As I look inside, I can't help but smile. It's filled with high school yearbooks, a cap and gown from some gradua-tion, some faded notebooks from "chemistry" and "trig II." And a couple of scrapbooks. Before I leave I will look up his picture in his yearbook, will read the puff pieces his bud-dies and girlfriends scribbled in the blank pages. *Hope we keep in touch. It was great getting to know you. Stay cool.* Maybe I'll add a little note myself. Something like, *I saw you.*

53

"THANKS FOR COMING OUT HERE," I SAY TO PAUL and Mandy, as we sit in my living room. "Your offices are great, but for a guy in my shoes, they're rather oppressive."

"It's a nice break for us, too," Paul assures me. He's wear-ing a colorful sweater and dark blue corduroys. My living room has three pieces of white cloth furniture that form a horseshoe around a glass table. Paul and Mandy take the two love seats across from each other; I sit on the couch, Paul to the left, Mandy to my right. As I look from one to the other, I can't shake the feeling that this is not unlike an interroga-tion.

"We might as well get down to it," Paul says. He's prob-ably got tennis with the mayor in an hour.

"Fire away," I say.

"Okay. First. Where were you on November eighteenth, in the late evening?"

"I was at work. The whole night." I've already told Paul this, and we've already gone over the botched alibi more than once. But we haven't gone into painful detail, because it wasn't so important if I admitted to the killing. Now it's pretty damn relevant. Paul wants to go over this again to verify we're on the same page.

"How late did you stay?" He knows this, too, at least what the sign-out sheet said.

"About three-twenty in the morning. I was working on a deal, we were hoping to close it the next day."

"Can anyone verify you were there?"

"Well, obviously, I signed out when I left the building." I think of the security lady, surprised to see me coming into the building from the back elevator, some time after three in the morning. Her explanation of why she was so surprised, I recall now so vividly that it makes my heart skip a beat: *I was a little confused, that's all. You came in the south entrance and walked all the way around to the parking elevator.*

But Roger Ogren has already talked to her, as has Cummings. She said, miraculously, that she didn't remember me that night. She checks the sign-ins, she assured both of them, and there's *no way* someone could have fudged the time sheet to make it look like they had been working all night.

"You put the time down, along with your name," Paul says.

"Yeah. I would have signed out at some time around three-twenty."

"And no sign-*in*."

"It's just like your guys' building. You only sign in if you arrive after seven. People who've been working all day only put down the time they leave."

"So the fact there is no sign-*in*, only a sign-*out*, means you didn't enter the building after seven P.M."

"Correct."

"So unless you pulled one over on the security guard—which she assures us you did not—that means you must've been in the building until three-twenty in the morning."

"Yes. Well"—and here we have carefully covered the mysterious entry by the McHenry Stern employee at three-ten—"right before I left for the night, I ran down the street to the all-night convenience store for some coffee. They have some flavored stuff that's much better than the swill in our vending machines."

"But you didn't actually go to the store," Paul says. Paul sent an investigator down to the store, and he noticed security cameras inside. Cameras that would have recorded me that night, had I gone in. Or *not* recorded me, had I not.

"No," I say. "As I was walking outside, I just decided that enough was enough. If I didn't get *some* sleep before the presentation, I'd look like hell warmed over. So I turned around and went back to the building. I went upstairs, packed up, and left for the night."

"At three-thirty."

"Yessir."

"You didn't sign out when you made the coffee run."

"No. If you're coming right back, they don't make you."

Take *that,* Roger Ogren. My tracks are covered. Physical evidence that I was working all night, objective proof on a piece of paper. Paul and Mandy, of course, understand this better than I, and we share a quiet moment of celebration, Mandy perhaps a little less enthused than the men.

Okay. Enough celebrating. We all know there are some holes.

"I got a call from Nate Hornsby that night, too. A friend of mine. Works in the foundation with me."

I thought you still might be at work, he'd said on my office voice mail that night, the message I heard the next morning. *I just tried to reach you at home, but you weren't around.*

"He called because a speaker we'd signed up for a foundation luncheon canceled."

"What time was this call?" Paul asks.

"Oh," I say, letting my eyes casually drift up to the ceiling, then back down at Paul, "sometime around nine-thirty."

That one silences the room. I have just given the approximate time of the murder.

"Nate will verify this?" Paul asks carefully.

I scratch my face and sigh. Paul's face drops a little with

my hesitation. Don't go south on me now, he's thinking.

"As I sit here now," I say, "I don't quite recall whether we spoke, or whether he left me a message on my voice mail."

Paul looks at Mandy, then at the floor. Just for a second, they're thinking, just for a second you had us thinking maybe you really *are* innocent. It's an awkward moment, my attorneys not wanting to know whether my memory is faulty or just convenient. But having a pretty good idea that it's the latter. Paul reaches to the table for the glass of water I served him.

Mandy finally chimes in. "The phone records will demonstrate that the call was made. But all they'll record is the connection, and the length of the phone call. The records can't tell us whether a human or a machine answered."

"If your voice mail picked up," Paul says, setting the glass back on the coaster, "it would take several seconds to play out your greeting, then who knows *how* long for him to leave a message."

"Was it a long message?" Mandy asks, revealing her spin on what happened. I look at her, and she quickly recovers. "I mean, did he say a lot—"

"I know what you mean," I say. "No. He had very little to say. The speaker canceled, let's talk about it tomorrow, that's about it."

"You were busy at the time," Paul says. "You didn't have time to talk."

"Right."

"So if you two did talk person to person, it would have been a short conversation."

"A minute or two, tops. From a phone record, it would probably be the same length of time as if he had left a message on the voice mail."

Paul actually smiles when I say this. There is no conflict for him in this. "Anyone else who could verify that you were working all night?"

"My secretary, Debra Glatz, should remember I was working late. In fact, I think I left her a voice mail before I left that night." I hope Deb will also remember the state of my office when she saw me the next morning, the empty food wrappers, the stale coffee. "I was getting a cold that next day, and I had hardly slept, and Deb told me that I should just go home. I told her I couldn't, with the meeting and all."

Paul's eyes narrow. "The message you left her is good. The part about you having a cold and not getting any sleep—well, as you can imagine, that could cut both ways."

The reason I didn't sleep, Paul is saying, and the reason I caught a cold, could be that I was busy lurking outside certain houses and murdering certain abusive doctors.

"What about anyone else at the office?" Paul asks. "Maybe other people stayed late—not nearly as late as you, of course—but maybe they saw you there."

"No one I can remember."

"I wonder if it would be worthwhile to interview your coworkers." Paul is looking for help from me here. He doesn't want to ask around, only to find that no one saw me there that night.

"I wouldn't bother," I say simply. Mandy scribbles something down on her pad. *He did it! He's guilty!!*

Then I remember Frank. "The partner I worked with on the project probably knew I was working late. Frank Tiller. He can't verify that I was there, but he *can* say that it was a big project, and it meant a lot to me."

Mandy scribbles that down in the notebook. "Are you guys close?" she asks.

"He's probably my best friend at the firm."

"What about Nate Hornsby?"

"Also a good friend."

"And your secretary?"

"We had a good relationship."

"You would expect all of these people to be cooperative with us?"

"I would think so." I haven't talked to any of them since my arrest. "So we're happy?"

Paul leans forward, resting his elbows on his knees. "Alibis are difficult things," he says to me, and somehow I sense that this is the beginning of a long speech. "You really stick your neck out when you file a notice of alibi. Technically, the state still has the burden of proving you guilty beyond a reasonable doubt. That doesn't change, *technically*. But in reality, when the defense says, 'He was at work,' it will become the defense's burden to prove this to the jury. In other words, you can forget about all the other deficiencies in the state's proof. You can forget about their inability to place you at the Reinardts' home. Forget about their weakness on motive. Forget about any other suspects we might suggest. If you tell the jury you were at your office, and they don't believe you, you will be convicted."

I examine my fingernails. "And you're worried we won't be able to prove I was at the office."

"Yes I am, frankly. And I'll tell you this. As soon as we file a notice of alibi, Roger Ogren will commit nearly all of his resources to disproving it. More than he already has."

My throat suddenly raw, I reach for my glass of water. My hand shakes as I bring it to my lips.

We sit quietly, each lost in his thoughts about the alibi. Me, thinking about how smart I felt when I left the building that night, after fudging the sign-out sheet. My attorneys, probably thinking that they have met yet another criminal defendant who has outsmarted himself.

54

RANDOLPH J. LARAMIE WAS AN ARCHITECT WHO came to this area in the late 1800s. He was credited with raising the community from a farm town to a commercial district. He reportedly built as many as a dozen factories after settling here. Later, he was elected mayor of Mount Rayford, then the largest town in the county.

The first building Laramie designed in Mount Rayford was a two-story brick school. Mr. Laramie purchased thirty acres of land to support it. By the 1960s, the school had a full-length football field and several baseball diamonds in its boundaries. The diamonds were authentic baseball fields, with wood fences spanning the outfield and sand covering the pitcher's mound, the baselines, and home plate. Little League played games there all summer long. Baseball had always been my best sport, and I played dozens of games on Laramie fields.

The greatest memory from my childhood came on one of those fields. For only the second time in the entire season of the nine-year-old Palomino baseball league, I hit a ball over the fence. Only this time it came in the bottom of the seventh inning—the last inning in that league—with a man on, in the championship game.

I didn't even realize I had hit a home run until the first-base coach, Mr. Ritter, yelled the news to me as I ran around first base. I looked up and saw the left fielder standing still, looking over the fence. I stared at him in disbelief, until I saw the pitcher, Joey Farley, throw his glove on the ground and walk off the mound.

I couldn't suppress the smile as I rounded second and turned toward my teammates, who were jumping up and down with their hands in the air. My dad was off the bleachers and grabbing the chain-link fence, shouting my name. As I reached third, one of the fathers, who was coaching third base, held out his hand for me to slap, shouting, "Atta way, Marty!" as my foot touched third base. My teammates joined me as I ran the final ninety feet to home. I jumped into the air and stomped on home plate with both feet. I felt my legs go out from under me as I was lifted into the air. Mr. Durkin, our other coach, shouted "MVP!" at me. And I tried to rear my head back, to see my dad again.

Landing on that white rubber pentagon was the single greatest memory from those years. So it only seemed fitting that this same site should memorialize my newest triumph: the burial of Dr. Derrick Reinardt.

• • •

The sand was hard on Thursday, November 18. Cold and very hard. It took me over half an hour to dig the ditch, scooping shovels full of heavy sand and carrying it a few feet away. The last couple of feet became soil, which was easier to lift. In the end, I looked into a four-foot hole right behind home plate.

With each shovelful, I peered around my quiet surroundings. I was on one end of a very open field, enough to be home to three baseball diamonds. The nearest street was more than a hundred yards away, and despite a still-strong wind, I would hear a car coming before anyone would have a chance to see me. It happened two or three times, in fact, while I was working. I heard the engine coming long before it came into view, and I fell flat to the ground. The cars always drove right along the stretch of road and out of my view. Were the passengers to look over at the fields, at most they'd see a mound of dirt. The nearest light was by the school, a good stone's throw away.

Behind the field I was on were trees and bushes, my best friends. If anyone did come around, I'd just pick up the shovel and run through the bushes to my car, parked less than a block away on the street. Not a foolproof plan, but about as good as I could do under the circumstances.

The hole sufficiently deep, I carried my shovel over to the car. I opened the trunk quietly. Dr. Reinardt was wrapped in two thick red-and-black flannel blankets. I caught a glimpse of his contorted face but looked away. I lifted the body out of the trunk and carried it over to the bushes by the baseball field. I returned to the car to get the clear plastic paint drop cloths from the car. I'd bought them months ago, with the ambition of repainting my kitchen.

First I laid out the plastic drop cloth like a picnic blanket. Then I rolled the doctor out of the blanket onto the plastic and removed my coat from the body. Then I rolled him over and over along the plastic, wrapping it around him as I went. I repeated the process with a second drop cloth. Plastic was no substitute for a coffin, but combined with the cold tem-

*peratures this time of year, I hoped the stench would be
stifled for some time.*

*The hole was not quite long enough for Dr. Reinardt's
body, but what did he care about comfort? I forced him down
into the hole, pushing on his chest with my foot. His head
stuck up awkwardly, his knees lifted up as well. Something
made me want to take one long last look at him, but it was
too dark. And I still had the mounds of sand to fill in. Besides,
Doc, I hate good-byes.*

Yes, I congratulate myself as I cruise along the highway, the
choice of Laramie Field was a good one. A random baseball
field in a suburb thirty miles outside of the city. There will
be little reason to connect me to it. I didn't go to Laramie
Elementary; I went to Washington School in Becker Heights.

And the likelihood of anyone discovering the body, at least
for a while, is slight. Nobody is playing on those fields in
March.

MOUNT RAYFORD
NEXT EXIT

I pick a Wednesday night for this last visit to Dr. Reinardt's
grave. Wednesday, March 2. Less than two weeks until my
trial. My attorneys have hit full stride now, poring over witness lists, drafting pretrial motions, and preparing testimony.
They filed a motion to dismiss the charges against me because there is no evidence that a murder was committed—
because there's no dead body. The judge ruled against us
because of my confession; he added he would not reward a
criminal by allowing him to profit from his ability to hide a
dead body well.

I have largely dropped out of the work on the case, my
role restricted to giving an occasional suggestion about a witness. Paul and Mandy continue to make suggestions about
Rachel—will the prosecution be able to prove we were
having an affair? I have put them off, as always. What can
they do but accept my story?

My lawyers and I had a talk about Rachel. Paul told me that we should consider suggesting that Rachel was involved in the murder, and how would I feel about that? I gave him something close to a green light. There are things he can do to suggest Rachel's involvement. He doesn't have any hard proof, of course, and if things got really tight I could always make it go away for her, confess to the whole thing. Short of that, however, the most he can do is draw some inferences. It's not much different than what Rachel is doing with me, giving the prosecution little nibbles to save herself but not dropping the bomb on me. At any rate, Paul never really asked my permission; he's made it clear that he calls the shots, and there's no way I'm changing lawyers at this point.

I park my car along the same side street I used last time. The air is crisp, only a slight breeze on my face. A far cry from last time, with the swirling winds.

I jog over to the bushes and work my way through them sideways, using the shovel to whack at the branches to clear a path. As I step through, looking out over the large school yard, the rush, the little thrill that I felt last time I was here, returns with a flourish. That there is no remorse, no pang of guilt, is not nearly as surprising to me as the fact that I actually enjoy the feeling. A part of me wants to dance now, to round the bases of the baseball field and slide into home plate above the rotted corpse. Why is there no conflict within me? Why am I not troubled by this?

I walk up to the chain-link backstop and look out over the baseball field. The bleachers along the baselines are gone now, as is the outfield fence. The school must have finally decided it didn't make sense to section off this huge space into a bunch of baseball diamonds. Even the pitcher's mound, I notice, has been flattened. I wonder if this is how the diamond looked on the night of November 18.

I walk around the diamond and lean against the backstop, very close to the burial site. I should be crouched down, I suppose, alert to every sound, looking for shadows. But I stand here with a sense of invulnerability, absolute power. Is this the feeling that flows through the veins of killers? Is this the stimulus they live for, not the actual killing, but the *control*? Is this what *I'm* living for?

I suspect it is. This, after all, is why I am here. Control. The thought has never left me over these past months, be it a distant awareness or a thundering strike of reality as I lay in the dark contemplating sleep: Michael Sprovieri, who *saw* me, might have followed me that night. He might know where the body is buried. It would be hard to believe, I realize; it would involve a number of assumptions I'm not ready to make. But it's there, regardless. And after days of fearing a flash bulletin on the news or a call from my attorney that they found the body, it has come to this. Control your surroundings. Eliminate any uncertainties.

The sand is uneven, I can see despite the dark. I did the best I could that night to smooth it over with the shovel and my feet. I guess it doesn't look half bad. Hell, no one's noticed almost six months later.

Yes, all in all, a job well done, I tell myself as I scoop the shovel into the earth. It's almost a pity to ruin it.

5 5

"HELLO."

"Hi, Marty."

"Hey, little sister. What's up?"

"Are you hanging in there?"

"Like a trooper. How are the little ones?"

"They're great. Tommy talks about you all the time."

"He's a sport."

"Do you know what tomorrow is?"

"Yeah. Monday."

"Marty."

"Really, Jamie. Today's Sunday, tomorrow's Monday."

"You know what tomorrow is, don't you?"

I make a noise.

"You *do* know, don't you?"

"Yes, sweetheart, I know."

"Well, I was wondering."

"Yes?"

"If I were there, I would want to take some flowers to the cemetery."

"So you want me to put flowers on her grave? Is *that* what you're saying?"

She sighs. "Listen, I don't want to have a fight, okay? I know you've got plenty on your mind right now. But she's our *mother*."

"She *was* our mother. She's dead now."

Silence. Then, softly, "The things you say."

"Sorry."

Sniffing on the other end.

"Really, Jame, I'm sorry. I shouldn't put this on you."

Another sigh. "I know you start things tomorrow. I wouldn't ask, but I really want to do something. If I could come out—"

"I told you, I don't want you coming here. I'll do it, okay? After the motions, I'll go out there and I'll put flowers on her grave."

"She liked lilies."

"Lilies, then."

"Very colorful. Get an arrangement."

"Fine."

"You don't mind, do you?"

"You know I do, but you know I'll do it for you."

"And tell her we love her."

"I'll tell her *you* love her."

"You love her, Marty. Whatever else, you love her. And you know it."

"I'll give her the flowers. I'll tell her you and the kids send their hellos. I'll even sing her happy birthday. Good?"

"Thanks."

ROGER OGREN WALKS INTO JUDGE MACK'S COURT-room with a new sidekick, a tall, grave woman in a long skirt and white silk blouse, with the posture of a marine. She strides ahead of Ogren and introduces herself to Paul as Gretchen Flaherty. She and Mandy smile warmly at each other and shake hands; old friends from Mandy's time at the C.A., I imagine. I wait for my turn, even hold my hand out, but she pretends not to see it.

A voice calls out from across the room. A young guy in a shirt and tie, his hair hanging down in his face, announces that the judge will see us in about ten minutes. I take a deep breath and exhale. Court proceedings, I find, are pretty much hurry-up-and-wait. This is especially true when your lawyer is Paul Riley. We have never made it from the front door of the criminal courts building to the courtroom without at least two or three people stopping and addressing Paul by name, either by extending a hand or, if their standing is sufficiently exalted, a slap on the back. Mandy and I will often stand idly by for ten or fifteen minutes while Paul catches up with whomever about whatever. Paul is never in a hurry; like most people of his professional standing, everything can wait for him, even a court appearance. Although we have managed to make it into court every time before the judge has entered, I always find myself sweating it as we walk briskly to the courtroom at a minute or so before the hearing. For today's ten o'clock hearing, we arrived at 9:58.

The clerk reappears shortly and tells us the judge is ready. Paul holds his arm out to his adversaries, after you. They walk in front of us, Gretchen Flaherty cutting a look in my direction but still not acknowledging my presence.

I whisper to Mandy as they walk away, nodding at Flaherty, "What's *her* story?"

Mandy gives me a look, rolls her eyes. She mouths the word: "bitch."

His Honor is not wearing his robe as we walk in. He is in a starched white shirt with a blue striped tie and gold cuff links. His frame is even more frail than it looked in the robe. He has bony shoulders and a skinny neck. He is coughing, as always, and I can't help but wince once or twice as he threatens to expel a lung. His whole body moves as he coughs, his shoulders chopping up and down, the flap of skin under his chin bobbing. He really doesn't look well. But his voice is clear and strong when he speaks, once again surprising me.

"We have a new face here," the judge says, with a tone probably reserved for women. Call him old-fashioned.

Roger Ogren introduces Gretchen Flaherty, who will be his assistant at trial.

The judge resumes his agitated mood. He shuffles around papers, looking for this or that, stopping occasionally to rub his bald, spotty forehead with his index and middle fingers, until the clerk comes in and shows him that it is the heap of papers sitting almost right in front of him that requires his attention. He barks at Ogren to raise his first motion.

The prosecution starts with the biggest pretrial motion: Ogren wants to keep out all evidence of Dr. Reinardt's abuse of Rachel. "The decedent's abuse of Mrs. Reinardt is not relevant to these proceedings," Ogren argues. "It would do nothing more than inflame the jury's passions and turn them against the victim." He carries on for a few minutes, talking about case law and fairness.

Ogren speaks deferentially, as any lawyer would to a judge. But he's also got sort of a know-it-all attitude. *Obviously,* he says about one case. *Clearly,* Your Honor. Ivy League, I'd bet my mortgage. I know he's the guy trying to send me to the chair, so I'm a little biased, but really, this guy is such a weasel. His chubby pink face, the stupid slicked-back hair, that sort of righteousness that must come with always being the accuser. The way he holds a cupped hand out in front of him as he speaks, like he's lecturing us all. You know that he was one of those kids who always got beat up on the playground, the kid whose hat you would yank off and make him be monkey in the middle. And I can see him just encouraging his tormentors, running from kid to kid trying to retrieve his hat, while it is passed just out of his reach to the next kid in the circle. He's a big prosecutor now, made a name for himself; maybe some of the wounds have closed. But you know that underneath that gray suit is the pudgy kid who still wonders what people are saying about him behind his back, whose eyes dart self-consciously around a room. The kid who is sizing everyone up, wondering whether they were one of those bullies who terrorized kids like him. Maybe this is what has inspired him to be a prosecutor, to be able to punish someone for his suffering. Professional success, after all, is the nerd's ultimate payback.

Mandy is handling the motions on our side. Paul will handle the majority of the trial, and this is his little present to her. Besides, Mandy has been in the criminal courts more recently than Paul, and she has tried some cases before Judge Mack. All convictions. So she's got more than her share of credibility.

"One of the potential theories the defense will be pursuing," Mandy says, "is that Rachel Reinardt was involved in the disappearance of her husband." Disappearance, not death. We're not conceding anything. "The fact that she was subjected to countless episodes of spousal abuse is highly relevant to her motive to harm her husband. It is, in fact, the primary reason the prosecution—the *prosecution* believed Mrs. Reinardt was involved in her husband's disappearance. Let's remember that they charged her with this crime. So I find it curious that they now argue that the abuse is irrelevant."

"Prior-act evidence is not admissible for this purpose," Ogren says. "The defense is trying to play the easiest card here, beat up the victim, make the jury hate him. But the character of the victim is not at issue here."

Mandy has been shaking her head while Ogren speaks. "The defense is absolutely entitled to pursue the theory that Rachel Reinardt was involved in the disappearance of her husband. Your Honor, she was *charged* with this crime! And the abuse she endured is her motive, at least one of them. We will argue that this is why she killed, or otherwise harmed, her husband. I submit, Your Honor, that it would be grossly unfair to allow us to argue that Mrs. Reinardt was involved in this crime but deprive us of the evidence that supports her motive."

Judge Mack raises his hand.

"Your Honor," Ogren says, "if I could—"

"No," the judge says. "The motion's denied. Evidence of abuse is relevant to Mrs. Reinardt's motive. And relevant *only* for that purpose. I will instruct the jury as such."

I quietly let out a sigh, not realizing that I had been holding my breath. In the space of less than five minutes, an issue that we have considered for hours, days, weeks has been settled. We will be able to tell the jury what Dr. Reinardt was doing to his wife. The judge will tell the jury that they can consider it only in regard to Rachel's motive, but it won't matter. The jury will be thinking of this poor victim as someone who got what was coming to him.

Mandy told me that the prosecutors have a nickname for Judge Mack: "Potluck." He tends to let in more evidence than some judges would. He thinks that the more you throw in, the closer you get to the truth. Score one for us.

Roger Ogren sits back in his chair, stoic, save for a curling of the lip. He shoots a look at Gretchen Flaherty. He knows he missed a big one. I wait for him to look over at me, but he doesn't. I had an oh-so-subtle smirk ready for him. Nah-nah-nah-*nah*-nah.

57

JUDGE MACK RAISES A FIST TO HIS MOUTH AND clears his throat, a painful sound resembling a car engine turning over. "Is the defense prepared to make its motions *in limine?*"

"We are, Judge," Mandy says. "The first motion we would raise is the motion to exclude certain portions of Rachel Reinardt's testimony. Your Honor, we expect that Mrs. Reinardt will testify that my client would often spend time outside the Reinardts' home in the evenings."

"Right, right. His obsession with Mrs. Reinardt."

"Yes, Your Honor, and it is inadmissible and prejudicial character evidence. The prosecution will attempt to prove that my client was standing outside the Reinardt home on the night in question, and they will use his supposed prior actions as proof of conformity. It is inadmissible, and it is *grossly* prejudicial."

Judge Mack rests his chin on his hand now, and sort of hums to himself. I fear for a moment that he will break into song, or fall asleep. His eyes roll over to Gretchen Flaherty. "Response?"

"Thank you, Judge. This evidence is not offered to show propensity. It is offered to demonstrate the state of mind of the defendant. It illustrates the extent of his infatuation with Rachel Reinardt in a way that no other piece of evidence can."

"Your Honor," Mandy says, "this is thinly veiled character evidence. They are offering this to make it more believable to the jury that my client was outside the Reinardts' house on the night in question."

"No," Gretchen Flaherty states decisively, "this evidence is—"

"I've heard enough," Judge Mack says. "This one kept me up last night, and that doesn't happen very often these days." The judge looks at the attorneys, not even smiling, but allowing them time to laugh at his little joke. "I do believe that this evidence could be relevant to the defendant's state of mind. For that limited purpose, it would be admissible. On the other hand, I'm not blind, at least not yet." The judge winks, I think at Mandy, when he says this. "I realize that this evidence carries the grave danger of being considered as character evidence, regardless of any limiting instruction I give. This comes down to a matter of weighing probity against prejudice."

The judge leans back in his chair. "This is, without question, the best evidence the state has that Mr. Kalish was taken with Mrs. Reinardt. If I exclude this, they are left with some statements the defendant supposedly made to Mrs. Reinardt, and some general observations from people that the defendant seemed interested in her. I hesitate to remove a piece of evidence that, in my mind, sheds significant light on the relationship between these two."

Come on, Judge. Enough of the potluck. Say "however." *However, I must exclude this evidence . . .*

"On the other hand—"

Close enough.

"—this evidence is quite prejudicial to the defense, not for the purpose for which it is admissible, of course, but for the purpose for which it is *inadmissible*. We all know that this evidence is going to make it more likely for the jury to accept that the defendant was outside the house on the night in question."

You could hear a pin drop in these cramped chambers. Aside from the evidence of the spousal abuse, this is the biggest ruling we will get on the pretrial motions. No, this is *bigger*. If the jury never hears that I used to stand outside her house, then the prosecution's circumstantial case becomes that much less believable.

The judge massages his forehead with his fingers. "Any of you have sinus problems?" he asks.

My mouth drops open. Sinus problems?

Paul doesn't miss a beat. "I sure do."

"Yeah, Judge," Gretchen Flaherty says, "the season came early this year."

What, the side with the most allergies gets the ruling? Fuck, I'm stopped up from May to September. Can I get the charges dismissed?

"Usually, it doesn't come until April at the earliest," says Judge Mack. "We get one god-dang warm spell and *bang*." He nods toward me, of all people. "Could I bother you for a drink of water?"

There is a water cooler behind me, one of those plastic bluish jobs. I stand up and pull a wax cup from the dispenser attached to the side. Shit yes, you can have a drink of water. I'll pour it down your throat myself, you give me the ruling.

All of us sit there as calmly as possible. Paul's foot swings ever so slightly on the crossed leg. Mandy's thumbs twiddle in her lap.

The judge has already screwed the top off of his prescription bottle. He accepts the cup from me without comment. He pops two pills into his mouth, pours in some water with a shaky hand, and thrusts his head back. His head falls forward again, and he coughs loudly. He puts his fingers in his mouth and removes one of the pills.

"The pipes don't work as well as they used to," His Honor informs us with a sour face. The pill goes back in, another drink of water, another head thrust, and we learn from his calmer expression that the pill has gone down.

The judge crinkles the cup in his hand and tosses it under his desk, hopefully into some sort of garbage can. Then he looks at Paul. "Well, I think the best thing to do is to let the evidence in."

58

MOM'S GONNA BE MAD. SHE SAID IF ME OR JAMIE *ever got sick, we're supposed to tell the camp instructors. That's what they told us the first day; I remember they made us repeat it back to them. Don't leave, they said. Talk to one of the instructors. No one's allowed to leave without telling.*

But that's just for little kids, like Jamie. I can leave if I want. It's only two blocks to my house. I'm old enough. I'm eight and a half years old. And I've got the key. I reach into my pocket and run my finger over the jagged side of the single key attached to the ring. I can go home if I want to. I don't need to ask permission.

I was standing over by the woods near the baseball diamond, and nobody saw me slip into the trees and cut through to the next street over. And now I can see my house. My stomach hurts and I feel kind of dizzy, and I can go home if I want to.

One of the counselors yelled at me today because I swore. But I'm old enough to swear. He's not my dad or my mom. He can't tell me what to do. And I'll go home if I want to.

The front door is locked. I figured Mom wouldn't be home yet, because she grocery-shops on Fridays. But I'm just gonna use the key. I'm gonna go upstairs and lie down.

I close the door behind me and think about getting something to drink. But I don't want to. I think I might throw up. So I go upstairs. I'm gonna lie down. Mom will come home and make me a peanut butter and jelly sandwich and some grape juice with ice.

I turn at the top of the staircase and head for my room. But I hear a sound behind me. I stop for a moment and hold my breath, but it's my mom's voice. She's laughing.

I could call out to her, but I don't. I walk toward her bedroom door. The lights are out; I can tell because there's a little crack between the door and the frame. It's dark.

Then I hear a man making a sound, a kind of grunting sound. Then my mom does, too. Like her stomach hurts. Then the man makes the sound again.

Someone's hurting my mom.

I tiptoe-walk to the door. I should push it open, but I'm scared. Maybe he'll hurt me, too.

I stand there. My hand is shaking hard, but I touch the door gently. Then I hear my mom laughing again. So she's okay.

So I just push it a little. Just enough to peek in.

I see the man first, just the curly hair and kind of a beard on his face, like my dad's on the weekend when he doesn't shave. He's lying on the bed.

Then my mom. She's on top of him. Her head is back, so she's looking up at the ceiling but her eyes are closed. She's breathing funny and making a groaning noise. She's naked. I can see her boobs. They're kind of flopping up and down as she moves. I saw them only once about a year ago when I walked into her bathroom and I surprised her and she told me I should knock before I come in because I'm a grown-up now, kind of.

The man pushes up with his waist and makes a noise. She does, too, a louder noise like she's almost in pain, like he's hurting her. Then his hands move from the sides and grab her by the waist. She circles her head around.

"Like that," she says. "Just like that."

I exhale and take a swig of the soda I brought with me to the cemetery. Well, happy birthday, Adrian. I hope you're resting comfortably up there. I'm sure you are.

Are you with Dad? Does he know now what he didn't know then? I turn to my father's tombstone, next to hers. The stones are small, raised slightly off the grass, with a concrete urn that rises from between them. I touch my father's marker, run my fingers over the outline of his engraved name.

Dad would understand. He would've understood then, too, with the same blend of practicality and love he brought to every situation. But I never told. Never told anyone, Adrian, what I saw you doing. I let you make a fool out of Dad, out of Jamie. I let you do it. I let you make me a conspirator.

Did you know? Did you figure it out, when the camp counselors told you I was AWOL for half an hour? Did you think, maybe just maybe, that I could've slipped home without you knowing?

I suspect not, but then, what did *I* know back then? Your naïve little boy didn't even know what he was seeing. All I knew is that I saw something bad. Bad enough that I knew I should slip back out of the house and say nothing. How bad, how deceitful, I did not know; it was just a general awareness that something covert, something seemingly so intimate, was not supposed to take place with someone outside your family.

ADRIAN VIVRIANO KALISH

1934–1996

DEVOTED MOTHER, LOVING WIFE

These are not the words I would have chosen. And probably not the ones she would have chosen, either. Who knows, maybe she *did* choose them—I really have no idea, Jamie exclusively handled the funeral arrangements—but I don't expect that Adrian Vivriano Kalish would have chosen to define herself solely by her kids, and certainly not by her husband.

I still remember Jamie's worn face at her funeral, her then-husband at her side. This was before Jeannette was born, four years ago, and Tommy was too young to comprehend a whole lot. Jamie absorbed the loss for all of us, took all of the pain for the remaining Kalishes (that being Jamie, me, and an aunt) and did a collective mourning. Jamie just stood there through the entire service, including the burial, with the same immovable expression, which I can't summarize in any other way but to say she was numb. She stared at the casket throughout the burial, never lifting her eyes, the only sign of life being the strands of hair that blew in her face.

And me? How would a bystander have summed up my appearance that day? Bored, probably. Distracted. That's pretty much the way Jamie described it to me the next day with a rebuke. But she was wrong. To say I was indifferent would be off the mark. Even after almost an entire lifetime of detachment, of nearly complete emotional (and in the later years, physical) separation, there was still something between my mother and me. I don't think there was ever a time in my life, in fact, when I felt closer to her than when she died. Not the tender kind of closeness, there was never that. And it wasn't born of sympathy, either; the anger hadn't subsided, not even temporarily, upon her death. But maybe by dying, she was now somehow inside me, etched in my soul, in a way she never could be during life. I could not shun her in death, could not scold her with silence, could not turn my back on her or sting her with a sarcastic remark. So somehow, in some small measure, I just accepted her.

The flower arrangement rests in the concrete urn, a truly beautiful array of purples and yellows and reds. This, I'm quite sure, she would have liked. I wasn't too receptive to Jamie's idea that I bring flowers, but the truth is that, for all my bluster to my sister on the phone, I was planning to come here today anyway. Haven't missed a birthday yet, Adrian. Probably never will. Don't ask me why.

I gently touch her headstone, like I rested my hand on hers the day she died. And like that day, no words will be spoken.

59

SEVEN WHITES, THREE AFRICAN-AMERICANS, AN Asian, and a Hispanic. Seven men, five women. These people will decide whether I live or die.

A multitude of others left the courtroom over the two days of jury selection, either happy to avoid service or disappointed not to be a part of a media spectacle. Regardless, they will tell their husbands or wives or children or friends that they came *this* close to serving on the jury for that murder of the doctor from Highland Woods. *Did you see him?* their friends will ask, referring to me. *Was he in the courtroom?*

All of them will answer yes, they saw me. *Well, what did he look like? Was he scary?* I sincerely hope that the answer to that last question is no. I have practiced, over the last few weeks, how *not* to look threatening. My smile in court can't be too big or toothy (can't look unremorseful), or too tiny (don't want to look cold-blooded); rather, just a polite, gentle, toothless smile that doesn't hide my pain but shows I'm making an effort to get through this. I've run through how I will sit at the defense table, too. Can't lean my head on my hand; it comes too close to looking bored or even disrespectful. Can't lean back against the chair and cross one leg over the other, either; it seems too flippant and overconfident. Sitting forward, hands resting comfortably in front of me, will be the position. Humble, composed, attentive, hopeful.

My movements, whatever they are—a turn of the head, a raising of the hand—must be at medium-speed. If I move too quickly, I might startle, give some indication of an impetuous, fiery side. Too slowly, I'm the calculating killer with ice in my veins.

Hair will be short and dry; no grease, no long bangs, just your average haircut, on the short side but not too short. Clothes will be unfashionable. Plain white shirts, button collars. I've got four suits that are either gray or blue, which I will alternate. I have picked out four ties, some of my least favorite, one a deep blue with cream paisleys, two red ones—one navy-striped and the other patterned with yellow teardrops—and a brown one with muted swirls of yellow.

I have practiced the look on my face for the different occasions. Eye contact with the jury, with rare exceptions, will be a no-no. But when it happens, I will be ready. No smiles, however appropriate. My lips will tuck in slightly—a grim pose—suggesting dignity, sadness, peacefulness. My eyes will narrow a bit, as if I were smiling, and the combination with my straight mouth will show the jury that I'm trying to be pleasant to them, trying to be polite—that these things are part of my basic nature—but in all my sadness and fear I cannot bring myself to smile. I will let them break the eye contact, unless they hold it for a long time, which I don't expect.

For any humor in the courtroom, I will give the smile I've decided on but will not laugh. I will be the one person who is unable to enjoy the moment. When Detective Cummings testifies, I will look at him curiously, mouth suspended slightly, eyebrows tilted to the center, eyes intense, head craned forward a little. If Cummings says anything controversial—anything that contradicts our story—I may even raise my hands off the table momentarily, lean back, maybe cast a glance at Mandy with disbelief, before returning my eyes to the witness, closing my mouth in frustration. During these moments I will not look at the jury, so my reaction won't seem contrived; it will just be a private moment with my trusted attorney, and if the jury sees it, well, so be it.

All of these things I have rehearsed in front of my bathroom mirror for the past two weeks. I brought in a chair from the kitchen table and just sat there, staring at my reflection, changing wardrobes and expressions and mannerisms and gauging imagined reactions.

Paul laughed at me when I asked him for advice. "The jury isn't going to think you live on welfare," he said. "They'll expect an investment banker to look like one. Flashy is out—we agree on that—but professional is not. You want to look neat." Paul was less flippant about my mannerisms. "Keep one thing foremost in your mind. You are innocent. You should be humble, easygoing, and calm. And above all, Marty, innocent. These charges are outrageous, and the inferences the prosecution is drawing from what evidence they have are absurd. You're a personable guy, Marty, a nice guy and a successful guy, who would have no reason to put his life in jeopardy by committing murder. The prosecution wants you to be an obsessive, brooding, jealous man capable of anything." Paul shook his head. "But that's not who you are. You just have to show them that. Be yourself."

So that's what I've practiced those two weeks, being myself as described by Paul Riley. On the bathroom counter, just across from the chair I had dragged in for my rehearsals, I placed a single sheet of white stationery from McHenry Stern, the words descending vertically with bullet points:

- professional

- neat

- innocent

- humble

- easygoing

- calm

- outrageous charges

- personable

- nice

- successful

- not obsessive

- not brooding

- not jealous

- not obsessive

- NOT OBSESSIVE!!

As expected, I did not sleep a wink either night. I was neatly combed and pressed today, but my face must have shown the strain of the last few months, the dark circles, the crow's feet that were not present three months ago, the permanent wrinkles etched now across my forehead. This, I realize, is not necessarily a disadvantage. Let the jurors see what this has done to me.

Seven men, five women. We had some image of the ideal juror—an intelligent, liberated minority. African-Americans, in particular, are wary of the criminal justice system, so the wisdom goes. And some women might be inclined to take the side of someone who killed a wife-beater, no matter the circumstances. Some men might, too. But above all, we wanted smart, open-minded people. There will be testimony that I lurked outside Rachel's house, that I was an obsessive, lovestruck child. We need people who will look beyond that. If there was one phrase that Paul uttered over and over again during the jury selection, it was keeping an "open mind."

Jamie calls me around eight o'clock. We say very little to each other. I can hear little Jeannette playing with her toys in the background. Not for the first time, Jamie offers to come to town to be with me. But I'm stubborn on this point. I don't want her here.

I lie on my bed and stare at the clothes sprawled on the floor. Tonight, for the first time, I do not pick up my underwear off the floor. I do not clean up the cartons of Chinese delivery. When I do get off the bed, I move gingerly, like an athlete with an injury. My hands are in a slight but permanent tremble; a dull pain has taken up residence in my gut. I lie on the bed with eyes open, not expecting or even wanting to fall asleep. I am numb, like my sister at my mother's funeral; maybe the analogy is apt, maybe we are looking at death from opposite sides here.

There is no remorse; really, there never was. There is no sadness. There is no fear. A defense mechanism, I suppose, a willful suspension of reality. I do not accept what is happening to me. I do not accept that I will spend the rest of my life in prison. I do not accept that I will be forced to breathe cyanide gas in a tiny little room while people watch me choke. I do not accept that my reputation has been destroyed. I do not accept that people will always wonder, even if I am acquitted, whether I committed this crime. I do not accept that a part of my sister's life has been destroyed.

I do not accept that tomorrow, twelve citizens will begin their judgment of me. I do not accept that tomorrow will come at all, because I have this time. So I watch the minutes slowly move around the clock, reasons blurring into outcomes, fears into acceptance, energy into surrender, time slipping away like sand through my cupped hand. But it is my time for now, and no one can take it away from me.

60

THE SIDE DOOR TO THE COURTROOM OPENS, AND A tall, thin, balding man steps through. He briefly stops to survey the packed courtroom. He's followed by fifteen others, most of whom also pause briefly to take in the impressive audience. Each takes his or her seat in the jury box and continues to look around the courtroom, for the most part avoiding any glances in my direction. This is fun for them, something they'll be able to tell their friends and family about.

Judge Mack explains to the jurors that an opening statement is not evidence, it is merely a recitation of what the prosecutor hopes the evidence will show. Finally, His Honor turns away from the jurors to Roger Ogren. My heart sinks.

"Is the prosecution prepared to give an opening statement?"

Roger Ogren stands. "Yes, Your Honor." He buttons his gray patterned suit and picks up a notepad. He walks over to the lectern, which is centered in front of the jury box, and places his pad on it. Then he steps to the side, squarely facing the jury.

Be prepared, Paul has told me. *If Ogren points his finger at you, be prepared to look the jury in the eye. Don't hold your gaze on any one of them too long. Don't challenge them.*

Ogren drops his head before beginning, then slowly lifts it. "This is the story of a man obsessed. A man obsessed with a woman who did not return his affections. This is a story about a man who murdered this woman's husband out of jealousy and rage. A man who *admitted* to doing it—who *confessed* to doing it."

Ogren turns and points at me. I stare back, not at the jury, but at Ogren himself. "That man is the defendant, Martin Kalish. The woman who was the object of his obsession is Rachel Reinardt. Her husband, Dr. Derrick Reinardt, is dead."

Ogren stops on that for a moment. "This is a story about a man who could not have what he wanted. A man who would make romantic advances toward Mrs. Reinardt. A man who would tell Mrs. Reinardt to leave her husband. A man who would stalk Mrs. Reinardt, who would stand outside her house at night, peering into windows. All of these overtures by the defendant were met with a very clear, very stern *no* from Mrs. Reinardt." Ogren scans the jury. "*No,*" he repeats.

"The defendant couldn't have what he wanted. And on November eighteenth of last year, after months of rebukes from Mrs. Reinardt, the defendant finally decided he would have what he wanted. It was finally time that Rachel Reinardt belonged to him. And *only* him."

I hold my breath, hoping to somehow stifle the pounding

of my heart. Some of the jurors are looking over at me. *This will be as bad as it gets,* Paul warned me this morning. *Remember you're innocent.*

"On November eighteenth, the defendant went to the home of Dr. Derrick Reinardt and his wife, Rachel. He stood outside that house, in the backyard, right by the back porch, and he waited. He waited out there, lurking outside their house, and he looked through the sliding glass door into the den. And he waited." Ogren's head moves as he looks at each juror. "He waited until Dr. Reinardt came into the den. Then"—Ogren's voice rises dramatically—"then the defendant finally fulfilled his dream. His dream of killing the man who stood between him and Mrs. Reinardt. She would now belong to *him.*"

Ogren pauses again. He walks over to the tagged wooden bench, sitting by the prosecution table. He picks it up and walks back over to the jury box. "The defendant took this wooden bench off the porch"—Ogren lifts it up to chest level—"and he threw it against the sliding glass door that separates the porch from the den." Ogren makes a throwing motion with the bench. Then he sets it down.

"And then," he continues, "the defendant was inside the house. He attacked Dr. Reinardt. He punched Dr. Reinardt. He struggled with him. Then he threw Dr. Reinardt to the ground. At this point, Dr. Reinardt was lying on the floor. He was not moving. He was not fighting. He was lying helplessly on the carpet of his den." Ogren lets that one sink in.

But something I've heard Paul say hits me here: *If you aren't going to be able to prove it, don't say it in the opening statement. Don't break a promise to the jury.* And Ogren is going out on a limb here. From what we know, at least, Rachel has said only that she saw the doctor and some unknown intruder struggling while she crawled into the living room to call 911. The stuff about Dr. Reinardt lying helplessly on the carpet—how will Ogren prove that?

"The defendant then went to the oak cabinet in the den," Ogren continues, "and opened it up. Dr. Reinardt was still lying on the carpet at this time." All right, we get the point.

"And the defendant opened that cabinet. He reached in, and he pulled out a handgun."

This is an interesting development; he's saying I knew where the gun was. We figured he'd say Dr. Reinardt pulled the gun out, and I disarmed him and used it on him. The problem with that, Paul pointed out, is that it makes the shooting look less premeditated. So Ogren is going for the better story: that I planned all along to use the gun, that I went to the oak cabinet when I walked in. Only problem is, how can he prove that? How can he prove I knew where the gun was?

"He pulled out a .38-caliber handgun, ladies and gentlemen. Dr. Reinardt's handgun."

I'm sure Ogren wishes like hell that he had that gun so he could hold it up impressively to the jury, instead of having to make the shape of a gun with his hand. But they still haven't found it.

"The defendant stood in Dr. Reinardt's den, ladies and gentlemen. He stood over Dr. Reinardt, who was lying there helplessly. He stood over Dr. Reinardt, holding Dr. Reinardt's gun. And then he fulfilled his dream. His dream of having Rachel Reinardt all to himself. The defendant pulled the trigger of that gun, and he shot Dr. Reinardt." Pause. "And *then* . . . he pulled the trigger *again*." Ogren takes two steps to his left, the jury following him, and stops again. "He killed Dr. Reinardt, ladies and gentlemen. He broke into his house and he killed him. And then he took the body away.

"The People will prove, beyond a reasonable doubt, that these events happened. The People will prove that the defendant went to the Reinardts' home that night for one reason, and one reason only: to murder Dr. Derrick Reinardt. We will prove that the defendant broke into that house and fought with Dr. Reinardt until he was on the floor, immobile, perhaps unconscious. And we will prove that the defendant then went to the oak cabinet, removed the gun, and shot Dr. Reinardt dead. We will prove that the defendant was desperately in love with Dr. Reinardt's wife, Rachel, and that this was the reason he killed Dr. Reinardt. How will the People prove this?"

Ogren doesn't have any charisma, no flare for the dramatic. He's very mechanical up there. But as I listen to him, I realize that this works pretty well for him. The sober prosecutor. No flash. All substance. When he was picking the jury, he made the mistake so many people make, didn't realize his own limitations, tried to be all cozy with them when it wasn't in his personality. He has overcome that now, unfortunately, and found his mark. Just the facts.

"You will hear from Mrs. Reinardt herself, the widow. Mrs. Reinardt will tell you that she met the defendant over a year ago. She worked with the defendant at the Reinardt Family Children's Foundation, a charity that she founded and ran. She will testify that the defendant became obsessed with her, that, in the defendant's own words, he had fallen in love with her. The defendant would follow her around at foundation functions. He would offer to give her rides home, which she usually refused. He would ask her out, ask her to spend time with him privately. He tried to persuade her to leave her husband. He would stand outside her house at night, just hoping for one glimpse of her." In my peripheral vision, I think I notice Paul's jaw clench. "Just like he stood outside her house the night he murdered Dr. Reinardt." My heart is racing. Some of the jurors' eyes go off Ogren, getting an image of me lurking outside Rachel's house. Paul stands and objects to the use of this evidence. Ogren isn't allowed to suggest that, because I allegedly visited Rachel's house earlier, it's more likely that I did so on November 18, too. The judge sustains the objection. But the jury heard it; the bell can't be unrung.

Ogren returns his attention quickly to the jury. "Mrs. Reinardt will testify about the night of the murder, too. She was in the den when the defendant crashed through the window. She will tell you that she heard the noise of glass shattering. She will recount for you how the defendant struggled with her husband. And as they struggled, Mrs. Reinardt crawled out of the den, through the hallway, and into the living room to reach a phone. She called 911, ladies and gentlemen, in an effort to save her husband. And we will play that tape for you. You will hear the cries of a woman desperately trying to save her husband."

The jury is fixated on Ogren again. The retired nurse steals a look in my direction. I look away.

"It was from the living room, just after she made her call to 911, that Mrs. Reinardt heard two gunshots. The two shots that took the life of Dr. Derrick Reinardt, her husband." Ogren's hands open slightly. "Mrs. Reinardt never saw her husband again."

Ogren moves on to other witnesses who will testify. He talks about Detective Cummings. From Cummings, Ogren goes to the confession. I admitted I killed the doctor, Ogren tells them.

I pick up only bits and pieces of what he's saying now. I'm thinking of Rachel. She told Ogren that I was following her around like a puppy. That I was desperately in love with her. This is not news to me, of course, but there's something about hearing it in open court that makes it more real, more tangible. More painful.

"Now," Ogren continues, "I want to talk about something else that you will hear about in this trial. You will hear, ladies and gentlemen, about a very painful subject. You will hear about spousal abuse." The jurors do not seem surprised; most of them already know about this. But I'm a little surprised that Ogren is bringing this up, even though Paul predicted he would so he could defuse the issue.

"Mrs. Reinardt was the victim of spousal abuse. It wasn't something that occurred very often, but it did occur at times. And yes, the night Dr. Reinardt was murdered was one of those times. He slapped Mrs. Reinardt in the face twice. That was all. I'm not condoning it." He holds his hands up. "I'm not. People who abuse their spouses should be punished. But they should not be murdered. Whatever Dr. Reinardt may have had coming to him, it's not death at the hands of a jealous would-be lover."

Ogren takes a step forward toward the jury. "Mrs. Reinardt

will testify that, in her opinion, her life was never—*never*—in danger that night from her husband. He hit her twice, and she didn't enjoy it, but he had stopped hitting her. She was upset, yes, but she was not afraid for her life.

"Mrs. Reinardt will also tell you that, obviously, she hated the fact that her husband hit her sometimes. But she'll tell you that she loved her husband, and she wanted to get him help. She thought, with counseling, maybe her husband would get better. She still loved her husband. She didn't want to see him dead. And any suggestion the defense might make about this will not square up with the evidence you will hear."

Ogren is doing a nice job of fronting this issue, taking some of the sting out of it. It's a nice seed to plant in the jury's head.

"Ladies and gentlemen, Gretchen Flaherty and I represent the People in this matter. Today is the People's day in court. And as the representatives of the People, we carry a burden of proof in this case to prove the defendant guilty beyond a reasonable doubt. We are happy to assume that burden. And we will *satisfy* that burden. We will prove, beyond a reasonable doubt, that the defendant committed this crime. We will prove that he killed Dr. Derrick Reinardt. That he did so in order to have the doctor's wife, Rachel Reinardt, all to himself. That he *confessed* to doing so to the Highland Woods Police Department. And that he committed this crime with premeditation. And at the end of this trial, we will ask you to return a verdict of guilty on the charge of first-degree murder. We will ask you to vindicate Dr. Reinardt, in the only way any of us can now. By convicting his killer."

By *killing* his killer, he means. Will this vindicate Dr. Reinardt? Will my conviction somehow add dignity to his life, his memory? Will his friends now say, ah yes, he tortured his wife, subjected her to years of abuse, and was killed for doing it—*but,* now that we've executed his killer, *now* he is vindicated?

Paul doesn't even flinch. He just sits comfortably, hands together on the table, watching Roger Ogren take his seat.

"Does the defense wish to give an opening statement?" Judge Mack asks.

"We certainly *do,* Your Honor," Paul says, rising to his feet.

The jury turns to Paul. He takes two steps away from the defense table, stopping between ours and the prosecution table. I turn my head to watch him. He pauses a moment, then opens his hands. "Mr. Ogren gave you a lot of answers. When this trial is over, you will have only questions. Questions like, how could Marty Kalish have killed Dr. Reinardt when he was *twenty miles away,* at work downtown? If Marty did this, then why didn't they find his fingerprints at the Reinardts' house? Why didn't they find follicles of his hair there? Shoe prints? Anything?

"Questions like, how does a police department arrest a man when there's no physical evidence—*no physical evidence*—that he committed this crime? When there's no proof that he was anywhere *near* the Reinardts' house on November eighteenth? And where is Dr. Reinardt now? Why have the police stopped looking for him?

"Questions like, why did the police arrest *Rachel* Reinardt for her husband's murder, and then drop all the charges?"

Paul surveys the jury, letting his questions find their mark.

"Your job is not to answer all of these questions. You only have to answer one: Did the prosecution prove, beyond a reasonable doubt, that Marty Kalish is guilty of murder? The answer to that question will be no."

I feel Paul's hands on my shoulders. "Marty did not commit this crime. He didn't kill anybody. Marty Kalish was at work at the time of this attack and he can prove it. The prosecution will argue that he wasn't at work, but even so they will not show you any proof—not any—that he was near the Reinardts' home that night."

Paul moves from me now, walking purposefully around the far side of the defense table toward the center of the courtroom, his theater. My emotions are swelling, Paul's comments finding a safer landing in my gut than anyone else's.

"Mr. Ogren told you that this is the story of a man obsessed. The evidence will show you that this is the story of a *police department* obsessed. Obsessed, as they should be, with finding the perpetrator of the most highly publicized crime in the history of the small, peaceful town of Highland Woods. But obsessed, as they should *not* be, with arresting someone, *anyone*."

Roger Ogren stands and politely objects. Paul is arguing, not simply reciting his prediction of the evidence. The judge sustains the objection.

"Mr. Ogren is correct," says Paul. "I should stick to what the evidence will show. The evidence will show that Dr. Derrick Reinardt disappeared from his house on November eighteenth. The evidence will show that when the police arrived on the scene, they found no clues. They didn't find fingerprints. They found some strands of hair, but none that were Marty's. They found no prints, no hairs, no carpet fibers, nothing that was attributable to Marty or to anyone else."

Paul takes a step toward the jury. "I want to underscore that last point. *Or anyone else.* The police found themselves with a murder, or a kidnapping, that made the front pages of the newspapers, and with no leads. No clues. Days and days went by, ladies and gentlemen, and they had nothing. Every day or so, a story ran in the paper. 'No Leads in the Reinardt Case.' No suspects."

Paul is a natural in front of the jury. He has a deep, resounding voice; he speaks slowly and punctuates his points like a TV anchorman. He speaks of the charges with indignation. He is sincere, not condescending or flashy. He uses his hands expressively but not nervously. He has mastered the art of the pregnant pause, taking a step or two to one side or another while he lets a point sink in. My spirits, in the gutter only moments ago while Ogren spoke, are lifted now.

He opens his hand to me. "So how'd they end up with Marty Kalish? Well, the police had conducted many interviews, many, many interviews. They talked to a lot of people who worked with the Reinardts at their charity. Marty was one of them. They asked him questions about Dr. Reinardt. About Mrs. Reinardt. One of the things they asked was, do you know if Mrs. Reinardt cheated on her husband? Marty thought that question was out of line, that Mrs. Reinardt wouldn't do something like that. He told the police so. And they marked that down, ladies and gentlemen. They marked that one for the file. Mistake number one for Marty: He got mad when they insulted Dr. Reinardt's widow.

"But even still, they had nothing on Marty. They will tell you that themselves: They did not consider Marty to be a suspect."

This was one of the benefits Paul was talking about when we tried to suppress my confession. In order to avoid the *Miranda* requirement, the cops had to say I wasn't a suspect when they interrogated me. And now Paul is using that against them.

"Another week, ten days, went by after they interviewed Marty. And still, nothing on Marty. And nothing on anyone else. More headlines. More pressure." Paul raises a hand. "I should clarify that. The police did have one suspect, ladies and gentlemen. But it wasn't Marty. It was Dr. Reinardt's wife, Rachel.

"The police were learning that Mrs. Reinardt was the victim of spousal abuse, just like Mr. Ogren told you. And that would supply a motive for Mrs. Reinardt to hurt her husband. And that stuff I mentioned about her cheating on her husband? Well, the police were starting to believe that, too. They didn't know for sure, but they were investigating that. It supplied a motive, and it supplied the second person who came through that glass door: her lover."

Roger Ogren starts to his feet but thinks better of it. He probably figures it's better not to look worried about this.

"I'm not saying this is what happened," Paul says. "But it was something they were thinking about. It made sense to them. So they kept an eye on Mrs. Reinardt. On December third, they sent an undercover officer to the Christmas party the Children's Foundation was holding. They watched Mrs. Reinardt."

Paul lets out a grave sigh. "Then, mistake number two for Marty Kalish. His mistake was going to the party. He was a volunteer, and he was invited, and he wanted to go. He didn't go to have a good time. There wasn't much of that at the party. The leader of the group was missing and presumed dead. His wife was grieving. But like so many other volunteers, Marty wanted to show his support. So he went, said a few words of condolences to Mrs. Reinardt, and left.

"But the police"—Paul waves a finger—"they thought it was odd that Marty just stopped in so briefly and left. That gave them strike two. So the next morning—we're talking over two weeks after the disappearance of Dr. Reinardt— they brought Marty back in for questioning. This time it wasn't a friendly visit to his house. This time, it was at the police station, in a small room, with other detectives watching behind the one-way mirror.

"The detectives who questioned Marty will testify in this case. They will tell you that at the time they questioned Marty, they had no reason to suspect him in this case. No reason. The only person they suspected at the time was Rachel Reinardt. And they wanted to know more about her. They just wanted to ask Marty about her.

"And that's what they did. When they got Marty to the police station, they asked him about Mrs. Reinardt. They told him that they suspected Mrs. Reinardt in her husband's disappearance. Marty said she couldn't have had anything to do with it. Ridiculous, he said. Then they asked him if *he* was having an affair with Mrs. Reinardt. He told them the truth. *No*. He wasn't having an affair with Mrs. Reinardt.

"Then they told him about how Dr. Reinardt abused his wife. How he beat her. And this upset Marty, like it would anybody. And they kept talking about that. About how he beat her. How he raped her. How he humiliated her. How he degraded her.

"Marty listened to what they said about Dr. Reinardt abusing Mrs. Reinardt, a woman Marty considered a good friend.

A woman whom everyone at the foundation admired. He listened to them go on and on about this abuse." Paul pauses a moment for effect. "And then, ladies and gentlemen, Marty made a mistake that will haunt him the rest of his life."

Paul and I have gone over this point many times. My favorite was the first time.

"I'm not sorry I killed him," I said to Paul.

Paul grimaced and blew out an exhale. "That's what you said?"

"I think so."

He seized on that, my qualification. "I know those inter-rogations can be pretty terrifying, Marty," he said. "Sometimes, they get you so tangled up, you don't know what you said."

That was the truth. I was in a bit of a fog at the end of that conversation with Cummings. I really was talking more to myself than him, anyway. I don't remember what I said.

"I remember saying, 'I'm not sorry,' " I said to Paul.

He waved his hands. " 'I'm not sorry' is fine. 'I'm not sorry I killed him' is not. Jesus, Marty, if you're not sure, then you certainly shouldn't admit to that."

"Well," I said, "what would be a better thing to say?"

"I'm not sorry he's dead," Paul tells the jury. "He said to that detective, who stood over him, describing the sordid, horrible details of Rachel Reinardt's marital life—he said, well, if that's true, then I'm not sorry he's dead."

A couple of jurors write in their books. One of them, an aerobics instructor, looks right at me. Paul continues quickly, holding up his hands.

"Now, we can all agree that that was a dumb thing to say. Marty would be the first." Paul shakes his head. "No question about it. A dumb thing. But it is not—and I think we can all agree on this, too—it is *not* a reason to charge someone with murder."

Ogren lifts his palms off the table, even looks at the judge, like he's about to object. But he just settles back in, once again preferring to look unpersuaded.

"So there you have it," Paul says. "Three strikes and

you're out. Marty mouths off when they accuse Mrs. Reinardt of adultery at the first interview. Marty stops in for a short visit at the Christmas party. And Marty says he's not sorry Dr. Reinardt, an abusive husband, is dead."

Ogren has had enough. He objects to the argument. The judge sustains.

"I apologize, Your Honor, and to the jurors," Paul says with a grand nod. "The evidence, as Mr. Ogren said. The prosecution will not offer one single piece of evidence—not a *single* piece—that Marty was in the Reinardts' house on the night Dr. Reinardt disappeared. They will not show you fingerprints of Marty in that house. They will not show you any hair follicles of Marty in that house. They will not show you any of Marty's blood in that house. They will not show you any of Marty's footprints in that house. And they will not put a single person on this witness stand"—Paul shakes a finger at the witness box—"who will say they saw Marty in that house that night. Not even Rachel Reinardt, who was *in* that house, who saw her husband struggle with whomever came into the house. Not even *she* will tell you that that person was Marty Kalish.

"Nor will the prosecution show you any evidence that Marty was *outside* the Reinardt house that night. They will not show you any evidence whatsoever that Marty was anywhere *near* the Reinardt home on November eighteenth.

"Mr. Ogren told you that Dr. Reinardt has never been seen or heard from since the night of November eighteenth. But they will not show you any evidence that Marty had anything to do with Dr. Reinardt's disappearance. You will learn that they searched Marty's house. They found nothing that shows that Dr. Reinardt was ever in Marty's house. No hair. No blood—they say he was shot twice, but no blood at Marty's house.

"You will learn that they searched Marty's car. But the prosecution will not show you any evidence that Dr. Reinardt was ever in Marty's car. Nothing.

"They will not show you any evidence whatsoever that connects Marty to the so-called murder weapon. No fingerprints on a gun. No gunpowder residue on his hands. Again, folks, nothing. Not a thing."

Paul has made his way back to the defense table. He stands so that we are across the table from each other.

"Marty Kalish has been accused of a terrible act," he says quietly, with a trace of bitterness. "For the last two and a half months, he has been faced with these incredible charges. He has had to live with it every day.

"Mr. Ogren said that this was the People's day in court. Well, you know what? This is also Marty's day in court. Marty has been waiting for this day ever since he was arrested. He has waited for this day, when he can come in to a court of law, and show you, twelve fair people, that he *didn't do it.*"

61

"THE PEOPLE CALL DETECTIVE THEODORE CUM-mings."

Detective Cummings looks much more presentable than he did the last time he testified against me. I figure it's a new suit. He wears a blue shirt and a patterned red tie. His wife must have dressed him. As he takes his seat in the witness stand, he raises his chin and moves his head around, uncomfortable with his closed collar. He's one of those guys who has the top button on his collar open, tie yanked down, before he's had his first cup of coffee in the morning.

This is the second time I've had to listen to Cummings give his credentials, and he plays it up well enough, but however you slice it he's telling us he's a lifer in a town where the closest thing to a major crime is when the high school cheerleaders *wet* the toilet paper before they string it over the football coach's front yard. He mentions sexual assaults and burglaries, which I assume means an eighteen-year-old feeling up a seventeen-year-old in the backseat and a skateboarder smashing a car windshield to swipe a radio. (Although in spite of my spite, I should admit he did a pretty nice job of tripping *me* up.)

Gretchen Flaherty is handling Cummings. Her posture is flawless, her dark hair pulled back tightly into a bun. She is not particularly attractive, her features a little too severe, but she looks about as good as she can today in a dark blue suit and silk blouse. Her arms are crossed, and she nods a little too often and a little too eagerly as Cummings speaks. She stands a foot or so from the lectern that is next to the prosecution table and tends to shuffle her feet back and forth. As Cummings talks, she peeks at her notes resting on the lectern. For some reason, this gives me a sense of comfort. She is nervous, too.

Cummings talks about his initial response to the crime scene. He describes the 911 call from Rachel. A young woman who was sitting behind the prosecutors wheels a cart carrying a large tape recorder to near the jury box. More questions between Flaherty and Cummings.

The large, circular reel on the machine begins to turn. First, static, very loud, which startles the jurors. The assistant adjusts the volume just before the voices start.

"Please . . . please . . . come quick . . . he's going to hurt me."

"Ma'am, where are you?"

"He's going to hurt me."

"Who is going to hurt you? Ma'am, where are you?"

"Please . . . my husband . . . please . . . oh God."

The courtroom is silent. The assistant turns off the tape and wheels the cart back behind the prosecution table. The jurors sit quietly, probably replaying in their heads the words they've just heard. *Please . . . my husband . . .*

"It was very cold in the house," Cummings says in reference to the crime scene, "with the glass door broken. It was a windy night." He gestures a lot as he speaks.

The prosecutor carries the wooden chair over to Cummings. "Yes, this was the bench we found in the victim's den. We believe this bench was used by the intruder to gain entry into the house." So that's what I did. I didn't break in. I *gained entry*.

Flaherty asks Cummings a few questions about the bench and admits it into evidence. Cummings then describes the den. "The coffee table was turned over. One of the cushions was off the sofa. There was a stain of blood in the middle of the carpet."

We stipulated that the bloodstain in the den was Dr. Reinardt's blood. Flaherty reads the stipulation to the jury, then turns to Cummings and asks him about it.

"It was approximately eighteen inches in diameter. There was a trickle of blood leading out of the den to the broken glass door."

As Cummings finishes his sentence, the young woman who pushed the tape recorder in front of the jury carries an easel over next to the witness stand. Flaherty approaches Cummings with some blown-up photographs and shows them to him. Cummings identifies them as accurate depictions of the crime scene. A police photographer took the pictures; Cummings watched him do it. Flaherty admits them into evidence and places the photos, one behind the other, on the easel for the jury to see. The easel is turned so that the defense can see it, too.

Cummings steps off the witness stand. Flaherty hands him a pointer. Professor Cummings points out the bloodstain, the coffee table, the cushion of the sofa. The next photo is a close-up of the bloodstain. Then we see close-ups of the trail of the blood leading to the glass door. The next photo shows the bar, with an opened door and the empty bottle of whiskey.

"Why was the cabinet door open?" Flaherty asks.

"Objection," Paul says, rising. "The detective would have to take a wild guess."

Well, okay, Paul, maybe not a *wild* guess. But Judge Mack sustains the objection.

Flaherty nods. "During the course of your investigation

that night, Detective, did you come to learn what was underneath the bar in that cabinet?"

"Yes. Dr. Reinardt's handgun was located in there."

"Did you find Dr. Reinardt's gun in that cabinet?"

"No, we did not."

"Did you find Dr. Reinardt's gun anywhere?"

"No," he says flatly. "We've never found it."

Flaherty pauses. She asks Cummings to return to his seat on the stand.

"Based on the condition of the room, Detective, did you form an opinion as to what transpired in that room on the evening of November eighteenth?"

"I did."

"What is that opinion?"

"Obviously, from the broken glass and the presence of the bench in the den, we believe the defendant entered the house by using the wooden bench to break through the glass. He attacked Dr. Reinardt. He threw Dr. Reinardt against the sofa. We believe he struck Dr. Reinardt while he lay on that sofa and then dragged him onto the carpet. Maybe he continued to attack Dr. Reinardt as he lay on the carpet. From the open cabinet door beneath the bar, we conclude that the defendant opened the door, removed the gun, and shot Dr. Reinardt with it as he was lying on the carpet. That would account for the large stain of blood on the carpet. And the few splatters of blood that appear several inches away from the big stain came when Dr. Reinardt was lifted off the carpet. As Dr. Reinardt was carried out of the den, he continued to spill blood on the carpet. All the way out the door, and onto the patio."

The next photo shows the blood on the patio. Flaherty next asks about Rachel.

"She was sitting on the stairs when I arrived at the house. She had a blanket thrown over her shoulders, and she was shivering."

"Did you speak with her?"

"I attempted to. She was practically incoherent. She would

alternate between sobbing and just staring into space. Obviously, she was very upset."

Flaherty turns to the subsequent investigation. First, they talk about physical evidence, or more accurately, the *lack* of it. They know Paul is going to make a big deal out of this, so they front it. It was a very cold night, Cummings explains. The intruder, in all likelihood, would be bundled up well. Hat, scarf, gloves. Makes it tough to find prints or hair or fibers. They found a couple of boot impressions in the mud on the path through the woods, and similar partial treads on the carpet of the Reinardts' den. At that point, the prosecution reads a stipulation into the record about the boot prints. They all came from a men's size-eleven Explorer boot, a boot that is sold all throughout the area.

They also tell the jury that I wear a size-eleven shoe. What is not read to the jury, but will be pointed out by Paul, is that they never found such a boot in my house. It got incinerated along with the rest of my clothes. I've had those boots for about six years, and almost never wore them. And, more important, never wore them into my house. I'd always toss them off in the garage, on an old newspaper. Ergo, no carpet fibers from my house. Nor could anyone the police interviewed testify that they saw me in these boots. They were a little tight on me, and I almost never wore them. In fact, as I think about it, the only time I've worn them in the last few years was to Rachel's; I needed them because there was so much mud by the stream near her place.

My special boots. Only for Rachel, and never brought into my house. Lucky me, I suppose, though not for the first time the thought crosses my mind: Did I know this day would come? Have I been preparing for this moment without knowing it? I want to think not, that my conscious feelings alone drive my actions. But I have come to a simple realization as I've pondered the events of November 18. I am not in control.

"Initially, we couldn't rule out that this was a kidnapping for ransom," Cummings says. "We tape-recorded all incoming calls to Mrs. Reinardt's home phone, beginning that very evening."

"Did Mrs. Reinardt receive any phone calls that next day?"

"Yes. The defendant called her."

I feel the jury's eyes on me as Cummings says yes. The woman sitting behind the prosecution table wheels the large tape recorder back in front of the jury box. More questions between Flaherty and Cummings.

This time, the volume on the machine is perfect. The first voice is that of Rachel's mother, answering the phone.

I watch the jurors. Most of them sit with wrinkled brows and slanted eyes, the height of concentration, hanging on every word.

"Mrs. Reinardt, this is Marty Kalish. I work at the foundation. I don't mean to disturb you. I just wanted to tell you that we're all praying for you. . . . Do they have any idea who did this?"

With this last statement from me, the accountant in the jury nods knowingly. The real estate agent sits back in his chair. About half a dozen pairs of eyebrows are raised. Already, I am tainted. If I knew Rachel so well, why did I have to introduce myself to her, tell her I worked at the foundation? And Jesus: *Do they have any idea who did this?*

The prosecutor is talking again. Cummings talks about his first visit to my house.

"Why did you go to the defendant's home?"

"Two reasons. One, because we wanted to speak with people who worked with Doctor and Mrs. Reinardt at the foundation."

"The Reinardt Family Children's Foundation?"

"Yes, that's right. The defendant was a member of that foundation. The Reinardts were chairs of the organization."

"What was the other reason?"

"The defendant's phone call to Mrs. Reinardt. He seemed very interested in knowing whether the police had any suspects." I see a couple of heads nod in the jury box. Yeah, they're thinking, he sure *did* seem interested.

I look over at Paul to see if he'll object, but he just runs a hand over his hair.

Cummings describes our first encounter. "We asked him fairly routine questions. We asked him how well he knew the Reinardts, whether he knew of anyone who would want to harm Dr. Reinardt."

Flaherty holds up a hand; Cummings is going too fast. "When you asked him how well he knew the Reinardts, what did he say?"

Cummings turns and looks directly at me when he answers, to be sure I know who's delivering the punch. Just like I looked into the doctor's eyes just before he died.

"He said he didn't know them that well," Cummings says. "He said that if the Reinardts saw him, they probably wouldn't even remember his name."

Some of the jurors have followed the direction of Cummings's stare, to me. I probably should look back at them, or stare Cummings in the eye. But I look at the floor. Again, the jury's thinking, why would I lie about my relationship with Rachel? Why be so secretive, unless I had something to hide?

Flaherty also notices that Cummings is looking at me, and she doesn't like it. She clears her throat loudly. "Did you ask the defendant anything else, Detective?"

Cummings turns to the prosecutor. "Yes. We asked him whether he had any reason to suspect that Mrs. Reinardt was involved in an extramarital affair."

"And how did the defendant respond?"

Cummings has this next line of testimony memorized. "The defendant said, 'I highly doubt *Rachel* is capable of adultery.' "

"He used Mrs. Reinardt's first name?"

"Yes."

"Describe his demeanor at that time."

"He was defensive. He snapped at me. He told me that I should show Mrs. Reinardt some respect."

"Detective, as a result of this conversation with the defendant, did you begin to suspect that the defendant was involved in Dr. Reinardt's disappearance?"

Cummings has to be careful here. If he suspected me, Miranda rears its beautiful head at the station house interrogation. Just because we lost that issue once doesn't mean we can't argue it again; we still have the appeal if I'm convicted. But the prosecution wants to walk the tightrope. They don't want it to look like the police were completely clueless when they brought me in.

"Well," Cummings answers, "let's say that I felt he knew more about Mrs. Reinardt than he was letting on. I believed he was hiding something. But I wouldn't go so far as to say I suspected him. I was trying to keep an open mind."

I lean back in my chair. An open mind, sure. I look over at Mandy and smirk. She returns a blank, solemn stare, reminding me without saying so that the jury is watching me.

"And after this meeting with the defendant at his house, did you take further steps to investigate his possible involvement in the disappearance of Dr. Reinardt?"

"Yes, we did. We met with the Reinardts' maid, Agnes Clorissa. We showed her a number of photographs, including the defendant's. Ms. Clorissa identified the photo of the defendant as someone she had seen at the Reinardts' house before."

Flaherty asks Cummings some more questions about the photographs he showed the maid. She hands these photos to Cummings, who identifies them as the ones he showed her. He confirms that he hasn't moved them out of order since he showed them to the maid. The photo of me was neither first nor last; it was the fifth one. The photos are admitted into evidence as a group exhibit.

"How often had Ms. Clorissa seen the defendant at the Reinardts' home?"

"Objection. Lack of foundation, and to the extent there is any foundation, it is based on pure hearsay."

Judge Mack sustains the objection.

Cummings goes on to explain that he put a tail on me after the maid identified me. Paul objects to any discussion about what the plainclothes detective saw at the Christmas party between Rachel and me. It doesn't really matter; that cop, Janet Brewer, will testify in this case, too.

Cummings testifies that he paid another visit to my house the following day. I accompanied them to the police station.

"The defendant was placed in one of our questioning rooms."

"Who was in the room with him?"

"At first, it was just me. I asked him again how well he knew Rachel Reinardt. He said again that he didn't know her that well. I told the defendant that we suspected that Mrs. Reinardt was having an affair."

"How did the defendant respond?"

"He said he didn't know anything about it."

"Please continue."

"I told him that we suspected Mrs. Reinardt might be involved in this."

I'd bet my mortgage on Rachel goin' down on this, he'd said to me at the station.

"And, Detective," Flaherty says dramatically, "how did the defendant respond?"

"He said, 'She had nothing to do with this.' "

"Those were his exact words?"

"His exact words."

"Did you ask him to explain that statement?"

"After that, he sort of clammed up. So I left the room for a while."

"Okay. Now, did you return to the police room where the defendant was?"

"Yeah, about a half hour later. I returned with Lieutenant Walter Denno."

"Did you continue to interview the defendant?"

"Yes."

Flaherty nods. "Describe what happened next, Detective."

"I continued to talk to him about Mrs. Reinardt, how we suspected she was involved. The defendant continued to deny this."

"So what did you do?"

"I finally told him that I didn't believe him, and that I was going to have to pick up Mrs. Reinardt for questioning. I was bluffing, of course. But I said it to him."

"What did the defendant say?"

"He said—actually, he shouted—'She had nothing to do with this!' "

"And then?"

"Then," Cummings says to the jury, "the defendant started shaking his head. And then he said, 'I'm not sorry I killed him.' Then he said it a second time." Once more, Cummings turns toward me. " 'I'm not sorry I killed him.' "

62

DETECTIVE THEODORE CUMMINGS REMAINS ON THE stand for the prosecution into the early afternoon. He describes interviewing people I worked with, how he attempted to determine my whereabouts on the evening of November 18.

We had to give the prosecution a written notice of our alibi, that I was working at McHenry Stern until 3:20 the morning following the murder. So Cummings describes how he checked the records at my firm and how someone using a McHenry Stern security card entered the building at 3:10, just ten minutes before I signed out for the night. He describes how I easily could have doctored the whole thing.

At the finish, Gretchen Flaherty reemphasizes my confession. "One more thing, Detective—you testified earlier that the defendant confessed to you on Saturday, December the fourth?"

"I did."

"Well, sir, let me represent to you that there may be some

debate over what words, exactly, the defendant used. So can I ask you to repeat them to the jury, sir?"

I expect Paul to object, but he just shakes his head in amusement.

Cummings turns to the jurors. "He said—and I quote—'I'm not sorry I killed him. I'm not sorry I killed him.' "

"He said the same thing twice, Detective?"

"He did."

"Any chance you heard it wrong? Any chance he said, for example, 'I'm not sorry he's dead'?"

"Absolutely *no* chance," Cummings says. "If that's all he'd said, I wouldn't have arrested him. I remember those words as plain as day."

Gretchen Flaherty takes her seat triumphantly.

Paul Riley walks to within about five feet of Detective Cummings and leans against the railing near the witness stand. "Good afternoon, Detective," he says politely enough. Paul starts in nice and easy. He will establish that this was a headliner case, and the cops weren't making any progress at the time they started looking at me. This was a big case, wasn't it? he asks. The biggest of your career? Lots of press. Lots of pressure to find the killer. Cummings fights with him a little on this last point. All cases are important, he says; there's always pressure to find the perpetrator. Oh, so this case was no more important than, say, a purse snatching? No no, he admits. It was a higher priority. Yes, he agrees, he was determined to conduct a very thorough investigation. Follow every lead.

Paul next turns to Cummings's theory of what happened on November 18. Cummings tells him what he has managed to piece together from the physical evidence. I forcibly entered the home of Dr. Reinardt by using that piece of patio furniture that sits over by the prosecution table. I struggled with Dr. Reinardt. I knocked Dr. Reinardt to the floor of his den. Then I walked over to the bar, opened the cabinet, removed the gun, walked over to the doctor, stood over him, and shot him twice. These, Cummings agrees, were the conclusions he drew from a very thorough investigation.

Paul has not gone out on a limb yet, not really pushed the detective at all. But his skill is nonetheless apparent in the courtroom. He stands with authority, decked out in his three-piece navy-blue suit, crisply starched white shirt, and subdued red tie, his hands resting comfortably in front of him, about three steps away from the lectern. His voice is commanding, his manner courteous but edged with an air of control: He will not tolerate evasion or equivocation.

And then we hit one of the high points, something that the prosecutors cannot fight in any way: the lack of physical proof. They dusted the den, the whole house, for fingerprints: not a one belonging to old Marty. No hair follicles matching mine. None of my blood on the carpet or anywhere else. Paul asks about the various strands of hair the cops found in the den. Four different kinds. Some matched Rachel's hair. Some matched the maid's. One, a piece of gray hair, is believed to have belonged to the doctor himself. Prior to trial, both sides agreed that neither party needed to call an expert to discuss the hair. We didn't challenge the findings because they didn't hurt us at all; and Roger Ogren was in no hurry to bring in an expert to say the cops found nothing good.

It's the fourth kind of hair found in the house to which Paul next turns his attention. "The final hair sample found was a long, dark curly hair."

"Yes."

"You found that long, dark curly hair in the den." Paul is going to say *long, dark, and curly* as many times as he can. The jurors occasionally glance over at my reddish-blond mop.

"Correct."

"You found one of the long, dark curly hairs on the couch."

"I believe we did."

"The same couch," Paul says with a turn to the jury, "where you claim there was a struggle between Dr. Reinardt and the intruder."

"The same couch."

"And you found another long, dark curly hair on the carpet in the den."

"Yes. But no one with long, dark curly hair confessed."

Paul turns to Judge Mack, who doesn't require any prompting. "That last statement is stricken from the record. Detective, that is improper, and you know it. You've testified before, sir; you know the rules. The jury will disregard the statement."

Cummings nods solemnly and mumbles an apology.

"To this day, Detective, you don't know who those long, dark curly hairs belong to, do you?"

"That's correct."

"Interesting," Paul muses. He does a little stroll along the jury box. He stops near the end of the railing, near an Asian woman, juror number six. Then he turns again.

"Detective," he says, "at the outset of this case, you believed that Dr. Reinardt's disappearance might be a kidnapping for ransom, isn't that right?"

"The physical evidence did not tend to point that way."

"Oh. Then why were you recording and tracing the incoming calls to the Reinardt house, Detective? For kicks?" Paul waves a hand flippantly. "To pass the time?"

Cummings smirks. "Obviously, we couldn't rule out a kidnapping."

"And it made some sense, didn't it? That Dr. Reinardt might be kidnapped?"

"Not really."

"Well, Detective—we're not just talking about your everyday citizen, are we? Wouldn't you describe Dr. Reinardt as a prominent member of the community? Ran in the big leagues? Mixed with the politicians? Chaired a well-known charity?"

Gretchen Flaherty objects. Compound question. The judge groans but tells Paul she has a point.

"I would say he was well known," Cummings says.

"And quite wealthy, too."

"He was, yes. But most kidnappers don't fatally shoot their victims first, Mr. Riley."

"Assuming he's *dead*. I mean, surely you don't know for a fact that Dr. Reinardt is dead, do you?"

Oh, he's dead.

"We believe he is," Cummings says. "We have every reason to believe it. But I can't say for absolute fact, no."

Unless he was holding his breath for over an hour.

"And you'd agree with me, Detective, that the presence of the blood in the house does not speak one way or the other as to whether this was a kidnapping. I mean, a kidnapper could very well use force in abducting his victim, couldn't he?"

"Anything's possible, counselor. But that's not a likely scenario."

Paul nods, one eye to the jury. "You base that on experience?"

"I base that on common sense and training."

"Training," Paul repeats. "You mean, classes? Textbooks?" The two men face each other a moment, silent. "My point being, Detective, you've never investigated a kidnapping, have you?"

"I've never been part of a kidnapping investigation. It doesn't mean I don't have training."

"You've never investigated a kidnapping?"

"No, Mr. Riley, I have not."

"Hmm. Well then, I'll have to ask you to base this on your—*training,* but I suppose it would also be possible that the kidnapper came into the house, and it was *Dr. Reinardt* who produced the gun, in an attempt to ward off his abductor?"

"It's possible."

"Isn't it also possible that Dr. Reinardt was not *fatally* shot?"

"I suppose."

"Maybe Dr. Reinardt was simply shot in the leg? That's possible, right?"

"Possibly."

"I mean, you have no idea, right?"

"I suppose anything is conceivable, Mr. Riley. Like I say."

"So what I'm getting at is"—and Paul moves toward Cummings—"Dr. Reinardt might still be out there somewhere, alive, and no one's looking for him."

This draws an objection from Gretchen Flaherty. Speculative. Argumentative. Compound question. The judge overrules.

"Highly unlikely," Cummings says, "but conceivable, yes."

"Well, Detective, there isn't any physical evidence in this case that would *disprove* that possibility, is there?"

Cummings searches for something. "I suppose if you killed someone, and threw him in an incinerator or buried him or something, you could always claim it was a kidnapping, and there would be nothing to disprove it. As long as you hid the body well."

Nice one, Teddy. Nice jab.

"Well, sure," says Paul. "Your scenario's possible, my scenario's possible. True?"

"Yours is possible. Anything's *possible.*"

"All these possibilities," Paul says absently, moving a few steps forward. "Now, I gather from your tone of voice—it sounds to me like you don't place much credence in my scenario."

"You're right about that."

"Well then, Detective, why don't you tell the jury what evidence you have to disprove my possibility? Since you don't believe it, tell the jury why. Because it seems to me, Detective, that there is not *one piece* of physical evidence to refute the possibility that Dr. Reinardt was kidnapped, and that he was alive when he left the house. And that he *still* is alive. Isn't that true?"

Cummings is agitated. "It's just such a ridiculous thought—"

Paul stands straight again. "But there's no evidence to *disprove* it."

"There hasn't been a ransom demand."

"A ransom demand, yes, yes." Paul brings a finger to his mouth. Jurors number nine through twelve are women, and

at least two of them—the accountant and the retired nurse—
seem to enjoy watching Paul in action.

"Well, indulge me another second, Detective. This lack of
a ransom demand you mentioned. Now, isn't it possible that
in the course of an abduction, Dr. Reinardt was shot but not
killed, but that maybe he died *later* from his wounds? I mean,
the kidnappers can't very well take him to a hospital. Isn't
that all possible?"

"Again, conceivable, not likely."

"So the kidnapping is pulled off *with force*—Dr. Reinardt
is wounded but not killed—then he is taken away to some
unknown location, where he dies from his wounds, maybe
that day, maybe the next. At that point, the kidnappers aren't
likely to make a ransom call, are they? For a dead person?
I mean, based on your *training,* sir—those books you read,
what the instructors told you at kidnapping school—wouldn't
that adequately explain the lack of a ransom demand?"

A couple of the jurors laugh at the detective's expense.
Gretchen Flaherty objects to the form of the question. Paul
volunteers to rephrase; he's happy to repeat his point.

"Isn't it possible, sir, that kidnappers abducted Dr. Reinardt, who ended up dying, and *that*'s why you haven't received a ransom demand?"

"It's pure fantasy, counselor. Your client confessed.
You're turning this into a wild goose chase when the killer
is sitting right over there." He points to me. Here you go,
Marty: Give 'em the dignified-calm-personable-easygoing-
innocent look. So what do I do? I look away from everybody,
toward the court reporter.

"I believe you're avoiding the question," Paul says calmly,
drawing the jury's attention off me and back to him, standing
near the witness. "Haven't I just given you an adequate explanation why there'd be no ransom demand?"

Cummings sighs in exhaustion. "Anything's *possible.*"

Paul wastes no time in moving on. All right, he says,
enough of this kidnapping theory, let's assume this was a
murder. Paul wants to talk about what I supposedly did with
the body after I left the house. He scores a little here. Isn't

it uncommon for someone to murder someone and then pick him up and run out of the house with him? Cummings says there's no set pattern to what people do in these situations. Paul jabs with him a little, draws a few objections from Gretchen Flaherty. Cummings won't budge, but Paul has made his point. So Paul returns to the assumption that I carried the doc out of the house.

"As an experienced investigator, where would you expect the intruder to take Dr. Reinardt?"

"We would expect Dr. Reinardt to be buried somewhere, or perhaps dumped somewhere, a landfill or something. Who knows? Maybe he was thrown into a river."

At Paul's request, Cummings summarizes the search for the corpse. The two rivers near Highland Woods, the Bailey River and the Swan Harbor River, were dragged with no success. Two landfills that service the county were searched, in part by Cummings himself. That one, I wish I could've seen, my favorite cop knee-deep in excrement.

The woods behind the Reinardts' house were also combed over.

"Do you believe that Marty Kalish took the doctor through those woods on November eighteenth?"

"We don't know. But it's likely. It's the most logical route."

"Any sign that Marty Kalish had been in those woods?"

"He didn't pin his business card to a tree, if that's what you mean." This draws a laugh from the gallery. None of the jurors laugh, I notice. "The boot prints match your client's shoe size."

"But you didn't find an Explorer boot at my client's house, did you?"

"No, your client wasn't dumb enough to leave those around for us."

"Well, let's be fair with this jury, Detective." Paul's tone carries a hint of a rebuke. "Do you have some way of knowing that Marty Kalish owned a pair of Explorer boots?"

"No, I don't. How could I?"

"My point is, you *don't*."

"I couldn't possibly, counselor."

"And size eleven is a fairly common shoe size for men, isn't it?"

"I wouldn't know if it's usual or unusual."

"Aside from this business with the boots, there's no physical evidence to suggest that Marty Kalish took Dr. Reinardt through those woods?"

"On November eighteenth, the winds were gusting at around thirty-five miles an hour. I can't imagine how we would be able to tell *who* was in those woods."

"So you have no idea."

Cummings sighs. "No."

"For Marty Kalish to have transported Dr. Reinardt to whatever location, wouldn't you expect him to use his car?"

"Objection. Speculative."

"Ms. Flaherty, you know very well that the question is proper. Overruled." Judge Mack is getting testy as his stomach growls. And this is about the fiftieth objection from Flaherty. If she thinks she's throwing Paul off balance, she should know by now that she's not. And the jury is getting a little annoyed with her. Their attention seems to heighten whenever the prosecutor objects; her complaints are magnifying the importance of the questions.

"Using his car would seem logical, yes."

"So you searched his car after you arrested him."

"Yes. Two *weeks* after the crime was perpetrated." Giving me ample time to clean the car out, Cummings implies. Actually, I needed only that night to do it. By the time the cops got to my car, you could've eaten breakfast off the trunk's carpet.

"You didn't find any trace of Dr. Reinardt in that car?"

"No."

Paul runs through the failed search. No hair. No blood.

"You search anyplace else?"

"After the defendant confessed to the crime, we searched his house." A nice jab.

"You searched Marty Kalish's home?"

So they run through the search of my house. Nothing any-

where, basement, garage, *nada*. Paul seems to be getting under Cummings's skin a little, the cop having to admit over
and over that he found nothing, coupled with Paul's incredulous inflection and his frequent glances at the jurors to see
if they share in his bewilderment.

"Frankly," Cummings says, "I wouldn't expect the defendant to be dumb enough to bring a dead body to his *house*."

Paul seems to light up at this comment. "Okay then, let's
talk about *anyplace,* Detective. *Anytime. Anywhere*." Paul
throws his hands into the air. "Dr. Reinardt's house. The
woods. Marty's house. Marty's car. You name it, Detective.
You tell *us*. I'm giving you the chance to name anyplace in
the world. You tell the ladies and gentlemen of the jury: Can
you identify for us, sir, *any* evidence that Marty and Dr.
Reinardt were together *anyplace, anytime,* on November
eighteenth or any time thereafter? Can you do that for the
jury?"

Cummings works his mouth, ending in a scowl. "We don't
know where he took him."

6 3

THE COURTROOM, IT SEEMS, IS A SECOND HOME FOR
Paul Riley, a home he's lived in a long time; he knows where
the floorboards creak, where the drafts are. He uses the space
to maximum advantage, moving about, seemingly lost in
thought, when he wants points to sink in for the jury, ap-
proaching the witness when he's cornering him on something, all the while setting the pace, controlling the reactions.
He has managed to dance around circumstances relating to
the doctor's death without, to my knowledge, causing offense
to the jury; if anything, he's starting to charm them. He is
for the most part courteous, able to rebuke the witness with-

out getting testy, but always aware of the right moment to raise his voice or his hands or change expressions, and drawing the jury into his changed mood. I've picked up on a tool he uses to emphasize a point: He refers to the jury in his questions when he really wants them to pay attention. *Tell the jury, Detective,* he'll say, and it's always a strong moment.

I've also noticed that Paul plays to the jury. At the hearing to suppress my confession—where there was only a judge, and it was a legal issue—Paul was much more subdued, his questions less speechy and more businesslike. In this setting, with laypersons who have seen plenty of courtroom drama on television, Paul relies considerably more on mannerisms and facial expressions and tone inflections. It's getting a little late in the afternoon now, a time when the jurors are starting to stretch a little and checking their watches, but Paul has done well to keep them relatively entertained. He has scored on the easy things—most notably the lack of physical evidence putting me at the scene—but he did better than I would have expected on the kidnapping angle, too. It actually sounded kind of believable.

"Let's talk about the conversation you had with Marty Kalish the day you arrested him," says Paul. "The day, as you put it, he *confessed.*"

"Fine."

"When you had this conversation with Marty, who else was in the room?"

"It was me, Lieutenant Walter Denno, and the defendant."

"Now, during this interview, did you tell Marty that you suspected he was having an affair with Mrs. Reinardt?"

"I asked him that."

"And he said no. But you thought he was her lover, didn't you?"

"I thought it was possible. That's all."

This is consistent with what Cummings said at the suppression hearing, that he didn't know whether Rachel had a guy on the side, and even if she did, whether that guy was me. Paul is probing this for the *Miranda* issue. Maybe, in his zeal to impress the jury, Cummings will go overboard and say he really thought I was the guy. In doing so, he might make it appear that he suspected me, and therefore should have read me my rights.

"I should add," says Cummings, "that we now believe there was no such affair."

Paul thanks Cummings for the clarification. "But at the time you questioned Marty, you certainly *did* believe that Mrs. Reinardt was having an affair."

"We suspected it."

"Okay," Paul says. "Well, since you were wondering about Mrs. Reinardt's extramarital love life, I take it that you were investigating Mrs. Reinardt's potential involvement in her husband's disappearance."

"Yes."

"Simply put, Mrs. Reinardt was a suspect."

"We were considering her potential involvement."

"And a lover of hers, if there was one, would be a suspect, too. Obviously."

"Yes."

"And it was frustrating, wasn't it, that you couldn't identify this so-called mystery lover of Mrs. Reinardt's?"

"I don't know if I'd say that."

"At the time you talked at the station with Marty, it had been sixteen days since Dr. Reinardt disappeared?"

"That's right."

"More than two weeks."

"That's right."

"All right," says Paul, "fine." What is left unsaid for the time being, but will be played up in closing arguments, is that the cops were looking at sixteen days of futility and dead-end roads right and left when they came upon me, the scapegoat.

"Now, at some point during the interview with Marty— closer to the end, I believe—you began to talk to Marty about the abusive nature of the Reinardts' marriage."

"That came up."

"You told him how, from your investigation, you believed

that Dr. Reinardt had been beating his wife for months."

"Yes."

"You told Marty that Mrs. Reinardt had been subjected to physical abuse."

"Right."

"Physical abuse in the form of repeated whips on the back with a leather belt."

"That's right." Some of the jurors recoil. Actually, Cummings is being generous with Paul here. We didn't actually go into the detail of the abuse at the interrogation, and shit, I'd heard about it already anyway. Paul's making it sound like they were educating me on the sordid details, and in the process turning me into a blithering idiot prone to say something dumb.

"You also told Marty about the *sexual* abuse Mrs. Reinardt had endured."

"Yes."

"And during this part of the interview, Marty seemed upset, didn't he?"

"I suppose he did."

"These things you were telling Marty, they seemed to bother him, didn't they?"

"Sure."

There. Paul has set the framework for the reason I said, *I'm not sorry he's dead.* Because I was so gosh-darned upset at what a cruel bastard the good doctor was.

Paul takes a step away from the lectern and inches forward. "Now, you testified earlier that Marty said, 'I'm not sorry I killed him.' "

"That's what he said."

"That's what *you* said, earlier today."

"That's what I said, and it's the truth. He said it twice."

"He said it twice," Paul repeats. He looks at the jury. "He said it twice. Did he say it in a clear voice?"

"Yes. Clear enough."

"Clear enough for you to hear it?"

"Yes."

"But—wasn't Lieutenant Walter Denno just outside the room at this time?"

"He was in the adjoining room."

"That adjoining room—you can see into the interview room from there?"

"Right."

"And you can hear into the interview room, too?"

"I wouldn't say *everything*," Cummings says. Again, well coached. At the hearing on the confession, Lieutenant Denno testified that he didn't personally hear me confess to Cummings. He said he was in the viewing room, but he didn't hear it. I've always kind of wondered why he said that, why he didn't just back up his detective.

"But certainly," says Paul, "from that room, you could hear anything that is said in a clear voice."

"Not if it's said quietly."

"Oh. Well, tell us, where was Marty at the time he supposedly confessed?"

Cummings is still a moment. "He was sitting in the chair."

"The chair," Paul repeats. "He was in the chair when he . . . *confessed*."

"Yes." Cummings is studying Paul now.

"And you're saying he *confessed* in a clear voice."

"Clear enough, I said."

"You're quite sure you could hear him."

"Yes."

"Was his hand over his mouth?"

"No."

"Was his mouth obstructed in any way, shape, or form?"

"No."

"Where were *you* sitting?"

Cummings's eyes dart about. "Across from him."

Fuck, I can *still* smell Cummings's breath as he stood over me. I don't know why he'd lie about this. He should just admit he was standing right over me. That would explain why he, and nobody else, heard me confess. But he doesn't want to admit that he was in my face. I guess it makes it seem like he was intimidating me.

"So he was speaking across the table from you."

"Yes."

"And he confessed in a loud enough voice for you to hear?"

"Yes."

"But not loud enough for Lieutenant Denno, in the adjoining room, to hear."

"I assume," Cummings says. "I can't speak for Lieutenant Denno."

"Fair enough," Paul says. "But to your knowledge, isn't it true that you are only the *only one* who heard Marty supposedly confess?"

"He was mumbling."

Jesus, Cummings is making this much tougher than it has to be.

"He was mumbling? Didn't you just tell us that he confessed in a clear voice?"

"I said clear *enough*," Cummings snaps.

"Oh, *I* see," Paul says sarcastically. "He spoke just clear enough so you could hear him, but he *mumbled* just enough that Lieutenant Denno, watching and listening in the viewing room, *couldn't* hear him. That's what you're saying."

I notice Gretchen Flaherty's feet shuffle as she starts to stand. Roger Ogren puts a hand on hers, and she settles back in.

"He spoke at a level I could hear," says Cummings. "It wasn't that loud. If the guys outside couldn't hear, I can't speak to that."

"Isn't it true, Detective, that at the time Marty Kalish gave this so-called confession, you were standing directly over him, with your hand cupped around his face?"

Cummings sits up in his chair. "That's not true."

It's *not* true, but it's what I told Paul. Cummings could fit that part.

"And isn't it true that you put your hands around Marty's throat?"

"No, sir." Cummings shakes his head vehemently. "Not true."

"And you told Marty that if he didn't say something quick, that you were going to haul Rachel Reinardt into the station and arrest her."

"That is absolutely false, Mr. Riley."

"Isn't it true that you were standing over Marty?"

"No, sir."

"And you were telling him over and over again about the abuse Rachel endured? The *rape* she endured!"

"I mentioned it, but it wasn't like you're saying."

Paul walks toward Cummings. "And isn't it true that when Marty gave this so-called *confession,* you were face-to-face with Marty?"

"No!"

"And *that*'s why Lieutenant Denno didn't hear what Marty was saying. Because you were in his face, grabbing on to him!"

"*No.* None of that is true."

Paul turns away from Cummings, toward the jury.

"No, sir," Cummings repeats.

"Well, regardless of how you tell the story," Paul says to the jury, calmer now but still with an edge, "you were the only person who heard this—this *confession.*"

Cummings runs his fingers over his thin hair on top. "That's correct, Mr. Riley."

Paul nods solemnly. "It's standard policy in your department to tape-record confessions, isn't it?"

"Where feasible," says Cummings. "It wasn't in this case."

"No?" says Paul. "Wasn't there a tape recorder in the room?"

"There was," says Cummings. "But the point is, we weren't expecting the confession. We were just talking, so there was no need to use it."

"And you told us, Detective, that Marty confessed of his own free will."

"That's right."

"Without the tape recorder on."

"That's right."

"But after he supposedly confessed—after he had done so,

as you say, in a voluntary manner—at that point, you didn't tape-record his confession, did you?"

"I tried to," says Cummings. "But he clammed up."

"Wait a minute." Paul raises his hands, shakes his head violently. "One second, he confesses voluntarily. The next second, you reach for the tape player, and suddenly Marty *won't* confess?"

That's actually the truth. There was something so final about that tape recorder. Thank God for that moment of clarity.

"Counselor, I can't explain why he stopped talking. But he did."

"So when you tell this jury that Marty Kalish confessed to murder"—now Paul turns back to Cummings and jabs a finger—"we have to take *your* word for it."

"It is the absolute truth."

"According to you."

"Yes, according to me."

"And *only* you."

"I guess so."

Paul pauses on that, then turns on his heels and moves to the left before squaring off. He nods absently. "All right. You arrested Mrs. Reinardt for the murder of her husband, didn't you?"

"Yes."

"You did so several weeks after Marty's arrest, correct?"

"Correct."

"But as we've established, even *before* Marty's arrest, you'd begun to suspect her."

"Right."

"One reason you suspected her, back then, was the rumors that she was having an affair."

"True."

"Another reason was the news that she'd endured all that abuse."

"Also true."

"Because these things gave her a possible motive to want to kill her husband."

"Potentially, yes."

Paul turns slightly toward the jury, raising a finger. "Tell me if this was another reason. You learned that on November eighteenth, the Reinardts' gun was downstairs, in the very den where these events transpired, stored in an oak cabinet. But you *later* learned that this gun was typically kept *upstairs,* in a nightstand by the Reinardts' bed. And you wondered, how did that gun get moved? Wasn't that another reason, Detective, to suspect Mrs. Reinardt?"

Many a juror is scribbling now.

"That was something we wondered about, yes."

"The fact that someone had moved the gun."

"Right."

Paul is planning to play this both ways, in closing argument. First, the evidence he just discussed is evidence of Rachel's guilt. Second, he will make the point that no additional evidence had surfaced from the time they originally suspected Rachel to the point they arrested her. So if the evidence wasn't sufficient *before,* why did they arrest her *later*? Because, Paul will say, weeks had passed since my arrest and my phony "confession," and they couldn't make one piece of evidence stick against me. So they hauled her in and gave her the choice: Tell us something bad about Marty and walk free, or risk the electric chair. They forced her to come to court and lie to save her own skin.

Paul turns to the judge. "Your Honor, I don't think I have any further—" He snaps his fingers. "Actually, there is one more thing I'd like to ask the detective. Just one more thing." He strolls toward the jury box. "While we're talking about the gun."

Cummings inhales. He knows he's almost finished. I happen to think he held up pretty well. Paul worked him over, but there was a lot to work with.

"Detective, you know that test you guys perform?" Paul waves his hand. "You know, that test where you look for the presence of gunpowder residue on a hand? To tell if that person has recently fired a weapon?"

"I know it," says Cummings. "But that test's no good if

you're looking at a hand sixteen days after it held the gun. No way residue stays on that long."

"I see." Paul stuffs his hands in his pockets as he inches toward Cummings. "Well, then how about less than one *hour* after?" Paul and his prey lock eyes; Cummings loses a little color as he watches Paul's hand leave its pocket and wave expressively. "Or even several hours after, but still the same night? The test is still helpful at that point, isn't it?"

"It could be," Cummings says sheepishly.

Paul smiles. "You see where I'm going, Detective. I'm talking about Rachel Reinardt. The only person who we all agree was in that house that night. You never, ever tested Rachel Reinardt to see if she fired a gun on November eighteenth, did you?"

Cummings's face transforms during Paul's lengthy question from embarrassment to annoyance to bemusement, so that when he says, "You're correct," he's almost smiling.

Paul lets out a sigh and, as he walks back toward the defense table—actually, he's just walking along the jury box—he shakes his head with disgust.

The gavel bangs, and the first day of my trial is over. We stand as the jury files out the door they came in through. Some of them are mumbling to one another as they leave, despite the judge's instruction not to discuss this case. I see now why Paul wanted to finish his cross-examination this afternoon. The jurors will hit their pillows tonight with the image of Cummings standing over me, the teary-eyed suspect. His hands around my throat. Rachel's untested hand the night of the murder.

The lawyers stand at attention until the jury is gone. Judge Mack begins his slow, almost painful descent from the bench. Behind me, I hear voices, the shuffling of feet, the clicking of briefcases.

Paul pulls his papers together and drops them into a folder. I touch his arm.

"That was great, Paul," I say to him. "Really. Thank you."

"It went well," he says modestly, as he places the folder into his briefcase. He takes in the compliment before adding,

"It's a little too early to get excited." Then he looks back at me, the guy who needs the reassurance. "But—it went well."

We plow through the mob that awaits us outside the courtroom and make it to the elevator. Several questions are thrown my way, but I just stare at Paul's feet in front of me, my attorneys and I shuffling along in tiny steps like some demented caterpillar. We take the elevator down to the underground parking lot and walk briskly to Mandy's Jeep. The lot is poorly lit and smells of gasoline. The only sound is the echo of our heels on the concrete.

I will congratulate Paul several more times today, tonight. I will silently beg him to do the same thing to every other witness who takes the stand.

I sit in the car as Mandy drives us off, and there are moments in the drive back to the law firm that my heart leaps, that I envision things I have not allowed myself to consider. I feel hope, for the first time that I can remember. The first sense that, yes, I might be acquitted. I might actually walk away from this. It's too early to get excited, Paul said, and he's right. But I am hopeful now. And with this first touch of optimism comes a horrifying feeling, a dread that slows my heart, puts a lump in my throat, fills my mouth with a damp, bitter taste.

I realize how much, just how desperately, I want to be free.

6 4

LATE NIGHT. MY SPIRITS ARE CHARGED NOW THAT the trial has started, now that I am finally rolling down a hill, however unknown the destination. I have to say I'm more optimistic than I've been, with Paul's job on Cummings today. But whether it's hope or fear, there is no chance I will be sleeping anytime soon.

Late-night television, for those unacquainted, brings little more than B movies, infomercials, syndicated shows from the sixties mostly, and an occasional good sex movie on one of the cable channels. After these two-plus months, if I have to watch another washed-up television personality from a twenty-year-old sitcom perform sit-ups on the latest ab-cruncher that folds neatly under my bed, I think I might just save everyone the trouble and put a gun in my mouth.

It's half past one, I'm trying to keep my mind off the case and on the intriguing saga of a man who fell into a vat of toxic waste, came out of it with superhuman powers, and now fights crime and occasionally gets the girl, when the phone jars me out of my stupor.

No. It couldn't be.

"Hello?"

"Hi." It's Tommy, whispering.

"What're you still doing up?"

"I dunno."

"Yeah? Lovestruck, are you?" Tommy and I have been talking about every other night lately, and he's been telling me about this girl, Bonnie Porter, who's been "bugging" him at school.

But Tommy doesn't reply with his usual denial, *gross* or *sick*. He doesn't speak at all.

"What's up, little man?"

His breathing is audible. "Are you going to jail?"

Oh, God. Jamie told him. We decided last week that he should know, that he should be prepared for the possibility so that my departure—if I have one—wouldn't be *that* abrupt. I figured she'd give me a heads-up first.

"I hope not, Tom."

"Mom says the police said you did something wrong. But you didn't."

"That's right, Tom. They say I did, but I didn't. I didn't."

"What did they say you did?"

So. Jamie hasn't gone into details. How to handle.

"Man to man, right?"

"Uh-huh."

"You won't tell Jeannie?"

"No."

"They think I killed someone, Tommy. But I didn't. I just have to convince them."

"Who got killed?" Cops and robbers. Good guys and bad.

"Some guy. But I didn't do it."

"You should tell them that."

This little kid can really reach me. Just tell them, and they'll believe you, because nobody's supposed to tell lies in an eight-year-old's world. How I wish Tommy could stay in that place. I scold myself now for the friendship, the new relationship I have formed with Tommy. I take this little boy, let him know I'm someone he can trust, a man he can talk to, and then head to jail the rest of my life. God, I have set this kid up for a big-time fall. What am I doing?

"I will, Tom," I say. "I'll tell them that."

"Promise?"

"Yeah. I promise."

"Are you gonna come visit soon?"

I close my eyes. The tears squeeze out, down my face. I'll try, I tell him.

65

I ENTER THE COURTROOM ON THE SECOND DAY OF my trial stirred but not shaken. The kinks are out now, and day two brings less of the nerves and more of the electricity. Roger Ogren and Gretchen Flaherty are already in the courtroom; they appear to hardly notice us as we take our seats. There will be no more greetings or handshakes between the two sides. The war has started, shots have been fired.

Mandy has commented on the difference between lawyers
in civil and criminal cases, the way they treat each other. On
the civil side, once the hearing or deposition is over, the
game face disappears. Lawyers will jaw for a while, converse
about all sorts of topics, their golf game, family, upcoming
trials, maybe even some off-the-record comments about their
own clients. But prosecutors, many of them take their job
more personally. They look at the defense lawyers as people
who are trying to help criminals avoid the law. They don't
buy into the whole system so much, that everyone is entitled
to a defense, blah blah blah. Some of Mandy's old buddies
at the county prosecutor could hardly look at the defense
attorneys.

I glance at the prosecutors more than once as we settle in.
I study Ogren's face, looking for any trace of despair,
recognition that his case isn't going so well. But to my dis-
appointment, he is all professional now, sticking a finger
down on the table as he makes a point to Gretchen Flaherty,
looking all confident and self-righteous. His choice of tie is
much better today, too, brown with flecks of red and black,
to match his charcoal suit.

The judge takes his seat at the bench moments later. He
talks to the attorneys, any last-minute things we need to wrap
up? Then he tells the bailiff to bring in the jury.

The sixteen citizens, twelve of whom will decide my fate,
enter the courtroom much more purposefully today, less
taken with the audience and their celebrity. A few pass a
glance in my direction, but most just eyeball their seats as
they file in. This is no longer just a show, just an idea to
them. They are dirty now. They have heard evidence, they
have begun to evaluate the case. I realize, with a shot of pain
to my stomach, that some of them have probably already
made up their minds about whether I'm guilty.

Gretchen Flaherty does a quick redirect on Cummings.
The lack of physical evidence was consistent with the manner
in which they believe I committed the crime, fully dressed
in winter garb to avoid leaving clues, ample time to clean
myself and my car up. And oh yes, I confessed in a clear

but quiet voice. Paul waves off the invitation to recross Cummings, as if everything he's said in the previous thirty minutes was meaningless.

Roger Ogren steps up to the lectern. "The People call Angela Siedlecki."

This is the neighbor who heard shots fired at the Reinardts' on November eighteenth. Paul says the main reason she's testifying is to confirm the firing of the gun and the timing of the events. Aside from this person, Rachel is the only person who can testify about that. Shows you how much confidence Roger Ogren has in Rachel.

Mrs. Siedlecki is a squat, overweight, middle-aged woman with brittle grayish hair, thick eyebrows, and a droopy chin. She takes the stand and looks around with wonder in her wide eyes. First time testifying? Wanna trade places?

Roger Ogren runs through her background. She married a Polish guy who owns a string of dry cleaners. She has lived next door to the Reinardts since they moved in three years ago.

"I'd like to turn your attention to the evening of November eighteenth of last year."

"Yes." She nods.

"Can you tell us what you recall about that night?"

"I was watching TV. I don't remember what anymore. I heard some noise outside."

"Describe what you heard."

"I heard glass shattering. I heard it twice. And I heard two loud pops."

"Do you recall what time it was when you heard these noises?"

"Not to the minute. But it was after the half-hour break of the show, y'know, when there are more commercials. It was probably five or ten minutes after that. So, maybe nine thirty-five, nine-forty." She snaps a finger. "It was—wait—it was a movie. . . ."

"That's fine, ma'am. What did you do upon hearing the noises?"

"Well, I listened for a moment. I wasn't really sure what

it was I heard. They weren't the kinds of sounds you normally hear. So I called the police. Just to be safe."

"What did you do next?"

"I looked out the window. There wasn't much to see. All I could see was the side of the house. The Reinardts have trees and shrubs all along the backyard, so it's hard to see much." She shrugs. "Everything *seemed* okay. I just waited for the police."

"Thank you, Mrs. Siedlecki."

The jury's eyes turn to the defense table now, and there is a slight elevation in their attention as Paul rises. After Paul's cross of Cummings, it is clear to all—most notably to Paul himself—that he is the superior trial lawyer in the room.

My attorney walks over to the lectern and gives a polite nod. "Mrs. Siedlecki, good morning."

"Good morning."

"Ma'am, you said you heard two pops."

"Yes."

"And you heard glass shattering."

"Yes. Twice."

"Isn't it true that you heard the pop sounds first, *then* the glass shattering?"

Ogren stands uncertainly. "Objection. He's mischaracterizing the testimony. She never said that. She said just the opposite."

"I'm not characterizing *anything,*" Paul says with a look of confusion. "I am cross-examining the witness. And I'd appreciate it if *she* answered, not Mr. Ogren."

"Proceed, Mr. Riley."

"Mrs. Siedlecki? Didn't you hear the pops first, then the glass shattering?"

Her brow wrinkles. "Well now, I think the glass shattered first."

"You *think.* So your memory isn't clear."

"I—think the glass shattered . . . first?"

"But you're not really sure, are you, Mrs. Siedlecki?"

"I'm pretty sure."

"Not positive?"

Mrs. Siedlecki considers that one, the ultimate commitment by a witness. I'm guessing she'd like to say yes, but there's something about that word—"positive"—that sends a hint of doubt into her watery eyes and curls her lips into her mouth. This woman strikes me as someone with a compromising personality, someone who likes to avoid the corners, so I'm surprised when she finally says, "I'm pretty close to positive, I guess."

"It was windy that night, wasn't it, ma'am?"

"Yes. Very windy."

"Enough so that you could hear it whipping up from inside your house, wouldn't you agree?"

"Yes."

"And your television set was on, you said."

"Yes," she says. "But—I think I can tell the difference between glass breaking and a gunshot."

Paul gives the jury another confused face. "Didn't you tell the police officer who interviewed you that you heard the pops first, then the glass shatter?"

"Did I . . . ?"

"I'm asking *you,* ma'am." Paul opens up the police report. "Didn't you say you heard loud pops and glass shatter?"

She pauses, her eyes on the report in Paul's hand. "I might have, I guess. They were close together."

"The sounds of the popping and the glass shattering came close together?"

"Yes."

"Within the space of, say, a few seconds?"

Mrs. Siedlecki thinks about this, her lips moving slightly. "Oh, I'd say about thirty, forty-five seconds apart, something like that."

"And as you sit here today, your memory is not clear as to which came first."

"Well, I always thought it was the glass first. But I'm not exactly sure, now that you mention it."

"Thank you, ma'am. I don't have any more questions."

Ogren stands back up. "You believe, Mrs. Siedlecki, that the glass shattered first, then the pops came."

"Well, I—I *think* so."

"Mr. Riley *suggested* that you told the police officer something different, that the pops came first. But you don't remember saying that, do you?"

She gives an exhausted sigh. "I mean—at that point—you know—the police were everywhere—and Derrick was gone— it was—" Her shoulders fall. "I really don't remember *what* I said to him."

"So you don't remember saying the pops came first, then the glass shattered."

"I don't remember, no."

Ogren sits down, and Paul stands back up.

"You don't remember what you told the officer about the sequence of the noises?"

"I just said that." Mrs. Siedlecki is a little bewildered about all of this. She didn't expect to be questioned on this point.

"Would anything refresh your memory?"

She shrugs. Roger Ogren's mouth opens, then he purses his lips.

"What about the police officer's notes? Might that help?"

"Maybe."

Ogren is back up. "Your Honor—"

"Just to refresh her recollection, Judge," Paul says. The judge waves him on.

Paul brings the report to Mrs. Siedlecki. "Take your time, please, and after you've read it over, let me know."

She takes her time, all right, putting on her glasses and peering at the paper. I don't know what could take her so long. The only sentence that matters is the one that says, *Heard shots fired and glass shatter.*

Finally, she hands it back to Paul.

"Now, Mrs. Siedlecki, do you remember what you told the police officer about the sequence of the noises you heard outside on November eighteenth?"

"Well, it sounds like I said the shots were fired first."

"So it does."

"Your *Honor*," Ogren says.

Judge Mack raises a hand, then shifts on an elbow to face

the witness. "Ma'am, we're interested in what your memory is, not what the notes say. You can use the notes to refresh your memory, not to quote them. Does looking at that report help your memory?"

Mrs. Siedlecki doesn't know come-here from get-away about her memory right now. "Well, I guess it does."

"All right, fine. Mr. Riley, ask about her memory."

"Thank you, Judge. Mrs. Siedlecki, let's put aside the notes now. From your memory now, do you remember what you told the police officer about the sequence of the noises you heard outside on November eighteenth?"

"I guess I told him that the shots came first."

"*Then* the glass shattering."

"Right."

"That's to the best of your memory."

"Well, yes, I guess." She makes a face, but doesn't say anything. She has no idea whether she's going from memory or the notes. I'm guessing it's the latter.

Paul is ready to end here, but he's not satisfied with her qualification.

"You would agree with me, Mrs. Siedlecki, wouldn't you, that your memory of this event was much better when you spoke to the police officer."

"I spoke to the officer that same night."

"Exactly. And your memory was much fresher *then* than it is *now*."

"That's for sure."

"Thank you."

Mrs. Siedlecki is all confused, chewing on her lip, as the judge announces a ten-minute recess.

66

"THE PEOPLE CALL OFFICER GEORGE FANDREI TO the stand."

Officer Fandrei is a young, clean-cut white kid of no more than twenty-five years. Lean face, tall and narrow, fair-complected, with an unfortunate mustache, thin and curved so that it creeps down each side of his mouth. Your basic suburban cop, decked out in full Highland Woods regalia—a uniform consisting of nothing but the color brown, save for the silver badge.

Gretchen Flaherty has this guy. She takes him through the basics first, full name, shield number, patrol unit. He's been on the force a little over two years. Graduated from a local high school, worked a couple of stints as a shopping mall security guard.

On November 18 of last year, Officer Fandrei responded to a 911 call from the Reinardt residence. Believed to be a domestic disturbance.

"Why was only one patrol car dispatched?" Gretchen Flaherty asks.

"Ma'am, this was a domestic disturbance. There was no report of gunshots. Typically, only one car would be dispatched."

"Tell us what happened when you arrived at the Reinardts' address."

"Well, I walked up to the door and listened for any sounds. But I didn't hear anything. So I knocked on the door, several times. When no one responded, I went inside."

"Did you announce your office?"

"Yes, I did."

"How many times?"

"I think just once. Mighta been twice."

"Did you announce it quietly?"

"No, ma'am."

"Will you say it now at the same level of volume you did that night?"

Fandrei draws himself up and gives us his best baritone: "PO-LICE!"

The point here, I guess, is that I still might have been in the house when Fandrei came in. When I heard him belt out his office, as they put it, I hightailed it.

"Describe what you saw when you went inside."

"Well, the first thing I saw was Mrs. Reinardt. She was lying on the floor in the living room. I could see her legs from the entranceway. So I walked in, and there she was. All sprawled out on the carpet. The phone had been pulled off of the little table that it was on. It was lying next to her."

"Describe how Mrs. Reinardt appeared."

"She was, you know, kind of off in space. Like she didn't even notice me. Her whole body was trembling. I think maybe her lips were moving, but she wasn't saying anything that I could hear. And her skin was real clammy. She had a cut just above her eye, and bruises on her face."

"So what did you do?"

"Well, I ran over to her. I asked her, 'Are you all right, ma'am?' But she didn't respond." The officer looks over at the jury for the first time. "She didn't even look in my direction."

"What happened next, Officer?"

"Well, I bent down next to her. I asked her if she was okay."

"Did she respond?"

"No. She didn't even look at me. She just sort of stared off."

"So what did you do?"

"I kept trying to talk to her. I asked her if she was okay. I asked her if her husband or boyfriend was in the house. I mean, the call was a domestic. I expected to see a guy somewhere."

"And she didn't respond?"

"No, ma'am. She just stared off. Her lips moved, like she wanted to say something. But she couldn't talk at first."

"What did you do next, Officer?"

"Well, I took off my jacket and placed it over her."

"Why did you do that?"

"Number one, because it was really cold in the house. That seemed weird, because I could feel the heat coming through the vent in the living room right by Mrs. Reinardt's head. But it was really cold."

"And what was the other reason?"

Fandrei stares at the prosecutor.

"Why else did you put your jacket over Mrs. Reinardt?"

"Oh. Because she might've been in shock. That's what you're supposed to do."

"So what happened next?"

"Well, I drew my weapon, and I called out for Mr. Reinardt."

"Did you get a response?"

"No, ma'am. So I started walking the downstairs floor. I went into the kitchen, and then into the den."

"Tell us what you saw in the den."

"Well, there was a very strong breeze. The curtain to the back door was flying around, you know, into the room, because of the wind. There were big chunks of glass on the carpet by the door. And there was a big spot of blood on the carpet. And little trickles leading out onto the patio."

"What did you do?"

"I had my gun drawn, like I said, and I walked toward the patio door. There's a light switch for outside, and I flicked it on. I looked through the hole in the glass onto the patio. But there was nobody outside."

"And what—"

"So I walked outside. I unlocked the door and slid it open, and I walked out onto the patio. And I looked around. I ran out into the yard and looked around. I shined my flashlight all over that yard. But I couldn't see anything. Nobody was out there."

"So what did you do?"

"I went back inside, and I radioed for assistance. I told dispatch we had a possible homicide and kidnapping."

"Then what?"

"Well, I thought maybe someone was upstairs. I hadn't looked up there. So I went upstairs and looked around. But there was nobody."

"Did you return downstairs?"

"Yes, I returned downstairs. I went over to Mrs. Reinardt again. I asked her what had happened. She didn't say anything at first. She just stared and trembled, you know, like before. Then I asked her, 'Did something happen to your husband?' And she grabbed my uniform. She said, 'My husband.' Actually, she kind of whispered it. I asked her if she knew who it was who broke into her house. She didn't say anything. I asked her if she had been hurt. She didn't respond."

Fandrei goes on for another ten or fifteen minutes, talking about how the other patrol cars arrived, as well as the detectives. They tended to Rachel, they went outside and tried to find where Dr. Reinardt had wandered off to. They thought the woods would be a good bet, and they searched them, but they found nothing. After a good half hour, they got the K-9 unit out to the scene, but the winds were way too strong for the dogs to be able to trace a scent.

Mandy gets to handle this witness. She looks really cute today. Her bushy hair sits on each shoulder. She wears a brownish coat with muted stripes, purple or red, I think. The painter in the jury box watches her with particular interest as she approaches the lectern.

"Good morning, Officer," she says.

"Good morning." Fandrei is a little more reserved now, furrowed brow, narrowed eyes, waiting for the enemy to cross him. I wonder if he has ever testified before.

"You were dispatched to the Reinardts' home at nine-thirty-eight on the evening of November eighteenth of last year, is that correct?"

"Nine-thirty-eight, ma'am, yes."

9:38 . . .

"And dispatch described the incident at the Reinardts' as a domestic dispute."

"Yes, ma'am."

"Dispatch did *not* say that the caller from the Reinardt home said she was in fear for her life."

"No, ma'am, nothing like that."

"You have handled many domestic disputes as a patrol officer, haven't you?"

"Yes, ma'am, I have."

"Before this date, November eighteenth of last year, you had handled a number of such disputes."

"Yes."

"Is it fair to say, Officer, that none of these other disputes involved a life-or-death situation?"

Fandrei looks off for a moment. "Well, one time some guy was waving a knife around, threatening to kill his wife."

"But he didn't."

"No. I don't think he was ever going to. He was just mad."

"Do you recall being dispatched to that incident? The one with the knife?"

"Yes, ma'am, I do."

"When that call came to you in the patrol car—well, let me back up. Were you in the patrol car when that call came in?"

"Yes."

"On that occasion, did dispatch tell you that the husband was wielding a knife?"

"Yes, ma'am, they did."

"So in your experience, if a situation involved a weapon, or immediate danger to someone's life, you would expect to be told that over the dispatch."

"Yes, ma'am, I most definitely would."

Fandrei is enjoying this line of questioning, and Mandy knows it. He is covering himself for why he took so long to make it to the house that night. They just said domestic disturbance, nothing about a gun or that someone was in danger. I don't know why the dispatcher was so calm; the 911 call sure sounded like more than a domestic dispute. Highland Woods' finest, at your service.

"So you had no reason to know about a gun being used at the Reinardts'."

"No, ma'am. No idea at all."

"You had no idea that, supposedly, someone had broken into the Reinardts' house."

"That's right. I didn't."

"You figured it was probably a bunch of shouting, probably nothing more than that."

"That's right."

"And you didn't arrive at the Reinardts' home until"— Mandy looks down at her notes—"nine-forty-nine, is that correct?"

One of the women, I think the office manager in the back row of the jury box, makes a noise. Eleven minutes to respond.

9:49 . . .

"That's right." Fandrei shrugs his shoulders apologetically. "Like I said, I had no idea it was a break-in. And I was clear on the other side of town."

The first siren had come much earlier than I expected. . . . How had they gotten here so fast?

Mandy doesn't push Fandrei on his late arrival to the scene. There's no need. The only point she will make is that they took a very long time before they got their act together and actually started searching for Dr. Reinardt.

"Once you arrived at the house, Officer, you say you knocked on the door."

"Yes, ma'am." He's glad to be on a new line of questioning.

"You knocked for quite a while."

"Well, I don't know. Pretty long, I guess."

"A minute's worth?"

"Oh, probably a little less than that."

"Okay. Then you went inside."

"Yes, ma'am."

"And you say the first thing you saw was Mrs. Reinardt."

"Yes."

"And as any good officer would do, you attended to her."

"Yes, ma'am."

"You checked to see if she was okay."

"Yes, ma'am."

"You tried to revive her."

"Yes, I did."

"You tried to talk to her."

"Yes."

"And that would have taken a minute or two as well."

"That sounds right."

"Then you walked around the first floor."

"Yes, ma'am."

"You went into the den."

"Yes."

"You saw the bloodstain."

"Yes."

"The broken glass door."

"Yes."

"Then you went out onto the patio."

"Yes."

"You looked around."

"Yes."

"You went out into the yard and shined your flashlight."

"Yes."

"You went over that yard pretty good, didn't you?"

"Yes, ma'am."

"You were very thorough, I imagine."

"Yes, ma'am, I was."

"Just looking around the patio and the yard, that must've taken at least five to ten minutes."

"Somewhere in there."

"But at least five minutes."

"Yeah, I'd say so."

"So from the time you first left Mrs. Reinardt, until the time you were finished searching that yard, you took anywhere from ten to fifteen minutes."

Fandrei crinkles his face and does the math. "That sounds pretty much on target."

"And it was after you returned into the house that you radioed for backup."

"That's right."

"Thank you, Officer. We have no more questions, Your Honor."

6 7

AGNES CLORISSA HAS BEEN THE REINARDTS' MAID for over four years. She moved to the area from Mexico City with her husband almost six years ago. She didn't live with them, but she would come to their house every weekday at six-thirty A.M. and make breakfast. She would stay at least through the early afternoon. She would also work in the evenings whenever the Reinardts did something social, which was about once every two or three weeks. Since about a week or two after the doctor disappeared, her time has been cut to three days a week.

She is a good-sized woman with big hands and a worn Latin face. The gray in her hair has almost completely overcome the jet black. She has declined the use of an interpreter, but her English is not so good. Roger Ogren does the best he can with her.

"Ms. Clorissa, have you ever seen the defendant before?" He points to me, and Paul tells me to stand.

"Jes," she says. "I seen him."

"Where have you seen him?" Ogren speaks verrrry slowwwwly.

"At the house."

"At the Reinardts' house?"

"Jes."

"How many times?"

She holds up two fingers. "Two times."

"Why was he there?"

"He come for the party."

"The party. Do you mean parties the Reinardts threw for their charity?"

"*La caridad*. Jes. The foundation."

"These were parties for the Children's Foundation?"

"Jes."

"Okay. Did you ever see the defendant talk to Mrs. Reinardt?"

"Jes."

"When was this?"

"Spring. April."

"April of last year?"

"Jes."

"At the Reinardts' home?"

"Jes."

"A party?"

"Jes."

"Were they alone? When you saw them?"

"Jes. He follow her."

"He followed her?"

"One time, I come into the keetchen. He come in to talk to her. She tell him, go away. He don' want to go. He talk to her."

"Do you know what he said to Mrs. Reinardt?"

Now I see why Ogren didn't want an interpreter. If the maid is going to repeat a conversation Rachel and I had, she has to appear to understand English pretty well.

"He say, what wrong? What wrong? He say, why do you avoid me? She say she don' want to be bothered. She say so."

I saw her break away from a group of two or three volunteers and walk into the kitchen from the living room. I was talking to someone, I don't remember who. I took the other route, down the hall, through the den, into the kitchen. I'd

*had a couple of scotches, and I was getting a little annoyed
at how she kept avoiding my looks all night.*

"Rachel," I said.

*She was over by the sink, opening a bottle of wine. She
turned her head and saw me, then turned back. "What is it?"*

*I walked over and leaned against the counter next to her.
"I was wondering if you were ever going to acknowledge my
presence tonight."*

*She shook her head as she worked the cork. "Please," she
whispered. "No one can know."*

*I replied, probably a little too loudly for her liking, "You
can have a conversation with me without it meaning we're
having an affair."*

*Rachel stopped her work on the bottle but kept her head
down. "Marty, please don't make this difficult."*

*I leaned into her. "Well, it's difficult for me, too. I mean
I know—"*

"Shh—"

*I actually raised my volume. "There's a difference between
discretion and completely avoiding me."*

*Noise from behind us, shuffling of feet. Rachel looked over
my shoulder; I turned around to see Agnes Clorissa.*

*"Sorry," Agnes said with uncertainty. I can only imagine
the look on my face.*

"How did Mrs. Reinardt appear at that time?"

Agnes looks at him funny. She leans forward. "I don' . . . ?"

"How did Mrs. Reinardt *look*?"

"She look . . . oh, *claro*. She look upset. Upset."

"How about the defendant?" Ogren points at me.

"He all red." She waves a hand down over her face. "Face
all red."

"His face was red?"

"Jes."

"Thank you, Ms. Clorissa. That's all we have, Your
Honor."

Paul stands up and walks over to the jury box at the far
end. "Ms. Clorissa, you were born in Mexico City, right?"

She is leaning forward as Paul speaks, her neck craned, her eyes intent. "Jes."

"You grew up there."

"Jes."

"You spent thirty-six years there."

"Jes."

"And you spoke Spanish."

"Jes."

"No English."

"*Poquito*. Leetle." She holds her index finger and thumb an inch apart.

"How's your English now?"

"Is okay." She nods.

"Does Mrs. Reinardt speak to you in English?"

Agnes smiles. "She speak Spanish."

"And you and your husband speak Spanish to each other?"

"Jes."

"All the time?"

"Jes."

"You live in the city here, correct?"

"Jes."

"You live at 106th and Caroway."

"Jes, I do. I take bus to Reinardts'."

"That is a Mexican neighborhood, pretty much, right?"

"Jes."

"Most of the stores you go to, they speak Spanish."

"Jes."

"Okay. Now, I want to talk about the time you saw Mrs. Reinardt and Marty talking in the kitchen, okay?"

"Okay."

"His back was to you, right?"

She looks at Paul with a contorted face. Paul stands there and waits for an answer. They stare at each other for a good ten, fifteen seconds. Finally, she says, "I don' understand."

"Marty wasn't facing in your direction, was he?"

She looks Paul over for a second with that crumpled face, then sighs. "I don' understand."

Judge Mack leans forward. "I wonder, counsel, if it would

be more appropriate to bring in an interpreter."

"Judge," Paul says with a hand up, "I would ask that she be asked these questions in English. If she claims to have heard a conversation in English, then I'm entitled to explore the credibility of that testimony. The jury is entitled to know whether she can really understand English that well."

The jurors, most of them, anyway, nod at this argument. The judge lets Paul proceed. Agnes is sitting up there bewildered, not sure what exactly is going on, but getting the idea that the heat is being turned up a notch.

Paul takes a step closer to Agnes. "Was Marty standing face-to-face with you?" He points at his face and to her, waving his finger back and forth. "Or"—he turns his back to her—"was he turned around?"

"Like—now," she says, wagging a finger at him.

"Turned around, you mean?" Paul cranes his head around to ask this.

"Jes."

"How far away from you?"

She leans over the witness stand—smacking the microphone in the process and treating us all to a nice reverberation—and points to a spot on the floor near Paul's feet. " 'Bout there," she says.

Paul takes two steps forward. "Here?"

"Jes."

"For the record, about"—Paul strides toward Agnes and stops at the witness stand—"six strides away from you."

"Jes."

"Marty was upset, you said."

"Jes."

"So he was talking fast." Paul nods his head agreeably.

She thinks it over and nods. "Jes."

"You came into the kitchen from the living room."

"The leeving room. Jes."

"That's where the party was."

"Jes."

"Was there music?"

"Jes."

"Loud music."

"I donno. Music. I donno loud."

Paul takes six strides back to his spot and keeps his back to Agnes, so he's looking out into the spectators' seats. "And you are testifying that my client said, 'Why are you avoiding me?' to your boss?"

You gotta love Paul. He threw in as many nouns and clauses as he could. He left out words like "Marty" and "Rachel" and substituted "my client" and "your boss." Agnes sits there, trying in vain to understand, but shrugging and sitting back in her chair before Paul has even finished his sentence.

"Joo talk too *fast,*" she says with a shake of the head. She knows what he's doing.

Paul keeps his back to her. "You are testifying that . . . my client said why are . . . you avoiding me to your boss?"

She still didn't catch it. Paul spoke slowly and loudly. Although he chopped up the sentence pretty good.

Agnes shakes a finger at Paul. "Joo try to trick me. Joo think I don' speak English mean that I am stupid."

Paul turns around to face her. "Not at all, Ms. Clorissa. Not in the least. I'm not saying you're stupid. I just wonder how well you can translate the language that you claim my client was speaking that night."

She folds her arms with a huff; no way she got that whole sentence. "I hear what I hear, okay? He ask, what ees wrong? Why do you avoid me?"

Paul turns sideways now, to the jury. "Isn't it possible that he said, 'Why are you annoyed?' "

"Jes. He say, why do you avoid me?"

Paul nods agreeably. Annoy, avoid. What's the difference?

Paul turns back to Agnes. "Did you see Mrs. Reinardt earlier that night?"

"I see her, jes."

"How was she acting?"

"Acting?"

"How did she appear?"

"Oh. I—donno. I don' remember."

"Is it possible she was upset earlier?"

"I donno, upset."

"Did you understand what I just said?"

"Jes, I understand. I say I donno."

"Isn't it possible she was mad earlier?"

"I donno."

"And isn't it possible that Marty saw that she was mad, or upset, or annoyed?"

"Objection," Roger Ogren says. "No foundation."

"Sustained."

"Isn't it possible that Marty said to Mrs. Reinardt, 'What's wrong?' because she looked *upset*?"

"Same objection, Your Honor."

"Sustained."

"And isn't it possible that he then said to her, 'Why are you annoyed?' "

"Same objection."

"This is different. Overruled."

"Then I object on the grounds that it calls for hearsay."

"Sit down, Mr. Ogren."

Paul turns his back to Agnes again, and walks toward the jury box. "Ms. Clorissa, isn't it possible that my client said to your boss, 'Why are you annoyed?' "

Agnes takes a second, eyes up at the ceiling. Then, from the heavens, she says, "Jes."

One of the jurors, a grad student who writes for a conservative newspaper, shakes his head and mumbles something, I'm going to guess not politically correct.

Paul moves closer to Agnes now. "Ms. Clorissa, you like Mrs. Reinardt, don't you?"

"I like her very much. Very much."

"And you remember when the police started to question her?"

She pauses. "When the police talk to her?"

"Yes. Do you remember when the police started talking to her?"

"Jes."

"You were afraid, weren't you?"

"Jes. They say she do this to her husband. I say no." She draws a horizontal line in the air.

"And you were afraid for her."

"Jes. I was afraid."

"And you wanted to help her."

"Jes. I tell her so."

"You *told* her you wanted to help."

"Jes."

"You and Mrs. Reinardt talked about that time when Marty and her were talking in the kitchen."

"We . . . talked . . . ?"

"You said Marty"—he points to me—"was talking to Mrs. Reinardt in the kitchen."

"Jes . . . ?"

"At that party?"

"Jes."

"You talked to Mrs. Reinardt about this, right?"

She nods. "We talk about it."

"And she told you what Marty said to her."

"Jes."

"*She* told you what words he used."

"She tell me what he say. I tell her what I hear, too."

"But she told you first, right?"

Agnes thinks about this for a moment. "She tell me, then I tell her."

Paul nods. "You wanted to help her."

"Jes, I wan' to help her."

"*When* did you talk about this?"

"I don' remember."

"After she was arrested."

"Jes. After."

"I see." Paul brings a finger to his chin, then wags it. "When you saw them in the kitchen, you walked in on that conversation, right?"

Agnes squints. "I saw them talking . . . ?"

"I'm sorry. I'll rephrase." Paul waves a hand, erasing the air. "When you first walked into the kitchen, Marty and Rachel were standing there talking. Right?"

"Jes."

"They were standing still, right? Standing, not walking."

"Jes."

Paul holds out his hands. "But Ms. Clorissa, you told Mr. Ogren that Marty followed Rachel into the kitchen."

"I say—?"

"You said he *followed* her. You said that."

Agnes Clorissa has less than a high school education and lives in a city where she hardly understands the native tongue. But English or Español, Agnes knows when she's caught. Her posture straightens, her face reddens. But she doesn't speak.

Paul's tone softens. "You didn't see Marty follow Rachel into the kitchen, did you? You couldn't have."

"He follow her."

Paul takes a step forward. "Rachel *told* you Marty followed her, didn't she?"

"She say he follow her, he follow her."

"But she told you, right? You didn't see it." Paul points to his eye.

"She tell me. I believe her."

"Oh, I'm sure you do, Ms. Clorissa. You'd believe *anything* she told you, wouldn't you?"

"Jes. I believe her always."

"Yeah." Paul pointedly turns to the jury, nodding. "And she told you about this—about Marty *following* her—she told you this after she was arrested."

"Jes."

"The same time she told you that Marty said, 'Why are you avoiding me?' "

"Jes."

"And you believed her."

"I believe her."

Paul lets out a soft moan, shaking his head. "All right. Fine." He blows out a breath and ponders things a moment. "Oh, yes," he says. "Ms. Clorissa, you have worked at the Reinardts' for several years, right?"

"Jes."

"During all that time, did they have a gun they kept in the house?"

"Jes."

"Where did they keep it?"

"By the bed."

"By the bed? In a nightstand?"

"Jes."

Paul glances at the jury. "Thank you, Ms. Clorissa."

Paul takes his seat. Ogren stands back up and approaches the witness stand. He speaks deliberately, and holds his fingers out like he's conducting an orchestra. "Ms. Clorissa, you are sure that the defendant said, why are you a*vvvoid*ing me?" The "v" sound that comes out of Ogren's mouth could have cut through a block of wood.

"Jes, that is what he say."

"And you heard him say, what's wrong."

"Jes."

"You understand that you must tell the truth, right?"

"Jes. I tell the truth."

"Ms. Clorissa, when you clean the Reinardts' home, do you open up cabinets and drawers?" Ogren uses hand gestures to illustrate opening things.

"No. Not usual. Sometimes."

"So if Dr. Reinardt had *moved* his gun from the nightstand by the bed to downstairs, in the cabinets by the bar, you might not know about that?"

"No."

"The gun could sit there for weeks without you knowing."

"Jes."

"Thank you." *Muchas gracias.*

Paul stands back up. "Do you know what the word 'annoyed' means?"

"I donno."

"Thank you, Ms. Clorissa."

We break for lunch. Agnes gets off the witness stand in a huff. Paul turns his attention to his notepad, avoiding the steely glance she throws him as she walks past. Mandy packs up her briefcase. I stand to stretch my legs. The spectators file out for lunch.

As always, I look for encouragement from my lawyers. "I thought that went pretty well, don't you?" I say to Paul.

He looks up at me with a poker face. "Jes," he says.

---

6 8

THE HOUR FOR LUNCH FEELS LIKE FIVE MINUTES, A quick cab ride to Paul's club, a Caesar salad I stare at more than eat. Then back to court. This afternoon, my secretary, Debra, is going to testify. She called me the day after the police and one of Ogren's cronies talked to her. By the time they got to her, they already knew about the sign-out sheet that bore my name at half-past three on the night of the doctor's death. And they knew I had been working on a big project that was about to close.

Deb remembered the Madison deal. She remembered my appearance that morning after the murder, how disheveled and sick I looked. She told me she was sorry that she remembered, but she had to tell the truth. I told her I understood. I really did. What's she supposed to do, risk an obstruction charge for me? I'd never have done that for her.

We were a little surprised that Ogren decided to call Deb as a witness. She can say some good things about me, too, including the fact that she believed I was working late on the night of November 18. Paul figured this is what happened: Ogren knows we're going to claim I was at the office, and he has to admit I was there, because of the sign-out sheet. His theory is not that I wasn't there—it's that I wasn't there until after Dr. Reinardt was killed. So Deb can talk all she wants about the food I left on my desk, the fact that I left her a voice mail at three-something that morning. None of that matters to Ogren, because he'll say that was part of my cover-up.

Gretchen Flaherty calls Debra Glatz to the stand at about one-fifteen. Her hair has been cut but not tapered, so it's still thick and bunched around her face but misses the shoulders. I catch her perfume as she passes our table. It reminds me of the office, of the people I will never speak to again, many of whom were questioned by the police and none too happy about it, from what Frank Tiller told me.

Deb looks very drawn today. Even with her customary makeup job, I can see the narrowness of her eyes, the redness in her cheeks. This isn't easy for her. She sits awkwardly in the witness seat, a diminutive woman surrounded by thick wooden railings. She has to lean forward to speak into the microphone.

Deb gives her full name, Debra Jean Glatz. Four years together, I never knew her middle name. She discusses her background, worked at McHenry Stern seven years.

"Do you recall the day of November nineteenth of last year, Ms. Glatz?"

"Yes."

"Did you see the defendant that day?"

"Sure, I saw Marty." She looks over at me now, for the first time. I give her something close to a smile, a little nod.

"Do you recall what time?"

She holds her look on me for a moment, then turns to Gretchen Flaherty. "It would have been around eight. My train gets me in at seven fifty-five in the morning."

"Can you describe his appearance?"

She nods, runs her tongue over her lips.

"Ms. Glatz? Please describe his appearance."

Deb blinks twice and looks down. "Nothing that unusual, I suppose. He looked a little"—she sighs—"I don't know, a little distracted, maybe. He had a big project he was working on day and night for the past two weeks."

"Thank you, Ms. Glatz, but I'm asking you to describe his *appearance*." Flaherty's a little harsh on her, I think. I wonder if it would have been better to let Ogren handle Deb.

"I just did," Deb says.

"Ms. Glatz, I realize this is not an easy situation for you. You were very fond of the defendant, weren't you?"

"I would say I still *am*."

"So this must be difficult for you, obviously. But please, if you could, tell us how the defendant appeared to you."

Paul stands. "I must object, Judge. The question has been asked and answered."

Judge Mack takes his hand off his chin. "Sustained."

Gretchen nods. "All right. You said he looked *distracted*. Did he seem well?"

Deb shrugs. "You'd have to ask him." It's not a bad answer, but she sounds evasive from the outset.

"Did he have a cold, Ms. Glatz?"

Deb swallows. "He sneezed a couple of times."

"Would you describe it as a bad cold or a mild cold?"

"Your Honor," Paul says. "Ms. Glatz didn't say he *had* a cold. And even if she did, I think Ms. Flaherty is asking her to guess."

"I imagine Ms. Flaherty is asking for the witness's perception," the judge says.

Deb is stoic. This is an answer she can fudge, without outright lying. She can say she doesn't know. Or that it seemed kind of mild, how the hell would *she* know?

"It was a bad cold," she says.

Or maybe not.

"Did you notice anything else about his physical appearance?"

Deb shrugs.

"How about his face, Ms. Glatz? Did he seem refreshed? Like he'd gotten a good night's sleep?"

"Judge." Paul is on his feet. "Really. How could the witness have any idea how to answer this?" This objection, it seems, is more for the jury's benefit: Yeah, how could *she* know? But I'm wondering if this is a good move on Paul's part. After all, my alibi is that I was working late. So what's the damage? Maybe Paul's just trying to throw off the prosecutor's rhythm, but we look like we're hiding something. The judge overrules Paul.

"He looked tired, I guess."

"And how about his hands, Ms. Glatz?"

Deb shoots a look at Flaherty. "His hand was kind of bruised."

"Bruised?"

"Yes. Bruised."

"How could you tell it was bruised?"

Deb touches her right hand with little enthusiasm. "His fingers were swollen and—a little discolored."

"Were they a purplish color?"

"Yes."

"Did you ask him about the bruises?"

"Yes."

"What did he say?"

Deb shakes her head slightly. "I don't recall specifically. He was busy getting ready for the big meeting he'd been working up to for weeks."

Atta girl.

"What did he say, Ms. Glatz?"

"He was much more interested in the contract I'd been revising for the meeting."

"Oh. So he was avoiding the question?"

"I didn't *say* that!" Deb snaps. "He answered me. He said he had bruised them playing basketball."

"Basketball?" Gretchen moves from the lectern, turned toward the jury. "Did you ask him when he had found the time to play basketball while he was working *day and night* on this project?"

"No, I didn't ask him that."

Gretchen Flaherty nods. "You know the defendant fairly well, don't you?"

"I know Marty pretty well."

"And have you ever known the defendant to play basketball?"

Paul is standing again, his arms out. "There is no foundation for that question. She was his secretary, not his social coordinator."

"Your Honor," Flaherty says, "I'm just asking for her own knowledge."

"Overruled."

"I don't know every activity Marty is involved in when he's not at work. If he plays basketball with his friends, I wouldn't know one way or another."

"But to your knowledge, he never played basketball."

"Like I *said,* I wouldn't know one way or another."

"Well, when the defendant told you that he had bruised his hand playing basketball, did that seem odd to you?"

Paul again, hands in the air. "What's next, Judge? His favorite movie?" A couple of the jurors laugh. The judge turns to the prosecutor, agitated like the joke is on him. He sustains the objection.

Flaherty purses her lips. "As you understood it, Ms. Glatz, the defendant had been working at the office very late the night before this day you noticed his bruised hand."

"*Objection,* Your Honor," Paul says. "Ms. Flaherty is leading her own witness."

"Sustained."

"Then I would ask for permission to treat the witness as adverse, Your Honor."

"Your Honor, really." Paul leaves the table and moves to the center of the room. Speech time. "Ms. Flaherty calls this witness herself, then she asks her to guess about whether he had a cold and whether he likes to play basketball. And now, when she doesn't get the answers she wants, she wants to *lead* her, too. Ms. Glatz is not adverse."

"I object to that speech," says Flaherty. "Your Honor—"

The judge raises a hand. "Go ahead, Ms. Flaherty. You can lead."

Flaherty turns on Deb with vigor now. "The defendant told you that he had been working well into the early morning of November nineteenth, didn't he, Ms. Glatz?"

"He didn't have to tell me. He had left me a message on the voice mail at about three-thirty the night before. The message came from his office phone. And he had—"

"But he *did* tell you, also, didn't he? He made a point of telling you he'd been working late the prior night?"

Paul hasn't taken his seat yet, and he turns to the judge. "Object to the form."

"Let's get on with this," the judge says.

"He told me," says Deb.

"And earlier that week, you hadn't noticed that his hand was bruised and purple and swollen, had you?"

"That doesn't mean it hadn't happened earlier in the week. I don't make it a point to examine Marty's hands every day."

I can't help but smile. Deb can get quite an attitude when she wants to. Although I'm not unaware that her defensiveness reinforces to the jury that she is trying to help me.

"Please answer my question. You hadn't noticed that his hand was swollen and purple earlier that week, had you?"

"No. All I'm saying is, it could have been, and I wouldn't have noticed."

"Ah, but you certainly noticed it on November nineteenth, didn't you?"

Deb folds her arms. "Yes."

"In fact, it was one of the first things you noticed."

Deb lets out an audible sigh. "I don't know if it was first or tenth or fifteenth. I was showing him the contract I had been revising. I was holding it, and *he* was holding it. His hand was right in front of me. I couldn't miss it."

"But you had been revising that contract all week, hadn't you?"

Deb pauses. "Yes."

"And yet, this was the first day you noticed his swollen purple hand."

Deb nods.

"Is that a yes?"

"*Yes.*"

Flaherty checks her notes on the lectern. Finally, she looks up. "Pass the witness."

Deb blinks and looks over at me. I look away but give her a brief smile. She did the best she could.

Paul stands at the lectern. "Ms. Glatz, can you describe how Marty's office looked on November nineteenth of last year?"

"Yes," she says with renewed animation, turning to the jury. "Well, the contract he had been working on was on his computer screen. There was a half-eaten brownie and a bag of potato chips on his desk. He had worked through dinner the night before and just ate some junk."

Gretchen Flaherty stands.

"He tends to do that when he works late," Deb adds quickly.

"Objection," Flaherty says with a cold look at Deb. "The witness has no idea if the defendant worked through dinner, or if he was even at the office at all. Move to strike."

"Judge," Paul says, turning to face His Honor, "Marty's secretary should know her boss's propensity to work late and eat junk food."

Judge Mack asks the court reporter to read back Deb's testimony. The reporter reaches back to grab the tape that spills from her little machine. She pulls it back, piece by piece, like she's pulling a rope on a ship.

The judge listens again to the testimony, then turns to Deb. "Ms."—he checks his notes—"Glatz, what time did you leave the office the day before this, November eighteenth?"

She looks up at the judge. "I'm sure the same time I always do. Four-thirty."

"All right, I'm going to sustain the objection and strike the last two sentences of the testimony. Just tell us what you know personally, Ms. Glatz."

Paul continues. "So there was a half-eaten brownie and bag of chips."

"Yes. And a cup of coffee, half full." Deb looks at me.

"What else did you tell them?" I asked Deb when she called me.

"That's it, Marty. Just about your fingers and the cold, and the document on your computer screen."

"Did you tell them how my office looked?"

"Well . . . no. I mean, I don't remember."

"You don't? Remember, you said, 'Nice breakfast,' and you pointed at it."

"I—did . . . ?"

"Yes, Debra. You did. You did." I sighed. *"I can't believe you don't remember."*

Silence at the other end of the phone.

"And there was also a cup of cold coffee sitting on my desk. I had drunk half of it the night before. Come on, you don't remember?"

Silence.

"It's important, Deb."

"Well, maybe . . ."

"I'm not asking you to lie, Deb. I would never, never do that. I'm just asking you to tell the truth."

"There was—a half-eaten brownie, and chips, and coffee. . . ."

"Right."

"And were there also papers spread out all over Marty's desk?"

"Yes, I believe there were."

"You also had a message from Marty when you arrived at work on November nineteenth."

"Yes. Marty had left a message on my voice mail."

"Does the voice mail tell you what time the call was made?"

"Yes. Marty left the message at about three-thirty in the morning. He asked me to do some more revisions on the contract for the meeting the following day."

"He left the message for you at three-thirty the prior night?"

"Right."

"And he asked you to do some more revisions."

"Yeah."

Paul looks over at the jury. "Now, Marty had a very big meeting on November nineteenth."

"Oh, *yes*. He had been working on the Madison deal for weeks. He had been stressed out about it all week."

"Marty had worked at McHenry Stern for seven years, is that correct?"

"Yes."

"And that meant he was a year, maybe two, from making partner at the firm."

"That's right."

"And—"

"It was very important to him."

"Making partner was very important to him."

"Very important. He talked about it all the time."

"And was this deal as big as any deal Marty had done since you worked for him?"

"Bigger," she says. "This was the biggest deal Marty had put together himself."

"Thank you, Ms. Glatz."

Deb starts out of her chair as Flaherty stands again. Deb settles back in.

"Just so we're clear," says Flaherty. "You don't have any personal knowledge that the defendant was working all night in his office on November eighteenth, do you?"

"You're right," Deb says, a little more comfortable now that Paul has built her up. "For all I know, he took out a couple of hours to play basketball."

A snicker from the jury. Flaherty just smiles. "Well, *whatever* he did, you have no idea, correct?"

"Correct."

"Now, Ms. Glatz, I believe you described the state of the defendant's office on the morning of November nineteenth."

"Yes. I did. Would you like me to describe it again?"

"No. Do you recall that you and I had a conversation about a month ago about this case?"

"How could I forget?"

"And that's when you told us about the defendant's cold, and his bruised hand?"

"Yes."

"And I asked you if there was anything that would make you believe that the defendant had been working late into the night on November eighteenth?"

"I remember you asked me. And I told you that he had left me the voice message."

"And then I asked you if anything else would make you believe that?"

"I remember that."

"And you said you couldn't think of anything else."

"I don't know if I said that or not."

"Well, you didn't say anything about food wrappers or coffee, did you?"

Deb thinks about this. "I guess I didn't." She *knows* she didn't. But again, she's straddling that line. She's not lying.

"So since our conversation a month ago, your memory has suddenly gotten much clearer?"

Deb does what she always does when she's cornered: She gets that pouty look and grinds her teeth. I hold my breath; I didn't tell my lawyers that Deb and I had talked.

"Ms. Glatz? Do you have an answer?"

"Just because there was food and coffee doesn't mean he was working late," she says. Not a bad answer; she didn't tell the cops because it wasn't necessarily relevant.

"That's true," Flaherty says. "For all you know, the defendant could have eaten that food at five o'clock the prior night, and not at three in the morning."

"Right."

"Or that morning, before you came in."

"Right."

"It doesn't say *anything* about what time the defendant left work the prior night."

"Right."

Score one for the prosecutor. "Even still," Flaherty muses. "You didn't remember the food and coffee on his desk when we talked, did you?"

Deb already gave a good answer for that: It had nothing to do with the questions she was asked back then. Or she could get all confused and act like she doesn't remember *what* she said, and the whole thing would be a wash to the jury. But she's on the spot here, she might not be thinking so fast. Or she might choose to tell the truth.

Come on, Deb.

"No, I didn't remember it then," she says sheepishly.

Flaherty stiffens, suddenly empowered. "And in between the time we talked and today, you now remember these things."

"That's right."

"Interesting," the prosecutor says. I believe, at this moment, that I have underestimated Ms. Gretchen Flaherty. "Tell me, Ms. Glatz, after you and I talked, did you talk to the defendant?"

All eyes on the jury fall on me. I try to look uninterested. Dignified-calm-personable-these-are-outrageous-charges-I'm-not-obsessive-easygoing-innocent.

"Yes."

Mandy, who has been scribbling notes, stops in her tracks. She doesn't look up, or even move. Paul's hands, which are clasped on the table, tighten up.

"You talked with the defendant."

"Yes."

"You talked about your conversation with me."

"That wasn't the reason I called. I wanted to see how he was doing."

"But you also talked about *our* conversation."

"Yes."

"Did you tell the defendant the things I asked you?"

"Yes."

"Did you tell him the answers you gave me?"

"Yes."

"And he told you about the food, and the coffee on his desk."

Deb pauses. Her eyes shoot briefly at me.

"The answers aren't over there," Flaherty says, pointing to me, actually walking toward me. "Isn't it true that the defendant told you to say that there was food and cold coffee sitting on his desk the morning of November nineteenth?"

"He didn't tell me to say that."

"But he told you about it, didn't he?"

"He reminded me."

"Oh, he *reminded* you. So he told you about the food and coffee, you said you didn't remember, and he said, well, now you do."

"Objection," Paul says. "It's a compound question."

"Well then, I'll be happy to break the question up," Flaherty offers, hitting full stride now. "Ms. Glatz, when you had this conversation with the defendant, he told you that there was food and coffee sitting on his desk on the morning of November nineteenth."

"He mentioned it."

"He mentioned it. And you told him you didn't remember that."

"I—I hadn't—it hadn't—"

"You didn't *remember* it at that time, did you?"

"I guess"—Deb looks down and takes a breath—"no."

"And he said, well, that's what happened."

"Something like that."

I grab Mandy's pen and notepad and start scribbling.

"So you're covering for him, aren't you, Ms. Glatz?" Flaherty gives her accusation quietly, with an edge of sympathy, making it even more deadly. "You're covering for your boss."

Deb's hands grip the railing. "I'm not lying. If Marty says it's the truth, then I believe him."

Flaherty nods, keeping her calm and getting further under Deb's skin in the process. "You accepted it as the truth, because he told you it was."

"If he says it's what happened, then I believe him."

The prosecutor bows her head slightly, like she's talking to a child. "But just for the record, when you were telling this jury about the food and coffee from your boss's desk— you didn't know that from your own personal memory."

"No." Deb is near tears now.

"You were telling us what your boss told you to say."

"I—he didn't—" Deb shakes her head as a tear falls.

Flaherty gives Deb a moment, so the jury can fully take in the protective secretary doing what her boss told her to do, before she thanks Deb quietly and sits down.

Paul reads the notes I've scribbled to him. Then he stands. "Ms. Glatz, did Marty ever tell you to lie?"

"No," she says, dabbing at her cheek with a tissue, "he didn't."

"In fact, he told you only to tell the truth, didn't he?"

Deb is pale now, and she has me to thank for this basting she took. She has every reason to crucify me if she wants to.

"Yes," she says. "He only told me to tell the truth. And that's all I have done."

"Everything you have said here, you believe to be true."

"That's right."

"That's all I have, Your Honor," Paul says calmly. That's all he has for Deb, he means. It is by no means all he has for me.

69

"SHE CALLED ME, PAUL. WHAT WAS I SUPPOSED TO do?"

"Tell her to call *us,* first of all," Paul says. "Don't talk to her your*self*! And if you *do* talk to her, *tell us* about it! Marty, haven't you learned *any*thing?"

We are in Paul's office in the law firm. He is hovering near his desk, pacing back and forth. He has spent the last ten minutes lambasting me. Mandy sits silently in the chair next to mine.

"Can you honestly say it would have affected the way you examined Deb?" I ask.

Paul looks at me with exasperation. "Is *that* the criteria you use in deciding whether to tell me something? Whether *you* think it will change the strategy?" He sits down in his chair, a tall oak chair with a maroon back. His glass desk is covered neatly with personal memorabilia, a pen set with a marble base, the inscription from one of our former mayors; a photo of his wife and three kids in a simple all-glass frame; a rectangular silver tray that holds his incoming mail; a glass ashtray that he fills with cinnamon candy. "I've seen dozens of people think they're amateur lawyers, think they know what's best for them. Let me tell you, Marty, they *don't.*"

"What we don't know can hurt you," Mandy says quietly, eyes forward. "You can't expect us to win this trial if we don't know everything. I wonder how many times we'll have to say that before you believe it."

I turn to Mandy. "Did you have something specific in mind?"

Mandy still doesn't look at me. "How would *I* know what I don't know?"

My relationship with Mandy hasn't been the same since I changed my story and said I didn't kill the doctor. There is something lost between us. Trust. It hurt her more than I ever would have realized. Since then, she has been nothing more than my lawyer. Sympathetic, attentive, supportive, polite in conversation, but distant. Not my friend. Not like before. It wasn't that I killed Dr. Reinardt, because I said I did all along. It was that I changed the story, that I didn't trust her and Paul to help me tell the truth. Paul welcomed the change in my story; Christ, he practically begged me to do it without saying so directly. But not Mandy. She was disappointed. I wasn't the person she thought I was. Whoever *that* was.

"So?" Paul says. "Any other surprises lurking out there for us?"

I say nothing.

"Do you want to walk out of that courtroom a free man?"

I stare at him.

"Because if there's some bombshell out there, and I don't know about it, I can't help you."

"I get the point." I rise from my chair, unsteady. "I have enough people trying to beat me up now. Including two people who have a metal chair and a cyanide pill with my name on it."

Paul shakes his head.

"I'm the client," I say. "*You* work for *me*. Got that? I will tell you what I goddamn *want* to tell you. And if that means we lose, well then, that means *I* lose, not you. You'll still get your fee, then you'll run off to your next trial and your next million. *You* won't spend your next five or six years waiting to die, meeting your friendly neighbors who think you're the next best thing to a woman. *You* won't taste cyanide gas while you try to breathe another breath." I head for the door, turning before I leave. "This is happening to *me*, not you. This is happening to *me*!"

70

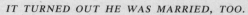

IT TURNED OUT HE WAS MARRIED, TOO.

He had a son I went to high school with. I actually liked the kid. I wonder if he knew.

I waited for her to leave the house first. At fifteen, I only had a driver's permit, but my parents had already handed down their old Chevy for when I got my license.

It wasn't hard to follow her. Once I saw her turn left out of the driveway, I knew she was headed for the main east-west street that essentially took you anyplace you were headed. There would be enough traffic so I could hang back but keep an eye on her. She wouldn't be looking for me, anyway.

They met at an apartment complex near the high school baseball field. The parking lot was bordered by a hedge. Once I saw her turn into the lot, I parked my car and sprinted along the hedge, keeping low.

They weren't even that discreet. It was pretty far removed from the main thoroughfare, a good three towns over from where both of them lived. Still, they could have waited until they got inside before embracing, running their hands over each other.

The winds are much calmer than they were six months ago. It's a pretty mild evening, no lower than thirty-five or so outside. I probably don't need a jacket; at any rate, I don't have one, just my suit coat from court today. There are no leaves this time, only a dry crumbly path for my wing tips to plod over.

When I make it through the trees into the clearing, I look up, as I always did. The stars are littering the sky tonight, promising, reassuring, casting a shiny silver light on my face, lending a dreamy quality to the scene. This is why I have always stopped here when I crossed through the woods—the surreal calm, the fantastic hope of a future with Rachel, all of this I could find in this impossibly vast sky. Now, as I gaze upward, the hope is for something that is surprisingly less urgent, but no less heartfelt. It is not simply that I want to be free. That is not nearly enough. It's that I want to start over. And for a moment I believe that I will never bring my eyes back down from the stars, that if I stare into them long enough I will be lifted from everything in my life, that I'll be given that clean slate. But I know that I will lower my eyes again, as I always do. Despite their majesty, their purity, their promise, the stars are impossibly distant.

I slow my pace to a walk now, letting the light breeze touch my face. I move slowly, savoring this moment, one of the last such ones I may have. The hill is just as steep as it ever was, but with all the running I've been doing, it is a much easier climb than it was on November 18, even with my shoes slipping on the grass. It's funny, my physical condition is the one thing in my life that has improved since I last stood here.

I park myself at the oak tree. I undo the top button of my shirt and pull down on my tie. And I watch the house.

The lights are on upstairs. It's dark downstairs, with the exception of the patio light, whose light does not reach the spot where I'm standing. The blind is pulled in the bedroom window. There is nothing to see. No silhouettes pass.

After a time, I slide down the oak tree and sit on the damp grass. I pull out a blade of grass and put it in my teeth, just staring up at the sky. Staring up at her, assuming she's up there. Knowing her, she managed to charm her way into the pearly gates. A flirtatious wink to St. Peter and all sins were forgiven. Come on in, Adrian. We saved you a good seat.

I never confronted her. Never told anyone, not Dad, not Jamie. Things just kept on, from that first time when I was eight. There was never a dramatic break, never a single defining moment in our relationship. It's probably because I was too young when it happened, didn't understand exactly what it was that I had seen, just knew that whatever it was, it was bad. I suppose if I looked back, there was a rift between us from that moment on, but if there was, it was subtle. It's funny, my first feelings of betrayal didn't involve my father at all. It was just me. She had betrayed *me*! But I was far too young to be independent from my mother, and she played the role of the nurturing mommy with great skill. So on we went for a good two years, me having some idea that my mom had done something bad, but not confronting her or myself about it; Adrian acting like nothing had happened.

But like with any other boys, it wasn't more than a couple of years later that I was sneaking into R-rated movies and catching the occasional porno supplied by a friend with an older brother. It was during one of those movies that the light turned on. Those films weren't exactly plot-intensive, but this one involved a woman who was cheating on her husband. There they were, all legs and thrusts, screwing away in the bedroom, and suddenly the woman was Adrian and the man was the same nameless, faceless man from that day. I knew then what my mommy had done to my daddy.

Still, I let it go. I pretended. It didn't happen. It was an isolated incident. When I was fifteen, I had my first girlfriend. I felt for the first time what it meant to have any sort of a romantic bond with someone. It was then that the anger began to swell. And I started watching my mother. I picked up on trends. She left, two mornings a week even before I did, to run "errands." And then I followed her and saw them. He was a real estate agent who worked on the PTA with Adrian. Early mornings were the best times, I guess.

I brush a hair off my face. Still no movement upstairs. I can't see her. Just the shade, colored yellow from the inside light.

That was my day, I guess, seeing Adrian and that guy. The loss of innocence. Doesn't everyone have a day like that, that one identifiable moment or shot of dread, where a child realizes for the first time that the world can be bad, where the roof is ripped off the shelter, and he understands that he'll need a protective coating for the rest of his life? Whether it's your parents divorcing, your mom getting cancer, the first time someone calls you "nigger," your dad losing his job. Maybe it's a testament to my upbringing that this moment didn't hit me until age eight. But this is the question I have never understood: Why can't I get past it?

Movement upstairs, I think, a brief silhouette past the shade. I wait for another pass. Just as I'd been waiting for twenty-some years. She was my cure. Rachel, this beautiful, sexy, confident creature, got me past it. I think of the good old days, standing out here, watching her. How very simple it was. The jolt to my heart, that burst of adrenaline I felt, when that curtain slid open on the glass door. That indescribable feeling of being off balance, panicked, excited, *alive*!

"I won't betray you." I will keep my commitment to you. I will prove to you, to my sister Jamie, to Adrian, to myself, that I can do it. No matter what happens. Because if they take everything else away from me, they can't take that.

I take a deep breath and rip a handful of grass out of the lawn. I notice a flicker out of the corner of my eye. I look back up at the bedroom window. The room is dark now.

There's something else. Something unresolved. My eyes move back above the house, to the sky. Then they close.

"Help me understand," I whisper absently.

71

I WALK INTO THE COURTROOM AT TWO MINUTES TO nine. Paul and Mandy turn at the sound of the doors opening. The judge is already seated on the bench. The jury box is empty. I mumble an apology to my lawyers as I take my seat between them.

"Perhaps now that Mr. Kalish has graced us with his presence," Judge Mack says, "we can begin."

I make a point of looking at the clock on the side wall and making a wrinkled face, what's-the-big-deal. The minute hand is two minutes shy of the hour. Then I look at the judge, who is staring down at me.

"Is there something you wanted to say to me, Mr. Kalish?" says Judge Mack.

Yeah, there is. The trial starts at nine. I'm on time. Go fuck yourself.

I look at the floor. "Nope," I say in a flat voice, hoping to convey utter disinterest.

The jury files in a moment later. Mandy pushes a notepad in front of me. "Forget about last night," it reads. "Don't cop an attitude in front of the *jury*!!"

I turn my head toward her without making eye contact. I move the notepad back in front of her and straighten out a hand for reassurance.

Roger Ogren walks to the lectern and calls Janet Brewer, the cop who spied on me at the Christmas party. I look over at Gretchen Flaherty. She performed well yesterday with Debra. And she, more than anybody, knows it. Today she holds her head a little higher, her back a little straighter. She is on her way up in her career, a promising young trial lawyer looking to use me as a notch, her first big one.

I recognize Janet Brewer as she passes the defense table on the way to the witness stand. I remember her from the foundation Christmas party. The short, gray-haired woman with her hair in a bun. I caught her eyeballing me as I made my way through the crowd aimlessly, waiting for Rachel to be alone. She looked away when I saw her.

Her hair is the same way today, pulled back severely. Her face is taut, her expression formal. She does not look like a pleasant person. Not that I expected us to become tennis partners.

"I was assigned to the Reinardt case," she tells us. "My assignment was to attend the Christmas party thrown by the Reinardt Family Children's Foundation. It was our understanding that Mrs. Reinardt was going to be present."

"And what was your purpose for being at the party?"

"To look for anything suspicious. The case was still in its preliminary stages, and we thought it was possible that Mrs. Reinardt was involved in her husband's disappearance. And even if she wasn't, we thought perhaps the person who broke in to the house was someone at the foundation. Someone who might be at the party."

"Okay. Where was this party?"

"At the Winston Hotel, downtown."

"What day was it held?"

"Friday, December third. In the evening."

"What time did you arrive, Officer?"

"About seven o'clock."

"What did you do?"

"I mingled. I made up some name and said I had just joined the foundation. I just sort of blended in."

"What time did Mrs. Reinardt arrive?"

"About seven-thirty."

"And did there come a time that evening that the defendant showed up?"

"Yes. The defendant arrived right at nine-thirty."

"Did you have occasion to observe him?"

See, this is why I find Ogren so unappealing. He uses phrases like "have occasion to" and "subsequent," like this

is how lawyers are supposed to talk. Did she *have occasion*
to see me? This is where Paul Riley shows his superiority in
the courtroom. He speaks the jury's language. *Did you see
the defendant?* Ogren is under the mistaken notion that he
appears more intelligent and authoritative when he uses
lawyer-speak, when really he just sounds overbearing and
self-absorbed. The things people miss about themselves.

"Yes," the detective answers.

"Please describe what you observed."

Officer Brewer bows her head a moment and clears her
throat, then looks up. She's got this testimony down pat.
Probably said it into the mirror a hundred times.

"The defendant spoke with a couple of people for a few
minutes. He turned his head often to look toward the door.
I looked over at the door. I saw Mrs. Reinardt."

"She was standing near the door?"

"Yes."

"Alone?"

"No. She was talking to two people."

"Go on."

"The defendant went to the bar and ordered a drink. Then
he spoke with another man at the bar. Then that person left,
leaving the defendant alone at the bar. He just stared toward
the door. Again, I followed his stare to Mrs. Reinardt.

"Then he had another drink, and then another. One person
approached him and tried to make conversation. I wasn't
close enough to hear what was said, but the defendant ig-
nored this person for the most part. He never once looked at
that person. He kept looking toward the door. Toward Mrs.
Reinardt."

"What happened next?"

"The defendant then started walking around the room, cutting through people. He kept turning and looking toward the
door. He walked through a bunch of people, not saying *anything* to *anybody*. Then a woman stopped him, and they had
a brief conversation. But in the middle of that conversation,
the defendant walked away from her, toward the door. I
looked over at Mrs. Reinardt, and the two people she was

talking to were gone. Now there was only a single woman talking to her."

"What did you see the defendant do subsequent to his conversation with this woman?"

"He walked up to Mrs. Reinardt. After a moment or two, the other woman left, leaving the defendant and Mrs. Reinardt alone."

"Describe what happened next."

"They talked. The defendant stood very close to Mrs. Reinardt. Closer than she *wanted,* it looked like."

"Objection," Mandy says. "There's no foundation for that remark. The witness has no idea what other people wanted or didn't want." Mandy has the same way of objecting as Paul, making a point to the jury at the same time she makes her case to the judge.

"Sustained."

Brewer doesn't even wait for another question. "Well, as he leaned in toward her, she sort of leaned *back.*"

"She leaned away from him?"

"Yes."

Bullshit.

"Please continue."

"They talked for about two minutes. The defendant put his hand on her arm as he talked. I believe Mrs. Reinardt started to cry. Then the defendant got even closer to her, and he said one last thing to her. Then he walked out of the party and never returned."

"He left the party?"

"Yes."

"What time was that?"

"Nine-fifty-five."

"But you said he arrived at nine-thirty."

"Yes, he did. He left the party only twenty-five minutes after arriving. Right after he finally got to talk to Mrs. Reinardt."

"Thank you, Officer Brewer. No more questions, Your Honor."

Mandy gets out of her chair slowly and walks halfway

between the defense table and the witness stand, her hands clasped behind her back. "Officer Brewer, you don't have any idea whether Marty Kalish was feeling sick the night of the Christmas party, do you?"

"Sick? He had three glasses of scotch."

"Which, if you aren't feeling well, is going to make you feel even worse."

"I don't know if he was feeling sick or not."

"You have no idea."

"That's right."

"So it is entirely possible that Marty showed up at the party, made a go of it, and decided that he just didn't feel well enough to stay."

"He didn't look like he had the flu."

"Oh, really? Did you take his temperature?"

"Of course not."

"As a matter of fact, you never got closer than, say, fifteen or twenty feet from Marty, isn't that right?"

"Something like that."

"So you were never close enough to Marty to have any *clue* whether he felt sick."

"*Obviously,* I can't say for certain whether he was sick or not. Most people with the flu don't throw down three glasses of scotch in the space of twenty minutes."

"I never said the flu. You did."

"Well, whatever."

"So I repeat. Isn't it possible that Marty went to the party, tried to make a go of it, then decided that he just wasn't up to it and left?"

The officer seems more amused by this than anything. "That is possible, yes."

Mandy nods and pauses. "You thought it was unusual that Marty went over to talk to Mrs. Reinardt?"

Brewer makes a face. "Well, he seemed pretty interested in speaking with her. He was looking over at her the whole time he was there."

"What I'm asking is, what was so unusual about the fact

that Marty went over to talk to her? I mean, what was so suspicious about that?"

This is a softball for Officer Brewer, and Mandy is hoping she'll take a big swing of the bat. Again, there is the *Miranda* issue for my appeal, should I be convicted. If Brewer says I was acting strangely—which obviously would have gotten back to Cummings—then that makes me all the more of a suspect when Cummings interrogated me the next day. It's a pretty good weapon we've had against the testifying cops in this case, preventing them from exaggerating my actions. Although every time I've heard my attorneys flirt with the issue, I've felt a shot to the gut. It's a good tactic, I realize, but also an acknowledgment that my attorneys are preparing for a guilty verdict.

Officer Brewer has done a pretty good job describing my behavior in her direct testimony, limiting herself to what I did, not how I seemed. Mandy is giving her another chance to step off the tightrope.

"The fact that he talked to Mrs. Reinardt?" she says. "I don't know. By itself, I suppose there was nothing unusual about that. Depending on what he said."

"You didn't hear what he said, did you?"

"I didn't, no. You'd have to ask Mrs. Reinardt."

Something tells me they *did* ask Rachel. I'm not looking forward to the answer.

"He wasn't acting strangely, was he?" says Mandy.

"I would say he seemed pretty interested in talking to Mrs. Reinardt."

"You considered that strange?"

"No."

"So he wasn't acting strangely?"

"I don't know if that's strange or not. He was interested in talking to her, is all."

"In fact," Mandy says, "you observed many people from the foundation approach Mrs. Reinardt that night." Mandy realizes she's not getting anywhere with her plan. Brewer is not going to comment on my demeanor, whether I was suspicious or strange. So Mandy is going to take that and use it to show I *wasn't* behaving suspiciously.

"Several people approached her, yes."

"Here was a woman whose husband had disappeared a few weeks earlier."

"That's right."

"And people were offering her comfort and support."

"I don't know *what* they were offering her."

"Because you weren't close enough to hear."

"That's right."

"So, Officer Brewer, isn't it possible that Marty simply showed up at the party to be a friend for Mrs. Reinardt, despite the fact that he was feeling sick?"

"Like I said, I don't know."

"So it's possible."

"How would I know?"

"You *don't* know."

"That's right."

"And it's possible that Marty waited his turn to talk to her, so he could show her his support, and then he left to go home."

"That's possible."

"Thank you."

Mandy walks over to our table and takes her seat. Gretchen Flaherty stands and says she has no redirect.

72

VICTOR SILAS LOOKS AT THE FLOOR AS HE WALKS past the defense table. He shifts around in the seat on the witness stand, adjusts the microphone, then his glasses, then his tie. He doesn't look in my direction.

Vic always seemed kind of stiff, so he's in typical form

today. But there's an edge to his voice as he speaks, and he is much quieter than usual. He licks his lips and fools with his glasses in between nearly every question.

"I work in the outreach projects," he says.

Roger Ogren opens a hand. "Can you explain that?"

"The whole reason we have the foundation is to help disadvantaged children. Some of it is just providing money to shelters and orphanages. But we also sponsor outings, athletic leagues, tutoring. The hands-on work."

"Did you work closely with the defendant?"

Vic nods reluctantly. "Marty was on the fund-raising committee. He did things like mail solicitations, speaking lunches, organizing some of the bigger events. I was on that committee too, at least in a nominal sense. In a way, *everyone* was on that committee."

The outreach people kind of looked down their noses at people like me, who didn't do *real* time, as they called it, spending time with the kids. They saw us as people who did the few hours a week to soothe our consciences, and mingling with pretty deep pockets in the process. There was always kind of a rift in the foundation between the money people and the "true" volunteers.

"Did you work closely with the defendant?"

"We ran around in the same circle of friends at the foundation."

"You mentioned the fund-raising committee. Did you also work with the defendant at some of these outreach programs?"

"Yeah. Marty did some of that work."

"Do you recall a fund-raiser in the spring of last year at the Pierce Museum?"

"Sure. It was probably the biggest thing we had ever put on."

"You attended that fund-raiser?"

"Yes."

"Did the defendant attend?"

"Yes."

"Did Mrs. Reinardt attend?"

"Yes, she did."

"Did Dr. Reinardt?"

The jurors, already attentive, light up at the sound of the victim's name. This is the first time they have heard him mentioned as a living, breathing person, and they no doubt are expecting this testimony to hold some relevance.

"Yes. He was there, too."

"Do you recall what time the party broke up?"

"People began to filter out at around ten-thirty. By eleven, pretty much the only people left were foundation members."

"Did that include you and the defendant?"

"Yes."

"Was Mrs. Reinardt still there?"

"Yes."

"Was her husband, Dr. Reinardt, still there?"

"No. He had left. He said he had been called away to surgery."

Okay, the jurors are thinking. Now we're getting somewhere. This is not the hard-evidence sort of stuff—time, place, opportunity. This is the juicy, gossipy stuff. Let's see what a slimeball Marty Kalish was.

"Was there any particular reason the foundation members were still there?"

Vic adjusts his glasses. "We had to clean up."

"What did that include?"

"Well, the theme was Vegas night, a casino. There was money all over the place, and pledge cards. Our job was to gather all the money and pledges and count them up."

"Was that a big chore?"

"Oh, yeah. We raised almost a quarter of a million dollars that night."

"Can you estimate how many foundation members stayed around that evening to record the money?"

Vic sighs. "I'd say about fifteen of us. The junior people got stuck with the job."

"Do you recall what time Dr. Reinardt left the party to perform his surgery?"

"Oh, I'd have to say around ten."

"What time did the junior volunteers start counting up the money?"

"About eleven."

"And the defendant was one of those people?"

"Yeah, Marty helped."

"How late did *you* stay, Mr. Silas?"

"It took us just past one in the morning."

"So, a little over two hours?"

"Yes."

"Do you recall what time the defendant left?"

Vic pauses and clears his throat. "I couldn't say for certain."

"*About* what time?"

"I'd say about eleven-thirty."

Ogren pauses, watching some of the jurors write this down. "An hour and a half before you. How did you know he left?"

"I saw him."

"Can you describe what you saw?"

Vic scratches his cheek. "I—a couple of us were talking to Rachel."

"Rachel Reinardt?"

"Yeah. She was thanking us for our work, that sort of thing."

"Where was this?"

"In the room where we were all working."

"Go on."

"Well, we were just talking a little bit. Then Rachel kind of looked off behind us."

"Did you turn around to see what she was looking at?"

"Yeah."

"And what was it?"

"Well, Marty was standing back away from us."

"The defendant?"

"Yes."

"Did he walk up and join your little group?"

"No. He sort of hung back."

Ogren sits back a moment, as the jury watches Vic.

"He hung back. Did he say anything at all?"

"No."

"Did it seem strange that he would hang back like that?"

"Objection."

"Sustained."

"Okay, what happened next?"

"Mrs. Reinardt excused herself, and she walked over to Marty."

"Then what?"

"Then they left."

"Together?"

"Yes."

"This was around eleven-thirty."

"Right."

"Was the defendant what you would call a junior member of the group, like you?"

"Marty joined after I did. Yes."

"You would have expected him to stick around and help count the money."

"Objection," Paul says. "Number one, lack of foundation. Number two, Mr. Ogren is leading the witness. Number three, it is irrelevant."

Judge Potluck shakes his head. "The question will stand. Sir, please answer the question."

"Well, there was no set rule or anything. We were all just volunteers. But I guess I thought he would have stuck around."

Ogren does that little nod he does and brings a fist to his chin. "Now, Mr. Silas, did you ever have occasion to speak with the defendant about that evening's fund-raiser?"

"I spoke with him."

"Can you tell us when, and where, this took place?"

"It was at a Chinese restaurant downtown, the following Monday. For lunch."

"Who was there?"

"Two other guys from the foundation, and Marty and I."

"Did you discuss the fact that the defendant had left the party with Mrs. Reinardt?"

"Yes."

"Can you tell us what was said?"

"Well, it was like we were sort of kidding around with him. You know, he had left the party with Rachel. I mean, it was pretty childish stuff. We were making sort of crude suggestions to him about what happened after he and Rachel left the party. You know, like they"—he waves his hands a little, searching for the words—"we were just suggesting that maybe something had happened between them. But we were just kidding around."

"What did the defendant say *had* happened between Mrs. Reinardt and him that night, after they left the party?"

"Well—I mean, he didn't—"

"Mr. Silas. Was one of the people at your table a man named Jerry Lazarus?"

"Yeah, Jerry was there."

"Did Jerry Lazarus say that he had tried to call—"

"Objection!" Paul says, interrupting Ogren. "May we approach?"

Paul and Roger Ogren walk up to the bench.

When I called your house, Laz had said to me at that lunch with his patented smirk, *and no one answered, I thought maybe you had car trouble or something.*

This is the statement Ogren was about to recite, establishing that I was not at home several hours after I had left with Rachel. The prosecutors questioned Laz about this after Silas told them about the conversation. Laz lied, said he had no memory of that. Nate Hornsby said the same thing. We might have to call one or both of these people to rebut Silas.

But still, I don't catch the drift here. Ogren has already told the jury, as has Cummings, that Rachel and I didn't have an affair. So why suggest that I was away from home for hours? Why suggest that I was at Rachel's?

I look over at Vic as the lawyers confer. He is looking at me as I turn to him, but then he breaks eye contact and plays with his glasses.

I think of how this case has affected my friends. I put words into Deb's mouth that came back to haunt her. Laz and Nate Hornsby flat-out lied to the police. Three people have been tarnished by this. Three decent people have gone against their better judgment and stood up for me out of some sense of friendship. None of them, I'm quite sure, believes that I am innocent of this crime. Jerry knows that I admitted to my lawyers that I did it. Deb and Nate, at the very least, are not sure. Part of them wonders whether I did it, whether I had it in me. But that hasn't stopped any of them from coming through for me. I wonder if I will ever be friends again with Nate and Deb. Whether this will always be a barrier. The sad thing is, that's the least of my concerns.

Paul walks back to his seat. Ogren returns to the lectern.

"The objection is sustained. The jury should disregard the question."

"Mr. Silas," Ogren continues, "I realize you say that everyone was kidding around at the table. But understanding that, did anyone ask the defendant what had happened between Mrs. Reinardt and him after the party?"

"I don't know if it was directly asked. It was a very sarcastic conversation."

Ogren is struggling with this. He takes a moment to gather his thoughts.

"At that lunch, did the defendant give any explanation for what had happened later that night, after he had left the party with Mrs. Reinardt?"

"Well—well, he—he wasn't *serious*."

"What did he say?" asks Roger Ogren.

Vic wears a troubled look now. "He said he had car trouble that night."

"He said he had *car* trouble?"

"Well—yes."

That statement, in isolation, might be confusing to the jury. They don't know what question I was answering. But I imagine they can guess. I was making an excuse for why I got home so late.

"Following that evening at the fund-raiser, did you continue to work in some of the foundation's outreach programs?"

"Yes."

"Did the defendant also work at these programs with you?"

"Yes, he did."

"Did you notice anything different about the way he conducted himself at these activities?"

Paul objects. "The question is vague. If Mr. Ogren has a direct question, let him ask it."

"All right," says Ogren, "I'll ask it. Mr. Silas, did you observe any differences in the defendant's interaction with Mrs. Reinardt at these activities?"

"I guess you could say so. I mean, who can really say?"

Vic, buddy, I appreciate your hesitancy. But it's a little late. If you were going to hold back, you should have done that when Ogren first interviewed you.

"Please tell us what you observed, Mr. Silas."

"I guess I would say Marty was more attentive to Rachel."

"Attentive?"

"Well, he spent more time around her. He—seemed like he was trying to be around her more, I guess."

"Would you say he followed her around?"

"Objection. Leading the witness."

"Sustained."

"Well, Mr. Silas, can you explain what you mean when you say he tried to be around her more?"

Vic shrugs his shoulders. "I guess you could say he followed her around a lot."

"Can you give us any examples of how he followed her around a lot?"

"Well"—Vic sighs—"like we had this basketball league we sponsored. We would load the kids into a couple of vans and drive them to the gym. Marty wanted to drive in the same van as Rachel. Rachel sat in the back with the kids, and Marty volunteered to drive the van. He wasn't supposed to, because he wasn't insured as the driver. But he sort of insisted."

"He was told at first that he couldn't drive it?"

"Yeah."

"How did he react to that?"

"He got mad. He said something like—well, he just wanted to drive that van."

Ogren adjusts his glasses. "Did you ever notice any reaction from Mrs. Reinardt when the defendant, as you put it, followed her around?"

"I don't know. Maybe sometimes."

"Can you tell about those times?"

Vic thinks about this. "Like one time, we were doing this play—I can't remember which one—but we were doing a play with a bunch of the kids. And we were setting up, you know. And Rachel, she's in charge, of course, and she was walking around, just supervising. Not necessarily doing anything, just walking around checking on other people. And Marty was following her, talking to her."

"How did Mrs. Reinardt appear to react?"

"She—I mean, I can't say for sure. But she looked like she was annoyed. She gave him kind of a mean look. And she said we didn't need two supervisors. That maybe he should try helping out, and not just following her around."

"Did examples like the one you just gave happen often?"

"I don't know. A few times, I would say."

"I see. Now, after that casino fund-raiser, was there anything different about the *extent* of the defendant's participation in these foundation activities?"

Vic swallows hard. He seems to be lost in thought, lost in *guilt,* maybe? Is he wishing he could turn back? "Could you repeat that?" he asks.

"Would you say that the defendant's involvement in the foundation increased, decreased, or stayed the same after the casino fund-raiser?"

"Oh. It seemed like Marty started attending more functions. He pretty much had stuck to fund-raising before. But after that big casino night, he started going to pretty much everything."

"Did you ever ask him *why* he started attending more functions?"

"No."

"Did it ever come up in conversation?"

Vic grimaces a little. "We may have teased him about it a little bit."

"How so?"

"Well, just making comments about him and Rachel."

"What kind of comments?"

Paul stands and objects. "The witness has testified that whatever comments were made were made in jest. I fail to see the relevancy of their content."

"The relevancy is in their effect on the defendant, his reaction to them," Ogren says.

The judge overrules. Ogren repeats the question to Victor.

"I don't know. We said things like, 'Doesn't Rachel look good today? How's Rachel doing?' Stuff like that."

"And how did the defendant"—Ogren opens up toward me—"respond?"

"Usually with silence. He wouldn't say anything at all. Sometimes he would get mad at us a little. But it was no big deal. I don't want to overstate it or anything."

Roger Ogren flips his notepad closed as Vic gives this answer. This was his last question, but he stops at Victor's last statements. He's clearly not satisfied with the way Vic qualified his answer. Finally, though, he thanks Vic and sits down.

Paul doesn't have much to ask Vic Silas. No, Vic admits, Marty never said anything about being romantically involved with Rachel. No, Marty never even said that he found her attractive. No, Vic didn't know me all that well; he was more friends with Nate Hornsby, who was my friend. We didn't talk very often, Vic and I.

I only half listen to Paul's examination. He's not going to get much out of Vic that is helpful. The jury must believe by now that I at least had some sort of crush on Rachel.

The court recesses for lunch. Mandy asks me, are we at least going to eat lunch together? I nod, yes. I'm not going to eat, anyway. My thoughts are not on lunch, or on Victor Silas. I can think only of what will come after lunch, when the prosecution in the *People* v. *Kalish* will call its next, and perhaps final, witness.

73

THE BAILIFF CALLS TO THE GUARD BY THE DOOR. "Rachel Reinardt."

I don't turn to look. I will let her fade into my peripheral vision as she approaches the witness stand. I will let the smell of her cologne reach me, will listen to the sound of her voice, before I actually look at her. This must happen in increments. I have to keep a grip on my emotions.

Rachel's shoes tap along the floor of the courtroom, virtually the only sound, certainly the only sound I hear. Her blue leather flats, sounds like. Good for walking a tightrope.

She told them I followed her around. The jury already knows this from Vic Silas. She said I seemed infatuated with her. That's subjective, something I can deny. She said I was outside her house sometimes. That hurts a little, but I can be the trusted friend who was worried about the spousal abuse.

It's her usual perfume. Nothing overpowering, just a light, springlike scent. My hands begin to tremble. I very casually place them facedown on the table. I nod my head a little to seem very casual; the jury probably notices I have not looked up. I turn to my left, to Mandy, who instinctively leans into me. She knows I have nothing to say, so she whispers, "No problem."

"Do you swear that the testimony you are about to give is the truth, the whole truth, and nothing but the truth?"

"I do." It's her voice, but not the one I'm accustomed to hearing. She is quiet, guarded. God, this must be so difficult for her. She has had to fight off a murder charge, find a middle road to cut a deal without really hurting me. And now she will walk an even thinner line.

Oh, she's so beautiful. Her eyes shine, her hair so delicate and luscious, cut into a bob with the ends curling onto her cheeks. Her thin, even eyebrows quiver slightly.

"Will you please state your name for the record?" Roger Ogren asks.

She brushes a hair off her face. "Rachel Ann Reinardt," she says quietly.

Rachel tells Ogren where she lives, what she does for a living, where she grew up. She talks about her husband very generally. They married just over five years ago, flew to Italy for their honeymoon, moved from downtown to Highland Woods three years ago and started the foundation.

"Mrs. Reinardt, do you know the defendant?"

She turns to me. She needs me, still, she is saying. Still. Hold me, make this go away for me.

"Yes," she says.

"When did you first meet him?"

"Marty started working at the foundation about a year ago."

"How did you first meet him?"

She pauses, her mouth opening slightly. "I think it was at my house. My husband and I would have the volunteers over from time to time. We wanted to express our appreciation for all of their hard work."

"And when was this first meeting with the defendant?"

"Probably close to Christmas, the year before last."

Ogren leans forward. "Mrs. Reinardt, I'll have to ask you to keep your voice up."

"I'm sorry," she says, raising her chin.

"Did you notice anything unusual about him?"

"No. He was a nice young man."

"Did you work closely with him at the foundation?"

"Not at first. Marty worked on the fund-raising committee. My husband was more involved in that side of the foundation. I was more involved in the projects."

"All right. Now, I want to take you to March of last year. Up until that time, had you worked closely with the defendant?"

"No."

"In March of last year, did the foundation hold a fund-raiser?"

"Yes, we did."

"Can you describe the fund-raiser?"

Her head makes a half turn to the jury. "The Pierce Museum lent us their Prehistoric Room. It's the biggest room in the museum. We had over a thousand people on hand. Politicians, business leaders. From around the country. It was our most ambitious fund-raiser to date." Her pride in her work lifts her voice, for the first time today, above the flat monotone.

"Do you recall if the defendant was present at that fund-raiser?"

She nods.

"Please give a verbal answer, Mrs. Reinardt."

"Yes. Marty was there."

"Did you speak with him that night?"

"I spoke with him briefly during the party. I really can't recall what was said."

You have to be the youngest person in this room, Mr. Kalish.

"It was just small talk."

"Did there come a time that evening that your husband was called away?"

"Yes. He was called off to surgery at the hospital."

"And he left?"

"Yes."

"What time did he leave?"

"About ten-thirty."

I'm sorry your husband had to leave.

I don't think he's sorry.

"But you stayed."

Rachel nods. "I stayed until the last guest left."

"And that was what time?"

"Maybe a little after eleven."

"Mrs. Reinardt—please—keep your voice up?"

Rachel shakes her head lightly. "I'm sorry. A little after eleven."

"Great. Did you speak with the defendant at any time after your husband left?"

"Yes."

Are you going to get home all right?

Why, Mr. Kalish, are you offering me a ride home?

"He approached me shortly after my husband left. He asked me if he could give me a ride home."

"How did you respond?"

"Well. My husband had taken the car. I needed a ride home."

"Did you accept?"

"Yes."

"When did you leave with the defendant?"

"Oh. Eleven-fifteen, maybe."

"Okay. You went to his car?"

"Yes. We walked to his car, and he drove me home."

"Did you have a conversation in the car?"

Rachel nods, her eyes fixed on the floor.

"Please give a verbal response, Mrs. Reinardt." Ogren's tone has hardened somewhat. He had to know Rachel would be less than enthusiastic today, but he seems concerned with her attitude.

"Yes, Mr. Ogren, we had a conversation in my car."

"What did he say to you?"

She looks up over Ogren's head, staring off for a moment. Slowly, her eyes fall to her lap. "He said I was—I was attractive. Things like that."

That didn't happen. I start to fall back in my chair but catch myself. She has to give them something. I knew this. I knew this.

"Did you respond?"

She shakes her head, her eyes glassy.

"Mrs. Reinardt? Did you respond?"

"No."

"Did he say anything else?"

Rachel wets her lips. "He said my husband—he—didn't appreciate me."

She has to give them something.

"Did he say anything else?"

"Well. He did say—he asked me for a tour of my house."

Have you ever been to our house, Marty?

Would you like a tour?

"He asked to come inside your house?"

"Yes."

"Did you agree to that?"

"Not at first. But he asked again. I didn't want to be rude."

"So you went inside with him?"

"Yes."

"And?"

"I—I started showing him around. But he—he just walked into the den and sat down. He asked me to fix him a drink."

"Did you?"

"Well, yes. I did."

"Where was he sitting?"

"On the couch."

"And you?"

"The couch."

"Right next to him?"

"No. But—he moved right next to me." The jurors are leaning forward now, straining to hear Rachel.

The judge steps in. "Please keep your voice raised, ma'am." Rachel nods.

"Okay." Ogren's voice has softened now. It doesn't take a genius to see what's coming. "So what did you two do? Did you talk?"

"We talked. We"—she lets out a sigh and blinks rapidly—"he was a little forward."

"Can you explain that?"

Rachel closes her eyes, reliving a painful fictitious moment. "Could I—could I have a glass of water?"

"Certainly," Ogren says, and the bailiff helps Ogren with the pitcher of water that rests on the clerk's desk, to the left of the judge.

Rachel accepts the glass and sips slowly before continuing. "He touched me. Maybe he—put his hand on my leg. I think he said I was attractive."

"You *think* or you know for sure?" Ogren might as well wave the immunity agreement in her face—comply or else. The harshness of his tone does not play well with the jury or with me, but Ogren is calculating here that he has to lower his thumb a little.

"I know for sure," says Rachel.

"Okay. Now, when the defendant touched you, and put his hand on your leg, and told you that you were attractive, how did you respond?"

"I didn't."

"Did you tell him to get out?"

"Well. It was more like I didn't respond to him. He would back off and apologize."

"But *then* . . ."

Rachel sighs. God, she's doing everything she can here. "Ev—every so often he would do it again."

"Okay. How long did he stay?"

"A while. He had three drinks." She looks at the jury a moment, then back at Ogren. "I should have just told him to leave. I know that. It was just—it never got confrontational. He would make a pass and then back off. I didn't really know *what* to do."

"That's fine, Mrs. Reinardt. We can stop talking about that now."

"Thank you."

"Following this evening, did you see the defendant again?"

She takes a deep breath. She nods, staring off into space.

"Can you give a verbal answer, Mrs. Reinardt?"

She focuses on Ogren again. "I'm sorry. Yes."

"When did you next see the defendant?"

Rachel looks reluctantly over at the jury box. "We have after-school tutoring programs. Monday through Friday. He showed up at the Monday program."

"That following Monday?"

"Yes."

"Did that surprise you?"

"Yes."

"Why?"

"He wasn't on the schedule."

"Schedule?"

"These programs start at four o'clock. We fit each child in once or twice a week for two hours. The volunteers have to leave work early to make it. And most of them can't be there but once a week, at most. So we have a schedule. We try to match up children with adults, to provide some measure of continuity. It's set long in advance."

"But the defendant just showed up?"

"Yes."

"So what did you do?"

"I thanked him for coming, but I explained to him that the schedule was filled."

"What did the defendant say?"

"He said that was fine. He would just help out however he could."

Ogren looks up from his notepad. "Were those his exact words?" he asks.

Rachel looks down. "No."

"What were his *exact* words, if you can remember?"

Rachel shuffles her hands in her lap. "He said he would be my personal assistant."

Ogren pauses, so the jurors can finish scribbling this down in their notebooks. "So, what happened next?"

"Well, we serve dinner every evening. So he helped get the food together."

"Was he working near you?"

She nods. "Yes."

"Can you describe your interaction?"

She looks at me briefly, no visible expression except a slight turn of her eyebrows. She's apologizing. Then she fixes on Ogren again. "He stayed very close to me. He would— touch me. He—put his hand on my shoulder. Things like that."

She has to give them something.

Ogren nods solemnly. "Did he talk to you?"

"Yes."

"What did he say to you?"

"He talked about the Saturday before."

"Can you be more specific?"

She stares at him, then closes her eyes. "He said we could have had a lot of fun that night."

"Did the defendant say anything else?"

Rachel clears her throat, bringing a fist to her mouth. "He said maybe we could try again sometime."

I make a couple of fists myself and rest them under my chin. I can't keep my legs still; my feet drum nervously on the wood floor. My mind is racing now, almost as fast as my heart. I want to get out of this chair so desperately. Take Rachel and run from the courtroom, run from this city, run from our lives.

74

RACHEL CONTINUES TO TESTIFY ABOUT SEVERAL foundation functions where I showed up. At all of these events, she says, I pretty much just stayed close to her. It made her feel uncomfortable, she admitted. She did everything she could not to encourage me. But I started becoming more insistent. I would ask her to dinner. I would assure her that her husband would never know a thing. She also talks about the night that her maid testified about, when I cornered her in the kitchen and asked her why she was avoiding me. And *her* English is quite good.

I watch the jury, trying not to be too obvious about it. They are troubled. Most of them have stopped taking notes and just watch her. The almost clinical aspect with which they have observed most of the witnesses is replaced by genuine empathy. Concern. The evidence against me has not been too strong, but Rachel's testimony, collectively, is beginning to hurt a little. She's trying to hold back for my sake, but I wonder if the jury is picking up on that, too. Paul told me all along that if the jury thinks I was in love with Rachel—supplying an obvious motive for murder—this would go a long way to gloss over other deficiencies in the state's proof.

Rachel finishes talking about the foundation basketball league, one time last September when I put my hand on her leg and told her I wanted to see her afterward. I can just imagine how it played out when they interrogated her. They had a full schedule of foundation activities, went through them one by one, and put it to her. *Did you see him at this one? What did he do? What did he say?* God, what she must have gone through.

Roger Ogren flips over his notepad on the lectern. "Other than seeing the defendant at foundation events, did you ever see him anywhere else?"

Rachel nods somberly. As the testimony has worn on, her resolve has begun to fade. She is fighting Ogren less now. Maybe she has realized, too, that she is better off being matter-of-fact about these things. God, I'm so sorry I put her in this spot. "I saw him outside my house," she says.

"He was outside your house?"

"Yes."

"When did *this* start?"

"September."

"Of last year?"

"Yes."

"Tell us about the first time you saw him outside your house."

"It was nighttime. I was upstairs, and I went to close the bedroom shade. I happened to look outside, at the backyard. And I saw Marty standing there in the lawn."

"What did you do?"

"Well—I didn't do *anything*. I was shocked."

"Did the *defendant* do anything?"

"He saw that I saw him. He waved to me."

"That's it?"

"No. He motioned to me to come outside."

"Did you?"

Rachel shakes her head no. "I closed the shade."

"Did you call the police?"

"No."

"Why not, Mrs. Reinardt?"

Her face softens. "I didn't want him to get in *trouble*."

"I understand. Did you ever see the defendant outside your house again?"

"Yes."

"How often?"

"Oh, I don't know."

"Every night?"

Her lips part, then she shakes her head. "I'd say three, four times a week."

"How do you know that?"

"I looked outside every night."

"How long did this continue?"

"It—well, until the day my husband disappeared."

Ogren lets this one sink in. The real estate agent in the jury box sits back in his chair and shakes his head grimly.

"Did you ever call the police?"

"No."

"Never? This whole time?"

She shakes her head forcefully. "I was stupid, I guess." She holds out a hand. "I thought the whole thing was harmless."

"Mrs. Reinardt, did you ever talk about this with the defendant?"

She looks at the floor. "Several times."

Oh, Rachel! You're saying *this*?

"What did you say?"

She told me to quit doing it, I suppose.

"I told him to stop."

"And how did the defendant respond?"

"He said he wasn't hurting anybody. He said, 'I can look, even if I can't touch.' " Her face turns sour as she repeats these words. This gets a few raised eyebrows from the jury.

Many of them scribble in their notebooks, no doubt repeating this phrase verbatim.

Ogren nods sympathetically. Then, quietly, "Did the defendant say anything else?"

"Not that I recall."

Ogren bends his knees slightly, impatient with his witness. "Did he mention your *husband* in this regard?"

Rachel sighs audibly. "Oh. Okay. Yes, he did."

"Describe that, please?"

"He asked if my husband knew about it."

"*Did* your husband know about it?"

"I didn't tell him," she says. "I thought it would make matters worse." Her face contorts, tears form. "God, I was so *stupid*." Her eyes close. Finally, she brings a hand to her eyes and sobs quietly.

Oh, Rachel. I'm surprised you held out this long. Hang in there, it can't be much more.

Mandy leans over to me and whispers. "What does she mean by that? Stupid?"

Ogren is in no hurry to ask the next question. The jury is captivated, and he is happy to sink into the woodwork. Even the judge, who normally looks forward impassively while he listens, has turned to watch Rachel. The prosecutor asks Rachel if she would like to take a recess. She waves him off without speaking.

Rachel finally manages to compose herself. She wipes her cheeks with a tissue from her purse and takes a deep breath.

"Mrs. Reinardt," Ogren says softly, "I want to talk for a minute about your relationship with your husband. Can we do that?"

Rachel fixes her hair and breathes through her mouth. "Yes."

"Okay. Did you have a good relationship with your husband?"

She lingers on that question. "We loved each other. We had our problems as well."

"Can you please discuss some of the problems?"

"My husband was a heart surgeon. He performed surgeries of many varieties."

"Were these life-and-death cases?"

"Often."

"And from time to time, did some of his patients—did some of them fail to—"

"He lost some of them." Rachel's eyebrows flitter, the only sign of emotion on her vacant face. "He did the best he could. He was one of the best surgeons in the country." She looks at the jury for validation. "Everyone said so." Many of the jurors acknowledge her with grim smiles or bowed heads. This testimony is not helpful to me, attributing some goodness to the victim, but Rachel is not calculating here, not straddling any line. She always saw the good in him, even at the end.

"Mrs. Reinardt, can you tell us about the effect these losses, these deaths, had on your husband?"

Rachel wets her lips and examines her hands. "He had a very difficult time with it."

"What do you mean by difficult?"

"I mean he—he took it personally whenever someone died on the operating table. In a way, he blamed himself, even though it wasn't his fault. He felt helpless. Sometimes he would wake up with nightmares. He'd wake up screaming—" Rachel stops and looks at Paul, who is on his feet.

"I apologize for interrupting, Your Honor. But I think we have once again strayed from the issues in this trial."

The judge nods. "I'll sustain that objection. I'd like counsel to approach."

Paul and Ogren walk up to the bench. The jurors watch Rachel, who dabs at her eyes with the tissue. Not a look in my direction.

The lawyers step back. Ogren goes directly to the issue now, the issue he tried so desperately to keep out of evidence, but that he will now try to front.

"Was there physical abuse in your relationship with your husband, Mrs. Reinardt?"

Rachel bows her head ever so slightly. "There was."

"When did this start?"

"It would have been—something like April or May."

"Of last year?"

"Yes."

"Your husband would strike you?"

"Sometimes."

"Was it . . . with his hand?"

Rachel looks out at the spectators, then the jury. Finally, her eyes glaze over. She is back in the house with her husband, clutching the pillow, or running through the bedroom. "His belt," she whispers. Her mouth twists, suggesting some bitterness perhaps. This I have never seen from Rachel. She has never condemned him for it. "He would hit me on the back with his belt."

Some of the jurors recoil again, even after hearing this for the second or third time, probably because now they are seeing the recipient of the abuse. Ogren keeps moving, trying to get through this topic as quickly as possible. He wants to front this evidence, but he doesn't want to dwell on the image of his beloved victim as a wife-beater. "Did this happen often?"

"It wasn't every night or anything like that." Rachel inhales deeply. "Every—every week, I suppose."

Ogren takes a step closer and almost bows his head. "Was there sexual abuse?"

Rachel has been remarkably calm through this. She holds her head up and speaks clearly, in a flat voice. "I wouldn't call it that. Sometimes we would be—intimate—when I didn't really want to. But I never told him that."

"You never told him his advances were unwelcome?"

"No."

"During these times, did he physically hurt you?"

"No. Nothing like that."

"All right. Now I'd like to talk about the week that your husband disappeared. Are you ready to talk about that?"

She nods her head, her wide eyes glossing over again, gazing at the floor. It's hard enough for her to relive these moments, to say nothing of the fact that she will have to navigate through the story without implicating me. Can I ever compensate for this? Can she ever forgive me?

"Did your husband perform any operations that week?"

"Several."

"Did any of his patients die?"

Rachel blinks several times. "He lost a patient that week."

"The week he disappeared?"

"Yes."

"Where were you that evening?"

"Home."

"Was your maid there?"

"Agnes left after she made dinner. About five-thirty."

"When did your husband come home?"

"About six o'clock."

"Describe what happened when he came home."

"He was very upset. He told me—he said—" Rachel tears up and shuts her eyes.

"What did he say, Mrs. Reinardt?"

"He said, 'I couldn't save him.' He kept saying that. 'I couldn't save him.' "

"Okay. Now, what did you two do?"

"We had dinner. I tried to get him to eat, but he wouldn't."

"And after dinner?"

"He went upstairs. He went up into the study to read some files."

"Did you visit him up there?"

Rachel's face tightens now, her eyebrows raised, as she keeps her eyes focused on the floor.

"Mrs. Reinardt?"

"I—went up to the study, yes."

"When?"

"About eight, I guess."

"What was your husband doing?"

Rachel's mouth comes open. Her breathing increases. "He was"—her eyes water up again—"he was reading the file on the patient he lost._Trying to figure out what mistake he'd made. He was crying." She brings a fist up to her mouth as the tears fall.

"Did you notice anything else?"

Rachel is sobbing now, speaking in short gasps. "He—was—drinking. He was—he had been—drinking."

"What did you do?"

"Nothing. I didn't do *anything!*" Rachel loses all composure now, crying uncontrollably with her hands over her face. Two—no, three of the jurors have joined her.

This time, it is the judge who asks Rachel if she would like to take a break. A good two or three minutes pass. The judge asks Mr. Ogren if he would like a short recess, but Rachel looks up and says she's okay. But still, Ogren gives her a good couple of minutes to get herself together, treating the packed courtroom to whimpers and sniffs. Despite the vicarious pain I'm experiencing, I'm grounded enough to realize that this whole scene is working out quite well for the prosecution.

Rachel finally continues to testify, breathing through her mouth. "A little while later, he came into the bedroom. I was sitting on the bed reading. He was—he had had a lot to drink." She takes a deep breath. "He was upset."

"What did you do?"

"I went to him. I tried talking to him."

"What did your husband do?"

"He became more upset. He wasn't himself. He—" Rachel covers her mouth with her hand, but she holds in the tears; after a moment, she removes her hand and speaks more quietly. "He hit me."

"Where did he hit you?"

Rachel points to her left cheek.

"He hit you in the face?" Ogren didn't seem ready for that one.

"Yes."

"What did you do?"

"I left the room."

"Where did you go?"

"I went downstairs. Into the den."

My pulse quickens now. We are in the den.

"What happened next?"

"I poured myself a drink. Then my husband came downstairs."

"And then what happened?"

"He came into the room. He was sort of stumbling. He could hardly stand. He said it was all his fault."

"What was all his fault?"

"The death of his patient. He said it was his fault. He was crying."

"What did you do?"

"I went to him again. To console him."

"What did your husband do?"

"He pushed me. He pushed a little harder than he meant to. I fell to the carpet."

"What happened next?"

"Then I heard the sound of the glass breaking."

No. That's when he fell on top of you. He was tearing at your clothes. God, Rachel, don't protect him *that* much. Tell them. Tell them the forewarning he had given you.

I know how it'll end.

He's going to rape me first. He said he'll rape me then kill me.

"What glass was that?" asks Ogren.

"The glass from our sliding door."

"Where is this door?"

"The door that leads to the outside patio. It's in the den."

"Okay. You heard the glass on that door shatter. And then?"

"Well—I looked up at the door."

She looked up at the door?

"And—what did you see?" Roger Ogren asks.

Even before Rachel turns her head toward me, before her eyes narrow ever so slightly and her jaw clenches, I feel it. I feel it in the contraction of my stomach, the tightening of my throat, the sudden chill in my body.

It's nothing more than a brief glance, but it's enough to signal me. I meet her stare for that moment. I wonder what she sees in my eyes. Pleading. Fear. Disbelief. But in the end, acceptance. I never once told her to lie for me.

She pauses a moment, her eyes facing her lap. A fresh tear falls from her cheek to her leg.

"Then I saw Marty," she says.

7 5

SILENCE, INITIALLY, AN EERIE MOMENT OF SUCH utter calm that I wonder if I actually heard Rachel correctly. But of course I did. Were there any doubt, the reaction of the jurors, the judge, the prosecutors, confirm it. I should try to read the map now, see where the testimony is headed, but for the time being, rational thought escapes me.

They made her say it. They threatened her, more than I could ever know. She tried to protect me but they gave her no choice: Tell the jury you saw Marty in your house or we'll put you next to him in the electric chair—

"The defendant?" says Roger Ogren, after a lengthy delay. Slowly his arm rises, like a drawbridge, finger directed at me. "It was the defendant whom you saw breaking into your house?"

"Yes."

"All right." Ogren is playing with time here, letting this revelation settle firmly into the jurors' minds. His next words are delivered gently. "Please tell us what happened next."

She holds up her hands unsteadily. "They struggled."

"Your husband and the defendant."

"Yes."

"Can you give us any detail?"

"No, I can't." Rachel brings a fist to her mouth, like she's about to cough. She pauses momentarily. "I—crawled out of the room. I went to the living room. I called emergency."

"Did you, in fact, call 911?"

"I know that I did," she says. "I don't really remember it."

"What happened next, Mrs. Reinardt?"

"A few seconds after the call—I heard it—I—I heard"—she covers her mouth again, trembles again with eyes squeezed shut, chest heaving—"the shots."

"You heard gunshots?"

"Yes."

"How many?"

"Two."

"You were still in the living room."

She nods. "By the phone."

"What do you remember next?"

"A police officer, standing over me."

"You had passed out, Mrs. Reinardt?"

"Apparently."

"Did you talk to the police officer?"

She sighs. "I don't remember."

"Did you tell the police that the defendant had broken into your home?"

"No."

"Well, did you *ever* tell the police that the defendant had broken into your home?"

"No."

"All right, Mrs. Reinardt."

Ogren returns to the prosecutor's table, where he huddles with Gretchen Flaherty. I turn to Mandy for the first time since the bombshell. For all her courtroom demeanor, Mandy, too, has been blindsided.

Rachel collects herself after a good five minutes of a silenced courtroom, my attorneys stiff as statues, the judge as alert as I've seen him.

Ogren motions to his clerk. They are going to play the 911 phone call again. Paul Riley stands and objects. It's already been admitted, we have stipulated to the contents, et cetera. But the judge allows it. Now, with the details fresh in their minds, the jurors once again hear Rachel's words.

OPERATOR: 911.

CALLER: Please . . . please . . . come quick . . . he's going to hurt me.

OPERATOR: Ma'am, where are you?

CALLER: He's going to hurt me.

OPERATOR: Who is going to hurt you? Ma'am, where are you?

CALLER: Please . . . my husband . . . please . . . oh God.

(END OF RECORDING)

The clerk wheels the giant recorder back behind the prosecution table. Roger Ogren stands front and center. "Mrs. Reinardt, you were afraid that the defendant was going to hurt you, too?"

Rachel adjusts in her seat. She gives a curt shake of her head. "I—I don't know. Maybe at that moment."

"All right, Mrs. Reinardt. Now, when, if ever, did you next speak to the defendant?"

"He called me the next day."

"At your home?"

"Yes."

"What did he say?"

Rachel has subtly transformed. Her anger, apparently, has overtaken her horror, and she speaks in a flat voice now. "He said he was sorry to hear about my husband. And he asked me if the police had any leads."

"And what did you take him to mean?"

"I don't understand."

"Did you take that as a threat?"

"Your Honor!" Paul Riley is on his feet. "Objection. It's a leading question, it is completely argumentative, and there is no foundation whatsoever."

The judge nods. "Sustained as to leading."

Ogren turns back to Rachel. "Can you describe the defendant's tone?"

"His tone?"

"Yes," says Ogren. "Was it friendly? Threatening?"

"Same objection," says Paul. "This is ridiculous."

"No, Mr. Riley. The witness can answer."

Rachel stares at the judge a moment, then looks off. God,

have they bullied her. But she's still fighting. "I didn't take it as threatening," she says.

Ogren deflates. Rachel will not help him here. "All right. What did you tell the defendant when he called?"

"I said no. They had no leads."

"Have you ever spoken to the defendant since?"

"No."

"Mrs. Reinardt, did there come a time during the police investigation that the police questioned you?"

"Yes."

"And they eventually arrested you."

"That's right."

"And yet, even then, you never told the police that the defendant was the one who attacked your husband."

"That's right."

"You were scared, weren't you, Mrs. Reinardt?"

"Objection! Leading."

The judge peers down at Rachel. "Mrs. Reinardt, were you afraid of the defendant? Is that why you didn't tell the police about him?"

Oh, Jesus. Now they're ganging up. Rachel looks up at the judge. There's something different about a question coming from the judge.

"It wasn't fear," she says.

Ogren steps forward, to reassert control. "All right, Mrs.—"

"There's another reason," she says.

"If we could, Mrs. Reinardt, I'd like to—"

"No." Rachel glares at the prosecutor. "I want to say this."

Ogren pauses, considering his moves. His witness is leading *him* now, and he is unsure of the destination. So am I. Finally, Ogren opens a hand.

"The reason I never told anyone about Marty—it has nothing to do with fear. I don't think Marty would ever hurt me. The truth is, I blame myself. It's my fault my husband is dead."

Roger Ogren nods. Rachel's trying to help me here, that much seems clear.

"I could have stopped him," she says. "I had the power to do something." She reaches into her purse and removes some papers. Divorce papers? She was going to leave her husband? Under the table, Mandy taps my leg. I turn to her and shrug.

"I went to see an attorney," she says. "About two weeks before my husband's death." She flips through the papers, to the last one. "Yes. November fifth."

None of the attorneys has any idea what's coming. Ogren, who probably is too far down this road now to cut her off, clasps his hands behind his back. "Why did you see an attorney?" he asks, no shortage of uncertainty in his voice.

Rachel unfolds the document and smooths it out on her lap. "William Bedford was his name." She sighs. "I wanted— oh God, I should have."

"Why did you see the attorney, Mrs. Reinardt?"

"He drew up a request."

"A request for what, Mrs. Reinardt?"

She pauses. The room is hers, once more. "For a restraining order against Marty."

"A *what*?" I am on my feet; I have kicked my chair several feet behind me. The rush from the chair, the impact of her words, leave me dizzy, unsteady.

Paul rises and grabs me. "Your Honor!" he shouts. "We've been given no notice of any such document! Move to strike this testimony."

Ogren walks toward the judge. "First I've heard of it, Your Honor."

Mandy stands. "Sit down, Marty. Sit."

I comply, as Paul and Roger Ogren approach the judge. I fix a stare on Rachel, who is reading the document. Two weeks *before* Dr. Reinardt died. Against *me*!

Paul is back now, taking a seat and shaking his head. Roger Ogren continues. "You got a restraining order against the defendant?"

"The attorney drafted one," she said. "We never filed it."

The prosecutor approaches Rachel. "May I see it?"

Rachel hands him the document. "It was November fifth," she repeats.

"Two weeks before your husband's murder?"

Rachel nods her head. "We were going to file it—at the last minute I changed my mind."

Ogren is leafing through the document. "Why? Why did you change your mind?"

"Because I was stupid," she says. "I thought it would embarrass Marty."

Ogren is still off balance. He reads through the document and asks her questions off of it. He was following you? Yes. He was threatening your husband? Yes. Paul objects furiously but to no avail. It's coming down like an avalanche now. I've given up any pretense of decorum, dropping my head into my hands and squeezing my eyes shut.

"Do you have anything else, Mr. Ogren?" asks the judge.

"Just one more topic," says the prosecutor. I hear his footsteps, his whispers with Gretchen Flaherty. Then his courtroom voice again. "Mrs. Reinardt, your husband had a gun."

The murder weapon. I look up at the witness. Rachel's eyes close. "Yes."

"Where did he keep it?"

She shakes her head, almost casually. "Usually upstairs. It would depend."

"Did you ever see that gun downstairs?"

She sighs. "Sure. It was an older model, kind of a relic, I think. I—I don't know anything about those things. But he would show it to people. He was proud of it. He showed it to some people at the last party we had at our house for the foundation."

"This was the April party? April of last year?"

"Yes."

"Was the defendant at that party?"

"He was there."

"Did your husband show the gun to the defendant?"

"I—I couldn't say for sure. I believe he was in the room, yes."

"And what did your husband do with the gun when he was finished showing it?"

This isn't happening.

"He put it in the oak cabinets below the bar. In the den."

"He did this in front of the defendant?"

"Again. I think so. I'm pretty sure Marty was in there."

"Do you know if your husband ever moved that gun back upstairs?"

"I don't know. The gun was more of a souvenir than any-thing else. I'm surprised it was even loaded."

Ogren looks up at the judge. "No more questions," he says.

Paul leans over, in front of me, to Mandy. "Do we start today?" he whispers.

"No," I say.

"We don't want to leave this in their minds tonight," Mandy whispers back.

"Mr. Riley?" Judge Mack calls.

"It doesn't matter, Paul," I say.

"Could we have a moment, Your Honor?" Paul asks.

"A very short one, counsel."

"*No,* Paul."

"We can't leave this hanging like this," Mandy says. "We have to go after her now."

"Paul," I say quietly, as composed as I can be. "Are you listening to me?"

He turns to me. *"What?"*

"We wait until tomorrow."

Paul studies me for a moment. Then he stands. "Your Honor, given the lateness of the hour, and the fact we've been completely blindsided with new so-called evidence, I would ask for an adjournment."

Judge Mack considers this, glancing at the clock. "Fine. We recess until tomorrow morning at nine o'clock."

I tell my lawyers I will meet them at their offices at six. I have an errand or two to run first.

I MAKE IT BACK TO MY HOME BY NINE-THIRTY, AF-
ter a two-hour meeting with my attorneys. Tonight I will add
some water to the Glenfiddich. I feel the need to keep my
wits about me.

I sit at the kitchen table and spread out, the prepared text,
already thought out, to my right. The yellow pad in front of
me, the pen in my left hand. I hold my hand up in the middle
of the pen, making the left-handed scrawlings of a right-
handed writer all the more difficult to read. Or trace, I should
say.

I am about halfway through the first letter when the phone
rings. I look up and see my reflection in the window. How
much life has drained from this pale, shadowy mug.

"Hello?" I say into the phone.

"Hello. Brett?"

"Speaking," I say. "Brett" was the first name I saw in the
first magazine I could find.

"This is Rudy Sprovieri," the voice says.

"Oh, are you going by *Rudy* now? I prefer Michael."

"Yes, well—I got your note?"

"Oh, good. I was afraid the parking attendant would lift it
off the windshield."

"I've been calling all night. I wanna know what this is
about. And who *you* are."

"Wasn't the note clear enough, Rudy?"

"No, as a matter of fact, it wasn't. 'There is something
you should know about your position at the company.' What
the hell does *that* mean? And who *are* you?"

"I'm a friend, Michael. Do you mind if I call you Mi—"

"*No,* I don't—will you please tell me what this is all

about? And why I'm not supposed to tell my wife?"

"Oh, no. *Don't* tell your wife. Don't tell anybody. Not until we can be sure."

I hang up the phone. It rings again, not ten seconds later.

"Listen to me. I want an explanation right now. You leave me this cryptic note on my car. It looks like a goddamn ransom note"—because I cut all the words out from magazines—"you tell me my position with the company is not secure—or whatever you meant. You tell me to be secretive. And then you won't tell me what this is about. What the hell *is* this? And who are *you*?"

Good for me that my number is unlisted. I'm sure Sprovieri checked with directory assistance.

"A friend, Michael," I say. "I'm a friend. Really, I'm a little surprised you don't recognize my voice." Probably because I've been talking out the side of my mouth, in a southern drawl.

Finally, an exhausted sigh at the other end. "I—have *no* idea why you're doing this. Are you going to explain this note to me or *not*?"

I cover the phone and take a moment. "If I was you," I say finally, "I'd burn that note. And I'd keep my eyes open at work. Michael, do not tell a soul about this."

"About *what*? Are you going to tell—"

"Ssshhhhhh. I'll take care of it. If anyone knows we're working together, it will make matters· worse. Don't tell a soul. And *don't* tell your wife."

"Listen, *Brett,* or whatever your name is, will you please—"

"Tell you what, Mike, why don't you call me tomorrow?"

"Listen to me—"

"No, no, Michael Rudolph Sprovieri. *You* listen to *me*. Relax. Call me tomorrow morning. What time do you get up?"

"I—well, I don't—maybe six-thirty."

"Call me then. I might know more."

The phone rings five or six more times tonight. My answering machine has been turned off since this afternoon, after court, and I just let the phone ring. Except the third time, when I answer but hang up after five seconds, saying nothing more than "Call me tomorrow" to Mr. Sprovieri.

It takes me almost twice as long to complete my work with all the noise. But what the hell. It makes it that much more enjoyable, too.

7 7

MY HEAD THROBS AS I SIT AT THE DEFENSE TABLE. Even adding the water, I overdid it a little last night with the scotch. By comparison to my lawyers, however, I look as though I slept like a baby. Mandy's eyes are red and puffy. Her hair, which never really sits in place anyway, takes on an even more frazzled look today, a little flatter and more disordered.

Paul isn't the kind to pull an all-nighter—I'm quite sure he didn't—but his face is drawn as well. For the first time today, he does not sit calmly, taking in the surroundings and chatting with various members of the law enforcement community who are on hand. Today, he flips through his notes, scribbling at times, mumbling to himself. Somewhere in there, he is probably cursing me for giving him only a few hours' heads-up before he cross-examines Rachel. But I know that, deep within him, the fire of a trial lawyer, ready to give the biggest cross-examination of the trial, burns bright.

Michael Sprovieri—I guess he goes by Rudy, his middle name—called me at six-thirty sharp this morning. I was just getting out of the shower. I played coy like I did last night, telling him to sit tight. Jesus, he has no idea who this "Brett" guy is or why he left some bizarre note on his car about his future with his company. He might find out soon.

The prosecutors, as always, were already seated in the courtroom this morning as I walked in with my attorneys. Ogren briefly looked up at us, and I made eye contact with him. I just nodded, kind of an eager, confident nod. He looked away, blinked a couple times, maybe wondering for a moment why the hell *I* seemed so chipper, before returning to his deliberations with Gretchen Flaherty.

The judge enters the courtroom and we all stand. His Honor speaks briefly to the parties. Paul tells the judge he'd like to approach the bench, a new matter has arisen. Paul and Roger Ogren argue quietly before the judge for several minutes. Ogren waves his hands in the air as he argues. Finally, in a huff, he returns to his seat. Paul walks calmly behind him. His Honor, Judge Mack, then calls for the jury.

Not a face looks in my direction as the jurors take their seats. I'm the killer now. None of them has any doubt about this.

Rachel walks into the courtroom and takes her seat in the witness box. She assures the judge she understands that she's still under oath. She is wearing a navy blue turtleneck and a reddish vest. She looks graceful and elegant. I will have to give her that. I will *always* have to give her that.

Paul stands and, for the first time, carries a binder with him to the lectern. He places it down awkwardly, pausing for a moment to be sure it will not slide off. This is not the way he likes to do it ("Notes are bush league," he once told me), but I haven't given him much time to prepare.

"Mrs. Reinardt, my name is Paul Riley. I would like to ask you a few questions about yesterday's testimony."

"Fine," Rachel replies. She folds one leg over the other and looks up innocently.

"If at any time this morning you would like to take a break, please let me know."

"Thank you."

"Mrs. Reinardt, you testified yesterday that your husband sometimes abused you."

Wow. He's going right after it.

"That's right. He did."

"Forgive me for being graphic, but you said he would whip you with his belt?"

She closes her eyes; her eyebrows lift slightly. "Yes."

"Forgive me, but when he would hit you, would he hit you just once and stop?"

"No."

"He would hit you more than once?" Paul scratches his face. He's not being offensive, but he's not being gentle, either. And the jury's picking up on the tension.

"Yes."

"Repeatedly, would you say?"

"Yes."

"About how many times?"

"I wasn't *counting,* Mr. Riley."

"If you could estimate . . . ?"

"Maybe—ten times."

"So in each one of these episodes, he would hit you approximately ten times, on the back, with his leather belt."

"That's right, Mr. Riley."

"And he would have sex with you against your will."

"What I *said* was he didn't *know* it was against my will."

"But against your will, nonetheless."

She sighs. "Yes."

"And obviously, these subjects are very painful for you."

"Yes, Mr. Riley, they are." A trace of anger in her voice.

"But, Mrs. Reinardt, you told a number of people about this abuse, didn't you?"

She glares at him. "No."

"No? Didn't you tell a number of women at the foundation that your husband beat you?"

"Marty," said Lieutenant Denno. "We know he beat her up. We know about that.

"Girls talk. Some of her friends at the foundation. She told them. I think she told you, too."

"I might have," Rachel says quickly. "I'm sure if I said it, I didn't go into detail."

"You don't remember?"

"No, I don't remember."

"So you weren't all that careful with this information?" Ogren objects. The judge sustains.

"Well, can we agree that you told *some* other people?"

"I said I don't remember."

"But you never told any of these people that Marty Kalish was"—Paul waves his hand with disdain—"*bothering* you. Did you?"

"I told that lawyer." Her face relaxes.

"Oh, we'll get to that," says Paul. "But other than that lawyer, you didn't tell anyone. True?"

"True."

"You didn't tell any of these people that Marty Kalish was the one who broke into your house on November eighteenth, did you?"

"You're correct."

"Okay. You started seeing a psychiatrist in May of last year, did you not?"

"Yes . . . ?" Rachel's eyes search Paul. Those long, thin eyebrows of hers arch.

"A man named Dr. Benjamin Garrett."

"That's right."

Ogren rises and objects. Doctor-patient privilege. Paul informs the judge that Rachel waived the privilege, allowed us to meet with him. Rachel confirms this for the judge. Ogren, it seems, had no idea.

Paul pauses. "You told your psychiatrist about the abuse."

"Yes."

"And with Dr. Garrett, you *did* go into painful detail, didn't you?"

"Yes."

"You told him about the belt, about the sex."

"Yes."

"You spoke freely with him."

"Not at first."

"But eventually."

"Yes."

"You trusted him."

"Yes."

"And you knew that he was sworn to a patient-psychiatrist privilege."

"I—well—it wasn't foremost in my mind."

"Yeah, but you know a psychiatrist can't repeat what his patient tells him. Everybody knows that, right?"

"I suppose so."

"And *you* knew that."

"I guess I did."

"So you knew that he couldn't repeat a word of anything—*anything* you told him without your permission."

"I guess—yes."

"And yet, Mrs. Reinardt, you never told Dr. Garrett that Marty Kalish was—*bothering* you?"

Her eyes narrow slightly. "That's right."

"You never told him, Marty Kalish stands outside my house at night."

"No, I didn't."

"You never told him, Marty Kalish makes passes at me."

"*No*. That wasn't the reason I was seeing him."

"You didn't tell Dr. Garrett that Marty Kalish was the person who broke into your house on November eighteenth, did you?"

"No."

"In fact, you never *once* mentioned his *name* to Dr. Garrett, did you?"

"No."

"Despite knowing that he couldn't repeat it if you *did* tell him."

"That's right."

"In fact, you told Dr. Garrett that you *didn't see*"—Paul waves a finger to emphasize each word—"the person who came through the glass door."

Rachel, stoic, allows a slow inhale, a blink of her eyes. "That's right."

"After Marty was arrested, you still didn't tell Dr. Garrett that Marty was the guy who entered your home on November eighteenth."

Rachel crosses her arms now. "No."

"In fact, Dr. Garrett *asked* you about Marty, after he was arrested, didn't he?"

"Yes."

"And you told him you had no *idea* if he was the person who attacked your husband."

"Something like that, yes."

"And after *you* yourself were arrested. Even *then*"—Paul stabs at the air—"you never told Dr. Garrett that Marty did it."

"I didn't tell him. No. I didn't tell him *ever*!"

"Despite knowing that he couldn't repeat it."

"That's right."

"All you talked to your psychiatrist about was the abuse."

"Yes."

"You wanted to make *sure* he knew all about *that*."

Rachel crinkles her face. "I don't know what you're suggesting."

"Your Honor," Roger Ogren says, "we object to the question as argumentative."

"Ahhh"—Judge Mack massages his face—"I'm going to sustain that objection."

Paul's eyes have never left Rachel. "Mrs. Reinardt, you told us yesterday that the abuse began in April or May of last year."

"That sounds right."

"Well, you said you first went to your psychiatrist in May of last year, right?"

"Yes."

"And I take it the abuse had already begun when you first went to him?"

"Yes. That's the whole *reason* I went to him."

"So you could tell him about the abuse."

"So I—yes."

"Well, how long after the abuse started did you go to see Dr. Garrett?"

Rachel frowns. Paul is pinning her down here, something she does not seem to enjoy. "A few weeks, I suppose."

"So it was probably April when this . . . *abuse*"—Paul

kinds of flips his hand as he says this word—"started."

Rachel's face goes cold with Paul's hesitation, which falls just short of sarcasm. She's getting the picture now. "That's right."

"How often did this abuse take place?"

Rachel draws another slow breath.

"Every week, I think you said?"

"Yes."

"And this was consistent, you said. Every week, you told the jury yesterday."

Rachel's eyes water. She blinks away the tears.

"Mrs. Reinardt—"

"*Yes*," she cries. "It was consistent. It was every week!"

Paul gives her a minute as she removes a tissue from her purse.

"Mrs. Reinardt, is it your testimony that you received bruises when your husband abused you?"

"Yes."

"Bruises on your back, I take it."

"That's right."

"Nowhere else, is that true?"

Rachel folds her hands. "I believe so."

"Well, you told us he hit you on the back. Is there anywhere *else* he hit you?"

"No."

"So if there were any bruises, they would have been on your back only?"

"I guess that's right, Mr. Riley."

"You never showed these bruises to Dr. Garrett, did you?"

Paul is bluffing a little here. We didn't ask Garrett this question.

"No, I didn't."

"In fact, you never showed *anyone* these bruises, did you?"

Scars you can never see.

"No, I didn't show them to anyone."

"You told people about this abuse, but you never actually *showed* anyone."

LINE OF VISION   391

She glares at Paul now. "What are you suggesting? That I made it *up*?"

"Please answer the question, Mrs. Reinardt." This is the first rebuke Paul has given her. The atmosphere in the courtroom has taken on a decidedly adversarial charge. "Isn't it true that while you *told* people about the abuse, you never *showed* the bruises to anyone?"

"I really don't know, Mr. Riley. I might have."

"Really? To whom?"

Rachel's face goes cold. She stifles, I think, an urge to look my way. We both know she showed me her scars. But she's no longer sure what I will say. Plus, that would be admitting to intimacy with me, which she surely will not do now.

"Who'd you show the bruises to, Mrs. Reinardt? Give me a name."

Over the last few questions, my eyes have peeked over at Roger Ogren. He is whispering to Gretchen Flaherty. He can't figure out what Paul is doing. After this last question, he stands. "Your Honor, may we approach?" Ogren turns to Paul with absolute disgust, as in how-could-you-beat-up-on-this-poor-woman-and-aren't-we-all-so-indignant. I notice, however, that the jurors are quite interested in this line of questioning. Paul has more than his share of credibility with them, and they're gonna give him some rope. Paul and Ogren huddle in front of the judge, who leans forward with his hand over the microphone.

Ogren doesn't understand why we would be questioning whether Rachel was abused by her dear husband. We were the ones who fought to get the evidence of abuse in front of the jury. The reason, Mandy told the judge, was it supplied a motive for Rachel to kill her husband or have him killed. Roger Ogren, knowing it was going to come in, talked about it first with Rachel to deflate the issue. But now, here we are, questioning the very evidence we fought for, suggesting that Rachel was *not* abused by her husband.

It was the subject of much debate last night in Paul's office. My lawyers batted it back and forth like I wasn't even in the room.

"The abuse is the only motive we have for Rachel," Mandy argued. She didn't want to challenge Rachel's story. *"Without that, we have almost no presentable reason why Rachel would want her husband dead."*

"But if we could somehow show that she was lying about it," Paul said, *"then we completely destroy her credibility. Completely. Totally. And after her testimony today, identifying Marty and everything, that may be more important than anything else."*

"The jury will hate us if we can't prove it," Mandy said. *"They'll think we're monsters!"*

"It can't be . . . excuse me for saying so, Marty"—the one time Paul acknowledged my presence during the conversation—*"but it can't be much worse than what they think of us now."*

I left them there last night, not knowing which viewpoint would win out. I shouldn't have been surprised that it was Paul's.

The lawyers step back, and Paul has the court reporter read back the last question.

"No," Rachel says, still seething, "I never showed anyone my scars."

"Scars," Paul repeats. "Yes, now that you mention it— whips on the back would actually leave *scars,* wouldn't they?"

Rachel looks at him, trying to read where this is going.

Paul saunters over to the jury box. "I mean, there's a difference between a bruise and a scar, right? A punch might leave a bruise. Turn black and blue, whatever, then go away. But a whip—repeated *whips,* like you testified to—would leave *scars,* wouldn't they?" He turns to Rachel now. "Well, *wouldn't* they, Mrs. Reinardt?"

"Your Honor," Roger Ogren interjects, "we object. It's a speculative question."

Paul turns to the judge. "I agree, Your Honor, and I withdraw the question." Then to Rachel: "Mrs. Reinardt, didn't, in *fact,* the whips from your husband's belt leave scars on your back? I mean, isn't that your story?"

Rachel caught the drift while Ogren diverted attention. She sits up straight. "It's the truth. But not permanent scars. They have healed. It's been six months."

"It's been *four* months," Paul corrects. "But even still. Since you have told all of us that you were abused, then I suppose that *during* the months of this abuse, you had scars from the whipping. True?"

Rachel holds her breath a moment, her eyes searching for a good answer. But all she says, all she *can* say, is "True."

Paul walks over to Mandy, who hands him the photograph. He shows it to the prosecution first, then approaches Rachel. She watches him with uncertainty as he hands her the picture.

"Mrs. Reinardt, do you recognize this photograph?"

She studies the photo and does a slow burn. I swear she shoots a look in my direction. Her jaw circles once or twice before she admits she recognizes the photo. "It was from a pool party last summer the foundation put on." Her voice is flat, even, the words coming slowly.

It shows a bunch of us around the pool. One of the little kids is jumping off the diving board, doing a cannonball. Rachel is sitting beside the pool, her back to the camera, in a bikini. Ready for the punch line? No scars on her back.

I am suddenly very pleased that I kept this scrapbook. The police removed it from my house, but we got copies from the prosecution. This is one of the things Paul told the judge before today's session started. Paul figured the judge would allow it in because it was in the prosecution's possession all along.

"This picture was taken in July of last year, isn't that correct?"

Rachel avoids looking at the photo now, lowering it to her lap. "Yes."

"If I told you it was July twentieth of last year, would that sound correct?"

"I believe that's right."

Paul reaches around and points at the photo. "Is this person by the pool *you*?"

Rachel's eyes never move off Paul. "Yes."

"For the record, you are the person with dark hair, sunglasses on the top of your head, sitting by the pool, just off to the right of the photograph, talking to an African-American boy who is sitting next to you. Do I have that right?"

"You do."

"Your back is to the camera?"

"It is."

Paul takes the picture from Rachel. "Thank you." He strolls over toward the jury and stops, turned toward them.

"Let's see . . ." Paul says absently. "July twentieth . . . four weeks in May . . ." He ticks off the math on his hand. "Four weeks in June . . . almost three weeks of July . . . oh, and sometime in April . . . That would make something like twelve or thirteen weeks from the time that *you* claim Dr. Reinardt started beating you. Does that sound right?"

"I never actually counted," Rachel says in a voice that could freeze the sun. Paul has her on the run here. And Rachel doesn't like to run.

"Well," Paul says, still turned to the jury, "four plus four is eight. Plus three is—"

"I guess it was something like that," Rachel says.

"So that would be about twelve or thirteen episodes of this abuse, by the time this photo was taken."

Rachel turns to the judge. "Do I have to put up with this? Do I have to relive every detail of what happened to me?"

Judge Mack leans in toward Rachel. "You must answer the questions, ma'am."

She turns to Paul again. "Yes. It was after several episodes. Scars *heal,* you know."

Paul ignores the last comment. "Judge, may we show this photo to the jury?"

The jury passes the photo around very slowly. Rachel's back is hard, taut, well defined under the string of her bikini top. And remarkably unscarred.

Rachel watches the jurors review the photo, holding it close and looking at her back. "Why would I lie about this horrible thing?" she shouts. "Why would anyone make something like that *up*?"

"A very interesting question," Paul muses, standing by the jurors still.

"I wouldn't. I *didn't*."

This is good for us, no question. But I'm not unaware of the risks. Paul is going all-or-nothing here. We don't have a lot to go on to prove that Rachel made this whole thing up. If the jury doesn't buy it, they will want to crucify me. But what Paul said to Mandy last night rings true: We didn't have much place to go but up after Rachel's testimony yesterday. And if the jury believes us . . . well, they seem interested so far.

Now the downside: This is all we have to offer. Just the one photograph.

Rachel continues to watch the jury, helpless. I'm sure she wants to go over there and yank the photo from the bank teller, who's had the picture pretty much pressed against his nose for a good thirty seconds. There's not much to see, pal.

"The tan hides the bruises," Rachel volunteers, like she's talking to that juror.

"The *tan*," Paul repeats. He leans over by the bank teller to inspect the photo again, just two guys admiring a shot of a beautiful woman. "Yes, I couldn't help but notice the tan. On your . . . *back*." He stands straight and turns to her. "How'd you get that tan, Mrs. Reinardt?"

That one stops her. Her face drops, her eyes darting from Paul to the jury, to the spectators. *This* is why I'm paying Paul Riley all that money.

"You got that tan from being out in the sun all summer, at the foundation functions. Isn't that right, Mrs. Reinardt? Wearing tank tops and swimsuits?"

All she has to say is, no, I got it lying out in my backyard. Alone. Where no one could see my scars. Christ, she could say she went to a *tanning salon*. But Rachel is far too flustered right now—she's great when she has time to think things through, but on-the-spot deception doesn't seem to be her game. She looks away from the jurors. Then her eyes move back to Paul, as he walks toward the defense table, where Mandy is holding another photograph. A photograph of Jerry Lazarus and me, mugging for the camera. Rachel is nowhere in sight in this photo. But Mandy keeps the picture turned toward her and me, so neither the jury nor Rachel knows what it portrays.

Rachel's eyes move to the photo in Mandy's hand. Paul takes it from Mandy and turns to Rachel. "C'mon, Mrs. Reinardt." He shakes the photo in his hand. "You exposed your back to the sun all summer at foundation functions, didn't you?"

"This is ridiculous," Rachel says, shaking her head severely.

"Mrs. Reinardt—"

"Yes! Yes!" She pauses and fixes her hair. Then she gently places her hands in her lap. "Yes. Of *course* I got it from the sun."

"Thank you." Paul hands the photo back to Mandy, walks to the lectern, and flips through his notes. "Now, aside from this lawyer of yours, I believe you testified that you never told anyone—not your psychiatrist, not your husband, not your friends, *nobody*—about the fact that Marty was hounding you. Bothering you. Making passes at you."

"Not at first," she says. She composes herself, no doubt relieved to change topics.

"That's right. Not at first. You eventually told the police, didn't you?"

"Yes."

"You told them that after they arrested you."

"That's right."

"After they charged you with murder."

"Yes. But you seem to forget, Mr. Riley, that I told that lawyer two weeks before my husband was murdered."

Paul smiles. "Oh, I haven't forgotten. That worked out pretty well for you, didn't it, Mrs. Reinardt?"

"Objection. Argumentative." It is Gretchen Flaherty making the point.

"Overruled."

"I don't know what you mean by that," says Rachel.

"Well," Paul says, strolling toward the jury box. "You knew your lawyer was sworn to secrecy, right?"

"I guess I did."

"He couldn't say a word about this restraining order business unless you turned him loose. Right?"

"I suppose that's the point of an attorney-client privilege, Mr. Riley. I'll bet your client has told you some things he wouldn't want *you* to repeat."

A nice stinger, sure. But the jury doesn't seem to approve. Some of the gloss is coming off our lovely witness.

"Oh, my client has plenty to say, Mrs. Reinardt," says Paul. "Let's focus on you for now."

"Let's." Rachel seems to have forgotten about the jury, about me. This is between Paul and her.

"Just to confirm. You knew that your lawyer had to keep quiet about the restraining order business until you gave him the go-ahead. Isn't that so?"

"That's correct."

"And I'm going to bet that you paid that lawyer in cash. Right, Mrs. Reinardt?"

Rachel pauses, her eyes drifting to the ceiling. "I don't recall."

Paul nods amiably. "Well, I'll be happy to subpoena your checking account records. And your credit cards. We can look for any payment to this attorney, Mr. Bedford."

Rachel's eyes narrow, seemingly in concentration. "I believe it was cash, yes."

"So there was no record of this transaction with your attorney."

"If you say so."

Paul does a slight bow. Then he brings a hand to his chin. "Now, the time this lawyer took to meet with you, the time he took to draw up this request for a restraining order. I imagine it cost you at least a thousand dollars. Does that sound right?"

Rachel shakes her head. "I don't recall."

Paul shrugs. He's toying with her. "We can bring Mr. Bedford in and ask him. Do we need to do that?"

"You can do whatever you like, Mr. Riley. But I believe your estimate was correct."

"About a thousand dollars."

"Sure."

"Maybe more," says Paul. "Maybe two."

"Maybe."

"So you paid this attorney anywhere from a thousand to two thousand dollars in *cash*."

Rachel is nodding while Paul finishes his question. "I didn't want my husband to know about it," she says.

"Well, sure." Paul raises his hands. "This way, *no one* could know about it."

"That's true."

"And as long as you didn't file this request with a court"— Paul turns to the jury—"no one would *ever* know."

"It's my personal business," she says.

"But it's always out there, right, Mrs. Reinardt? In case you need to spring it."

Roger Ogren rises. "Objection. The question is argumentative."

"Sustained."

Paul points to Roger Ogren. "You never mentioned this to the prosecution, did you?"

"No."

"You didn't tell the police, did you? Even after they arrested you."

"No, I didn't."

"So like I said before," Paul says, "this worked out pretty well for you. This was your ace-in-the-hole."

"Same objection. Argumentative."

"Sustained."

"I mean," says Paul, walking slowly, one hand out, "as long as you don't file it with the court—as long as this document does not become public—you can say anything you want, right? You could have your attorney draft any kind of document you want, right? It doesn't have to be true. There's no one to challenge it. You could draft a restraining order against the president of the United States, couldn't you? As long as you didn't actually file it with the court. No one can challenge your allegations."

Ogren stands, maintaining the calm that Rachel is showing. "Judge, I have to object to this—the question is compound and entirely argumentative."

The judge raises a hand. "Let's do one question at a time, Mr. Riley."

Paul continues without acknowledging his instruction. "You never planned to file this, isn't that true, Mrs. Reinardt? You could write whatever you wanted in this petition because you knew you would never have to *prove* it in a court of law."

"That's not true."

"You just wanted to keep it in your purse and wait until you needed it, right?"

"No."

"This was just another part of the plan, wasn't it, Mrs. Reinardt?"

One of those rare moments follows. The judge, the jury, the prosecuting attorneys feel it. Paul himself takes a breath. A shift in direction. We are doing more than just destroying Rachel's credibility now.

"Plan?" Rachel says, confused. In her confidence she almost laughs. She is daring him, perhaps. Give me your best shot, Mr. Riley.

Paul grows comfortable with the silence surrounding him. A trial lawyer's number one goal, Paul has told me, is control. For the moment at least, Paul has regained control, the total attention of the room.

"Your plan to kill your husband and frame my client."

Something out of a movie, murmurs behind me, the jury squirming, the judge banging his gavel. Paul is in no hurry for the next question. He looks almost with amusement at

Roger Ogren, who has risen and moves to strike the question. "There is absolutely no evidence of any such plan," Ogren says. "For God's sake, Judge, the only so-called evidence they ever had to accuse Mrs. Reinardt was the spousal abuse—and now apparently they're suggesting that the abuse never happened! They have no basis whatsoever for these accusations." Even as he speaks, his eyes dart toward Paul. The prosecutor is wondering if he has just uttered famous last words.

"Back it up with facts, Mr. Riley," the judge admonishes.

"Sure, Judge." Paul wraps his arms across his chest, then brings a finger to his mouth. "Let's see."

Rachel watches Paul, her eyebrows raised, her mouth twisted in a dare. Her anger, her sporting side, has gotten the better of her. There is no pose for the jury, no humble, sympathetic posture.

Paul takes a couple of steps toward the jury and just stares over the heads of the jurors. This is Paul's thoughtful pose, letting his tongue roll around his cheek, clearly enjoying the weight of all eyes upon him, basking in the attention he commands. Finally, he turns on his heels toward Rachel.

"Oh, I know," Paul says, wagging a finger. "Mrs. Reinardt, why don't you tell the jury about Rudy Sprovieri."

Rachel's face breaks ever so slightly: the momentary part in the straight line of her mouth, the drop of her eyebrows, the subtle cock of the head. She starts, her mouth moving without a sound for a moment, her eyes darting from Paul to Ogren to the floor, where they remain, moving about wildly like she's looking for a contact lens she dropped. Then the recovery: A quick blink, and she snaps back to form, calculating, wary. But she's not ready for this, and it is a long moment before her mouth closes to a tiny "o," and, looking up at Paul with an expression of bewilderment and probably terror, she painfully pushes out the air. "Who—?"

"Rudy . . . Sprovieri," Paul repeats, ever so innocently. "You seem surprised. You haven't heard the name before?"

"No, I"—she crosses her arms—"I've heard of him. He's a friend."

"A . . . friend." Paul approaches Rachel. "How *good* a friend?"

"A—good friend, I guess?" She looks over at the prosecution table. Her cheeks have lost all color.

"A good friend." Paul nods and looks at the jury. Then back at her. "How'd you two meet?"

"Objection," Roger Ogren says. "This is entirely irrelevant."

The judge waves Ogren off again without speaking.

"We met at the tennis club," Rachel says.

"When was this?"

"I don't know. I'd say—maybe January of last year."

"January. That would be—about three, four months before you started seeing the psychiatrist."

"Something like that."

I hear a ruckus behind me. I turn to see Billy Colgan, one of the associates from Paul's firm working on my case, who has just slipped into the courtroom. He is out of breath and red-faced. Mandy turns to Billy, who nods and proudly hands her a slip of paper with three phone numbers on it, then a stack of papers with court seals on them.

Paul looks over at us, watching Colgan hand over the documents, then returns to Rachel with a smile. "Are you still good friends? You and Rudy?"

"Yes, I'd say so."

"How often do you two talk?" Paul is almost sweet as he asks these things, like he's prodding a reluctant friend about the details of her lover.

Rachel, for her part, has finally gotten her balance. She assumes a tone of disbelief, confusion. Her face is in a permanent crinkle now, her shoulders slightly raising with every question, as if she can't understand *why* we're talking about *this* guy.

"I really couldn't say *how* often we talk."

"Once a week?"

"Not that often."

"Once a *month*?"

But even still, Rachel hasn't had time to prepare for this

questioning. Her eyes are intent; beneath them her mind is in overdrive trying to get ahead of Paul, looking for the traps that await her.

"I don't know, Mr. Riley. I really don't remember."

"No? Was there a time when you talked to him every day?"

"No!" Rachel shifts in her seat, startled at the volume of her own voice. "No. Never *that* often."

"Did you talk to him yesterday?"

"No, I certainly did not."

"Okay . . . let's say, since . . . last Christmas. Have you talked to him since *then*?"

"Maybe . . . I don't know . . . maybe."

"Have you *seen* him since then?"

"I really don't know."

"He lives just a couple of blocks away from you, doesn't he?"

"That's right."

"Ever been to his house?"

Another pause. I really have no idea if she's been to his house or not. But if she *has,* she has to be careful here. "I'm not sure. I might have."

"You don't remember if you've been to his house?"

"No, Mr. Riley, I do not."

"Do you know if Rudy Sprovieri is married?"

"Ummm . . ." She ponders this with that contorted expression. "Yes, he is."

"Ever met his wife?"

"No."

"Does she know about you?"

"Objection!" Ogren yelps, jumping to his feet faster than I thought he was capable. "The question is without foundation and it is completely suggestive. Your Honor, he's— counsel is making it appear that something nefarious was taking place between these two. That is a completely baseless accusation."

Nefarious, Mr. Ogren? Baseless, you say?

"The objection is sustained," Judge Mack says. He turns

to Paul. "Mr. Riley, you've overstepped your bounds. The question is stricken from the record."

"Well then." Paul clasps his hands in front of him. "Let me be more direct."

Rachel holds her breath.

"Mrs. Reinardt, isn't it true that at the time your husband disappeared, you were having an affair with Rudy Sprovieri?"

"What!" Rachel gasps.

Paul takes a step forward. "Isn't it—"

"No! Absolutely *not*."

"And aren't you *still* having an affair with him?"

"No! What kind of person *are* you?"

"And didn't you and Rudy Sprovieri plan to kill your husband *together*?"

Ogren is on his feet now, complaining up a storm. The spectators are making quite a bit of noise themselves. Rachel, during all of this, looks around in horror, her eyes sweeping the jury, the gallery, and past me—but she catches my eyes and returns to me, the disbelief gone now, just a cold dark stare. I maintain eye contact, allowing the slightest of smirks.

Paul and Ogren approach the bench. Judge Mack bangs his gavel for order in a suddenly noisy courtroom. After a decidedly brief moment, the judge sends Ogren to his seat. Paul has the court reporter read back the question.

Rachel is fuming now, tears all down her face, her throat full. "No. We didn't plan *anything* together."

"You lied about the abuse, Mrs. Reinardt, didn't you? That way, if you killed your husband yourself, you had a built-in defense!"

"No! That's a lie."

"And you drew up that petition for a restraining order just in case, isn't that true?"

"No!"

"Just in case you needed to frame *Marty* for the murder!"

"No!"

"And, Mrs. Reinardt, as part of your plan, wasn't Rudy

Sprovieri supposed to *threaten* Marty to keep quiet about your and Rudy's affair?"

"No! *None* of that is true!"

"And just last night, didn't Rudy Sprovieri call Marty and threaten to *kill* him if he told anyone? Wasn't that part of the plan?"

"No! There was no *plan*. This is all wrong!"

"And don't you know for a *fact* that Rudy Sprovieri called Marty last night?"

"No."

"And again this *morning*? *Threatening* Marty? *Threatening* him not to spill the beans about you and Mr. Sprovieri?"

"My God! No! No no *no*!" Rachel slams her hands down on the railing, half out of her chair now. "I can't *believe* you're saying these things! It was *Marty* who did this!" She points at me. I shake my head sympathetically. "I *saw* him! Didn't you hear me? I *saw* him!"

Paul brings his hands together at his waist, watching, with no lack of amusement, Rachel's tirade. Ogren stands and asks for a recess, a brief one, just five or ten minutes. Paul says he has no problem with that, but he would like a moment of the judge's time once the jury is excused. So the jurors leave in whispers and contorted faces, Rachel gets up in a heap and storms out of the courtroom, and from the sounds of it, a good number of the spectators leave in a hurry. Paul hands the prosecution several sheets of paper and addresses the judge while Ogren flips through them furiously. For the record, Paul tells Judge Mack, based on the new circumstances of these phone calls from last night and this morning to my house, he is issuing subpoenas for the phone records of Michael Rudolph Sprovieri at his home and his place of business, as well as the phone records of three pay phones in the lobby of the building Mr. Sprovieri works at. For the last three months. He hopes the prosecution will cooperate to obtain these records with all due speed.

The judge might be disinclined to allow these motions if it will delay the trial. Paul has told me this. But what Paul doesn't know is that there will be a delay anyway. Within the last few minutes, the Highland Woods Police Department has learned the whereabouts of the body of Dr. Derrick Reinardt. Roger Ogren will hear about this soon enough. What with the autopsy and all the other tests they will perform, this trial will have to be postponed. At the *prosecution's* request.

But Ogren doesn't know this yet, and he is indignant at the mention of the subpoenas and furiously argues against Paul, babbling about red herrings and goose chases, waving his arms in the air and, at one point, slamming his fist on the table and knocking a stack of papers to the floor. Paul, in turn, is incredulous. Isn't this about truth, Your Honor? Does the prosecution really have a problem in unearthing the *truth*?

This word, as always, brings a smile to my lips. Truth. *Each side gives their own version of what happened,* Mandy once said to me, *and somewhere in the middle lies the truth.* Somewhere in the middle. That elusive middle. A middle that we just might reach.

But I doubt it.

BOOK THREE

78

COUNTY ATTORNEY PHILLIP EVERETT STANDS TO deliver his closing statement. His suit is a smart double-breasted gray pinstripe, with a blue-and-silver tie that he has knotted perfectly. He buttons his coat as he stands, first pausing and making a slight turn to the gallery of spectators, taking in his moment, acknowledging the crowd, even giving a brief nod to Roger Ogren. Then he approaches the lectern, square in the center of the jury box, set back about five feet, where his notes have already been placed. The jury is depleted after a lengthy and emotional trial, but they know now that the end is in sight, and they know what awaits them. They will have to make a decision that will affect the lives of at least one man, and probably to some degree their own. And depending on how they decide, they might face the question of imposing capital punishment. Sending a man to his death.

The press has berated the prosecution of late for the Reinardt murder case, very bad timing for Everett, who is said to be ready to announce his Senate campaign in the coming weeks. So what does Everett do? He says, you want it done right, you do it yourself. He rolled up his sleeves and participated in the end of this trial, and now will close it off. If he gets a conviction, he is the tough prosecutor who gets things done. If he loses, he is still the man who supports his underlings in a time of crisis, not afraid to take the shrapnel. I must grudgingly credit him with a heady political move.

I look across to Roger Ogren and Gretchen Flaherty. They sit composed and attentive. Before the proceedings began today, Ogren actually gave me something like a nod, a just-doing-my-job. Maybe he's reconsidering my guilt. Maybe, guilt or not, he doesn't enjoy this part of it, taking another person's liberty and maybe his life.

Phillip Everett takes two steps from the podium and laces his hands together at his waist. The jurors are fixed on him; I have noticed their reaction to his appearance in this courtroom the last few days, the seemingly heightened importance attached to this case with the participation of a man all of them have seen on television. Does this favor the prosecution, I wonder. Not for the first time, a shiver runs through me. Can the life of a man depend, in some small part, on the fame and importance of the person who is prosecuting him? Can his fate rise or fall on the added credibility of his accusers? I want to believe not. I want to believe somehow that the jury sees this for what it is—politics, desperation, maybe even an indication that the state's case is weak enough that they have to bring in the big gun. But Dad didn't raise no fool. The prosecution's chances of a conviction have increased.

"Ladies and gentlemen," Everett says quietly, "I want to thank you for your participation in this trial. It's been a grueling few weeks, for us as well as for you, *especially* you, and all of us realize that. We have asked you to take time away from your families, from your work, from your lives. And on behalf of the People, I want to thank you."

The prosecutor looks down humbly and pauses. "But this is one of the most important tasks you will perform in your lives. The room we sit in"—he looks around reverently and lifts out his hands—"is a court of law. A court of justice. And we ask you to do only what is just. What is just for the people. What is just for Derrick Reinardt."

The prosecutor turns and points at the defense table. *Don't shrink away if he points at you,* Paul reminded me over and over again. *Look him in the eye.*

But seeing the prosecutor's finger, I let out a very quiet groan.

"The defendant *murdered* Dr. Derrick Reinardt on November eighteenth of last year. He entered his house by smashing through a glass door. He shot him twice, in cold blood, while

Dr. Reinardt lay on the floor helpless." He turns back to the jury. "*Helpless*."

This is not the first time I've heard Dr. Reinardt described as "helpless" that night. For the longest time, I greeted that characterization with scorn. Now, I realize, it probably wasn't far off the mark. The way his eyelids froze as he realized death was coming. The way he tried to move his leg, in a vain attempt to push himself away from me, as I stood over him with the gun.

I shake my head out of the dreamy trance I tend to fall into when I think of that night. I promised myself I would listen to every word of Everett's close.

Everett stops and swings out his arms. "And you know what? His plan worked. It worked to perfection. For months, nobody had any idea where Dr. Reinardt was. Nobody had any idea it was the *defendant* who was involved. Nobody knew. His plan *worked*."

I wipe the perspiration from my forehead; to my surprise, even after all this time, I am still so affected by hearing these descriptions of the Reinardt murder.

"And *why* did the defendant do this? He did this so he could spend his life with Rachel, the doctor's wife. He wanted to marry her, so he could spend the millions of dollars Dr. Reinardt had worked hard for. The oldest motives in the book, ladies and gentlemen: love, sex, lust"—he turns back to the defense table again—"and greed."

Greed. There's a new one. There has been almost nothing said at the trial about Dr. Reinardt's wealth. Those are the kinds of mistakes you would expect, I suppose, from someone who is joining the trial late. I notice Ogren grimacing at the remark, too. I wonder what he thinks of the job his boss is doing on this closing argument.

The prosecutor lets go of his faraway look now and slaps a fist into his hand. "The evidence against the defendant is overwhelming. The police recovered a .38-caliber gun from the defendant's basement, hidden in a wooden chest underneath assorted memorabilia—I guess this was just another *souvenir* for the defendant. And you heard the testimony:

This was the gun used to murder Dr. Reinardt."

Now he's ticking off the facts on his hand. "We found sand in his basement that matches the sand from the baseball field in Mount Rayford where Dr. Reinardt was buried. You heard the testimony. A direct"—he slaps the back of one hand into the palm of another—*"match."*

The prosecutor turns on his heels now and glances at his notes. "And let's *talk* about the baseball field. When the police uncovered Dr. Reinardt, what did they find? A crumpled ATM receipt. A receipt that reflected a withdrawal from the *defendant's* checking account. Probably fell right out of his pocket while he was bending over and throwing the doctor into the hole he'd dug."

I fold one leg over the other as the prosecutor continues. The gallery seats, especially the front row spot I have been given out of courtesy, are so much more comfortable than sitting at the defense table.

Where to begin. The phone records that Paul subpoenaed showed repeated phone calls to Rachel's house in January and February. Some came from Rudy Sprovieri's house, but most came from the pay phones in the lobby where he worked—a blatant attempt, Paul told the jury in his closing argument at my trial, to keep the calls from registering to Rudy's name. There were also several calls from his office to mine, only days after the murder, which I now affectionately refer to as the I-saw-you calls. Finally, the records showed several calls to *my* house, including three calls the night before Rachel's cross-examination and one the next morning—these were the calls Rudy made after receiving my note, but which Paul claimed were phone calls in which Rudy threatened me to keep quiet.

The day after Rachel's cross-examination at my trial, Detective Theodore Cummings of the Highland Woods Police Department received two very startling videotapes in the mail. These videotapes were made on January 3 and January 15 of this year. They were fairly low on quality—the maker's no Hitchcock—but quite scintillating in content. The star of the films was Rachel Reinardt, her costar the dashing Rudy

Sprovieri. The first film began in the back of a motel off Route 41, an hour out of the city, where our costar got out of his red BMW, looked around once or twice, pulled his jacket collar up around his face, and hustled around to the front of the hotel. Rachel showed up about ten minutes later, dressed in a smashing winter-white leather coat, parking her car right next to Rudy's, in the back of the lot, out of sight. The stars returned to the parking lot roughly an hour later, five minutes apart, presumably satiated, and drove away.

The sequel—"Rachel 'n' Rudy Do the Town"—was located on the north side of our commercial district, Rachel ducking into a hotel with several shopping bags, which made her entry through the door just difficult enough so that the director got a good long close-up of her before she went in. Rudy showed nothing but his profile on the way in, but he made a nice pose as he exited the hotel an hour later.

Over the next two days after the receipt of these tapes by Cummings, there was not a peep to be heard from Roger Ogren. My defense attorneys had no idea the tapes even existed.

On the third day, reporter Andrew Karras of the *Daily Watch* received the same package of videotapes, with an anonymous letter, scrawled haphazardly in red ink, wondering why the police hadn't made this video public or, at the very *least,* told my defense attorneys about these tapes. This very issue was then the subject of a front-page article in the Metro section the next day by Mr. Karras, entitled "What Are the Kalish Prosecutors Hiding?"

Paul Riley, celebrated defense attorney, was indignant in the judge's chambers that day. If the article was true, it corroborated his theory that Michael Rudolph Sprovieri was having an affair with Rachel Reinardt. It was, without a doubt, *Brady* material, meaning it was something the prosecution was required to turn over.

Roger Ogren reluctantly confirmed that he had the tapes but said that their authenticity was still an issue, and wasn't it oh-so-convenient that these tapes *suddenly* popped up? Paul Riley was beside himself. What was Mr. Ogren suggesting?

That these tapes came from the *defense*? What possible reason would we have to withhold these tapes for so long? And
what proof was there that we had *anything* to do with those
tapes? Who knows *who* made those tapes?

The only person, besides me, who could have answered
that question was Gregory Quillar, a former private investigator who served as the choreographer, director, and exec-
utive producer of those videos, and who signed an exclusive
distribution deal with me, the delivery made in a shoe box
at his offices many weeks ago. Mr. Quillar is contemplating
retirement now after receiving a very tidy fee from the Martin Kiernan Kalish Defense Fund. Payments in cash, of
course.

"We know that he was having an affair with Mrs. Reinardt," Phillip Everett continues, waving his arms as he
walks along the jury box. "He's admitted that much."

He admitted that much because he had no choice after the
videos.

The jury in my trial saw the videotapes and read the phone
records, all of which completely impeached Rachel's testimony. But the topper, no doubt, was when an anonymous
caller informed the Highland Woods Police Department that
the body of Dr. Derrick Reinardt could be found beneath a
baseball field at Laramie Elementary School, in Mount Rayford. This call was made just after ten A.M. from a phone
booth by a gas station in Mount Rayford, presumably by
someone who saw the burial rite take place on November 18
and had been reluctant to come forward. That same day, Greg
Quillar caught the twelve-fifteen flight for a much-needed
and much-deserved trip to Bermuda.

The police dug up two other baseball fields before they
reached the one I used. Finally, they found Dr. Reinardt,
somewhat decomposed and wrapped tightly in plastic. Roger
Ogren, as expected, asked for a delay in the trial to perform
an autopsy and other tests on the doctor—tests that revealed
very little, except that Dr. Reinardt died from two very sharp
bullets in the chest. And, oh yes, they found Rudy's ATM
receipt—which I had removed from Rudy's jacket pocket

during one of my trips to his house—right alongside the doctor. They *had* to turn over the receipt to Paul.

At this point, Andrew Karras was running daily articles in the Metro section of the *Watch,* wondering why the police weren't investigating Rudy Sprovieri. The phone records, the videotape, the ATM receipt. Didn't they care about the *truth*? Would C.A. Phillip Everett see Marty Kalish convicted at any cost? Is that the kind of character we look for in a senator?

But the prosecution resisted, despite the pressures, and the trial resumed about a week later. Paul decided not to call me as a witness after all. The only witness we called after the body was found was Rudy Sprovieri.

Rudy refused to answer Paul's questions, citing the protection against self-incrimination. You should have seen the look on the jurors' faces the first time Rudy pleaded the Fifth. We proved it was Rudy's bank account on the ATM receipt. We proved he had called me, over and over. We proved he and Rachel were having an affair. And we put plenty of dents in Rachel's testimony. We had more than reasonable doubt. The jury took less than an hour to come back "not guilty."

Now, Andrew Karras cried in his article the next day, *now* are the police going to go after the *real* suspect, Rudy Sprovieri?

So the police searched his house. They found Dr. Reinardt's gun in Rudy's wooden chest in the basement—which I placed there after removing it from its hiding spot behind the gas station. They also found granules of sand in the basement, sand that I had removed from the baseball field and sprinkled in Rudy's carpet down there. They had no choice but to arrest him.

Rachel skated out of this, just barely. The prosecutors considered voiding her immunity deal based on perjury. She convinced them, somehow, that the only thing she said that was false was that she saw *me* coming through the door. She claimed that she *assumed* it was me but never actually saw me. Yes, indeed, she said, it could have been Rudy who came through. As for her lying about the affair, apparently that fib

was not "material" enough to constitute perjury. That's how
my lawyers explained it to me, anyway. So in the end, the
prosecutors weren't too pleased with Rachel, but they knew
they couldn't prove perjury to void the deal, and besides,
they needed all the witnesses they could get against Rudy.
So they held to the deal, and Rachel testified in Rudy's trial.
She admitted to the affair. She said Rudy was the jealous
type. That was about it, from what I understand.

Everett is actually doing a pretty nice job on this close.
Not as good as Ogren did at my trial—and Ogren had a
whole lot less to work with—but not bad.

"So what does the defendant do, in the face of this insur-
mountable evidence? The gun found in his house, the ATM
receipt found at the burial site, the sand from that baseball
field in his basement carpet? *What* does he say?"

Everett opens his hands in wonder. "He says he was
framed, ladies and gentlemen. Set up. Set up by Marty Kalish. He says *Marty Kalish* must have made all those phone
calls from his building and his house. Now, I have to wonder.
What about the calls that came from the defendant's *office,*
calls that were made to Mr. Kalish? Does the defendant claim
that those calls were made by Marty, too? What, did Mr.
Kalish sneak into the defendant's office and make all those
calls, with not a witness to notice, or to stop him, or to ask
him, hey, who are you and what are you doing in Mr. Sprovieri's office? Ridiculous, ladies and gentlemen. Smoke and
mirrors.

"And what about the calls from the defendant's *home*? Are
we to believe that Mr. Kalish broke into the defendant's
home and made all those phone calls? With absolutely no
sign of forced entry? Is that a *credible* explanation?

"And what about those threatening phone calls the defendant made to Marty Kalish during Mr. Kalish's trial? How
does he explain *that* one? He says, Marty *told* him to call
him. You saw that note he showed you. All those words cut
out of magazines, like a ransom note or something. Pretty
smart, when you think about it. He knows he can't imitate
Marty's handwriting, so he makes up this note out of words

from magazines." Everett laughs. "Boy, I thought I heard 'em all."

The County Attorney shakes his head. "And I suppose Mr. Kalish also put the ATM receipt next to Dr. Reinardt's body. Boy, that Marty Kalish must have been pretty busy. He must have been one very resourceful fellow."

Please, you're embarrassing me. Let's leave it at this: I have my moments.

79

"WHEN ARE YOU COMING?"

I can't suppress a smile at my nephew's enthusiasm. "A couple of days, little man."

"You're still staying with us, right?"

"For a while, Tom. Until I can find my own place."

Until I can find a job, too. The career opportunities for Marty Kalish have hit a wall here. I'm clean on paper, but there isn't a firm in the city that would take me.

Not that I'll miss the work. I need to do something that reaches people, not their wallets. I still have a little savings left. I'm considering grad school again, getting a master's and teaching. There are a couple of universities out by Jamie, but I'm leaning toward elementary education. Who knows? The beauty is in the possibilities.

"Here's Mom."

"Hi!"

God, she sounds so much like our mother. "Hey, Jame. You're sure this is okay."

She covers the phone, speaking to little Jeannette in the background, something about not drawing on the floor.

"Are you kidding?" she says. "Tommy can't wait. Neither can I."

Neither can I. The shadow will always follow me here. There was some degree of vindication after my acquittal, but only some. And after Rudy's trial, where I testified, there was plenty of lingering doubt about my involvement in the events of November eighteenth of year last. I guess I invited it with my testimony. But I had to hold up my end of the bargain. Marty Kalish never welches.

Rudy Sprovieri's defense attorney, Terry Galbraith, didn't expect to see me that morning, or any morning. He remained seated and scowling, his hands resting on a considerable paunch. His tie was askew and stained. "What can I do for you?" he asked.

"I'm willing to help you," I said. "But I need some information."

Galbraith was stoic, revealing nothing, his hands raised in a steeple. "Go on."

"Let's keep it hypothetical," I said.

Galbraith waved a hand. "Okay."

"Okay. Hypothetically, I know who made those videotapes of your client's secret interludes with Rachel."

"That's not terribly surprising."

"I'm sure it's not. But hypothetically, there's more."

"More of the same?"

"Something different."

I've got audio, Greg Quillar told me, when he turned over the videotapes.

"Hypothetically, I have an audiotape of your client and Rachel. Hypothetically, this tape depicts a rather sordid sexual encounter."

Galbraith's eyes narrowed. "I assume you're going to tell me about that."

"Have you ever heard of a rape fantasy?"

The expression on the face of Rudy's attorney was one for the record books.

"Apparently, the two of them liked to stage one. A rape, that is. It was a first date, it seems, that turned violent when Rachel just wanted to give a kiss good night."

Galbraith wrapped his arms around his chest. "Why are you telling me this?"

"I have some questions."

"Your curiosity is not my concern."

"Your client getting off murder charges is very much your concern. You get some answers from Rudy, you give them to me, and I can deliver an acquittal. And I keep the audiotape buried."

"I'm not making any promises," he said.

"It's a two-for-one, Mr. Galbraith. A couple of answers for a not-guilty, plus, for a limited time only, this lovely audiotape. Take it to Rudy. He'll say yes."

Well, Rudy *did* say yes. So I got my answers. And I did my part for him, too. I was called to testify at Rudy's trial, and Terry Galbraith threw the questions at me, one after another.

Mr. Kalish, you buried Dr. Reinardt at that baseball field, isn't that true?

You buried the gun used to kill Dr. Reinardt, didn't you?

You broke into Rudy Sprovieri's house.

You removed the ATM receipt from his coat.

You placed that receipt next to Dr. Reinardt's dead body.

You hid the murder weapon in Mr. Sprovieri's basement.

You placed the sand from the baseball field in his basement carpet.

You made those phone calls to Rachel Reinardt.

You placed that note on Mr. Sprovieri's car.

I answered every single one of Mr. Galbraith's questions the same way. "On advice of counsel, I decline to answer on the grounds it might incriminate me."

Oh, the prosecutors almost came out of their skins when they heard me. Really, it was their fault. After my acquittal, Roger Ogren had made noise about trying me for obstruction of justice, claiming I tampered with evidence and framed someone else. They tried to interview me, and Paul Riley told them I wouldn't talk without total immunity from prosecution. Of course, they balked. So without immunity, I had every right to take the Fifth.

Well, the tide turned in favor of Rudy after my testimony. By remaining silent, I essentially confirmed everything Rudy's attorney was saying. I hid the body. I hid the gun. I broke into Rudy's house. I planted the evidence, made the phone calls.

The headline in the *Watch*—"Second Acquittal in Reinardt Murder"—was not nearly as titillating as the sub-heading beneath: "Suspicions Turn Back to Original Suspect."

They can turn back all they want. I can't be retried for murder, and they don't have any hard evidence on obstruction. Paul Riley has inquired at the prosecutor's office, and they have closed the case.

But getting away from the circus is not the only reason I'm looking forward to the move. "I can't wait to be with you guys," I tell Jamie. It's time to turn the channel to real life. It's time for things I never realized I wanted.

80

NOVEMBER 18 OF LAST YEAR. SOMEWHERE CLOSE TO ten o'clock.

Still no sign of Rachel. Looks like the show won't go on tonight.

I look back at the den again. I stuff my hands in my jacket pockets and stomp my feet in a feeble attempt to keep warm. I fix on the staircase in the hallway, my eyes tearing from the wind.

I jump at the sight of her, my one and only, my beautiful Rachel, the ink-black hair to her shoulders, the shapely outline, even from a distance the shiny amber eyes. My hand leaves my pocket just in time to grab the tree to keep my balance. She must have been in the living room, not upstairs. Or did I miss her coming down the stairs?

I can't make out her features very well; I'm too far away to see the expression on her face. She's wearing a whitish blouse and blue slacks, not her ordinary attire for the occasion—she usually opts for a negligee, sometimes surprises me with some outfit like a schoolgirl skirt and knee-high socks. But tonight, as she walks along the tiled hallway in a semicrouch, almost tiptoeing yet moving with some urgency, Rachel is anything but provocative, her whole body wearing an obvious pain, maybe fear.

Scars you can never see.

She reaches the den, still crouching sheepishly, one hand tucked under her shirt. She walks to the bar. Her back is to me as she reaches the counter, a deep mahogany brown. She keeps looking up at the ceiling, probably listening for her husband upstairs? At the bar, she raises a trembling hand to the ice container. She removes a couple of cubes but knocks the tumbler sideways, the ice spilling onto the bar and floor.

Her head turns upward again.

It's only when he drinks.

She sets the glass upright, stuffs some more ice into it, and reaches for a bottle of liquor. She fills the glass and tries to gather the spilled ice. But her hand is shaking so hard that she can barely put the cubes back into the container.

The other hand remains tucked under her shirt.

She looks up again, but this time not straight up at the ceiling. This time, she looks more toward the staircase in the hallway. Her hands are still now.

A clumsy, uncertain foot stomps onto that last stair, then into the hallway. Dr. Reinhardt is wearing an oxford shirt, haphazardly tucked into his pants with the sleeves rolled up. His movements are slow and awkward. He stops at one point in the hallway and reaches out to the wall to steady himself.

The doctor can't see Rachel yet; she is still by the bar, against the front wall of the den. But now Rachel has placed the drink on the bar; she is reaching behind the bottles of booze that line the countertop. She pulls the bottles back and reaches out with her other hand. I catch a glimpse of shiny steel as she raises the object over and behind the bottles.

I shift and feel the wood from the Reinardts' deck. I'm only about twenty feet from the glass door now. The deck is raised three steps off the grass, leaving me the perfect amount of space to crouch down from their view. I reach up to the deck for balance and realize that my hands, like Rachel's, are trembling.

The outside porch light is off, so they can't see me unless they're looking. And as Dr. Reinardt enters the den, he is not looking out the glass door.

He stops and just stares at Rachel. She reaches for the glass on the bar, but the doctor, without moving, says something to her that makes her put her hands at her sides. He says nothing more, just glares at her.

Rachel fidgets. She brushes back a strand of hair from her face, then puts her hands at her sides again. She's talking to him, her head moving compliantly, but he doesn't respond. Finally, she picks up the glass and offers it to her husband. When he doesn't take it, she sets it down on the bar near him. The doctor lashes out with his right hand, knocking the glass and its golden contents to the carpet. Rachel instinctively steps back, says something in apology, then crouches down to retrieve the glass and ice. She is facing me now. For the first time, I see her face. I can make out cuts and bruises on her cheeks.

Scars you *can* see.

Rachel stands now, turning away from me and toward her husband. Her hands raise in compromise; she's trying to calm him.

The doctor staggers toward his wife, who holds her ground. They are face-to-face now. As slow as he's moving, his right hand rises in a flash, fist half closed. Rachel's head whips to the right, her hair and arms flying wildly, her knees buckling as she falls backward to the carpet. She lands awkwardly on an elbow, then rolls over so she's facing the carpet. The doctor nods approvingly, that's-what-ya-get, as Rachel brings a hand to the developing bruise below her eye.

Rachel slowly makes it to her feet again, her hand returning to her cheek, her entire body trembling.

"I know how it'll end," she told me only a few days ago. "He told me how."

Dr. Reinardt approaches her. He grabs her by both arms, shaking her. Rachel breaks a hand free and swings it lifelessly toward his face.

I am on the deck now, crouched down like a catcher, as I watch this silent horror movie, no sound but the *thump-thump, thump-thump* of my pulse. The only thing separating me from the sliding glass door is the wooden bench and the picnic table.

"Tell me how, Rach."

Dr. Reinardt reasserts his grip on Rachel. He pulls down on her, forcing her to the carpet in a vise grip. Once on the floor he tears at her blouse.

"He's going to rape me first. He said he'll rape me then kill me."

I grip the wooden bench and slowly rise.

The glass shatters on the impact; it takes a second blow of the bench to create the considerable, if jagged, hole.

Dr. Reinardt's head moves slower than normally would be expected at the sight of a home intruder. Rachel, lying prone, grips his arms tightly. He begins to yank free, his superior strength overcoming both his intoxication and his wife.

"What—" Dr. Reinardt lifts himself up, freeing himself from Rachel, as I pull my second leg through the gaping hole, my other foot crunching the glass farther into the carpet.

Dr. Reinardt absorbs the impact of my charge; we linger together a moment, locked in a tense draw, our taut frames forming a tent over Rachel. I loosen my left arm and drill it into the doctor, somewhere near the jaw. He grunts, releasing his grip.

I break free. He grabs for my ankle, but I make it to the bar, reaching over the bottles.

"What—" Dr. Reinardt freezes, his arms slowly rising in surrender. "Wait—listen—"

"Shut up!" Saliva flies from my mouth. The gun is out in

front of me, my arm trembling. "Move out of the way, Rachel." The mention of her name settles me.

She complies, moving from behind her husband toward me. Her husband watches all of this, alternating between terror and confusion. His eyes return to me. "I—know you," he says.

"You're not gonna hurt her again." I raise the gun higher, at the face of Rachel's husband.

Rachel holds her breath.

Sobs now, audible crying from Dr. Reinardt. His pants colored with urine; his knees buckle. "Don't," he pleads. "God, *don't*."

I blink furiously, my body in a tremble. Rachel stands to the side, watching me; her husband barely stands at all, nearly falling to his knees, showing his palms in pathetic surrender.

I steel myself. "It's over now." I've visualized this moment time and time again, but never quite like this. Dr. Reinardt, soiled and quivering, the shattered door as a backdrop, the cold air whistling into the warm den, my beautiful Rachel to the side, her blouse torn, watching me, waiting for me to save her.

It crashes over me, an avalanche of images. Rachel, lying flat on her bed, writhing in pain as her husband whips her with his belt. Rachel silently screaming as the doctor raises his hand to her. Our life together, a quiet place in the country far from here, Rachel doing her charity work, I'm working out of my home, maybe some consulting. Then I see my nephew, Tommy, in his late teens, developing into a young man, his jaw squaring, his voice dropping to an alto, his hair cut short—visiting me in prison.

I let out a nervous sigh. It will be okay now. I know it with a certainty that has no basis in reason. I have no plan, no guarantee of a life with Rachel. What I do know is that Dr. Reinardt will never again lay a hand on my one and only love. And that is enough.

The gun is at my side now, brushing my thigh. I offer no resistance to Rachel's hands. She places one on my wrist;

with the other she takes the gun away from me and steps aside. I pause a moment, staring at my empty hand as the adrenaline decelerates.

Dr. Reinardt exhales with relief. "Thank God," he mumbles. "Thank God."

I look up, not at Rachel, but at the man barely standing across the room. I begin to speak, a warning to the doctor, but my voice is drowned out by the explosion. In my peripheral vision, I see a flash of light from Rachel's extended arm.

The first bullet hits square in the doctor's breastbone. He stumbles backward a step, frozen for a beat, before he looks down as if he's spilled coffee on his tie. The second bullet comes before he can look up; the hole is not discernible from the first, the shots nearly identical in their location.

The blood spreads across his white oxford like a spilled drink on linoleum. Dr. Reinardt limps forward two, three steps, his legs heavy, his hands at the wound, before he falls backward to the carpet.

Rachel turns the gun on herself.

"No!" I cry. I lunge toward her. She wrestles away from me and puts the gun to her temple. Her face contorts with tears.

"Let me do it," she pleads. "My life is over. I'm going to jail."

I grab her arm that holds the revolver. Rachel doesn't resist; she lets me take the gun from her hand before she collapses to the floor. I drop to my knees. "No one's going to jail," I say. "He was going to kill you, Rachel."

"Oh, *think* about it, Marty!" she cries. She sits up, waving her hand around the room. "Think how this looks!"

I stand and pace, the gun still in my hand. I walk over to the doctor, tiptoeing around his body. I lower myself so that we are face-to-face. The doctor stares vacantly at the ceiling with frozen eyes.

"Give me back the gun," she says. "Let me end this. You can still have a life."

I stand. "An intruder broke in," I say, unzipping my coat.

"You couldn't see who it was." I point at the splintered glass door. "An intruder. You got that?"

"What—what are you going to do?"

I have already rolled the doctor over, fitting a sleeve of my jacket through one of the doctor's limp arms. I work quickly to wrap the doctor in the coat. I stuff the gun in my pants and approach Rachel. I squat beside her, cup her face with my hand. "I don't *have* a life without you," I say.

I walk to the glass door, unlock it and slide it open, shards of glass falling with the movement. I return to Rachel's dead husband, lifting him, propping him up until I get a shoulder under his heavy frame.

"An intruder," I repeat. "You didn't see him." With the doctor over my shoulder, I turn awkwardly, taking tiny steps, until I face the openness of the backyard. Then I break into a slow sprint.

8 1

JERRY LAZARUS RUNS A HAND THROUGH HIS CURLY hair. He exhales slowly, taking in everything he's just heard.

"Bet you didn't figure it that way," I offer.

He cocks his head. "You're right about that."

"You thought I did it."

Jerry fixes on me. "I thought you had good *reason* to do it."

"Saving the abused wife."

"Well." Jerry followed the trial, of course. He knows we disputed the abuse. "I guess I didn't know what to think."

"Join the club."

"So he got what was coming to him."

"Oh, Jerry. The whole thing was set up."

Laz sits forward, his elbows on his knees. "Explain that."

"Rachel wants her husband dead."

"Why's that? Because of the abuse?"

I let my eyes wander to the hardwood floor. "Because she wanted to be with Rudy."

Jerry nods solemnly. He can see the tension here. "She can't just leave him?"

"I don't know." I sigh. "Maybe she was afraid of being left with nothing. I don't know, maybe she really hated the guy—I mean, he seemed like a class-A jerk to me."

"Maybe he *did* abuse her."

"Nah." I purse my lips.

"How can you know that?"

"Well, Rachel *did* show me some scars on her back once."

Jerry's face falls. I have conceded something now, something he long suspected but never confirmed.

"But it struck me, even then," I say.

I brought a trembling hand to her back but didn't make contact. Three, four, five lacerations, long spindly scars forming a gruesome road map down the center of her back. I remembered then her wincing while we had made love earlier, as I sank my fingers into her back.

Guilt was the first thing that I felt. How had I not noticed these before? How long had this gone on, and I hadn't noticed?

"We had been together many times," I say. "And until that time she showed them to me, I had never felt anything like that on her back. If you believe her testimony at trial—and the stories she was telling some of her girlfriends at the foundation, not to mention her shrink—she received weekly beatings on her back, yet I never noticed a thing."

"So—what are you saying?"

"It was her and Rudy, part of the plan. He put those scars on her back the night before she showed them to me."

Jerry perks up. "That's a big leap."

"It's no leap at all. Got it from the horse's mouth."

"Rachel?"

"Rudy," I say. "He and I had a little chat."

"You talked to Rudy?"

"Well, through his attorney. Before his trial, after mine. He needed me. I traded for some information." I blink and avoid Jerry's eye contact. The details of my deal with Rudy need not be shared with him. "So," I continue, "she loaded up on painkillers, he took a belt to her. All to show me the next day."

Jerry nods slowly. "She wanted you mad enough to kill him."

"And I was."

"Wait a minute." Jerry rises from the couch, wandering over to the mantel by my fireplace. "Dr. Reinardt *was* abusing her. You witnessed it yourself, that night."

"Wrong."

"Then what did you witness?"

My face colors, I can feel it. "Rachel had a thing—she liked being overpowered, I guess. She liked to pretend that she was being sexually assaulted."

"Rudy told you that, too?"

"Well." I smile sheepishly. "Rudy confirmed it. I already knew it. Not from personal experience, that was never my thing. But let's say I have indisputable proof."

Jerry's eyes circle. Again, details I will not share. "So what you witnessed, the doctor throwing her down, tearing at her blouse—"

"—was foreplay."

"Jesus Christ."

My friend paces the room now, a hand to his mouth, working all the angles. He stops a moment. A finger rises from his cupped hand. "If she staged this whole thing, she had to be pretty sure you'd show up."

"True."

"How'd she know that?"

"Well, let's say it was not unusual for me to appear in her backyard on Thursday nights."

"Her backyard?"

"She knew I'd be there," I say. "Let's leave it at that."

"Okay." Jerry holds on that one, eyebrows raised. He won't inquire, but it sure seems odd to him. He snaps back to attention. "But here's where it breaks down, I think. She not only had to know you would be there, she also had to know for sure that you'd rescue her—that you'd break through the glass door. I mean, this whole scheme rests on knowing that you would do something incredibly brave, incredibly *stupid*, really. Was she *that* sure of what you would do?"

"She didn't have to be sure."

"Explain that."

"Don't get me wrong—she wanted me to come in. She wanted me to kill him. That was always Plan A."

Jerry begins to pace again. To some extent he is enjoying the mental game, a lawyer's game. "Tell me about Plan B."

"If I didn't come in."

"Right, if you didn't come in."

"Then she kills the doctor herself. Self-defense." I reach under the coffee table and remove the piece of paper, the transcript of Rachel's 911 call to the police. "Read this."

Jerry comes over and takes the paper. "Right. Okay?"

"Read it again."

OPERATOR: 911.

CALLER: Please . . . please . . . come quick . . . he's going to hurt me.

OPERATOR: Ma'am, where are you?

CALLER: He's going to hurt me.

OPERATOR: Who is going to hurt you? Ma'am, where are you?

CALLER: Please . . . my husband . . . please . . . oh God.

(END OF RECORDING)

"Who's going to hurt you?" I ask.

Jerry's eyes slowly rise from the paper. "My husband," he says.

"Rachel was a smart one, I'll give her that. That dialogue is vague enough to mean *either* someone is going to hurt her and her husband, *or* her husband is going to hurt her." I raise my hands. "She had both contingencies covered. She could explain it away later, either way."

Jerry shakes his head. "But she made this call after you left. Why the need for mystery?"

I shake my head, too. "She made the call beforehand."

I jumped at the sight of her, my one and only, my beautiful Rachel. She must have been in the living room, not upstairs. Or did I miss her coming down the stairs?

The first siren had come much earlier than I expected.

How had they gotten here so fast?

"Remember the testimony of the responding police officer," I say. "The 911 call came at nine-thirty-eight. He got to the house at nine-forty-nine." I wag a finger. "And I remember very specifically the timing."

Still nothing upstairs. Nine-thirty-seven. My anxieties getting the better of me, images running wild in my mind, but the truth is, no one's home.

I jumped at the sight of her, my one and only, my beautiful Rachel.

"By my watch, nine-thirty-eight is almost exactly when I first saw Rachel. And what happened after I saw her—their little sex game, my grand entrance, the whole thing—took probably a little under ten minutes." I sit back in the chair. "I heard the sirens when I was in the woods." I exhale. "She made the call before the doctor was downstairs."

"Wow." My best friend stuffs his hands in the pockets of his khakis. "And that's why she told people about the abuse. The psychiatrist, her friends—"

"Right. If she has to do it herself, then she has a dozen people, including a shrink, testifying that she was a battered spouse. And the story she was telling me—the abuse was escalating, the doctor was talking about killing her—I'll bet you green money she told the same thing to everyone else. Then she's got the 911 call, too. 'I tried to call the police, they were too late, I thought he was going to kill me, I couldn't wait any longer.' She would've walked away scot-free."

"Holy shit."

"But, Jerry—she knew I'd come in." I shake my head, partly in admiration for her skill. "She worked me for weeks about the abuse. 'It's getting worse, he's talking about killing me.' She told me that the doctor had even shared with her *how* he was going to kill her. He was going to rape her first, then kill her."

Jerry returns to the couch. "So you thought you were witnessing the final act."

"Right on."

Jerry's hand grabs my kneecap. "She played you good, my friend."

I give a faint smile. "You have no idea how well she played me. I mean, sure, I remove the body and hope everything will go away. But then I discover she's having this affair with Rudy. And what do I do? Do I lash out? No. I rationalize the whole thing. She was abused and scared. People in those situations do all sorts of things that aren't in their character. They say some rape victims become promiscuous, hate themselves. I don't know. So I cut her a break. Then she cuts the deal for immunity, and still I give her the benefit of the doubt. Christ, she implicates me at trial—she I.D.'s me in open court as the guy who came through the door!—and still I rationalize it. I figured they made her say it."

"I guess love is blind, deaf, *and* dumb."

"Well, I don't know. Maybe that was it. You know what it really was—" I hold the thought a moment, shaking my head.

"If it's the Marty Kalish I know," says Laz, "then I know what it was. You blamed yourself."

I hiccup a laugh. "I did," I say. "I felt guilty about the whole thing. I felt like it was my fault. The way I saw it, I escalated the whole thing. Not only did I break in, I went and got the gun and held it out. Sure, she brought it down for protection, but it's a whole other thing to actually use it. I could've just broken in and confronted the doctor, maybe even knock him around a little. I didn't have to get the gun. The way I saw it, I practically handed this battered woman a loaded weapon. So even when it looked like Rachel was something less than the person I thought she was—you know, Rudy and the whole thing—I kept coming back to the fact that if it weren't for me, she wouldn't be in this mess to begin with."

Jerry considers this. "You're a better man than I," he says. "So what finally changed your mind?"

"Well, the damn restraining order bullshit." My hands are on my face, rubbing my forehead. "I mean, she went to that attorney two weeks *before* the doctor's death. We were going along great—we had never been closer. There were no *threats,* no *stalking*. There was no fucking reason to prepare a court order against me, for chrissake, unless she wanted to show it to someone later. Like after I murdered her husband." I hurl a pillow across the room, then deflate in embarrassment. Maybe I haven't put this *completely* behind me. "After she testified about the restraining order, I revisited everything. The fact that I had never noticed the scars before she showed them to me. The timing of her 911 call, the fact that the cops were there when I was barely out the door."

"Right, right."

"She wanted me to get caught, right there in her house. She wanted the cops to find me in there, smoking gun in my hand, standing over a dead cardiologist. And her tune would have changed the moment they showed up. 'Marty's been stalking me. He's been threatening me. Wanna see my re-straining order?' Oh, it would have been precious."

"And if you don't come in," says Jerry, "she does it herself and has a great story to sell. Right, right."

I feel the blood rushing to my face now. Jerry does, too, and feels the need to move me off the self-pity. "Answer me this," he says. "How'd you figure out Rudy and Rachel were carrying on?"

The change of subject brings some relief. "Oh, that was actually pretty easy. Rudy may be handsome, but he's not so smart." I hold out my hand. "I'm getting these calls, right? These anonymous calls, telling me he saw me, I should turn myself in."

"Yeah." Laz already knows this much, from Rudy's trial.

"So I'm wigging out, right? I'm combing through neighborhood directories, racking my memory, trying to figure who could have seen me carrying the doctor out, and who would have recognized me."

"Right."

"So then I'm arrested. The papers say I confessed. I don't hear from the caller. But I need to know. So remember when I called the newspaper and told them I'm innocent?"

Jerry laughs. "Yeah, Paul wasn't too happy with you."

I nod. "I was fishing him out, making him think maybe I'd had a change of heart. And it worked. He called me again. And for once in this whole damn mess, I wasn't the puppet. I was the puppeteer."

"Tell me."

"He kept saying, 'I saw you.' I pushed him. What did you see? You didn't see anything. I got him worked up a little. And then he blew it."

"How?"

"He said, 'I saw you kill him.' "

Jerry claps his hands together. "And that's when you knew he was full of shit."

"Right. Because a real eyewitness would have seen different."

"You should've finished law school."

I grimace. The last thing I'd ever do now. "So then I knew that this caller was part of something with Rachel. I mean, of course, wearing the blinders like I did, I still didn't make out Rachel for being evil. But I had a pretty good idea that this caller had something going with Rachel. So I hired an investigator, he followed Rachel, and he got them on video."

"So that was you who sent the tapes."

"Sure."

"One more question," says Jerry. "Something that doesn't fit."

"Okay."

"Why does Rachel let you talk to her psychiatrist? I mean, at that point, the abuse doesn't help her. There's no self-defense argument. She's better off denying the whole thing, or at least not making a point of confirming it."

"Yeah, I thought about that," I say. "I think what it comes down to is this—if there was one thing that Rachel had to be sure of, it was that I was under control. She probably considered the possibility that I could've caught on to Rudy. I don't know. The shrink confirmed the abuse for me, in case I had started to doubt it. I mean, who lies to a shrink, right? I think she was just making sure that my strings were pulled tight. That, no matter what else I might suspect, I would always have sympathy for her."

"I need a beer." Jerry heads for the kitchen. I do a slow exhale. This is actually therapeutic, spilling it all to Jerry. I stretch out my legs, let out a soft groan.

"Here's what *I* think." Jerry has a beer for me, too, and he taps my bottle in a toast. "I think my friend Marty Kalish wasn't nearly so dumb and blinded by love as he makes himself out to be. I mean, sure, like you said—you repeatedly cut her slack while she was turning the screws on you. Definitely, that's pathetic." He smiles, then points at me. "But all the while, as you're rolling along to trial, thinking the best of Rachel, blaming yourself, you're getting ready for payback if necessary. You're making videos, planting evidence in Rudy's house, making all those phone calls to Rachel from Rudy's home and work. My guess is, you didn't plan on using that stuff unless Rachel pulled the trigger on you. But she did, and you were more than ready to respond." He takes a swig. "So give yourself some credit."

I raise my bottle. "Flashes of potential, what can I say."

Jerry shakes his head, a mouthful of beer delaying his response. "What I'm saying is, beat yourself up all you want for having a blind spot, but you had one foot on the ground the whole time."

I smile at my friend. This sounds more like a parting message, a keep-your-chin-up pep talk. My eyes fill; instinctively, I look away, but I want to say this to his face. "You were the only one, you know. You never left my side."

Jerry shrugs it off, typically him. I don't know if we'll ever see each other again. If we do, it will be on his visit. After tonight, after one more good-bye, this city has seen the last of Marty Kalish.

8 2

HIS WIFE HAD A SHOWING AT HER ART GALLERY every Thursday night, didn't get home till midnight. That's what the police report, the neighborhood canvass I peeked at during the visit to Paul's law firm, said about Mrs. Sprovieri. And Dr. Reinardt performed surgery every Thursday night. A perfect arrangement for Rudy and Rachel. Both spouses gone. Let the show begin.

I am standing in Rudy's bedroom, where Rudy used to stand, looking through binoculars like he used to, at the same house he used to watch. Every Thursday night. Ten o'clock.

There she is, through the darkness, the line of vision that Rudy and I shared. Maybe it was love; I'm not sure I'll ever understand that word. It was more like a promise, hope, the dream of something so disarming, so consuming, so addictive that it took complete control of me.

I can't really speak for Rudy. Maybe he didn't feel it. Maybe it was just an affair, just sex with a gorgeous woman. I prefer to think otherwise. Maybe it's easier for me to believe that Rudy was as taken as I.

Oh, the laugh the two of them must have had when they realized I was standing outside Rachel's house, that I was watching, too. Does that make me a voyeur twice over, peeping on someone else's Peeping Tom show? I know one thing it made me—a pawn in their plan. They had me on remote control, as long as they pulled their caper on a Thursday evening.

It was August of last year when I decided to pay her a Thursday night house call. I knew the doc wasn't around, working late and all, and I thought maybe-just-maybe she'd be up for a visit. We had been together a few times at that point; I still wasn't sure how Rachel viewed things between us.

I didn't drive. I walked a walk that became a ritual, through the woods into her backyard. I stood out there in the backyard for about an hour and a half, the old insecurities rising to the surface, mustering up the courage to knock on the door, cursing myself for my pathetic state. Telling myself to turn back, move on, but knowing in my heart that I wouldn't.

Then the curtain slid open.

I figured she saw me out there, all wishy-washy, and decided to give me a reason to smile. What else was I supposed to think? I didn't know there was another guy, a block away, with binoculars. Oh, well. It's not the worst I've been humiliated.

The room, like every other in the Sprovieri house now, looks different from any time I've been here. Boxes scattered, most shelves empty now, some even gone, leaving the brackets jutting nakedly from the wall. Rudy's wife is selling the house and moving; until then, she is living downstate with her mother. What Rudy will do now—what Rachel will do, for that matter—is anyone's guess but mine. I won't waste the energy.

I raise the binoculars again. She is upstairs, walking around in a white undershirt and sweatpants cut off at the knee. Her hair is up in a ponytail, something I've never seen on her before. It suits her. She walks into the master bedroom and flicks on the light. First she pulls down on the sweats, wiggling out of them. I feel the adrenaline, that familiar rush. Then the underwear. She reaches her arms behind her back and pulls the T-shirt over her head, facing me, naked. For a moment, just one deluded moment, I think she will start swaying side to side, will move her hands along her body, will even whisper to me.

Are you ready, Mr. Kalish?

I think maybe I am.

Now she is applying some lotion to her face. She pauses and looks into the mirror, her hand dangling in the air, her long neck craning forward. What she sees in her reflection, I don't know. I guess I never did.

What was it? What was it that drove them? What made her not only want to cheat, but kill her husband? What made my mother stray from Dad, from Jamie and me? I always blamed it on sex. Stupid me, never a fulfilling relationship in my life, I thought sex was the poison in the drink. I never allowed for any other factors—trust, security, friendship, intimacy, communication, shared experiences, unconditional commitment.

Oh, why didn't I give you the chance to explain? I could have forgiven you. How could an ignorant eight-year-old, a naïve teenager, understand what was happening between you and Dad? I'll never know the answers. I have to live with that. Jamie will never know the questions—she will remember her mother as she always has. I will try to see her through Jamie's eyes, too.

I gather my jacket and head for the door. It's time for me to go.

AS GOOD AS GRISHAM, OR YOUR MONEY BACK!

If you do not agree that *Line of Vision* was as good as the last John Grisham novel you read we will refund your purchase price of *Line of Vision*.
To take up this offer, please complete the information requested below and send this page and your receipt for *Line of Vision*, to us at the stated address.

Offer applies to UK and Ireland and is valid for copies purchased up until 31st October 2008.

Full Name.................................

Address.................................

....

....

I did not like *Line of Vision* as much as the last John Grisham novel I read because

....

....

....

....

Please send this page and your receipt to:

Line of Vision Offer
Quercus Books
21 Bloomsbury Square
London WC1 2NS